A KILLER CLOSES IN

Dakota thought about Black Oak, slowly sinking into a morass of unpaid bills. Her father's legacy to her. If she were ever to restore the ranch to its former glory—

But you're not keeping Black Oak, a stern inner voice said.

She unlocked the driver's side door. That was when she noticed the sheet of paper on the windshield. Probably an ad. She slipped it out from under the windshield wipers.

Abruptly, a chill sprang up, flattening the piece of paper against her hands. The sky darkened. Dust shuttled across the dirt lot; debris pelted her legs. She started to ball the piece of paper up, then decided she might as well see what they were selling.

In the last red light of day, the letters might have been etched in blood.

Capital letters.

Short and to the point.

ACCIDENTS HAPPEN. ASK YOUR FATHER.

* * *

"*Dark Horse* marks the arrival of a most welcome new talent in romantic suspense. Margaret Falk joins the ranks of Nora Roberts and Janet Dailey with her wonderfully fresh tale of mystery and romance. Gripping—satisfying—a keeper!"

—Carol Davis Luce

MARGARET FALK

ZEBRA BOOKS
KENSINGTON PUBLISHING CORP.

ZEBRA BOOKS are published by

Kensington Publishing Corp.
850 Third Avenue
New York, NY 10022

First Printing: September, 1995

Printed in the United States of America

This book is dedicated to
Vicki Lewis Thompson

Acknowledgments

While I have strived to portray Quarter Horse racing as accurately as possible, I have bent a few facts for the sake of the story; in particular, the American Quarter Horse Association's policies on blood-typing. Any inaccuracies concerning Quarter Horse breeding, training and racing are due to assumptions on my part and do not reflect on the experts I spoke with, who answered every question I thought to ask. Many thanks to Amy Owens, Lesli Groves, and Dan Fick of the American Quarter Horse Association; Officers John Cheek, of the Tucson Police Department, Bob Wagner (retired) of the Chicago Police Department, James McSwane and Bobbie Miller of the Lincoln County Sheriff's Department; Pete Siminski of the Arizona-Sonora Desert Museum; Bob Lewis of Rillito Racetrack; Maria Bennett of the Santa Cruz County Racetrack; Aleta Walther, James McKnight, Bob Allison, and Norm Amundson of Ruidoso Downs Racetrack; Jann K. Jones, trainer; and Ellen Cockey, race rider. Thanks also to Sinclair Browning, Vicki Lewis Thompson, Glenn McCreedy, Rob Cohen and Tracy Bernstein. And finally, thanks to Zip Peterson, the racehorse trainer who, for well over a year, answered all my questions with wit, generosity and grace. May this year bring you another Contessa Cash.

dark horse: *n.* a superior running horse whose ability is not known to the other entrants [orig.: inspired by a practice in which unscrupulous trainers altered the appearance of a known favorite in order to raise the odds against him; this was done by dyeing the coat dark to cover any recognizable markings]

Prologue

Still simmering from the confrontation at the Steak Out, Coke McAllister forced himself to ease up on the accelerator. That smart-ass deputy might be out looking for drunk drivers tonight. After three Scotch and sodas, Coke didn't want to risk it, even though all he'd had in the last hour was coffee, on top of a big steak dinner.

He was extra careful on Arizona Route 83, observing the speed limit exactly. Even so, he breathed a sigh of relief as he reached the turnoff for home.

As the dirt road reeled out before his high beams, Coke cursed himself for shooting off his big mouth. He'd planned to hold off until he was sure, maybe even catch the bastard in the act. As it was right now, he didn't have any proof. And wasn't likely to, not after showing his hand like that. Shouldn't have said anything, but he was so damn mad—

The road curved to the right. As Coke turned the wheel, the pickup shimmied a little. He wished now he'd driven the new truck, even though he would have had to stop for gas. The steering mechanism on this old boat had a lot of play in it, which might make him look drunker than he was. At least he was almost home.

Why couldn't he have kept his mouth shut? He winced and rubbed his forehead. *Think of something else.*

Dakota. His mind fixed on the image of his daughter with relief. Tomorrow he'd give her a call. He'd even fly her out here, and he could spend some—what did the shrinks call it?

quality time?—with his only child. As Coke drove the ranch road, his urgency grew. Suddenly, it was the most important thing in the world that he see Dakota again.

He hoped she wasn't too busy to come.

Coke glanced at the rearview mirror, and his heart skipped a beat. A dark shape hurtled up behind him. "What the—"

On impulse, his foot punched the accelerator.

Suddenly, headlights flashed on, their reflection in the rearview mirror nearly blinding him. "Damn fool!" he muttered, shoving the mirror sideways. But he could feel the bar lights mounted on top of a truck aimed at the back of his neck. They flooded his cab with white light.

What was the guy doing? He yanked the mirror back into position, squinting against the brightness.

Adrenaline ran through him as he saw the flat board across the front grill, the tire lashed to the board. The truck behind him surged forward. If he came any closer, they'd lock bumpers.

Coke felt a jarring thud as the two vehicles connected. Suddenly he was going much faster, as if his truck were on skis.

As the truck pushed him forward over the unraveling road, Coke was struck by the realization that deep down, he'd been expecting something like this all along.

Part One

The Santa Cruz County Futurity

One

No use putting it off.

Dakota McAllister crossed the scarred red floor of her father's study, lifted the videotape from the top of the beat-up television set, and inserted it into the VCR.

Removing a pile of *Speedhorse* magazines from the couch, she sat down and pressed the remote button. The gears engaged and her father's image flickered on the screen.

She had tried to prepare herself, but nothing could ready her for the ache in her heart at the sight of him whole and strong again. Coke McAllister wore one of the flannel shirts he favored, the sleeves rolled up to reveal weathered, work-beveled forearms. He looked much younger than his sixty-seven years. How could such vitality, such overwhelming self-confidence and charisma, be extinguished as if it had never been?

The image blurred. Tears, unshed from the time she learned of his death, pricked at her eyelids.

Dakota looked out the picture window at the hilly, oak-studded pastures of her father's Arizona ranch, and willed her vision to clear. She rewound the tape to the beginning. If this was Coke's last chance at life, she needed to give him every millisecond he was entitled to. Even if that life was only an illusion; a few feet of videotape.

Coke McAllister leaned back on the sway-backed plaid

sofa in the barn office, his arms resting along its top. He
could have been in the room with her. "Are we rolling,
Norm? All right. This tape is for my only daughter, Dakota
McAllister, in the event of my death." He paused, cleared his
throat, and stared straight into the camera. "Dakota, we
haven't seen much of each other lately. I'm sorry about some
of the things I said. See? I can admit when I'm wrong. If you
want to be an actress, you have my blessing. I still think it's
a crapshoot."

He couldn't help it. Even on this posthumous tape, Coke
McAllister had to have the last word.

"God knows all I ever wanted was for you to be happy. Of
course, your idea of happy and mine are different." He made
it sound endearing. Dakota had to remember the kind of person he was, how he had tried to control everyone around him.
A benevolent dictator was still a dictator.

"You already have my will, so you know I'm leaving
Black Oak to you. I'm sorry to saddle you with all the debts,
but I did leave you a way out of this sorry mess." He leaned
forward, elbows propped on his knees, and interlocked cal-
lused fingers. "Listen good, pumpkin. I have a horse in my
barn that can make the difference between bankruptcy and
putting Black Oak back on track. I know it sounds like I've
been smoking somethin', but this filly can save Black Oak."

Dakota opened her mouth to protest, and laughed as she realized it was futile to argue with a videotape.

Coke answered her unspoken argument. "I know you don't
want this white elephant, and the way it is right now, I can't
blame you. But you're the last of the McAllisters. There's a
responsibility with that. My father built this ranch into the
finest quarter horse ranch in Arizona. But you know how it
is in this business, princess. One day's chicken is another
day's feathers. We're sure gettin' the feathers, now." His
laugh was affable, self-deprecating. The kind of laugh she'd
always associated with two men: Coke McAllister and Ron-
ald Reagan.

"I know what people are saying, and it isn't true. We've always worked hard to produce sound horses. If I thought one

of my horses would break down, I wouldn't let him run. No matter what the pressure. I want you to believe that, even if nobody else does. If you ever knew me at all . . ." He paused, passed a hand over his face, and Dakota realized suddenly how old he looked. Old and sad.

She had to look away. Her gaze fixed on the bright red gas pump, circa 1920, that stood like a sentinel in the front yard.

"I'm as much at a loss as anyone about what's happening," Coke was saying. "At first I thought it was bad luck. But I'm beginning to think that someone has it in for me. Now, don't call me paranoid. Bad luck is one thing. But this has been much more than a run of bad luck. Something's going on with my horses. You know how I feel about that, Dakota. I don't care if someone picks a fight with me, but if they'd stoop to hurting a dumb animal . . . I'm getting off the subject. Whoever doesn't want me to prosper won't have to worry much longer. I'm no spring chicken anymore. Frankly, I'm getting damn tired."

He rubbed the spot between his eyes with his thumb and forefinger, a motion Dakota had seen many times. She was surprised at the way that simple action tugged at her. "I don't know what I can say to convince you that Black Oak is where you belong. You're headstrong, just like your mother. From day one she tried to pit you against me, and maybe she's succeeded. It's too bad I won't be around to find out which side you come down on.

"Dakota, I'm counting on the fact that there's more McAllister in you than you know. You're plain folks, like me. I'd bet the farm on it." He laughed at his own joke. "I *am* betting the farm on it."

Coke stood up and walked to the door. On the wall of the office hung a dozen rust-splotched metal signs from bygone eras: Edison Lamp Company, Sinclair Oil, Royal Crown Cola. Coke looked back at the camera a couple of times and motioned for his audience to follow him. Dakota grinned. No doubt he got the idea from his favorite TV show, "This Old House." She could almost hear him say, "Let's see if the homeowner's in."

Coke paused beside a stall. A nameplate fastened to the bottom half door read, SHAMELESS.

"What do you know," Dakota muttered. "The homeowner's in." A horse poked its dark head over the stall door; a feminine face, tranquil brown eyes, inquisitive muzzle. A crescent moon rode high on her forehead. "This is the one," Coke said proudly. He rubbed the filly's neck affectionately and repeated, "This is *the* one. The horse who's gonna win the All American. Hold on to her, Dakota. She'll make you a fortune." The certainty in his voice sent a shiver up Dakota's spine.

For a moment she wanted to keep the filly just to please him. The reaction wasn't foreign to her. As a little girl, she would have done anything to please him.

Back in the office again, Coke wrapped it up. "I wish I could get you to promise me you'll give this filly her chance. We never were good face-to-face, so I'm having my say where you can't talk back. Keep her, even if you have to sell every other horse on Black Oak. At least for the summer. That's all she'll need to convince you—one million dollars if she wins the All American. See if I'm not right."

Suddenly, Dakota's finger found the button again, and froze him in the frame. *At least for the summer.*

He knew he was going to die before the summer.

He knew he was going to die.

Why hadn't it occurred to her before? Why should a man in good health—even a sixty-seven-year-old man—go to all the trouble of making a videotape for the purpose of telling his daughter to keep one horse?

Coke McAllister didn't have some virulent form of cancer that would rush through his body like a forest fire. He didn't have heart trouble.

Three weeks ago, on the way home from a Saturday night of dinner and drinks with friends in Sonoita, Coke's truck had crashed into an oak tree on Washboard Road. He'd been killed instantly. His blood alcohol level was just under the legal limit.

He couldn't have known he would die.

Stunned, Dakota set the remote down. She'd heard of animals knowing they were about to die and going off to find a quiet place. Had it been the same way with her father?

Had he sensed his impending death?

She was surprised at the bleakness that assaulted her. He had been alone here, fighting an uphill battle, pitied by most of his former cronies in the racing industry, without his family to support him. She shouldn't feel guilty about it, but she did.

Although Dakota couldn't imagine her father committing suicide, she wondered if despondency over Black Oak's downfall had led indirectly to his death.

"I'll probably never know," she muttered as she pressed the remote button once more.

"So that's the story in a nutshell," Coke McAllister said. "You decide. You should know—" Again, he rubbed the bridge of his nose. "I thought you oughta know how much I . . . care. Care about you."

Something tightened in her chest. Why couldn't he just say that he loved her? What was so hard about that?

"One more thing. If you need a hand, ask Clay. He knows me better than anyone else. Despite the trouble you two had, he'll help you. Well, that's it. Hold on to her, Dakota. This one's special."

The picture turned abruptly snowy.

Dakota hit the STOP button and closed her eyes. She'd wondered how Coke would work Clay Pearce in. There was no doubt he'd do it, just as he had taken a few cheap shots at her mother. That was his style. He had to play with her emotions even after his death.

That was the kind of man Coke McAllister was.

TWO

There was more gossip than usual this morning over ham and eggs at the Cactus Flower Cafe. Everyone was talking about the Black Oak dispersal sale.

They wondered what Coke would say about his daughter selling off all the Black Oak horses so soon after his death. To think people once considered her a local girl. Of course that was a long time ago—almost ten years—and she'd been living in Los Angeles all this time. L.A. was a long way from Sonoita, and not just in distance.

Sonoita, Arizona, is literally a wide spot in the road. A four-way stop sign regulates traffic at the juncture of State Routes 82 and 83. The hamlet provides the outlying ranches with a post office, the Santa Cruz County Fairgrounds and racetrack, a few restaurants, and a strip shopping center. Surrounding grassland bows like wheat to the edge of clean blue mountains. From a distance, the rolling hills could pass for velvet, brushed here and there against the nap to reveal pale gold, fawn, and silver, the grasstops spit-shined to a platinum gleam.

The line between the bright grass and the pulsating sky is sharp, intimidating. The sky takes up two-thirds of the landscape. This portion of Santa Cruz County is a great-hearted, beautiful country that tugs at the heart, whispering promises of the kind of timeless, solitary freedom that will forever elude human grasp.

Today, however, Sonoita's visitors were of a more practical

bent. Megatrucks towing horse trailers cruised up to the
crossroads and turned north on Highway 83. The corner store
was already doing a land-office business, and the Steak Out
looked forward to a big lunch rush.

The entrance to Black Oak was marked by turquoise and
silver balloons, Coke McAllister's stable colors. By nine-
thirty, two off-duty deputies in orange vests were directing
traffic up the dirt road to Black Oak.

Dakota watched from an upstairs window as the cars pulled
into the dirt lot that had been cleared near the barn area. The
late-model Mercedes-Benzes, Cadillacs and one-ton dually
trucks made a striking contrast to the dilapidated structures
and overgrown fields.

She glanced at her watch. It was almost ten.

Dakota started down the stairs, thinking that at least she
was dressed for the occasion in a lightweight oatmeal linen
jacket and skirt. The white, boat-necked silk shell suited her
coloring, bringing out the topaz of her eyes and the sheaf of
wheat-gold hair that fell to her padded shoulders. It was a
classy outfit, the kind of suit any spoiled Beverly Hills bitch
would be proud to model as she sold off her father's beloved
ranch before the ink was dry on his death certificate.

Alice, the housekeeper, was dusting the table on the landing. At the sight of Dakota, her lips tightened into a line and
she wielded the duster like a broadsword, sending a flurry of
dust motes into the air.

Dakota suppressed the apology that came to her lips. Did
the woman think she *wanted* to see Black Oak go to some
Fortune 500 exec with a yen to play weekend cowboy? Or
worse, developed into a planned community? She could see
the billboards now: THE MEADOWS AT BLACK OAK. FINANCING
AVAILABLE. FROM THE NINETIES. She hated the idea of seeing
the broodmares and foals and stallions parade into the ring
and then out to the horse vans parked by the barns, taking the
heart's blood of Black Oak with them.

As she walked through the sunny foyer, Dakota tried not to
look at the photos lining the walls, but it was impossible. Her
eye had always been drawn to fine horses. There was no

dearth of them on the whitewashed walls, posed in the winner's circle at Tucson's Rillito Racetrack, her father holding their bridles and beaming with pride. Dakota knew their names, race records, and eventual fates, just as some people memorized the begats in the Bible: Moltaqua, American Flyer, Shasta Pine. Most of the photographs were black and white, when her father was a young man. It was another era, the glory years of the late 1940s, when Tucson was the capital of quarter horse racing. Did the handsome, cocky young man in the photographs have any inkling that Rillito Racetrack, the busy hub of quarter horse racing, would become a wishbone for elected officials, horsemen and developers? Or that his own famous Black Oak Farm would slip into oblivion? Could he have foreseen that the white-painted pasture fences would peel and sag, that with every strong breeze more of the faded Spanish tiles would slide from the roofs?

No. Coke had the heart of a gambler.

Dakota paused, unwilling to cross the threshold and meet with the unpleasantness on the other side.

She remembered her father's face as he spoke into the camera, capturing his imagined audience with those intense tawny eyes, so like her own. "Hold on to her, Dakota. This one's special."

This one. How many "this ones" had there been in the last ten years?

But maybe Shameless *was* special. Coke had certainly put his money where his mouth was. He'd paid her nomination fees faithfully since she was a yearling, for the Triple Crown of quarter horse racing: the Ruidoso, Rainbow and All American futurities, run at Ruidoso Downs, New Mexico. It was a lot of money to put out on an untried colt, a year before it would even run. Futurities were always a gamble, but because hundreds of owners made relatively small payments throughout the year, the end result was big money to the winner. Owners of a promising young horse had only two choices: pay incrementally larger fees as the year progressed, dropping out any time (should the colt be unable to run), or pay a whopping supplemental fee to get into the race. The supplemental fee for the All American—the crown jewel of quarter horse racing—was fifty thousand dollars.

One million dollars went to the winner.

If you had the right horse, it was a great investment. Shameless, sired by Black Oak's premier stallion, Something Wicked, might be that good. Coke had only let her run full out once, and the pace had been blistering—

Dakota shook her head, hoping the motion would clear her mind. That was not a bug that would bite her again. Selling her father's ranch was an unpleasant task, but it had to be done. She would do it because otherwise the creditors would do it for her, and because this was not her world anymore. It hadn't been for ten years.

She would go home to L.A., forget all about Shameless and her father and the memories—both good and bad—that clung to Black Oak.

Steeling herself, Dakota opened the door and strode out into the sunshine.

The day wore on like a record whose needle was stuck in a groove, replaying the same depressing refrain. At noon, the proceedings broke off for a catered lunch in the gaily striped tent on the lawn, but Dakota wasn't hungry. She'd seen too many of her father's beloved horses parade through the portable ring to a lukewarm reception and uniformly low prices.

Restless, she walked down the row of stalls in the two-year-old barn, catching snatches of conversation as potential buyers looked over the horses on this afternoon's program.

She turned the corner and bumped into a woman deeply involved in conversation. "Excuse me," Dakota said.

The woman dismissed Dakota with a curt nod and leaned toward the man she was talking to. The epitome of cowgirl chic, the woman was so thin that her leopard-print sweater looked as if it hadn't left the hanger. Black leggings, lizard-skin cowgirl boots, a black Bolero hat ringed with conchos, and hunks of glittery jewelry completed the look. Dakota started to walk around her. The man, who had been half in shadow, turned slightly.

A jolt of recognition shot through Dakota. "Clay."

From his six-foot-two height, Clay Pearce studied her with midnight eyes that revealed nothing more complicated than pleasure. "McAll—Dakota. I was looking for you."

Dakota's throat closed. She fancied everyone in the barn could hear the pounding of her heart. When at last she could unstick her tongue from the roof of her mouth she asked Clay, "What are you doing here?"

Clay gestured with his program. "There are a couple of broodmares I like. You're looking well."

The woman glanced at her. Her face was as flawless as any top fashion model. The pageboy bangs under her hat were deep henna red. The color just missed clashing with her coral lipstick. "Clay, if you want to see that filly you're so crazy about, we'd better hurry. They're about to start." Her voice carried the unmistakable drawl of west Texas.

"Just a minute, Rita. I'd like you to meet an old friend of mine."

Friend? Dakota thought with unaccustomed bitterness.

Despair assailed her in a staggering wave. Her divorce from Clay was the biggest failure of her life. She had assumed that her feelings had gone the way of the memories she'd so carefully blocked out. But now . . . he looked so damn good it squeezed the heart. The ten years had made him even more handsome and assured, endowing him with an aura of masculinity that a boy of twenty-two could not hope for. He was nothing like the pathetic lovesick fool of her fantasies. The one who had paid for dumping her in a thousand ignominious ways—by drinking himself into oblivion, gambling his money away, visiting hookers and catching a dread disease.

If any of these things had happened to him, it certainly hadn't left its mark.

"Dakota, this is Rita DeWeil. Rita, Dakota McAllister. She owns the filly, and everything else on this farm."

The woman's stainless-steel eyes sharpened to a knife

edge. *"You* own Black Oak?" Her tone implied that she found it hard to believe.

Dakota attempted a smile. "As strange as that may seem."

"It's a shame you have to sell now, when prices are so depressingly low," Rita DeWeil said. She took Clay's arm and tilted her perfect profile up to his. Dakota had the feeling that everything this woman did was for effect.

She had to admit the effect was stunning.

"Come on, Clay. I've just got to see the Something Wicked filly," the woman said, no doubt referring to Shameless. "No matter how fast you say she is, she's still an untried filly. I doubt she'll break the bank."

"You go on," Clay said. "I want to talk to Dakota for a minute."

Dakota felt her face grow hot. Her heart jackhammered in her chest, so wildly that she imagined it would shake her off her foundations. "That's all right, Clay. I'm pretty busy myself right now." She turned to go.

His hand clamped on her wrist, gentle and strong at the same time. "I have to talk to you. Now."

Dakota pulled her hand out of his grasp as if she'd been bitten. She stared into his eyes, and saw that he was serious. "All right," she said, trying to keep her voice steady.

Rita DeWeil's wide mouth straightened into a slash. "Well, hurry up. Once the bidding starts it'll be hard to find a seat. So terribly nice to meet you, Cheyenne."

"That's Dakota. We're a different tribe altogether."

"Dakota." She made it sound like an unsavory sex act.

Then they were alone. Dakota tried to regain control of her emotions, but it was difficult. Clay always had been larger than life, and now, standing in a shaft of sunlight, the dust motes snowing down around him, he seemed to contain a magnetic field that held her in its sway. What made this man stand out so completely? His hair, shiny and dark as sable, the strong, well-drawn features? Other men were just as good-looking. No, his presence commanded people to pay attention to him. Even as a boy that had been true, but it was many times as potent, now. He looked nothing at all like the redneck Clay of her revenge fantasies; he wore a jade-green chambray shirt, sleeves rolled up, and pleated tan trousers. She remembered the sandcast silver and turquoise bracelet on one wrist, part of the Pearce family collection.

At one time, she'd been part of the Pearce family collection. And she'd felt about as useless and ornamental as that bracelet on his forearm.

The silence grew awkward. At last, Clay said, "I'm sorry about Coke."

"Thank you for the flowers, they were beautiful." Did she have to sound like an automatic recording? It was obvious that he'd rattled her.

"Didn't you get my calls? I left two on your answering machine."

Startled, she asked, "When?"

"Thursday."

"I've been here all week."

"Hasn't Norm talked to you? Given you any advice?"

What did her father's lawyer have to do with him? "If you'll forgive me, I don't believe that's any of your business."

He sighed. "Maybe not. But I promised Coke I'd try."

"Try what?" Her father had always gotten along well with Clay. Coke had been against the divorce. There were times when Dakota had wondered just whose side Coke was on. "What is this all about, Clay?"

"You know he wanted you to keep Black Oak."

"I can't."

"You can't, or you won't?"

"I don't have the money. This place is falling apart, there are creditors at every door, and—" She broke off. "I don't have to explain anything to you!"

"You haven't found a buyer yet, have you?"

She shook her head. Norm had told her it probably wouldn't happen anytime soon. People weren't in the market for big horse ranches, and Black Oak was isolated enough that it was unlikely developers would want it, either. The Meadows at Black Oak were a long way off yet. She hoped a breeder would buy the ranch, but most of the serious quarter horse breeders liked Texas.

She only hoped the sale of the broodmares and yearlings would help pay the property taxes and give the creditors something to chew on until she could find a buyer.

"Some horses aren't on the program," Clay said.

"I'm keeping Cochita." Coke had given Cochita to her for her sixteenth birthday. "She and Canelo Red are going to my stepfather's place."

"He was a good stud in his day. I'm glad you're keeping him."

The last thing she wanted was Clay Pearce's approval. "Norm's negotiating with the Lone Star Stallion Station for Something Wicked and a few of our best mares, but we're keeping them through the summer. We'll honor the outside mares already booked to him this spring." She realized she was babbling. "Now, if you'll excuse me, I have to be g—"

Again, he grabbed her hand. She couldn't suppress the shudder that went through her. "You know Coke didn't want you to sell that filly."

She was tired of taking the blame for this. Tired of all the free advice and resentful looks. From her father's lawyer to the pool man, everyone was an expert on her affairs. "Do you think I do? I have no choice!"

"You have money."

"You're talking about my trust fund? There's not enough money in ten trust funds to keep this ranch afloat!"

"I'll bet it's enough to race one filly one season. If you knew what a mistake you're making! Christ!" He shoved his hands in his pockets. "Do you have any idea what kind of payoff you'd get if you won even one of those races? Look what your father's already put into her. Three thousand dollars in nomination fees alone, feeding, vet bills, training—"

"It's peanuts compared to what I'd have to pay just to get her to the trials in Ruidoso," snapped Dakota. "I'd have to ship her, stable her there all summer, find a trainer, pay another thirty-five hundred dollars in nomination and entry fees—and there's no guarantee she'd even get in the race!"

He looked at her with new respect. "You have thought about it, then."

"Of course I've thought about it!" What did he think she was, anyway? A complete novice?

"Then you know, with an untried filly, even with the potential she shows, you won't get anywhere near the price you'd get for her if she won even one of those races. The Ruidoso Futurity trials are in May. The Rainbow in July. You could triple your investment and restore your father's reputation at the same time. As it is, you're pouring all the money that went into her right down the drain."

"It's better than pouring it down a black hole," Dakota retorted. "And that's what horseracing is all about! What right do you have to tell me what to do, anyway? You gave up that privilege a long time ago."

She'd struck home with that one. At last Clay said, "You're right. I shouldn't be pushing you like this."

"No, you shouldn't," she agreed.

He grinned. To her dismay, his grin was even more disarming than it used to be. "I'm going to make one last pitch, and after that I'll leave you alone. Deal?"

Dakota was surprised at the bleakness she felt at the prospect of Clay leaving her alone. She lifted her chin. "Try your worst."

"Every man has a dream, McAllister," he said, using her last name as he'd always done, even when they were married. "Your father believed this filly could win the All American. Do you really want to deny him that last wish?"

His words might have come from inside her own mind. She'd played this particular tennis match in her head since she'd watched her father's videotape. "Even if I wanted to keep her, it's too late. The auctioneer won't let me pull her out now."

"You could buy her back. The consignor may bid on any horse in the sale. Norm told me the estate will guarantee your personal check for up to fifty thousand dollars. He put that stipulation in himself."

"Why'd he do that?"

"In case you changed your mind."

"And why would he think I'd change my mind?" But she knew. Clay had persuaded him. Seething with anger, she said, "I'd appreciate it if you'd stay out of my business affairs in future."

"I only made the suggestion, knowing what your dad would want. Norm agreed. We both thought you should have the option."

"You must think I'm made of money."

His eyes, dark as the night sky, scrutinized her. She knew he was assessing the cost of the suit she was wearing. Quintessential rich bitch, compliments of her mother. And, of course, her stepfather, who had made a fortune in personal computers back in the eighties. The man she owed her allegiance to, far more than to the domineering man who had been her blood father.

"Darling." Rita DeWeil was back. "They're about to bring out the Streakin Six mare. You promised you'd tell me how much to bid."

Darling. She left no doubt how she felt about Clay.

For his part, Clay certainly seemed to like it. He pushed away from the barn wall, his body loose-muscled and fluid as a cat's. "I'm sorry, Dakota. I promised your dad I'd try. I hope next time we meet under better circumstances."

And then he was gone.

Dakota walked through the cool, shadowy barn, painfully aware of her heart slamming against her chest wall, the blood thumping in her ears. Just the sight of Clay had sent adrenaline rushing through her like an undammed river, carrying with it all the disturbing debris of a decade ago. Memories, uprooted from a past she'd thought long buried, surfaced on a current of panic, anger and despair.

Judging from Rita DeWeil's possessive attitude, Clay had moved on. Why couldn't she?

But I have, a defiant voice in her head answered.

In L.A., Dakota's life ticked along at a satisfying pace. She had just signed with the William Morris Agency—no mean feat for an actor—and had landed small parts in three movies.

That was her world. There was no room for a man like Clay Pearce in it. None at all.

Here at Black Oak, Dakota was out of her element. She was the bad guy about to sell the ranch that had been in her family for over one hundred years; the fool about to throw away a chance at the All American Futurity. From the moment she arrived, the pressure to keep Black Oak had been unrelenting. Pressure from the Black Oak employees, pressure from Norm Fredman, and now, pressure from her ex-husband.

Dakota dragged her mind back to the present, shutting Clay behind the door she had thought was bolted, boarded up and cobwebbed with age.

This might be her last chance to look at the filly in her possession, the last chance to prove to herself she was right in selling her.

She reached Shameless's stall. Most people were at the auction, so Dakota had a few moments alone with her. Maybe she could puzzle out just what made this horse a potential All American winner.

If winners were selected solely on looks, it would be no contest. In the dim light of the stall, her coat had the muted sheen of dark velvet, but Dakota had seen her in the pasture. Outdoors, the highlights on the filly's flanks and muzzle ran the gamut from rich mahogany to the color of burnt buttered toast, depending on the angle of the sun.

Shameless was perfectly balanced. She had inherited her sire's strong sloping shoulder, fine head and glorious symmetry. Although Something Wicked was mostly thoroughbred, he sired quarter horses exclusively. This was not unusual. In the last forty years, thoroughbreds had been used to refine the racing quarter horses, but the breed itself originated in Virginia in Colonial times. A sturdy pony who could run blistering short match races, the quarter horse later moved west and began his career as a cow pony. Now he had come full circle.

From her dam Shameless had inherited the quarter horse muscularity and powerful hindquarters that could propel her far beyond any thoroughbred up to a quarter mile. Her dam was Dash To Judgment, sired by the most successful quarter horse stallion in recent years, Dash for Cash. That quality showed.

But more than the filly's quiet beauty, Dakota was arrested by a less tangible quality. This horse knew she was special. It showed in the way she stood, head slightly raised, ears casually pricked toward Dakota. Like a queen granting an audience, she waited politely for Dakota to state her case.

Dakota had seen the filly close up twice before in the last few days, and each time she had the same reaction. Excitement tingled in her stomach and goose bumps fanned out on her arms. A recognition of excellence vibrated in her soul with the perfect sonority of a tuning fork.

She was so taken aback by the feeling that for a moment she did not register the sound of the loudspeaker. "There will be a break of ten minutes."

People began emerging from the tent. Several of them made for the dark filly's stall. Reluctantly, Dakota left her, more confused than ever. She wandered through the barns, mindful that her decision might well have been the wrong one. Fortunately, she didn't run into Clay and his new love interest.

Ten minutes later she found a seat toward the back of the tent. Several rows ahead, she could see Clay seated next to Rita DeWeil.

Again she felt the wave of grief crash into her. Why did she still feel this way? Clay had every right to keep company with any woman who appealed to him. But when she saw Rita DeWeil lean against Clay, her mouth pressed intimately to his ear, Dakota felt as if she'd been blindsided.

"Number twenty-six," the auctioneer said. "This is a Something Wicked colt out of the Three O's mare, Trudy C." Dakota glanced at her program and her heart raced. Shameless was number thirty-one.

Two other colts and a broodmare were led through the ring to unenthusiastic bidding. Maybe the filly would go for peanuts, too. Dakota felt an odd stirring of hope.

"Number thirty is Darkscope, an eleven-year-old stallion by Certain Something out of Waterwitch. He's a full brother to Something Wicked, and has earned a total of $9,583 dollars on the track. Who wants to start the bidding at five thousand?"

Dakota doubted there would be any takers. Although Darkscope was a handsome horse—in fact he bore a striking resemblance to Something Wicked—he had been a big disappointment.

The gavel cracked, shaking Dakota from her reverie. "Sold to Dan Bolin for three thousand five hundred dollars," the auctioneer said. "Mr. Bolin, you sure got yourself a deal."

Dakota watched as the bay stallion left the ring. She was surprised that Dan Bolin, the man who ran Black Oak's breeding operation, would waste his money on Darkscope. He, of all people, should know that even though Darkscope was a full brother to Something Wicked, he had proved to be a dud in the breeding shed as well as on the track.

She didn't think any more of it, because a hush had come over the crowd. The filly was up next.

The auctioneer cleared his throat and looked at the crowd. Dakota became aware that she was clutching her program in a death grip.

"The next horse on the program is number thirty-one, a dark bay or brown filly by Something Wicked and out of the Dash for Cash mare, Dash to Judgment. She is nominated to the Ruidoso, the Rainbow, and the All American Futurities. Now folks, this here is the best bargain at this sale. She's ready to go. Bill, you go on, bring in Shameless now and show these good folks what I'm talkin' about. I'm starting the bidding at ten thousand."

Considering that several of the Black Oak horses had sold for a thousand dollars or less made this a big deal.

From the moment the filly stepped into the ring, there was only Dakota and Shameless, the distance between them telescoped until Dakota fancied she heard the filly's hoofs patter on the tanbark like cats' feet.

"Ten, ten, who'll give me ten thousand? Seven? Is that all you're gonna offer for this fine filly? I'm embarrassed for you, that's what I am. You are insulting this filly. Now folks. I know you're thinking about Something Wicked's get having their share of lameness. But this filly is sound as a dollar. We've got the X Rays to prove it. Ask the doc over there. He'll tell you. Who'll give me ten? Seven? All right, seven, then. Seven, seven, who'll give me ten? This filly is nominated for the *All American,* folks. She could win the Ruidoso three months from now, and then you'll be cryin' in your beer. Eight thousand, now that's more like it. Eight, eight, ah-gimme ten—lady in the black I got eight-five, gotta eight-five, gotta eight-five gimme ten. Over there I got nine, nine, gotta nine, gimme that ten thousand, hep-de-hep-de ten thousand, makin' it hep-de-hep de ten-thousand how 'bout twelve. Twelve thousand, over there, I see you Mister Earle. Gimme that fifteen thousand, gimme fifteen, fifteen, I gotta fifteen thousand fifteen fifteen who'll gimme seventeen—"

Rita DeWeil lifted her program. What did a man like Clay Pearce see in that woman? Aside from the fact that she looked as if she'd stepped off a *Cosmopolitan* cover?

Dakota couldn't conceive of Rita DeWeil owning her father's horse.

"I gotta seventeen, seventeen, who'll gimme eighteen—eighteen! Who'll gimme twenty?"

No one was biting.

"Anybody else? Come on, folks, anyone wanna steal this fine filly? All right. Seventeen thousand going once—"

Rita DeWeil would get Shameless.

"Going twice—Is that a bid, ma'am?"

The person in front of her swiveled in his chair and caught Dakota's eye. He wasn't the only one.

The bid spotter pointed right at her. She realized her hand hung up in the air like some incredible weight creaking on overloaded pulleys.

"Eighteen! I gotta eighteen, Miss McAllister, I got eighteen, gimme twenty—"

Panic beat frantic wings in her throat. What was she thinking of?

Rita DeWeil's rolled program shot up in the air, and relief flooded through Dakota. It was all right, all right, she was off the hook.

"Twenty thousand. Is that all you'll pay for this fine filly? She's *ready to go,* folks, can't you see that?" The auctioneer shrugged. "All right. It's your funeral. Going once, going twice—"

She saw her father leaning toward the camera, plaid shirt rolled up on tanned arms ... *This is the one, Dakota.*

Dakota held up one finger.

"Twenty-one thousand, to Coke McAllister's daughter. This is a lady's war, am I right or wrong, here, folks? What about you in the leopard sweater, leopard sweater, come one, give me two, in the leopard sweater—Twenty-two! Twenty-two I gotta gotta twenty-two who'll gimme twenty-five!" He paused, wiped the sweat out of his eyes with a handkerchief and stared straight at Dakota. "Miss McAllister, you gonna let this filly go for twenty-two thousand dollars?"

Suddenly, Clay Pearce turned around in his seat. She was too far away to read the expression on his face.

He must have encouraged Rita to buy the filly. So much for that pretty speech he'd given her earlier. Maybe he felt he'd done his duty by asking her to reconsider selling Shameless, and now he could support his girlfriend with a clear conscience. Well, she thought grimly, we'll see about that. Doubly determined, Dakota held up three fingers.

"I got twenty-five thousand, twenty-five, twenty-five, how about you in the leopard sweater?"

Clay faced forward again, but not before he whispered in Rita DeWeil's ear.

"Thirty, gimme thirty, she's a steal for thirty," implored the auctioneer.

But Rita DeWeil shook her head. Did Clay tell her to stop bidding?

"Sold to Coke McAllister's daughter!" The gavel cracked.

Dakota wasn't prepared for the elation she experienced. By all accounts, she should be devastated. She had just bought her own horse back for the highest price of the auction.

Three

This year, Trish O'Neill's birthday fell on a Saturday. Her parents took her and her two younger brothers to the Cactus Flower Cafe in Sonoita to celebrate. It should have been fun. Trish ordered her favorite lunch, a grilled cheese sandwich and pickle chips. But today her favorite lunch tasted like cardboard, all because of that stupid flier—the one advertising the Black Oak dispersal sale.

She'd seen it on the way back from the bathroom. As she went by, Trish always stopped to look at the shelves marked AUNT LAURA'S PANTRY at the end of the lunch counter, which displayed embroidered fishing scenes, peanut brittle, and homemade pie. Usually, she glanced at the bulletin board on the wall beside it, too, even though they never advertised anything interesting, just county fair horse races and bake sales.

When she saw the flier, Trish's stomach bolted up into her throat and nearly choked her. She'd sat down hurriedly, every extremity tingling.

"Honey, would you like to open your presents before we have the cake?" her mom asked.

Trish nodded. That queer jangly feeling in her stomach wouldn't go away. She thought she might just hurl her favorite lunch right up.

Her father leaned forward. "Is something wrong, sweet pea?"

She swallowed and smiled faintly. "No. Nothing." She

reached for the gift bag, halfheartedly picked through the tissue paper inside, and withdrew a makeup set.

"What do you think?" Her mother was beaming. "This is your Sweet Sixteen, so we thought we'd get you something a little more adult."

"It's great." What her mother didn't know was that she had been wearing makeup since the sixth grade. Just another dirty, sneaky lie in a whole shitload of them. As she opened the rest of her presents, Trish tried not to think about the biggest lie of all, but it was impossible.

It lived with her every day and every night. It got so that she couldn't look anyone in the eye. She was afraid of the men she saw in town, most of whom were friends of her father's, people she'd known all her life. Any one of their friendly faces could be a mask.

She wanted to scream at them: "I don't know who you are! I don't know!"

She'd actually thought today would be different. The place had been empty when they came in, and she sincerely wished it would stay that way. The only other person in the cafe other than her family was the waitress. The waitress was safe . . . maybe.

Coming to the Cactus Flower Cafe on her birthday was a tradition. The idea of spending her birthday as she had the last several birthdays was comforting, familiar. It was almost as if she could go backward from that night three weeks ago, back to Before. Before she lost her virginity to Billy Taylor, before she saw what happened on Washboard Road.

Some part of Trish knew that the burden she carried was too heavy for a sixteen-year-old. But what could she do? She'd promised Billy she wouldn't tell. There were good reasons for not telling.

Very good reasons.

"Who's this from?" Dad asked, handing Trish a sloppily wrapped gift.

Ken, who was only a year younger, grinned sheepishly. "Mom's gonna kill me."

Trish tore the present open and forgot, just for a moment,

the feeling of doom that had been hanging over her head. "Guns 'n' Roses! All right!"

"Ken, I told you I don't want that kind of thing in our house," Mrs. O'Neill said, but Trish, who had learned every nuance of her mother's voice, could tell her rebuke was only a token one.

The door squeaked open. Two men entered the cafe.

Trish unconsciously braced her legs, ready to run.

One of them walked into the side room and sat down, but his companion stopped at the O'Neill table. He stood over them, tall and menacing. Trish just knew he was scrutinizing her, maybe wondering if she was the girl who went with Billy Taylor. Billy Taylor, who drove a '65 Valiant.

"Greg! How're things going?" The voice boomed above her.

Her father stood up. "Hey, Jimmy." They shook hands. "It's my little girl's birthday today, so we're celebrating."

Trish stared at her plate. If she didn't look up, Mr. Meeghan wouldn't see her face.

"Her Sweet Sixteen," Trish's mom said.

"Congratulations," Meegan said to Trish. "Kiss any boys yet?" He didn't wait for an answer but started talking to her dad.

He wasn't interested in her.

It wasn't him.

Still keeping her face tilted away, Trish helped her mother clear away the wrapping paper from the table and put it into a plastic bag, half listening to the two men. They were talking about Mr. Meeghan's new truck.

"Man alive, this Cummins Turbo Diesel's something," Mr. Meeghan said, removing his straw cowboy hat. The patch under the arm of his white shirt was yellow. "Talk about pulling power. Don't know the horses are even back there."

Maybe Mr. Meeghan was *pretending* disinterest. Maybe he wanted her to let her guard down; maybe he was using his conversation with her dad as a chance to study her.

He did just buy a new pickup, didn't he?

Trish's dad motioned out the window of the brick restaurant at the horse trailer parked out front. "You goin' to the sale?"

"Thought I'd pick up a couple of mares. Oughta go pretty cheap, what with people being so leery of that Something Wicked line. I've seen stables with a run of bad luck before. There's nothing wrong with those horses."

A new pickup. To replace the bashed-in one.

Her father lowered his voice. "Boy, that was a shock. Hard to believe Coke's gone."

"Damn shame," Mr. Meeghan said. "I guess his daughter'll be all right, though. Heard he left behind a pretty big insurance policy."

Greg O'Neill grunted. "Probably all go to the bank."

Trish's heart pounded so hard that she just knew everyone could hear it. She reached for one of the loose ribbons, pulled a little too hard, and knocked a ceramic mug over. Coffee ran off the table onto the floor.

"Trish, I wish you'd be more careful!" her mother said.

Hands shaking, face hot, Trish tried to soak up the mess with a paper napkin. "I'm sorry." She felt like crying.

"It's all right." Her mother went over to the counter and brought back a wad of napkins. Dad and Mr. Meeghan didn't seem to notice.

". . . Wasn't an accident," Mr. Meeghan said.

Trish mopped up the coffee, straining to hear.

"You think he ran his truck into that tree on purpose?"

"I'm just telling you what I've been hearing. We all know things weren't going good."

Her father shook his head. "Coke? Suicide? I can't see that. If a man wanted to kill himself, there are a lot easier ways to do it."

Trish felt light-headed. She saw it as if it were last night; headlights spearing the darkness, the screaming engines.

"Guess we'll never know for sure." Mr. Meeghan clapped her father on the shoulder. "See you, Greg. Maddy." He nodded to Trish's mom. "And happy birthday, Trish. Hope it's a good one."

* * *

It had been an unseasonably warm night for January. Trish
told her parents she was going to stay at her friend Dawn's
after singing in the choir concert at Patagonia High School.
Dawn had agreed to back her up. The real plan was to go
with Billy Taylor to Greaterville.

Greaterville was a ghost town. At the time it seemed like
a great adventure, going to a ghost town at night. The idea of
necking in some spooky place where there might be ghosts
sounded cool. And so they'd driven north on Arizona 83 and
turned off on the Greaterville Road. At the fork in the road
Billy turned left. It seemed like they drove forever, and yet
there was no sign of a ghost town. It was a moonless night,
completely dark, and the road was so rough that they almost
got stuck twice.

Gradually it dawned on Trish that Billy didn't know where
Greaterville was any more than she did. Uneasiness quickly
spread from the pit of her stomach to her limbs. It was isolated out here. They might have been the only people in the
world. The vague notion that she was a moorless little boat in
a dark sea solidified, until it bordered on panic. "Let's go
home," she'd begged him.

"It's around here some place."

"I want to go home."

Billy sighed. "All right."

Trish was relieved when they reached the main road. So relieved that when Billy suggested they park for a while, she
was more than happy to oblige. They pulled off onto Washboard, a graded dirt road that served a couple of ranches in
the area, and looked for a place to park.

That night Trish and Billy went all the way. Aside from the
guilt—that's what you got for being raised a Catholic—she
was glad they had done it at last. She loved Billy; they'd be
getting married in another couple of years anyway. What
were they supposed to do, wait all through high school?

To tell the truth, it was kind of a disappointment. What was
the big deal? She thought as she sat next to Billy in the back-

seat pulling on her jeans, the air blowing cold on her knees. The only things she'd remember were how her head had been wedged against the Valiant's armrest, and a ripping pain that warmed into pleasantness, and the fierce concentration on Billy's face.

Was she really different now? Like maybe there was a presex and postsex Trish? She finished dressing while Billy left the car to take a leak. Now it felt cold. She realized she was shaking. A wind had sprung up. A tree branch raked the windshield, and a whistling sound eddied at the windows.

They had driven off the road a ways, following a track that was little more than a tall hump of grass between two ruts. When Trish heard the engine, her first inclination was to duck. Common sense told her the driver wouldn't even notice Billy's Valiant, but adrenaline kicked in, her mind roiling with images of being discovered out here by the sheriff—or worse, her own father. She knew she looked guilty as hell.

The sound came closer. Trish peered out the back window. Two sets of headlights appeared in the distance, the second pair nearly obscured by dust. As they approached, Trish realized they were trucks, not cars, and they were going fast, bumping and rattling over the rough road. There was something about the speeding trucks that scared her to the core.

She wished Billy would come back. Where was he, anyway? How long did it take to pee?

They were still a long way off but coming straight at her, one set of headlights just in front of the other.

There was a bend in the road just before where she and Billy had driven off to park. Logically, Trish knew the trucks would not continue in her direction, but she was scared just the same.

And then something happened that crystallized her fear.

The headlights behind advanced until they were hidden by the bulk of the pickup in front. There was a muffled thump, and the pickup weaved back and forth before shooting forward again.

"Billy!" Her voice was a tiny wail.

The other truck hung on its tail like a terrier. In the glare of the pursuing vehicle's beams, Trish could tell that the truck in front was white.

Fear gripped her in its sweaty fist. Where the hell was Billy?

They were closing fast, now. The truck behind was actually pushing the other one! Their engines rent the air, screaming like wild animals in a fight to the death.

Their lights blanched the interior of the Valiant. Trish's first instinct was to bolt, but she was paralyzed with fear. They'd never make the curve. They'd come right up here, and she'd be found the next day in Billy's car, miles from where she should have been, smashed and bloody—

Almost to the bend.

The truck in the lead accelerated. With a scream of rubber, he slalomed into the turn, back end fishtailing. Dust showered the air like fireworks.

He'd made it!

Relief washed over her. The pickups hurtled through the night, disappearing over a hill. Trish fumbled with the door handle and bolted out of the car, looking for Billy.

It was so dark she couldn't see anything. And cold. Now it was really cold. Rubbing her arms, she jogged through the tall grass. "Billy?"

"Over here." He was up on the hill.

She ran as fast as she could, her breath coming in short gasps. As she reached the top, Billy stepped forward and gathered her into his arms.

The banshee scream of engines seized the night. Thump. Squeal.

"Jeez! That guy's fucking crazy!" Billy said.

Below them the two trucks arrowed down the straight part of the road. Their lights were only pinpoints now in the hanging dust; white, red, white, red. Billy held her close, the fingers of one hand rubbing her scalp through the ribbons of her hair in a rhythmic, comforting motion. Trish wasn't so afraid now. She'd accepted the impossible, that one guy was trying to run the other off the road. She felt an odd air of detachment creep over her. It looked like a video game from here.

The back headlights eased up. Wham! Dropped back.

"Jesus!" muttered Billy. "They're headed toward Dead Man's Curve!"

Trish knew Dead Man's Curve was up the road somewhere. A lot of kids had wiped out there; one man had even died, giving the curve its name.

But this wasn't real. They'd slow down before then, wouldn't they? Trish squeezed Billy's hand, and he squeezed back. The simple action comforted her. It wasn't real. It couldn't be. These guys were just playing chicken.

Playing. Chicken.

Wham! This time the white pickup veered to the side, out of control. Its headlights lit up a shiny yellow diamond: a curving arrow and the number below it—fifteen. Fifteen miles an hour.

A video game, she told herself sternly. Her teeth gritted together so tight her jaw ached.

Did she imagine she saw the figure in the truck was fighting the wheel?

Just like a video game.

The pickup skidded, hurtled across the road—

Not real.

—and slammed sideways into an oak tree.

The sound of the impact carried up the hill, a loud smack, and then there was the tinny sound of loose metal scraping as the truck rolled over, once, twice, and landed upright on its wheels. It coasted down the slope into another tree.

The second truck had slowed for the turn, but not enough. It fishtailed, tires slewing out of control, and sideswiped the sign. The driver managed to straighten out and accelerated, engine screaming.

Then there was quiet.

The smashed truck's hood liked like an accordion. Steam rose into the cold night. There was a tinkle of glass. It didn't look all that bad, though. At any minute Trish expected the driver to open the door, jump out and wave at her, like the race car drivers did. *It's all right!*

No one jumped out. No one waved.

She could hear something hissing. The truck's lights were still on, and that was the spookiest thing of all. The headlights bathed the tree, etched the lacy oak leaves silver.

Takes a licking but keeps on ticking.

That little bit of black humor shook her out of her apathy. The man needed help, if he wasn't already dead.

"Jesus Christ," Billy said.

"We've got to go down there," Trish heard herself say.

"We can't!"

"We have to." She was quaking now, her limbs energized. She started to run down the hill. "He might be hurt!"

He caught up with her, grabbed her arm. "No, Trish! We'll get in trouble!"

"You stay here, then. I'll go." The rage she felt for him was icy hot.

"You're crazy!" But he followed, then passed her. They ran down the hill and across a broad stretch of field, up another, smaller rise and down the last slope that angled to the road below. Her breath came in harsh gasps, but her legs felt strong.

They were halfway down the slope when she heard the drone of an engine. Instinctively she edged over to the oak tree to her right.

"Hear that?" Billy demanded. "There's a car. They'll see him—"

"Shhh!" Her heart had forgotten to beat. She recognized the sound of the engine, although it was choppier.

The truck cruised slowly into view.

"Is that—?"

"Quiet!" she whispered savagely. Fear slithered through her extremities like mercury, silvery and toxic.

There was something wrong with the truck. The engine kept missing. It shuddered to a halt, backed up, and turned so that its headlights fixed on the wreck.

"Holy shit!" Billy muttered.

Trish couldn't swallow the lump that had formed in her throat like a dry pill. Her heart thumped in her chest.

The truck idled. White exhaust burbled into the air. Trish could feel her foot going to sleep.

"What's he doing?"

The door squeaked open, and a dark figure walked over to the wreck, silhouetted against the white light. The figure gave the impression of heft, but that could be deceiving; the bulky vest and billed cap he wore were a kind of uniform around here.

He stood there for what seemed like centuries. He rubbed his arms as if he were cold.

Trish's foot writhed with pins and needles, but she dared not move.

The driver turned, walked back toward the truck.

Unconsciously, Trish shifted her feet.

A rock, dislodged by her shoe, trickled down the slope. To her ears it sounded like an avalanche.

The figure below glanced up.

Looked right at her.

She felt like a rabbit pinned in the headlights.

The figure swiveled his head to the left, then the right, as if listening. Then walked with slow deliberation to the truck.

He got in, slammed the door. Backed up, turned around, and drove away.

The chugging engine was gradually lost to the hum of the night.

"It's eleven-thirty," Billy said at last. His voice was an octave higher. "If I don't get back soon, we'll be in deep shit."

"We're gonna be in deep shit anyway."

His eyes caught hers. They were unreadable.

"We've got to report it," she said.

"No we don't."

"What do you mean, no we don't?"

"What did you see exactly?"

"A murder!" She could hear her voice, high and frightened. She sounded like a little girl.

"Exactly? You saw some guy run the other guy off the road. Did you get a good look at the guy? I didn't."

"No, but—"

"So what's the point? We didn't see enough to help any-body." He reached out and tipped her chin up with his fingers. "You know how your parents feel about me. If they know we were together that'll be it. They won't let you near me."

"But he killed—"

He touched a finger to her lips. "They'll know. They'll be able to tell just by looking at you—everything you feel shows on your face. If they know we were out here, they'll know what you and I did."

She saw her father's face in her mind's eye, and that did it. Billy was right. Nothing they had seen would help the sheriff, but it could hurt her real bad.

But Billy wasn't through. "If that guy ever finds out we saw him, you know what would happen, don't you?"

"He didn't see us," she whispered.

"No, he didn't. But if we told . . ." Billy let the answer hang in the air.

She thought of the man staring up into the darkness, right at her. Wondered if he'd seen their car. Maybe he already knew who they were.

But if he didn't . . .

Billy was right. It would be suicide to tell anyone what they saw.

"You can't tell anyone about this," Billy said firmly. "Anyone."

Four

As Dakota hunched her shoulders inside the fringed suede jacket and pulled her black Stetson lower over her ears, she reflected that the phrase "morning after" was remarkably apt. But how many people suffered from a twenty-five-thousand-dollar hangover? It was a sure bet that if she stayed here much longer, she wouldn't have any savings left.

Dakota doubted she'd see a check on her father's life insurance policy anytime soon; when they billed for the premium they wanted it right away, but she knew they'd keep their money as long as they could. If she cashed in a couple of CDs she'd have enough money to juggle Black Oak's finances for a while, *if* nothing unforeseen happened.

What am I thinking? This is the horse business. Something unforeseen always happens!

Cold wind harried streamers of dirt and clear plastic cups across the lot where only yesterday trucks and horse trailers had been crammed together like RVs on a Mexican beach. The voices were stilled now; only the wind rang hollowly through the metal pipe corrals. Most of the Black Oak horses were gone. Even though there would be mares coming in to be bred to Something Wicked, by summer they would be gone, too, and then the barns would take on the staleness of structures that had outlived their purpose.

She had to get away from the oppressive emptiness. There was only one thing that would soothe her: a ride in the hills.

Dakota tucked her ponytail into her collar for added

warmth, donned her gloves, and strode across the drive toward the barn. A retinue of ranch dogs trotted at her heels. The two golden retrievers belonged to her. She'd named them Affirmed and Alydar after the great rivals who had swept the thoroughbred Triple Crown in 1978. Like their namesakes, the dogs were big strapping animals with reddish-gold coats and generous hearts.

Dakota was glad she'd brought them with her. She had planned to fly out for the dispersal, but there just happened to be an audition in Yuma last week for a location film. Since Yuma was halfway to Sonoita, Dakota decided to drive. It worked out well; she had room in her Toyota Forerunner for a few of her father's things, and transportation while she was here. Dakota preferred driving her Forerunner to Coke's new Ford monster truck, which she would probably sell.

He'd been driving the old farm pickup at the time of the accident. It, of course, had been totaled.

As she reached the barn, Dakota heard a laboring engine coming her way, and shielded her eyes against the bright sun.

A fifties-era turquoise pickup with an Al Jolson grin wheezed up the dirt road and parked nose-down on the small grade near the barn. Its occupant was a thin man, wearing a flannel shirt and goose-down vest. A lumpish teenage girl slid out of the passenger side.

As he approached, Dakota realized that her impression of middle age had to be adjusted upward. The man must be sixty. His hair was as black as an Apache's—probably dyed—and his face was scored and weatherbeaten from the wind and sun. She wondered if his bloodshot eyes were a result of the cold wind, or if he drank.

"You must be Coke's daughter." He put out a hand. "Name's Jerry Tanner."

She noticed his handshake was anything but firm, and was surprised. Horsemen usually had a good grip.

"Sorry about Coke." She could smell his breakfast on his breath. "He and I went way back. This here's my daughter, Lucy."

The girl wore a plum-colored goose-down jacket, dark blue

jeans and scuffed work boots. Brown hair sheathed her head like an ill-fitting helmet. The hairstyle was meant to appear elfin, and would have, on a petite person.

"Lucy." Dakota smiled at the girl, who squinted at her from colorless eyes sunk into a complexion like uncooked dough. Baby fat, Dakota thought sympathetically. "What can I do for you, Mr. Tanner?"

He grinned. "It's what I can do for you. Did Coke ever mention me?"

"I've heard your name," she said, although she couldn't remember where.

"I worked with him for the last couple of years. Training his horses."

"I thought he trained them all himself."

"I had his Ruidoso string when he was in California," he said. "Up until about a year ago. He and I didn't agree on whether or not to race a horse. I decided to resign." There was a hint of smugness in his voice. Suddenly, Dakota remembered the newspaper photo she'd come across in her father's papers. A horse running on three legs, broken leg flopping, eyes bulging with pain and terror.

"You heard of Blue Kite?"

Blue Kite. That was the horse's name. Dakota nodded, feeling ill. Another one of her father's mistakes in judgment?

"I thought he wasn't up to snuff, an' I told Coke so. Turns out the colt broke his leg. 'Course," he hastened to add, "it was bad luck. Could've happened to anybody."

But it had happened to her father. And there were plenty of other accidents, too.

"I'd like to work for you," Jerry Tanner said. "I heard you're keeping the bay filly, and I was the one who first put a halter on her. She works real kind for me."

Dakota stared at him. Yesterday, when she bought Shameless, she hadn't even thought about who would train her. Coke had always been more interested in the racehorses than the breeding operation, and so he had left Dan Bolin in charge of the ranch, while he took care of the racing stable. No doubt there was a big hole in the filly's training, and

she'd need a trainer soon if she was to be ready for the
Ruidoso Futurity. Still, Dakota didn't really know anything
about this man.

"I hear you're gonna run Shameless in the Ruidoso. It'll be
tight, but I can get her ready." He dug into his pocket, pulled
out a cheap wallet, and produced a curled photograph. It
showed her father and Jerry Tanner smiling at the camera.
"There we are, in happier times."

He knew the filly. He knew her father. The part of her that
thrived on reassurance wanted to jump at his offer, but her instincts told her to go slowly.

"Know why he called her Shameless, don't you?" Tanner
pocketed the wallet and retrieved a crumpled pack of Luckies
from his breast pocket, shook one out, and lit up. "Named her
after Garth Brooks's song. Really liked it—said it described
how he felt about the people he loved and let down. He was
always talking about how he wished he could make it up to
you . . . for not being there."

Icing on the cake. Thick and gooey, the kind that made you
gag. Not that she didn't believe him. It was just like Coke to
name a horse after a song. He'd named her after the place
where she'd been conceived, a town in North Dakota where
he'd been rodeoing. But Dakota couldn't see Coke confiding
in anyone, and it wasn't in him to blame himself for the de-
terioration of their relationship. Unless he'd changed a lot in
the last few years.

Tanner laughed shortly, waxing reminiscent. "He played
Garth Brooks over and over on that old cassette player of his.
Like a broken record."

Dakota's own taste ran from Bonnie Raitt to Puccini. She
didn't like country-western, perhaps because Coke had played
it so often when she was younger.

"So . . . What do you say?" he asked hopefully.

"I'll have to think about it." She knew her father had mentioned his name, a long time ago. It was something important,
and favorable—although Tanner certainly hadn't impressed
her so far. "What do you charge?"

"I'll be taking my own string up to Ruidoso, so I could just put the filly in with them. Shouldn't be too expensive. Coke's cabin's up there. I'd like me and my daughter to stay there, if it's all right with you. We can get by with a small salary and living expenses. And of course I'll be getting a good percentage when the filly comes home a winner. We could negotiate that."

"I don't know," Dakota said at last. She didn't want to be rushed. Already, she'd paid a small fortune for Shameless, and she didn't want to make a mistake now.

Jerry Tanner came one step closer, and she got another whiff of coffee, cigarettes and ham. "You're wondering if I'm any good," he said, motioning to the rust-mottled truck. "It sure don't look like I got rich training horses. Thing is, it's tough out there with the recession an' all. If you ain't one of the top guys, nobody wants to know you. Your dad believed in me, though. I'm sure he must've mentioned me." He paused, looking like a gambler about to play his trump card. "We were in the army together. If it wasn't for me he wouldn't have had any horses *to* train."

Everything fell into place. Jerry Tanner had been the man who saved Coke's life in the Korean War.

The trainer was looking at her, his expression hopeful. "He never told you how I saved his life?"

"Yes. Yes he did. I'm sorry I—"

"It's all right. It was a long time ago. It was Coke who got me to come out here. He was the best friend I ever had, aside from that little setback we had over Blue Kite. I think if he'd lived, we would've ended up friends again."

Suddenly, Dakota wanted to ask him about that incident, and a host of other things. Wanted to see her father through his friend's eyes. Maybe then she could understand him more, know why he had treated her mother the way he had. And why he had been such a stranger to her.

Jerry Tanner handed her his card, all business, now. "I'm takin' my horses up to Ruidoso first week of May. I'll be glad to bring your filly with 'em."

Dakota was still coming to grips with the fact that this was the man who had saved her father's life. "You live in

Sonoita?" she asked, wondering why it was she'd never met her father's savior before.

"We do now, ever since I hooked up with Coke again. Before that, we moved around a lot." He motioned to his daughter. "Lucy goes to school here."

Lucy's bangs fell forward over her eyes as she patted Alydar, whose back end wriggled engagingly. Dakota felt a stab of pity. It must be a hard life, moving around with the races. Summering in one place, wintering in another.

Jerry Tanner stuck his thumbs in his belt loops and looked down at the ground, rocking on his heels. "You probably have a lot on your mind, what with Coke just dying and all, but I wouldn't leave that filly too long. She'll need to be in top shape if she's gonna run against the best horses in the country."

Dakota wanted to hire him on the spot. He was the obvious choice. He'd worked with Shameless before; he knew her. And more important, he was the man who had saved Coke's life. Obviously, Coke had trusted him. Despite the hint of desperation in Jerry Tanner's eyes, his obvious attempts to ingratiate himself, she wanted to believe that his desire to work with such a fine filly had made him overeager. And of course, he had a teenage daughter to support. "Thank you for coming by, Mr. Tanner. I do have a lot to think about, but I'll probably call you in a few days and we can talk about it some more."

"Thank you, ma'am. You hire me, you won't be sorry."

Dakota watched father and daughter climb into the cab of the old Chevy truck. She saw the truck roll down the incline, heard Tanner pop the clutch and the engine cough to life.

A faulty starter, probably. How impressive could you get?

Dakota shook her head and wondered how it happened that Jerry Tanner was the answer to her problems.

Five

The oak tree leaned over the curve, its shadow pooling on the dirt road. Bunches of golden Arizona cottontop shivered in the breeze, their frayed topknots opaquely translucent, like pearls.

The tree's wound suppurated; black sap trying to heal the traumatized bark. Dakota stepped down from Cochita.

So this was where it had happened. Her mouth went dry as she saw the sparklets of turquoise glass mixed with dirt, gravel, and a few black threads of blown retread.

It seemed unreal to her, as if this tragedy had happened to another person. She had seen Coke only a few times in the last ten years, and every single time they'd fought. Maybe it was the only way they could maintain any kind of relationship at all. Two strong wills in an endless tug-of-war over unimportant things, so busy fighting over petty details that they never noticed there was nothing else between them.

Had it always been that way?

Her childhood had been happy. No major traumas, no verbal or physical abuse. Coke wasn't around all that much—he spent a great deal of time traveling during the racing season—but she remembered good times with him. He took her to basketball games. He gave her a horse of her own for her fifth birthday over her mother's objections. Every December, he took her up to the nearby mountains to find their Christmas tree. And when they stayed at the cabin in Ruidoso, they would fish in the creek below the house.

Sometimes Coke would take her fishing at Bonito Lake. Just the two of them, father and daughter, for the whole day. In fact, it was her mother who had always been the odd man out, until Dakota turned ten. That was when her parents divorced, and she and her mother moved to California. She'd never gone fishing with her father again.

Suddenly, the grief that had eluded Dakota since she'd learned of Coke's death crashed into her. Her heart dropped like ballast into a deep void that terrified her, for it was a place in herself she had not known existed.

Tears blurred her eyes. Coke might have been stubborn and opinionated, but was still her father. And now he was gone.

She was so distracted she didn't hear the three-wheeler until it shot over the hill. Cochita heard it, though. She jumped straight into the air like someone lit a cherry bomb under her.

Dakota, who had grown up with the First Law of Horsemanship—never give up the reins without a fight—found herself ploughing through the dirt, the leather tearing off her glove and burning a furrow in her palm before jerking out of her hands. Cochita took off for home.

The asshole on the ATV gunned his motor, described a doughnut around the tree, and drove off in the other direction. Dakota doubted he was too put off by the sight of her middle finger, but she was heartened that her reflexes were still in working order.

Her hand felt like someone had sewn gravel into it with an upholstery needle. She stood up, slapped her hat against her jeans, and started walking up Washboard Road. The entrance to Black Oak was about four or five miles from here, she guessed, and then it was another three miles to the main ranch house.

She heard a truck engine and, whispering a fervent prayer of thanks, stuck out a thumb. A Dodge Ram 350 drew abreast of her. "You make it to the buzzer?"

Of all the damn people to show up on this lonely road, it had to be her ex! "What's that supposed to mean?" she demanded.

"You look like a bronc just threw you. Just wondered if you made the time."

"Very funny."

He leaned over to the passenger side and opened the door. "Go ahead and get in."

The thought of owing Clay anything, even a ride home, made her cringe.

He folded his arms over the steering wheel. The sun picked out the dark hairs on his strong, bronzed hands. Hands that had once known Dakota intimately. "It's a cold day for a walk," he said. "Particularly such a long one."

The wind burrowed into the nooks and crannies of her jacket, but Dakota wasn't sure if it was the cold or the memory of Clay touching her that made her shiver. What made her react like this? He wasn't offering to have sex with her, just drive her home.

"I was headed over to your place anyway."

Dakota realized she had no choice. "Thanks," she said, hopping in.

"I'm glad living in L.A. hasn't taken away all your horse sense, McAllister." Clay aimed the heater vent in Dakota's direction.

"The name's Dakota." She knew she sounded prickly. "I'm sorry," she added, trying to keep her voice steady. "I'm just mad. Some jerk on an ATV came flying over the hill and spooked Cochita. He could have killed us both."

"They're tearing hell out of the public land around here."

"If Cochita's hurt—"

"She looked fine to me. Last I saw her she was kicking up her heels and congratulating herself on giving you the slip. You must be out of practice."

"I am not!"

"You can't be any great shakes if a twenty-year-old mare can throw you."

"She didn't throw me. Besides, you know what she's like."

"Wily as a coyote, slippery as an eel." Clay quoted Dakota's long-ago description of Cochita. "As I recall, she used to toss you once a week."

Dakota didn't want to talk about old times. "What did you want to see me about?"

"A couple of things. For one, I've got a couple of mares I'd like to breed to Something Wicked. And I wanted to thank you for buying Shameless back."

"I didn't buy her for you."

"Okay, you bought her for Coke. 'Course, if you weren't so damn pigheaded, you wouldn't have had to buy her back in the first place, but progress is progress."

"Coke was my father, not yours."

"I'm glad to hear you admit it."

She didn't deign to answer, and they rode in silence to the ranch. Dakota was relieved to see the buckskin mare in the corral; at least the old girl hadn't paid for her fun with a heart attack. The stud manager, Dan Bolin, was carrying Dakota's saddle and bridle back to the barn. When he saw her, he grinned and gave her the thumbs-up.

Clay followed Dakota across the faded bermuda lawn to the house. She was aware of him at her elbow, and hoped he wouldn't touch her. She didn't think she could stand it if he did. As they gained the walk, Clay said, "Coke said he was going to have the place painted this summer."

Dakota stared sadly up at her childhood home, thinking of all the things her father never had a chance to do. The house would still be painted—but only to help it sell.

The rambling white hacienda once defined Spanish-style elegance. In the twenties, Dakota's grandfather had owned a Hollywood movie studio. He'd hosted hunting and packing trips for his fellow movie moguls and weekend getaways for stars and rodeo queens. Poolside parties and lavish dinners had been a daily affair at Black Oak.

Dakota reflected that what had been in vogue in the twenties looked strangely out of place now. The red- and white-striped aluminum awnings hooding the windows would have looked more suitable on a funeral home. Rust streaked the stuccoed walls under rain gutters badly in need of repair. The arched picture windows were too narrow. Inside, built-in bookcases, cabinets and cubbyholes conspired with the myriad of photos and western paintings on the walls to imbue the house with a cluttered, genteel shabbiness.

Alice was vacuuming. "Let's go to the study." Dakota walked through the foyer, crossing a series of terraced, sloping floors which followed the topography of the hill. Clay paused at the blue French doors opening onto the courtyard and gazed at the view: flagstone paving, a swimming pool, and beyond, a belt of fat Aleppo pines. The pool looked like a rectangular-cut aquamarine, sparkling in the sunlight. It, like the house, had seen better days. Years ago, there had been a fountain in the shallow end. Now only a plastered-over pipe remained. The two-tiered diving board stand looked like an oil derrick. Dakota tried not to think of all the times she and Clay had competed with each other, doing back flips and somersaults off the high board, or sunned near the pool's edge, talking about their future together.

"Can you still do a perfect belly flop off the high dive?" Clay asked her.

"Can you still do a perfect swan dive off a Brahma bull?"

He grinned. "I guess neither of us is what we used to be."

As they entered Coke's study, Dakota looked around the jumble of horse blankets, tack, newspapers and magazines piled everywhere, wondering where Clay could sit. She'd been afraid to throw anything away, since there were any number of personal and business papers in among them. "Excuse the mess. Coke wasn't much of a housekeeper."

She'd loved to spend time in the study when she was a child, listening to Coke conduct business with various horsemen or tell stories over drinks with friends. She used to gallop her stick horse over the expensive Oriental rugs, and many of the divots and chips in the red enamel poured concrete had been from her rough play. Only Coke's collection of Americana—jukeboxes, signs, neon, and refurbished gumball machines—was new to her. It had been a late hobby.

Clay moved a horse blanket and sat down on a faded sofa. "I've always liked this room. It's got a lived-in quality."

"That's right. You spent a lot of time here." She tried to keep the accusation out of her voice, and failed.

"You never liked that, did you? The way Coke and I remained friends after the divorce."

"Why should I care?" But she knew her feelings showed in her voice.

"You tell me."

Dakota sighed. She knew she had no right to be jealous. But she also knew that her father had enjoyed playing people off against one another, and doubted his side of the friendship had been entirely innocent. She motioned to the bar. "Can I get you anything?"

"No, thanks."

"You said you had some mares for Something Wicked?"

As they discussed the mares, Dakota tried to maintain a professional distance. This was a business transaction. But she couldn't ignore the way his shirtsleeves were rolled just to the elbows, revealing the long muscles of his forearms. Or how his booted ankle rested negligently on his knee, or the way his faded jeans fit his trim hips like soft old velvet, remembering how she used to run her hand along his flat belly, pretending her palm was a car going over a road that dipped and swelled, slowing to a crawl over "the speed bump"—and suddenly she was whopped hard by the searing memory of the two of them tangling in wet-hot sheets of a summer's afternoon, her fingers unzipping jeans just like these, marveling at his smooth bronze skin.

In that one bittersweet instant, she was overwhelmed by the memory of being eighteen and in love for the first time, her whole future stretching out before her like a day at the beach, before the grief, the anger, the disillusionment set in, and wished with all her heart she could go back to that time and start over.

For one instant. Then she regained her sanity. She cleared her throat and tried to focus on the air just by his right ear. "Then it's settled. You can send the mares anytime this month."

Although their business was concluded, Clay made no move to leave. Did he guess how he'd affected her? "It just occurred to me that I put you in a bind yesterday," he said.

"What do you mean?"

"When I talked you into keeping the filly."

"You didn't talk me into anything. I make my own decisions."

"Do you have to be such an independent *bruja?*" He'd always called her that—Spanish for witch—and the memory jolted her. "I thought you could use some help."

"Help?"

"You'll need a trainer."

"I have a trainer."

It was Clay's turn to look nonplussed. "I don't see—"

"I got one this morning."

He digested this information, his dark eyes skeptical. "Do you mind telling me who it is?"

"His name is Jerry Tanner."

"Jerry Tanner? Are you kidding?"

"What's wrong with him?"

"I wouldn't let him near one of my horses."

"Coke did."

That stopped his gallop. Clay rubbed the back of his neck with his hand. "Did you also know Coke fired him?"

"Mr. Tanner told me about that. He said he had a disagreement with Dad over Blue Kite."

Clay snorted. "Some disagreement. Did he tell you he ran that horse against Coke's specific instructions?"

Dakota's stomach sank. "He said Coke wanted to run him."

"And you believed him." Clay's eyes narrowed. "Didn't you know your father at all?"

"I think you'd better go."

Clay stood up. "Just for the record, Jerry Tanner was responsible for that colt being destroyed. If you want to hire him, it's your business. But if I were you I'd think about that filly, and what you might be risking." He walked toward the doorway.

Dakota felt as if she'd been socked in the stomach. No one accused her of cruelty. Least of all Clay Pearce! "Just a minute!"

He turned to face her, his dark eyes challenging.

"Can we talk like two reasonable adults?" She sat down to keep her legs from shaking. "It's taking me a minute to get all this. You're telling me Jerry Tanner lied to me."

"If he said he didn't want to run Blue Kite, yes."

"But he meant a lot to my father."

Clay sat down on the sofa opposite her. "You mean because of what happened in the war."

She nodded.

"Tanner's been collecting for a long time."

"He saved my father's life!"

"He didn't have to make a career out of it. Coke gave him his start as a racehorse trainer. Gave him good horses, a high salary. He treated him like a younger brother, always forgiving his mistakes, even the big ones.

"When Tanner showed up again, Coke hired him on the spot. It never made sense to me, because it was obvious he was no good with horses, and Coke wasn't a tolerant man."

"Maybe Tanner was a better horseman than you thought."

Clay shook his head. "I saw him in action. Coke got so tense watching him try to load a high-strung colt he bit a cigarette in two. You could practically see his blood pressure rise. Didn't say a word, though." He shifted slightly, ran strong fingers through his dark hair. She wondered if he did it on purpose. Why would he bother to make her want him again? Just to show he could do it? "Every time I asked him about Tanner, he'd clam up. Even after he told me about what happened in the war, I didn't understand it. Jerry Tanner is bad news. Even Coke fired him—too late for Blue Kite."

"Obviously, you know more about Jerry Tanner than I do." She caught his gaze, was disconcerted by the disturbing scrutiny in those eyes she knew so well. "I'll have to think about it. If you could give me some names of trainers." She paused, self-conscious. "I really don't think you and I should do business, in light of our . . . past association."

"You think I'm here because I want a job?"

"Well, you offered—"

"I didn't get a chance to offer anything. I'm not taking on

any new owners." There was something final in his tone that snapped her to attention. "Half the horses I run are horses I raised, and I'm waiting for the day when I won't have to train for anyone else. I have no interest in training Shameless."

She was surprised at the bleakness that this remark elicited.

"Ron Spackman has a good-sized stable right here in Sonoita. He might be full up, but it's worth a try. I've written the name of a couple of other trainers on the back." When he stood up and handed her the card, their fingers brushed. Dakota felt as if she'd just touched an exposed wire.

She drew back, her face burning. She could still feel the residual warmth of his fingers on the stiff paper. This was ridiculous!

"You'd better do something soon," Clay said. "As it is, it's going to be a rush getting Shameless ready for the Ruidoso. I'll bet she hasn't set foot on a track in three weeks."

"But surely someone would have continued her training."

"Who? Dan's got his hands full with the breeding operation."

"You think I shouldn't run her?" Hadn't he told her only yesterday that the filly had a chance to win the Ruidoso?

"I'm not the one to make that decision."

It was all too much. She'd just paid a fortune for this racehorse, had no one to train her, and a pile of bills as high as the barn door. On top of that, here was her ex-husband, smirking about how she had to make some important decisions pretty damn fast! "Well, could you at least help me decide? Preferably before I send out the next payment?"

"Hey, don't bite my head off. If she were mine, I'd aim her for the Santa Cruz Futurity instead."

"The Santa Cruz Futurity. But you said . . ." Dakota was utterly confused now. If she stopped making payments on the Ruidoso, she'd lose all the money Coke had paid so far. "Why would you do that?"

"She'd have a real good chance of winning it. You know how two-year-olds are at the beginning of the season. All over the track, bumping into each other and gawking at the crowd. But she's got such raw talent that even if she doesn't get a good trip she'd probably make up for it. That wouldn't happen at Ruidoso, with the best colts from all over the country running. When she's more seasoned, I'd go to Ruidoso."

"The point's moot, anyway, if I can't find a trainer."

"You could start her out yourself, until you find someone."

Dakota stared at him, unable to believe what she'd just heard.

"It's easy enough to get a trainer's license. You helped your dad train the Black Oak horses."

"Coke made all the major decisions."

"Coke said you've been training show jumpers in L.A."

"As a hobby." Training her stepfather's show jumpers was a far cry from training a racehorse.

"But if the money's tight—"

"It's not that tight. Besides, I'm going home in another week."

"That soon?"

"I have a life, Clay. It just doesn't happen to be here."

"I suppose so. It's been good seeing you, though. Better than I thought it would be. You've changed."

Part of her wanted to know what he meant by that, but she refused to play his game. "Thank you for the Clay Pearce seal of approval."

"Still sarcastic, I see. You always sniped when you felt threatened."

"I'm not threatened by you."

He shrugged.

"Why would I be?" she added, and knew instantly she had made a serious mistake. *The lady doth protest too much.*

"No reason, except for the fact we were once married, and we never did hammer out our differences."

"You really think you're something, don't you? Perhaps you should go on 'Donahue' and talk about yourself, how irresistible you are to women. Get this straight, Pearce. Just because I fell for you once doesn't mean that I haven't learned a lot about men since then. We don't have any differences anymore, because we aren't even in the same universe!"

To her surprise, he looked serious. "You never wonder if we gave up too soon? Not once in all these years? I have.

There have been times, McAllister, when I've kicked myself for letting you go."

"You didn't let me go, as I remember. You told me to go. Big difference."

"I told you to make a choice."

"My husband or my career? What kind of choice is that? You said I've changed. It's a pity that you haven't. Your knuckles are dragging on the ground, you're such a Neanderthal. Does Rita get to have a career, or is she confined to a hobby or two?"

"I imagine Rita does what she pleases."

"I'm happy for her."

"You don't sound like you are. And as far as Rita goes—"

"Look, Clay." Suddenly her head ached. "I've been through a rough couple of days. I just want to put my father's affairs in order, find a trainer for Shameless, and go home. I don't need any more complications, and I sure as hell don't need a hard time from you. Surely you can understand that."

"You know I always got a kick out of hanging you out to dry, McAllister, but you're right." His mouth straightened into a line and his eyes darkened. "I'm sorry."

"Apology accepted."

"Friends?"

"Friends." Again, bleakness swept over her. How could she be friends with this man?

Speed bump.

He fed a quarter into the candy-apple red gumball machine and a gumball tumbled into his hand. He tossed it into the air and caught it. "Hope Spackman works out okay," he said, walking toward the door.

"Pearce."

"What?"

"Thanks for looking out for me."

He saluted smartly. "Yo, General." And then he was gone.

Clay's truck bumped along the road in the direction of the brick ranch-style house on the hill. His ancestral home of-

fered none of the nostalgic splendor of Black Oak. Built by
his father, it was the second house erected on Pearce land.
Plain and utilitarian, the modest dwelling was far more practical to keep up than the back lot hacienda of the McAllisters.

McAllisters and Pearces had been friends close to one hundred years; ranchers who shared common backgrounds and
attitudes. Marrying Dakota had been the most natural thing in
the world for Clay.

It was also natural for him to offer her his help now that
Coke was gone. But he had not expected to be attracted to
her. He'd assumed those feelings had died a long time ago.

So what was all that bull about how he regretted their
breakup? Where the hell did that come from? He didn't mean
it. He didn't even know her anymore, let alone love her.

Dakota had every right to be angry. No wonder she called
him egotistical. She must have thought he was flirting with
her just for the hell of it, when in reality the words had just
. . . slipped out.

Clay passed the house, glancing at the far hill. Some trees
and plants had been delivered for the wolf enclosure. It had
been Rita's idea, even though the run already had plenty of
native oak and grassland. He thought the increased activity
might do more harm to the reclusive animals than good, but
somehow Rita had gotten permission from U.S. Fish and
Wildlife to put the plants at the far edges of the enclosure, to
enhance the wolves' "natural habitat."

The truck phone rang. "I've been trying to reach you for
hours," Rita said. "Did the plants get there?"

"I'm looking at them."

"There was no trouble? I've been having a terrible time
getting that nursery to do anything. I don't even know if the
grasses are the right kind."

"I'll check on them later. I'm on my way to the barn."

"Maybe I should come by."

He rubbed his eyelids. "It wouldn't be a good idea. I have
to play catch-up with the horses."

"Oh, all right. I'll see you tomorrow morning?"

When he paused, she muscled through. "You said you'd

take a look at the horses. They came in today, and I want to know they traveled well. If you won't train them for me, the least you could do is look them over. *I* sure don't know anything. You chose them, after all."

"It'd be early. Before the track opens."

"How early?"

"Six-thirty."

"I'll set my alarm."

"All right."

"You know, Clay, you could still go to the rally. I haven't canceled the room yet."

"I can't. I'm sorry."

"If you change your mind, I'll be leaving around four on Friday."

When he didn't reply, she added, "You'd make a big difference, Clay. How many people actually have a mating pair of Mexican wolves?"

"They're not mine. You know that as well as I do." The Mexican wolves didn't belong to anybody. Clay had only donated acreage to the government for the wolves' temporary home, since a portion of the Bar 66 Ranch offered enough space for them to roam in their natural habitat. But freedom was only an illusion; the area was enclosed by a ten-foot-high chain link fence. Clay had come to call it "the compound."

"You could take more of an interest," Rita said.

"I thought the point was to leave them alone."

He was greeted by a long period of silence. When at last she spoke, her voice was brisk. "Well, then. I'll give you a call."

"I'm looking forward to it."

Her goodbye was cool.

Rita was used to getting what she wanted. He wondered if anyone had ever said no to her before.

He'd noticed—too late—that Rita DeWeil never did anything half way. She threw herself into a cause, bringing to it all the considerable resources of a widow of a prominent Phoenix developer. Right now, she wanted to save the Mexican wolf from extinction.

As Clay drove toward the stable, he avoided thinking about Rita and thought about the wolf instead. Although the Mexican wolf had ceased to be a threat well over thirty years ago, memories around her were long. There were things you just didn't do and harboring wolves was one of them. A lot of people viewed him as a turncoat.

He didn't completely understand why he was doing it himself. Such a cause should be an anathema to him. He had seen enough kills—by mountain lions, since there were no wolves left—to have a visceral hatred for any predator. He'd seen cows searching for their calves, their agonized cries excruciating, while their offspring lay nearby, torn to pieces.

His instinct had always been to protect the young and weak. Three generations of ranchers had bred it into the bone. Every time he saw a calf or colt being born, every time he doctored an animal or reunited a baby with its mother, he was overwhelmed by a warm feeling of pride and a joy so deep it choked him. They were so helpless, so gentle, so trusting—and they depended on *him* to keep them safe. He was their shepherd.

But wiping out a whole species sat wrong with him. His view was ruled by logic, not emotion. If a man started tossing out undesirable species right and left, the world would be a lousy place to live. If it survived at all.

He shook his head. You'd think God-fearing Christians would understand that, but a lot of them couldn't get beyond the man's dominion over the earth crap. It didn't take a genius to see every living thing had been put here for a reason, and if you fiddled around with it long enough, the whole thing would come down like a house of cards. There would be no calves, no colts. No people, for that matter. Which, judging from the current state of the world, might be a good thing.

He parked beside the barn and checked on the horses. Although his racers had regular grooms, Clay liked to brush down each one himself every couple of days or so. It was important that he be familiar with them, know them physically and mentally. He checked their legs every day.

Clay led his All American hopeful Dangerously out of his stall and cross-tied him in the aisle. "Let's see what we've got," he muttered to the chestnut colt, running his hand along the animal's legs and squeezing gently. All the while he spoke in soft, calm tones. No heat, and the puffiness was just about gone.

Training two-year-olds, who were technically still babies, was akin to weight training in humans. A young horse's legs were never meant to carry his own weight at a full-out run; they had to be built up artificially, just like the muscles of a weight lifter. You stressed them slightly, then rested them, then stressed them again, until the blood supply to the feet increased and the joints, muscles, and ligaments became stronger. No pain, no gain.

The irony wasn't lost on him that the whole idea of racing two-year-olds was unnatural.

Clay put the colt back in his stall and headed up to the house. His mind kept returning to his encounter with Dakota. He was glad he'd talked Rita out of buying the filly. Shameless was meant for Dakota. Dakota was still her father's daughter, whether she knew it or not.

The thing he had to keep in mind, though, was that she was no longer his wife.

Six

Dakota spent the rest of the day looking at the books for the stud farm. She could tell Dan Bolin didn't like it; twice he'd told her that Coke had always left that part of the business to him. It had worked that way for twenty years, so why change now?

"Norm's already looked at the books. He said they're fine," he'd protested.

"You know as well as I do that the only money coming in right now, other than from the auction, is from the stud and boarding fees. I have to know where we stand before I can make any decisions about what to do with the ranch."

"I have my own system."

"I'll put everything back the way it was, don't worry."

Grudgingly, he left her alone in his brick office. She noticed him from time to time through the window, hands shoved in the pockets of his jeans, looking like a captain without a ship. He was a big slow-talking redhead whose freckles had long since run together into a mottled tan. Up until now Dan had always seemed easygoing. She wondered if he resented her interference because she was a woman. Just yesterday, when she'd asked about the incoming mares, he'd told her not to "worry her pretty head" about them, then pointedly asked her when she planned to return to L.A.

Come on, McAllister, she told herself sternly. *You can't take every little remark personally.* "Pretty little head" was just an expression, probably one he'd learned at his father's knee. No doubt it was just as he'd told her, that he had been in charge so long it was hard to give up control.

Looking at the morass of ledgers, loose Post-it notes, and papers, Dakota realized just how Dan had managed to keep control. No one else would want to touch it. Dan's "system" was a complete mystery to her, and the records she did manage to locate were hard to understand. One note attached to a loose veterinary bill said, "Ongoing problem. See file," but she found no file under the horse's name. What did he do, file by coat color? After a couple more "see file" notes, Dakota realized that none of the mares sold at the dispersal sale had a file. In fact, the filing cabinet drawer marked MARES—BLACK OAK was empty. She wouldn't be surprised if he'd thrown out the files after the mares were sold, although that was no way to run a business.

Dakota made a mental note to ask him about them. For now, the only information she had on those mares was what had been written in the sale catalog. She supposed it wasn't important. In fact, none of what she did this afternoon would make an ounce of difference one way or another. She was wasting her time. Trying to look busy, as if it mattered to anyone but herself. Dan sure didn't want her help.

Dakota sighed. She'd promised herself she would look at the books, and that was what she'd do. First, she had to find a way to organize this mess so she could begin to make sense of it.

A great person for lists, Dakota found a legal pad and divided the stock into categories: the horses that had already gone to their new owners, the mares that would remain at Black Oak through the summer, and the outside mares booked to Something Wicked. There were over one hundred of these spread out over the next couple of months.

She was relieved when Alice brought her a late lunch, a tuna fish sandwich on one of her father's plates. It was one of those cheap ceramic plates you could get at Blakely's gas stations in Arizona during the fifties, depicting desert plants in oranges and greens. Coke had collected the whole set, much to her mother's dismay. Mom detested what she called the "junky giveaways," but Dakota had always liked them.

As she ate her sandwich, Dakota glanced at the calendar. There were reminders penciled in for the April payments to keep Shameless in the running for both the Ruidoso and Rainbow Futurities. They totaled nine hundred dollars.

Nine hundred dollars, and here was Clay wondering aloud if Shameless would even be ready for the Ruidoso Futurity. That was a lot of money to spend if you didn't even think you had a chance in the first place.

Dakota stood up, stretched, and rubbed the crick in her neck. Dan could have his ship back. She went along to say hello to Shameless, who was picking daintily at her haynet like a diet-conscious lady at a salad bar.

"So if I fork over the nine hundred bucks," Dakota asked her, "do you think you can win at least one of those races?"

Shameless lifted her queenly head and stared Dakota down, then with quiet deliberation swung her hindquarters around so that Dakota was treated to a view of her superbly muscled backside. Talk about a snub!

"I'm sorry I doubted you. Really."

"You done in there?" Dan Bolin stood in the barn aisle and jerked his thumb at the office.

"For now."

He turned away. Suddenly it occurred to her that Dan would know what shape Shameless was in. "Dan."

The stud manager paused, his features stamped with resignation.

"It's been three weeks since Coke died. What's been going on with the filly? Has anyone continued her training?"

He shrugged. "Coke did everything himself. I've been turning her out in the pasture during the day so she wouldn't get barn sour." He looked anxious to get away from her. "Anything else?"

"No. Thank you." Then she remembered the files. "Oh . . . Do you have the files on the Black Oak mares?"

He shifted his stance, shoving hands into jean pockets. "Why?"

Annoyed, Dakota said, "Because I'd like to see them."

His mouth set in a stubborn line. "The mares're already sold. I don't see why—"

"I don't care about that. I want to see them." Did he have to make every issue a tug-of-war?

"They're at the house," he mumbled. "I'll have to look for them."

"Thank you."

She felt like an intruder in her own home. This wasn't Dan Bolin's ranch. Until someone bought Black Oak, it belonged to her.

At that moment, Dakota fervently wished she could just dump everything and drive back to L.A. Tonight. Forget the filly, forget her father.

Forget Clay.

That night she called the trainers Clay had recommended. Nobody seemed eager to talk. One said his stable was full up, and the other said it was too close to the Ruidoso Futurity, to call him back in a few months.

Ron Spackman returned her call last. She crossed her fingers.

He was sorry, but it was too late for the Ruidoso in May; he couldn't take her.

"If she's not ready, we don't have to run her," Dakota said.

"Sorry. Can't do it."

Frustrated, Dakota demanded, "But why not?" She regretted the outburst immediately. She couldn't force the man to take her horse.

"I don't want to take any chances."

"What do you mean? What chances?"

Spackman paused. "I just don't want to risk it."

"Risk *what?*"

"Look, Miz McAllister, I've got some valuable horses in my barn. One of 'em's slated for the All American. I can't afford to have anything go wrong." He lowered his voice.

"Things get around in this business. Don't say I told you, but a lot of people think someone had it in for Coke."

Had it in for Coke? Dakota remembered the videotape. Hadn't Coke said something along those lines? "Are you telling me no one wants to train my filly because Coke had enemies?"

"I have my owners to think of. Sorry, but that's the way it is. I hope you find somebody." And he hung up.

Stunned, Dakota set the phone down and stared at her father, who smiled down at her from one of the many eight-by-ten glossies on the wall, holding the bridle of another winner.

Seven

At seven the following morning, Dakota hitched a horse trailer to her father's truck and drove Shameless to the Santa Cruz County Fairgrounds. She'd worry about finding a trainer later. Today, the filly was going to the track.

As she pulled up at the stable area, the gate man's eyes widened at the sight of the Black Oak trailer.

Dakota breathed the crystalline air deep into her lungs, exhilaration swelling her heart like wind filling a ship's sails. In this instant, the rare, cutting beauty, the grandeur of this high valley, seemed locked in a silent prism. Gradually, the sounds of the racetrack came through: country music on a radio, snatches of conversations in Spanish, the squeal of an angry horse, the faint growl of a down-shifting semi out on the highway. Against the backdrop of sparkling grassland and clean blue mountains, the pageantry of morning on the backside unfurled before her, as familiar as the old clothes she wore.

Several horses were already warming up on the track, some galloping, some walking and trotting alongside their pony horses. Riders led their charges to and from the track. Hot-walkers were set up by each shedrow, looking like stripped-down carnival rides, the horses tied to them trampling the same radius over and over. A horse received a bath after a workout, its coat gleaming like dark caramel. There was no shade here, anywhere, but it wasn't yet hot enough for anyone to notice.

Without warning, Dakota was hit by memories she'd thought long buried. It was as if she'd never left. The backside was an exclusive club, and she'd been a member. Once. Dakota had forgotten how just being here grabbed the heart and squeezed, how her stomach warmed with nervous excitement.

I'm only here temporarily, she warned herself sternly as she unloaded Tyke, the Black Oak pony horse. Inaptly named, the big paint was more than a match for Coke's heavy western saddle. Dakota would ride Tyke and lead Shameless around the track. A walk or slow jog twice around would be sufficient for today, just enough to reacquaint the filly with the racetrack and let her remember the feel of the saddle and bridle. Tomorrow Dakota would pony the filly again, and if everything went well, she'd let her stretch out into a slow lope. By the end of the week, she'd like to have a rider up and start galloping a mile.

This is just a stopgap measure, she reminded herself, until I find a trainer.

Better, right now, to err on the side of caution. If Dakota was careful, she could do little harm to the filly in a week, and just maybe, a little good. Surely she'd find a trainer by then. Unless they all felt the way Ron Spackman did.

His words haunted her. *Someone had it in for Coke.*

"Want me to tack her up?" asked Judy, the groom who had always accompanied Coke to the races.

Dakota nodded. "I don't know her quirks. She'll be nervous enough, without a stranger saddling her." But as Judy readied Shameless, the filly was calm, almost aloof.

After Dakota had mounted Tyke, Judy handed her Shameless's lead shank. Here goes nothing, she thought, biting her lip. I just hope I don't end up eating mudpies in the middle of the track. The good ol' boys would sure have a field day with that.

She led Shameless to the gap which opened onto the track and started around the dirt oval. Nerves caused Dakota to hold onto the lead too tightly, making Shameless angry. The filly tossed her head and kicked her hind legs out. Dakota gave her more rope. It would be better not to fight her so much. She wanted the filly to walk as calmly as possible.

Shameless was worlds away from the tame show jumpers Dakota handled back home.

Everyone was watching her. She could feel it. By now, they knew that Coke McAllister's daughter was here, with the filly she'd bought back for a ridiculous price at the auction. A lot of them didn't remember her from ten years ago, and the ones who did probably thought California had softened her up. Dakota knew she was viewed as an outsider, and it rankled her. Wasn't Black Oak once the premier quarter horse ranch in Arizona? How could they forget? And yet, just from the way they looked at her—as if they were weighing her mentally—she knew any respect her father might have garnered did not apply to her.

She gritted her teeth, forced herself to sit straighter. Held her head high. Tried to get back into the rhythm, remember how it used to be. They kept toward the outside, staying out of the way of the serious runners.

Dakota began to regain her confidence as they reached the backstretch. The filly bounced against Tyke's sturdy side like an overgrown puppy, her mouth on his neck as if he were nothing more than a stick to be fetched. Still kicking her hind legs out, but because she felt good.

Testing. Looking for weakness.

As they came around the last turn, Dakota noticed Clay mounted on a horse before the grandstand, staring at the far side of the track. He must be watching one of his horses gallop. When he saw her, he waved, and Dakota lifted her hand slightly. The filly tossed her head in anger.

Damn, she was strong. "If you can run like you pull, you'll be all right," Dakota muttered.

Just then two horses shot by her like a bullet. The filly jumped sideways, then lunged forward. Dakota could almost hear her arms rip out of their sockets.

Shameless took off.

Helplessly, Dakota watched the horse's bunching hindquarters and felt the sting of dirt clods. Despair gripped her.

She knew that chasing the filly would only make her run faster.

She was a witness to a disaster.

Her eyes registered Clay, only a hundred yards ahead. He wheeled his mount and started down the track—facing the same direction as Shameless—and waited for the filly to come even with him, his right arm outstretched to catch her.

Dakota saw Shameless head straight for them, at the last minute trying to swerve—

A crash was inevitable.

Dakota closed her eyes, preparing for the thud of colliding flesh.

It never came.

A kaleidoscope of motion, sound, fragments coming together.

Dakota's heart lurched. She couldn't breathe. The filly shied. Clay's horse ran alongside her now as he made a grab for her lead.

And caught it. Already slowing down, already uncertain, Shameless came back to him like a rubber band.

And then Clay leaped to the ground, holding Shameless as she pivoted around, her eyes wild.

Thank God! Dakota said, or thought—she wasn't sure which—as relief doused her in a warm bath. She could feel the freezing trickle of sweat under her arms. Shaking, she managed to slide down from Tyke without falling on her face. She didn't know how she managed to walk the distance between them.

The danger over, mortification set in. She could have caused a serious pileup, been responsible for hurt riders, destroyed horses.

Even now, Dakota knew she faced disaster. The filly could have been ruined for good.

Dakota stared at the blur of slender legs, unconsciously expecting to see splintered bone held together only by bloody wraps—the horror of a broken, dangling limb. One misstep on the track and the filly's ankle could have been shattered. She'd have to be destroyed.

No blood. The filly was putting her weight down on all four legs. Clay soothed Shameless, rubbing her neck and speaking softly, giving her the time and freedom to calm down.

"Is she all right?" Dakota asked, feeling like the lowest worm on the face of the earth.

"Looks like it."

She closed her eyes, swallowed. Maybe she'd gotten out of this unscathed. Shaking, she knelt down and felt the filly's legs.

"You won't know until later."

"I know," she said.

"Here." Clay handed her a cup of black coffee.

Dakota sat miserably on the wheel well of the Black Oak farm trailer, still shaking. She'd always despised people who gave in to self-pity, but right now she couldn't help the tears that brimmed in her eyes.

I've ruined her. I know it. I've ruined my father's horse.

Not only that, but she felt utterly helpless—something else that was completely foreign to her. Clay had done everything. He'd rented a stall, applied cold to the filly's legs before wrapping them, and all the time Dakota just stood off to the side, like a zombie.

She was really good in a crisis.

"We'll know more later," he said, sitting beside her.

Dakota stared straight ahead, seeing nothing. "You have your own horses to deal with."

"They're being seen to," he said simply.

"I could have killed—"

"You didn't."

"The filly could be crippled."

"So far so good. She didn't get far."

"Thank God."

As she stared unseeingly at the mountains, Clay spoke to her, his words comforting. It happened, he told her. Horses got loose. They hurt themselves and others. She was lucky, everything turned out all right, the jocks who were working those two horses had come too close, it was their fault.

But Dakota knew better. She hadn't been able to control her horse. She hadn't paid attention to her surroundings.

She'd failed. And suddenly she couldn't hold the tears back. Clay held her, stroked her back, told her it was all right, and she pressed her face into his shoulder, trying to stifle the sobs that shook her body. The irony was not lost on her. Here was her ex-husband, the man she'd tried to forget, holding her in his arms. And worse, she didn't have the strength to resist him.

She might as well admit it: Coke McAllister's daughter was a— "Weenie," she mumbled.

"Weenie?" Clay's voice vibrated against her cheek. "What?"

"I'm a weenie!"

Clay laughed. His laughing made her feel better. Suddenly the world didn't seem so bleak. Before she knew it, Dakota was laughing, too. Out of relief or hysteria, she didn't know.

But the fear that Shameless might be ruined for life sobered her up. Real fast. She drew away from Clay, put her head in her hands. "I could have caused a really bad pileup. Everyone here must hate me."

"You're blowing it out of proportion."

She glared at him. "You think so? I saw their faces. They expected me to fail." She swiped at a tear that threatened to drip off the end of her nose. "I can't believe, after all these years, that they could act that way. I suppose it's because Coke . . . Coke . . ." She couldn't continue.

"You think most people believed that stuff about Coke?"

"Why wouldn't they?"

"You don't drug your own horse when you *know* it's going to show up in a test. You don't run a horse you know will break down. Not when you have horses that are *that* good. Everyone knows that Coke couldn't have changed that much—or gotten that stupid."

"Then you believe it, too. That someone was trying to hurt his reputation?"

"Coke made a lot of enemies. He was responsible for one jockey's suspension at Los Alamitos. The guy was one of the top money-earning jockeys in the country this year. He's been suspended for a year, and he'll probably lose three hundred thousand dollars from missed rides. That's a conservative estimate. And you've already met Tanner. I'll bet losing his job didn't go down too well." Clay took a sip of coffee. "Coke was a good man. He didn't like to see horses abused, and he spoke up about it. That cost a lot of people a lot of money."

Dakota shivered. It wasn't the cold morning, but the idea that Coke was hated that much.

And where had she been when he needed help? Of course, Coke was too stubborn to admit he needed someone—anyone.

Clay stood up. "Will you do me a favor?"

She nodded. At this moment, she'd do anything for him.

"I want you to pony Budget Taco for me."

"I can't."

"What's the first thing you learn when you get on a horse?" He answered for her. "When you fall, you get back on."

"But I might cause an accident."

"You won't. You were getting the hang of it. I saw you. It just happened that you got unlucky."

Unlucky. Like Coke.

"Dakota, if you don't do this, you'll never live it down. These guys admire guts. If they sense a weakness, they'll eat you alive."

"I'm getting a trainer."

"I'm not talking about training a racehorse. I'm talking about self-respect."

That did it. This man had always known which button to push. She stood up. "Where is he?"

"That's my girl."

"I'm not your girl."

"So I'm not politically correct."

As they headed for his horses, she said, "What in the hell kind of name is Budget Taco?"

Eight

"We've got a problem." Dan Bolin stood in the foyer.

Dakota had come back around noon, still shaken from the filly's disastrous first outing. She'd called the vet before ponying Budget Taco, but had reached his answering service. After waiting an hour, Dakota decided it would be awhile before he returned her call, so she came back to Black Oak. She knew what to do: apply cold treatments to her legs twice a day, and watch Shameless like a hawk. When Dakota thought about what *could* have happened . . .

"Did you hear me?" Bolin asked.

"Sorry, I was thinking of something else."

"It's the vet. We haven't paid him in awhile. Swears he won't touch another horse until we do."

"How much do we owe?"

"Eight hundred and thirty dollars."

She stared at him in disbelief.

Dan shrugged. "Your dad always budgeted for vet bills, but since he died . . ."

"I see." Dakota followed him out to the barn, where Jared Ames, the vet who saw to the Black Oak horses, leaned against his truck, arms folded across his chest. Tall and completely bald, the vet had a perpetually dissatisfied expression, his mouth bracketed by deep grooves. Today, he looked more put out than ever.

"I'm sorry for the inconvenience," she said, feeling small.

"I've got bills, too, you know."

"I'll write you a personal check. Will that be all right?"

"That'll be fine." But his sour expression didn't change.

After she'd paid him, Ames agreed to drive out to the track and look at Shameless.

"I thought he was on the staff," Dakota told Dan, after the vet's van disappeared down the road.

"Not for the past couple of years. Things haven't been going all that well, so Coke had to stop paying him a salary and called him out as needed. Jared took it as a personal insult."

Just another dissatisfied customer in a whole line of them, she thought.

Even though she knew Dan Bolin didn't like it, Dakota went to his office again and spent a few hours going over the stud farm books. It was difficult to get a handle on the operation.

When Dakota had asked Dan anything about the day-to-day operation of the ranch, he gave her grudging, piecemeal answers—if he bothered to answer her at all. But as sullen as he was, Dakota felt sorry for him. She'd heard from Alice that his wife needed a heart transplant. That must take a horrendous toll on him. No wonder he resented her moving into his territory. The stud farm was probably the only place where he *had* control.

He still hadn't given her the files. It had become an unspoken battle of wills. Feeling petty, especially in light of Dan's personal problems, Dakota left a message on his answering machine, asking him to leave the files at the house when he came by for evening feeding. When she returned from getting the mail, she saw them stacked neatly on the side table in the foyer, no note attached. Well, she'd won that one, but it seemed a hollow victory.

She prepared herself a grilled cheese sandwich and iced tea, then went to her father's study. The sun had slipped below the horizon, submersing the study in gloom. The answering machine blinked. She played back the message and heard her mother's cool, disapproving voice, asking her to call back as soon as possible.

After what happened today with the filly, Dakota didn't feel like tiptoeing through a verbal minefield with her mother. Eileen Wood hated Black Oak, and made her feelings known at every juncture.

Dakota could imagine what her mother would say about Shameless.

She glanced at the painting of her father and his favorite racehorse above the mantel. How in God's name had she gotten into this? It wasn't as if she *wanted* to be here.

But as much as she longed to go home and resume the life she knew, Dakota couldn't leave yet. She hated loose ends, hated a mess. And this was a huge mess.

She'd been the one to put the filly in danger; she had to make sure Shameless was all right. After her humiliation today, Dakota wanted a second chance to prove she could handle a racehorse. She was still Coke's daughter. Even though they hadn't been close for years, she wouldn't denigrate his memory by running away. McAllisters didn't do that.

Dakota leafed through the broodmare files, wondering why she bothered. It was hard to concentrate on the dry facts and figures distributed here and there on each page, which mostly referred to the mare's "produce"—her foals—and the times she was bred. After a cursory glance at them, she gave up.

Feeling restless, Dakota looked through one of her dad's photo albums. It was dominated by enlarged photos of racehorses, but the family photographs were there, too. There was Maggie, Coke's first wife, a slight, dark-haired beauty who could ride racehorses with the best of them. Dakota always felt that Coke had been so devastated by her untimely death from cancer that in his second marriage he'd held some portion of his love in reserve, guarding against further hurt. Perhaps that was why Eileen was so bitter.

Dakota turned the page and came face-to-face with herself as a child, a skinny, tanned towhead who looked so happy in the photos. She tried to reconcile that child with the person she was now.

There were the pictures of her wedding at the Arizona Inn. It had been a beautiful summer night, and Dakota had been nineteen. The happiest night of her life—or so she'd thought at the time.

Her mother's last words to her before she walked down the aisle were, "I guess you're pigheaded enough to go through with this, but it won't hurt you in the long run. You're young enough to bounce back."

Coke had no such misgivings. He stood there in the receiving line, looking as proud as if he were holding Tailwind's bridle in the winner's circle after the Barbra B Stakes. That's the philosophy of the good ol' boys around here, Dakota thought. Win a stakes race, marry off your daughter to another member of the club. That made a successful man.

Clay was good-looking, for a college kid. He looked a lot better now—

She slammed the book shut. That was then. This was now. The life she'd planned for that night ended less than a year later, and most of the erosion of their marriage had happened long-distance. The only people who made out were the lawyers and AT&T.

As she stood up, Dakota's hip bumped the side table, dislodging another stack of papers.

She picked them up. Mostly correspondence with Coke's lawyer, Norm Fredman. They should be filed. Dakota got the box of files she'd bought in Tucson, set them down on the couch beside her, and started sorting through the letters.

One letter in particular caught her eye. Norm had sent it to her father when he was at Turf Paradise in Phoenix last fall.

She stared at the page, trying to absorb the full impact of its meaning.

> Harassment is a difficult charge to prove. I hope you have done what I suggested and kept a detailed account of every incident of vandalism. At least you'll have a record of dates, times, etc. We can use this in the appeal at Turf Paradise.
>
> I believe the ruling will go our way, especially in

light of the problems you've been having. Fortunately, you have a lot of friends in the business, and character witnesses will work in our favor. In the meantime, keep writing that journal.

Dakota guessed the ruling had to do with Coke's suspension at Turf Paradise, after one of his horses tested positive for drugs after a race. Clay didn't seem to think her father would do such a thing. Not just because it was dishonest, but because it wouldn't have been smart. And Coke had always been smart.

Kept a detailed account.

Dakota glanced around. Somewhere in this study must be a record of every bad thing that had happened to the Black Oak horses.

What if whoever had it in for Coke didn't stop at sabotage? What if Coke's death wasn't an accident?

Don't be ridiculous.

Crack! The brittle sound—like a breaking twig—made her jump. With relief, she realized it was just the house settling. But her heart continued to pound, and her pulse throbbed in her ears. She glanced at the black expanse of glass in the picture window, saw the reflection of a wild-eyed young woman in a cluttered room.

Anyone could see in.

Feeling suddenly vulnerable, Dakota fumbled for the lamp switch, turned out the light and peered out, letting her eyes adjust to the darkness.

Nothing, of course. Just moonlight on grass, dappled by a few trembling shadows from the juniper trees. The ranch was miles away from civilization. Who bothered to close their curtains out here?

There was another crack as the plaster settled again, like a distant gunshot. Laughing at her overactive imagination, Dakota pulled the curtains and started looking for her father's journal.

Nine

Shameless hadn't come out of the ordeal unscathed after all. Dakota discovered that there was some minor swelling in the filly's ankle. In a week Doc Ames would look at her again, and they'd know if she could go back to the track. But Dakota was nagged by worry.

She was not in the best frame of mind when Jerry Tanner showed up at the house.

From the way he hopped down from his truck, it was clear he thought he had the job. Dakota braced herself for a confrontation. "So, Miz McAllister. What's the story?"

It had always been difficult for Dakota to say no to people, so much so that she had practiced before the mirror for occasions just like this. "Mr. Tanner, I'm very sorry," she said as calmly as she could. "I've thought it over, and the truth is, I can't hire you."

He gaped at her. "You said we had a deal."

"I said I'd think about it."

"You led me to believe I had the job! You led me on!"

"Mr. Tanner—"

"You owe me, lady!" His whining tone grated on her. How had her father ever put up with him? "I saved your father's life! You wouldn't even be here if it wasn't for me!"

Dakota was aware of the core of anger in her chest. "I've made my decision, Mr. Tanner," she said, trying to keep her voice from shaking. She didn't want to participate in a shouting match.

"Goddammit!" He kicked the dirt with one filthy boot. "Why? You liked me just fine the other day. What happened to change your mind? You owe me that, you can't just tell me no without givin' me a reason."

"I did as you recommended. I talked to some people."

"Who? Whoever it is, he's a goddamn liar! I'll sue his ass, that's what I'll do! I'll sue him for slander! You promised me that job."

He leaned toward her, his breath—as usual—revealing what he'd eaten for lunch. Onions. "You really think you can train that horse yourself?" He laughed. "I know what happened at the track yesterday. You know what they're saying? You couldn't handle a poodle on a choke-chain."

"Get out of here." Now her voice *was* shaking.

"I hope you and your goddamn filly roast in hell!"

Anger stabbed behind her eye, a dull blade. "Get out of here or I'll call the police."

"You can't treat Jerry Tanner like this and get away with it!" He got into his truck and slammed the door.

His exit was spoiled somewhat by the fact that the truck's starter ground to a standstill, and he had to push the truck down the hill to get it going.

It wouldn't cost that much to go to the junkyard and find a starter that worked. How could she have ever entertained the thought of hiring such a man?

He'd had the gall to threaten her. He was obviously the type who thought the world owed him a living. Clay was right. Tanner had made a career of collecting on an old debt. And when her father finally had enough, Tanner blamed him, too.

You couldn't handle a poodle on a choke-chain. Heat suffused her face. On that score, he had hit close to home. So everybody was talking about her performance at the track.

She had half a mind to stay here and show them.

Still shaken from the confrontation, Dakota drove out to the road to pick up her mail. There were six mailboxes serving the ranches in the area; Dakota opened the big one emblazoned with the silhouette of a running racehorse.

The envelope from the insurance company was ominously thin. Holding her breath, she tore it open with clumsy fingers and withdrew a single white sheet of paper. "Dear Miss McAllister: We regret to inform you that pending further investigation, we are deferring payment . . ."

Stunned, she stepped backward against the mosaic of rock lining the roadbed, slipped on a shard of broken bottle and almost fell. Her hand flailed for the mailbox and she steadied herself.

It couldn't be. There had to be a mistake.

Scanning the letter quickly, Dakota saw the word "suicide."

Suicide?

"No way," she muttered. No way would Coke kill himself.

Suddenly, the sun seemed so bright it blinded her. She shut her eyes. Darkness swarmed under her eyelids, punctuated by darting colored dots.

Dakota stuffed the letter into the pocket of her jeans, slammed the mailbox shut, and stalked to the Forerunner. Her heart pounded as she slid behind the wheel.

Suicide.

Dakota swiped at her eyes, tasted salty tears at the back of her throat.

She peeled out of the clearing and sped down Washboard Road. Soon she found what she had been looking for: a rough-looking track that required four-wheel drive. The vehicle was made for that kind of road, and Dakota tackled it with grim determination and lightning reflexes. After an hour of concentrated off-roading, she came out on State Route 83 and raced down the highway, rolling up the windows and plugging in a CD of *Italian Opera's Greatest Hits.* She sang at the top of her lungs along with sopranos and tenors alike. Dakota knew her untrained voice didn't sound that hot, but driving her truck was like being enclosed in a world of her own making, and she soared along with "Un bel di" and "Nessun Dorma." She loved Puccini, the uplifting feeling his music gave her, the all-encompassing scope that made the whole world seem tiny by comparison. Grief and joy could not coexist, and Puccini's arias left no room for self-pity. When at last she came back down to earth, Dakota drove back to Black Oak, her head clear.

Ten

Clay realized he could look at Dakota McAllister all day. Although her wheat-blond hair had been french-braided into pigtails, she looked anything but provincial. Her clothing was nothing spectacular, either, but on that lithe body, the red-and-black-checked flannel shirt, faded jeans, and boots worked together to form a whole that transcended its parts. He imagined burying his nose in the shirt; fancied he could smell the clean, line-dried crispness along with the dusky scent of skin lightly tinged with soap. If he remembered correctly, she liked a no-frills soap: Ivory.

This wasn't the woman he'd seen at the auction, the aloof beauty in the tailored suit. This woman seemed more at home in boots and jeans.

Dakota looked as if she belonged here.

She must have sensed his presence, because she glanced up from where she knelt, one hand still passing over Shameless's ankle.

"How is she?" he asked.

Dakota stood up and brushed her hands on her jeans. "There's still a little heat. I guess we'll walk again today."

"I meant to tell you before, you're welcome to use my hot walker."

She shaded her eyes against the brilliant sun. "Thanks, but I'd rather walk her by hand. I've got the luxury, since she's the only racehorse I own."

"Have you found a trainer yet?"

She shook her head.

"What are you going to do?"

Dakota untied the filly's lead rope. "I don't know. She might be ready to go back on the track next week. I've got to start galloping her soon. When she's fully recovered."

Clay fell into step as Dakota and the filly started on the first circuit of grounds. Why was he drawn to her? The basic argument between them had never been resolved; in fact, it had worsened. She'd wanted to be an actress and live in L.A. He could never live there. He loved the life he had.

He'd learned quickly enough that living apart was not a marriage at all. And yet Clay couldn't fight his attraction for her. He had managed to keep his distance all week, even though she drew him like a magnet. Every day about this time she'd walk the filly around the grounds for a half hour or so, and every day he'd kept himself from coming by. Today, he'd given in, telling himself that he wanted an update on the filly's condition.

"I've been meaning to thank you," she said now, looking straight ahead. "For rescuing Shameless."

"After all the work you did ponying Budget Taco for me? It's a bargain."

"Budget Taco, Rocket Taco, Naco Taco." Dakota named three of the horses in Clay's stable. "If you send them out as one entry, do you call them the Taco Brothers?"

"The Flying Taco Brothers to you."

"Are all of them fast?"

"As a matter of fact, none of them can run a lick. They're pretty, though. I'm thinking of having them bronzed."

Dakota laughed. It was a nice sound. She tilted her face toward him. In the morning light, her complexion reminded him of a firm, golden peach. "I've been meaning to ask you about your folks," she said.

"Dad and Sandy are still living in Tucson. They bought a little ranch out near Bear Canyon. Just a few acres, enough room to keep his polo string."

"He still plays?"

"He'd play polo in heaven, if they had a team."

"It must have been hard for him to leave here," Dakota said. "I remember that summer he sold the cattle. It was a sad day, the end of an era."

"Like the dispersal sale at Black Oak."

Dakota bristled. "I couldn't do anything else. If you knew how much in debt Dad was."

"I'm not criticizing you. You've had to make some tough decisions."

She looked away. "And your mom? How is she? Does she like Florida?"

"She loves it. Still bitter about Dad, but I think it's more the principle than anything else. Frankly, I think she's happier without a man in her life." His sister, he told her, was married for the third time and living in Wyoming. He gazed out at the undulating hills of gray-green grass, the sun-bleached sky. "Another Sonoita ranching family bites the dust."

"You're still here."

He laughed. "Yes, I'm still here."

"How's the racehorse business? You making any money?"

Clay glanced at the nearby shedrow, where a wasp-waisted thoroughbred was bucking and whirling as it circled on the hot walker. "I'm breaking even."

"Don't you want to do anything else?"

"Is there anything wrong with what I do?" he asked, feeling suddenly annoyed.

"No. I just thought . . ."

"Go on." He'd heard it before, ten years ago. He'd also heard somewhere that people didn't change, they just got more so. Obviously, Dakota felt the same way as she always had about his choice of a career.

"I did it again, didn't I?" she asked wryly. "You must think I'm a godawful snob." She turned her tawny eyes—so like the color of the Sonoita grassland in winter—full on him. "Thanks for your help, Clay. I shudder to think what would have happened if you hadn't been there the other day. You saved us from . . ."

"Disaster?" he supplied.

"Sure catastrophe."

"Don't you mean mass destruction?"

She laughed. "Thousands maimed."

"That's what friends are for. We help our own."

"I'm still one of you?" she asked, and he thought she sounded playful.

"Don't you think you are?"

"I don't know." Her voice was thoughtful. "I guess I forgot how potent this place is . . . the hold it still has on me."

They walked on, the silence growing awkward. Dakota stared straight ahead, holding the shank close to the filly's jaw with her left hand and stroking the shining dark neck with the other.

"Clay?"

"Yes, McAllister?"

She didn't protest the name. "Was there anything wrong with Dad?"

He grinned. "Besides being pigheaded?"

"No. Seriously wrong. Maybe he'd been to the doctor recently?"

"As a matter of fact, he did have his checkup in January. I remember because he boasted about it. Said he didn't have to worry about cholesterol and 'all that crap.' His doctor said he was in great shape."

"Then I don't understand it." She pulled a piece of paper from the rear pocket of her jeans. "I got this yesterday."

He read the insurance company's letter with growing disbelief. "This is garbage."

She looked relieved. "That's what I thought you'd say."

"What are you going to do now?"

"I don't know. How do you contest these things? I have to talk to Norm." The filly's head jerked up and her ears strained forward. She stopped walking as an exercise boy riding a colt approached them. "You want to take a look?" Dakota asked her. "I guess you're entitled." They stood there for a minute while the horse and rider walked by, then started walking again.

When Dakota spoke again her voice was barely audible. "What if it wasn't an accident?"

"I don't believe Coke would kill himself."

"I'm not saying that."

He caught her meaning. "You think he was murdered? You've been watching too much television."

"You can't deny someone had it in for him. Maybe they hated him that much . . ."

"Just because someone wanted to make trouble doesn't mean they'd kill him."

"He was sixty-seven years old. In great condition."

"Even sixty-seven-year-old men in great condition sometimes drink a little too much and drive their trucks into trees."

"Didn't the sheriff wonder why he was driving so fast?"

"I don't know."

"It says here that the insurance company made their determination because of a number of factors. He was one step away from bankruptcy. He'd taken out this huge policy only a couple of months ago. He was driving at a high rate of speed when he crashed. To them, that spells suicide. And don't tell me you haven't heard the rumors."

Clay didn't deny it. "How could he be sure that crashing into that tree would kill him? Why didn't he just shoot himself?" He regretted his callousness immediately.

Dakota looked stricken, but to her credit, she soldiered on. "Because the policy would only pay for *accidental death.*"

There was no reply to that.

"On the videotape, he hinted that he didn't expect to be around much longer. He said . . . he said for me to keep the filly through the summer. The only way Dad would kill himself was if he found out he was going to die from something." She took a deep breath. "You know, debilitating. He prided himself on being tough, macho. Hemingway killed himself for the same reason, so Coke could justify it to himself. But if he was healthy . . ."

"He was healthy."

"Maybe he lied to you. Maybe he was sick—and just didn't want to tell you. He did take out that big policy . . ."

"You know what I think? Coke knew he wasn't getting any younger, and he wanted to do something for you. He felt bad about the divorce, and I think he wanted to make it up to you in some way."

"By taking out an expensive insurance policy?"

"Coke could get morbid sometimes. Living alone like that, he used to say fatalistic things all the time. I remember one time he told me that he'd finally found the horse of his dreams, but he probably wouldn't be around to see her run."

Her eyes sparkled avidly, hard as gems. "That's exactly what I mean! Why would he say something like that, unless he knew he was going to die? Couldn't he have suspected that someone had it in for him?"

"Coke was a shedrow philosopher. One of his favorite themes was how the people responsible for the great horses never lived to see them win. Coke was superstitious, like every other trainer I know."

"Why don't you want to train other people's horses?"

It caught him off guard. "I don't want anyone looking over my shoulder, telling me what to do." That was only part of the truth, but he didn't want to talk about what had happened to a promising colt when his owner insisted he run the horse too soon, against Clay's better judgment. He'd had high hopes for Expect a High. Instead, the colt had ended up hopping on three legs fifty yards past the finish line, the horse ambulance blocking him from view of the stands as the track vet humanely destroyed him. The nightmare of every horseman, to come back from a race with an empty halter. Every time a trainer sent a horse out, it was a gamble. The best trainers made the fewest mistakes. If the mistake had been Clay's alone, he could have accepted it.

Someday, if his breeding program was successful, he'd be accountable only to himself. And that meant he'd better get back to work and stop flirting with his ex-wife. "I've got to go. How about dinner?"

She hesitated. "I don't know if it's a good idea."

"For Christ's sake, we've been divorced for ten years. What do you think I'm going to do? Carry you up into the mountains and chain you to a tree?"

Dakota grinned. "I'd love dinner."

"Good. I'll pick you up at four." He strode toward his own shedrow, only looking back once. Dakota walked her dark filly, and there was a sadness in her expression that tore at his heart.

She'd looked everywhere. No journal, in any form; spiral notebooks, ledgers, legal pads. *Nada.*

Dakota wondered if her dad was organized enough to keep a journal. Just because Norm told him to do it, didn't mean he had. Coke had always hated paperwork, one reason he let Dan Bolin run the stud farm as if it were his own.

As she searched, Dakota tried to push Clay from her mind. What had possessed her to accept his invitation? She should never have agreed to go to dinner with him.

Not because she didn't trust him.

But because she didn't trust herself.

Why am I so damn self-destructive? she thought as she searched through another pile of papers. Her stomach was a cauldron of elation, anxiety, and strangled hope. She told herself that going out with Clay was just about old times.

Then why was her heart hammering? Why was her mouth dry?

Concentrate! Surrounded by a sea of papers, Dakota closed her eyes. Maybe it was time she talked to the sheriff. Surely, he would tell her what happened. She found the number and called the sheriff's department. The dispatcher told her the deputy who investigated the accident was on vacation. "He'll be back late next week. Ask for Derek Blue."

So much for instant gratification.

Still restless, Dakota finally abandoned her search in the afternoon and went down to the breeding barn. Something Wicked's dance card had been full since mid-February, and she wanted to catch his command performance.

Although Dan Bolin didn't look happy to see her, he said nothing.

Something Wicked was magnificent. A solid-colored bay, his power and vitality showed in every glistening muscle. He made her think of a tightly coiled spring. Dakota noticed that Shameless had inherited his proud carriage, the strong shoulder, the symmetry of legs and back. Her head was more feminine, but she had the same boldness in her eyes.

The stallion charged toward his mating, his whole body rumbling with loud neighs. It didn't phase him one bit that the object of his affections was a dummy mare with a fake vagina.

Breeding quarter horses these days was an antiseptic affair. Stallions were much too valuable to risk in a live mating. A fractious mare could kick out and injure him for life. With the antibiotics and extenders breeders now added to the semen, a single stallion could impregnate well over two hundred mares in a single season. Breeding was a science where centrifuges mixed the semen, a mare was inseminated by syringe, and a stallion spent its considerable vitality making love to a dummy.

Rita DeWeil parked her Cadillac in the dirt lot fronted by a strip mall of brick shops. It was ten minutes to four in the afternoon. In the time it took to put her car phone in the glove compartment, several other cars had pulled up around her.

One of the finest Italian restaurants in the country, Er Pastaro was located in Sonoita, right smack in the middle of nowhere. They didn't take reservations, so you had to be there right when it opened in order to get a table.

"Mrs. DeWeil," greeted the tall blond woman in white blouse and black apron. "How are you today?" Her French accent was charming.

Rita replied she was fine thank you. No, nobody would be joining her. As she sat down at a table in the small, rosily lit room, Rita tried to stifle her anger. It was Friday night. Clay should be here with her, but she couldn't even call him. She was supposed to be in Tucson.

Her stomach clenched as she thought of what she was missing. She'd made reservations at Loews Ventana Canyon

Resort—adjoining rooms. She'd told Clay that the committee had allocated the money for their stay, but that wasn't true. Rita had paid for it herself, and now she had to absorb the loss. It wasn't the money. She had plenty of that. What bothered her was the night she'd missed. Walking up to the waterfall that cascaded down the desert mountain in the dark, a romantic dinner, dancing close at the Flying V, maybe a dip in the Jacuzzi. And then . . .

She sighed, her body quivering with a mixture of sexual tension and longing. It would have been so wonderful. She had never wanted anyone more than she wanted Clay Pearce—and she wanted him all the time.

She spread a linen napkin on her knee and ordered a glass of chardonnay. That was when she saw him.

The hostess led Clay Pearce to a table across the room.

One of the ranchers at the table next to her leaned over to his friend and muttered, "The wolfman cometh." And they both laughed.

But Rita barely registered the words. She was too busy staring. At Dakota McAllister, looking cool and elegant in a black off-the-shoulder dress that hugged every curve.

The bitch.

Dakota was washing her hands after dinner when she saw Rita DeWeil in the mirror behind her. Rita wore a scoop-necked cold-shouldered purple blouse decorated with long fringes, nail heads, and conchos, and a black drop-yoked broomstick skirt that fell to the middle of her alligator boots.

She might have been hosting the Country Music Awards, except for her expression. Her face had the same smooth mask as Dakota's mother had when she was angry. But the perfect makeup couldn't hide the two points of red on Rita's cheeks, or the eyes that drilled like steel bits into the mirror. Dakota could feel the seething anger behind the mask, understood the control the beautiful woman exercised to keep from unleashing it on her.

Rita's smile didn't reach her eyes. "You're Dakota

McAllister, aren't you? I thought you'd be back in L.A. by now."

Dakota opted not to reply.

"I understand you and Clay were married once."

Dakota lifted her gaze to the mirror, stared Rita in the eye. "Yes, we were."

"I suppose he took you out tonight for old time's sake. He's told me all about you."

The woman's hatred surrounded Dakota in a noxious cloud. "Oh?"

Rita sketched her top lip with red lipstick. "Uh-huh. He called it an unfortunate mistake. You two were so young, he said neither one of you knew what you were doing." She pressed her lips together a couple of times, reminding Dakota of an exotic fish sucking water. "I suppose there's a temptation to try to revive old love affairs, recapture your youth . . ." She tilted her head to the side, flashing Dakota with her perfect profile, and her swan neck gleamed alabaster in the golden light. "But it's never a good idea."

"What makes you think I want to 'recapture my youth,' as you put it?" Rita might be a year or two younger—max—but at twenty-nine, Dakota hardly qualified as elderly.

"I'm talking hypothetically. I hope I haven't offended you. It's just that sometimes people get . . . ideas, and it's really pathetic when they act on them. I wouldn't want to see that happen to you." She turned to the side, admiring her lean body in the mirror. "Clay's happy now. Why dredge up all that stuff, when he's put it all behind him?"

Dakota turned to face her. "Why, indeed?"

"So I take it you'll be going back to L.A. soon."

"I'll go back when I'm ready."

Her lips tightened. "You aren't too quick, are you? Let me spell it out. Clay's already involved."

"With you?"

"With me."

Dakota forced her own smile. "Then you have nothing to worry about, do you?" And she walked out.

* * *

As Dakota walked back to the table, still shaken from her conversation with Rita, it came home to her how deep the rift had grown between Clay and herself. Years of changing, growing, of meeting other people had caused a chasm so wide that it was obvious they could never find the common ground they'd lost. Not that she wanted to.

Dakota had no doubt that a man like Clay must have someone in his life. Maybe several someones over the last ten years.

She'd known her share of love affairs. She'd lived with Peter for three years, had been relieved when he decided to call it quits, because the magic hadn't been there for her, either.

"Was that Rita you came out with?" Clay asked, as she sat down.

Her reply was barely out of her mouth when he stood up and walked toward the front of the restaurant. He caught Rita at the door, and they spoke briefly. Probably, Dakota thought uncharitably, he had a lot of explaining to do.

Clay sat down opposite her. "You want coffee?"

"No, thank you. It's getting late."

"It's not even six o'clock."

"All right, what I meant to say was it's getting late for *me.*"

"You go to bed with the chickens?"

Dakota clamped down on her reply. She had no right to expect anything from him. He was the soul of generosity to take her out for old time's sake, to save her damn horse's life, to make her quiver every time he accidentally brushed against her.

But Clay had already caught on. "Did Rita say something to you?"

"Nothing that a rhinoceros couldn't deflect."

"Rita can be possessive."

"Does she have a right to be?" Dakota blurted it out.

"No one has a right to own anyone."

"You're dodging the question."

"Why, is it important to you?"

She'd walked into that trap with her eyes wide open. "Not especially."

"You never were a good liar, McAllister."

Dakota wanted to wipe that grin off his face. "And humility was never your strong suit, *Pearce!*"

He laughed. "I guess not."

A tall cowboy whose belly rolled over his silver belt buckle walked past them. Verne Shumway, a local rancher, had known Dakota since she was a little girl. He nodded a brusque acknowledgment to her, and ignored Clay.

"I thought Verne was a friend of yours."

"I'm not on good terms with a lot of the ranchers around here."

"Why?"

He tapped his fingers on the tablecloth, something he often did when he didn't want to talk about something. "It's a long story."

"I want to hear it."

"I didn't think there was time," he said, pointedly looking at his watch.

She couldn't keep from grinning. It was rare to see Clay squirm. "Stow it, Pearce. I want to know why I'm not the only one who's unpopular around here."

"As unpopularity contests go, I win hands down." He ran his fingers through his dark hair. "You had no idea you were in the company of the wolfman, did you?"

Dakota stared at him. The wolfman?

"I'm the guy who's threatening their whole way of life. I'm a traitor to my own kind."

"Could you be more specific?"

"You've heard about the reintroduction of the Mexican wolf?"

"I read something about it."

"I donated some of my land to U.S. Fish and Wildlife to keep a couple of the wolves until they're released. If they're released."

Dakota couldn't believe what she was hearing. *"You're*

doing this? The two-time bull-riding champion at the Fiesta de los Vaqueros Rodeo, the guy who majored in Ag. at the U. of A.? Have you lost your mind?"

He grinned. "I've been accused of it before."

"That's something a Californian would do! Not a third-generation rancher in Sonoita. Don't you want to have any friends left?" But secretly, she was pleased. There had always been that perverse streak in Clay that defied categorization. He was one of the few people she knew who didn't give a damn what other people thought of him. "How did this happen?"

"Until a couple of years ago, I thought pretty much what everybody else did about wolves. That it was a damn good thing we wiped them out. I thought we ought to skin the tree-huggers and mount their heads on a wall. I've seen fresh kills, plenty of 'em, as you have. Calves torn up and just left there, uneaten—as if it were some kind of sport. The thought of bringing back a killer like that curdled my blood."

"What changed your mind?" Fascinated, Dakota leaned forward.

"A couple of things. For one, a trip to the Desert Museum," he said, referring to the desert zoo in Tucson where animals lived in their natural habitat. "And Rita—"

"Rita?" Dakota's stomach tightened.

"She got involved in it shortly after she came here. Pestered me to read about them, and I realized they'd ceased to be a threat years ago. Here in Arizona, we practically eradicated a whole species, well after they stopped being a threat to livestock. Even in the sixties, there were bounty hunters for the government looking for them, trying to hunt them down to the very last wolf. And they pretty much did. There are only about thirty of them left in the U.S., all in captivity."

"That happened in our lifetime? It's hard to believe."

"I figured it was people with my mentality who let it get out of hand, ranchers like me. I wanted to make up for it, so I offered my land."

"I'd like to see them sometime."

"That would be difficult. The female might even be pregnant now, and they're very shy. The less they see of humans, the better. In fact, I only saw them close up once, when the Fish and Wildlife people released them into the pen. But I've got a strong pair of binoculars. There's a moon out tonight. Want to give it a shot?"

"I think I'd better get home." She was tempted, though. Sorely tempted. But she was beginning to like Clay too much, and she'd been down that road before.

"McAllister, you're as head shy as a pasture-raised colt."

"With good reason," Dakota said as lightly as she could. "If you'd like to continue the metaphor, I don't take kindly to a saddle, and you broke me once."

His mouth quirked and his eyes looked grim. "Maybe," he said, as he helped her on with her coat, "we broke each other."

Eleven

After administering an ultrasound test Tuesday morning, Jared Ames declared Shameless fit to run. She could begin her training in earnest.

As he loaded the ultrasound equipment into his battered truck, Dan called to him from the barn. "Dwayne says you can pick your van up any time. Said it was the solenoid."

Ames turned to Dakota. "Need anything else?"

"No, thanks."

Before the words even left her mouth, he slid into the old Ford, threw it into gear, and shot out of the yard in a cloud of dust. In a moment he was just a dark blue speck on the horizon.

"How do you like that?" she asked Shameless. It was plain the vet didn't like her. Probably because Coke hadn't kept him on salary. "The sins of the fathers," she muttered.

The filly poked her head over the stall door, captured Dakota's shirtsleeve in her lip, and leaned her head against her new mistress.

"We've had a shaky start," Dakota told the filly. "But tomorrow, we'll try again." Soon, she knew, she'd have to make a decision: whether to aim for the Santa Cruz Futurity or the Ruidoso. To bring a horse up to racing form took, on average, a full ninety days. The Santa Cruz Futurity Trials were run seventy-four days from now. But Shameless had already been in racing condition before her three-week layoff.

It would be tight, but depending on the filly's ability to bounce back—

Suddenly, Dakota realized what she was doing, planning the filly's regimen way too far in advance, as if she were training the horse herself, instead of looking for someone else to do the work.

How quickly she'd worked herself back into the fabric of Sonoita. Every day this week she'd flung the covers away at five in the morning, eager to check on her All American horse, not realizing how seductive this world was, how it could pull you in. . . .

Just what Coke had counted on.

She'd better widen her search for a trainer, if she wanted to get out of here before it was too late.

The next day she drew up a chart and wrote in "gallop" for each day of the week. She would have to condition the filly slowly, letting her stretch out in a long, lazy gallop, building the distance up first to a mile, then a mile and a half until, by the end of the month, Shameless would be able to gallop two miles without effort. She hoped.

She felt a rush of pride as she watched the filly come back from her first gallop, still eager and dancing a little jig. Lori, Clay's regular exercise rider, had agreed to ride Shameless today. As Dakota took Shameless's bridle and led them slowly back to the gap, she asked, "How'd she go?"

Lori patted the smooth neck. "She's something special. I can't explain it, but when you get on a horse like this, well, you just know they're winners. I could feel it the minute I got on her. She's full of run."

Lori's words stayed with Dakota the rest of the day. After spending so much time with Shameless, grooming and walking and bathing and bandaging her, she knew the filly pretty well. After her initial aloofness, Shameless had proven to be an overgrown baby like most two-year-olds. But today, when Dakota had put Lori on her back before the gallop, the dark filly didn't butt her head playfully against her, or look around at the other horses and riders. Today she had walked straight ahead, her massive shoulders and hindquarters moving with purpose. There was something about her that seemed bigger, more impressive—as if she had grown overnight. Maybe it was the strong way she pulled at the bit, or the look in her eye.

Full of run.

After putting Shameless up in the stall she'd rented from the track, Dakota put a line through the word "gallop," and tried not to gloat.

Later that day she finally got to the broodmare files Dan had left for her. She was almost positive they'd kept three of the best mares sired by Something Wicked, and yet she saw no file on them. All their names began with the word "wicked," so they were hard to miss. Obviously, Dan had been sloppy in gathering up the files. She knew he'd resent her bringing it up, but curiosity had gotten the better of her. She'd better gird her loins for another battle.

She opened the manila folder marked PEACOCK LADY. Her eye ran down the list of foals Peacock Lady had produced over the last eight years, automatically lingering on two entries which marked the foals as deceased.

The phone rang. "Dakota? Are you there? Please pick up if you're there."

Dutifully, Dakota did. "Hello, Mom." She closed Peacock Lady's file and set it on the stack, her mind lingering on the poor dead foals. They'd been around long enough to have names. No doubt, each of them had a story that would break her heart.

"How'd the audition go?"

"I haven't heard anything."

"Do you want me to call your agent? See if he's heard?"

Abruptly, Dakota was visited by a clear image of her mother in a black swimsuit sitting up on the chaise beside the pool, cordless phone clutched against her ear, her face smooth as a river rock. Dakota's career had always been the most important thing in the world to Eileen Wood, since her own had never gotten off the ground.

"Well?" Eileen demanded.

"No. I'm sure if they wanted me for the callback, they would have gotten in touch by now."

"You shouldn't take any chances. Maybe they got your number wrong. I'll call the agency—"

"They're busy," Dakota said. "They represent other people besides me, Mother. Big stars." She felt the noose tighten around her neck, as it always did when her mother tried to take over.

"If you worked harder, you'd be a big star, too. When are you coming home?"

"I don't know."

"The sale was last Saturday. I don't see what you're waiting around there for. Norm can take care of anything that comes up."

Dakota looked at the mantel clock, racking her brain for an excuse to get off the phone. None came to her. "I have some things to do."

"I knew it."

It's none of her business, Dakota reminded herself. I don't have to explain a thing.

"Your father's tied up the will in some way, right? He's found some way to make you keep Black Oak. I knew you shouldn't have gone out there."

"He didn't do a thing," Dakota lied.

"What about the audition next month? You'll be back by then, won't you?"

"I don't know."

"You don't know? This is your *career* we're talking about! Whatever you're doing in that backwater can't compare to landing a regular role in a soap opera!"

Suddenly, all this religious striving to make it to the pinnacle of her art—to become a regular character on a soap opera—struck Dakota as absurdly funny. She compressed her lips to keep from laughing.

"How did the sale go?"

"Pretty good." She tried to keep from laughing aloud, almost choked.

"What are you laughing at? Dakota?"

"I'm just fine, Mother. But I have some news you might not like. I bought a horse."

"What? Why would you do a thing like that? David has two show jumpers that aren't doing anything while you're gone—"

"A racehorse. And you know the real kicker? It was my own horse! I bought my own horse, Mother."

A long pause. "You're out of your mind."

"I guess so. Anyway, I don't have a trainer yet and I've got to get her started, so it might be awhile before I can come home."

"What are you talking about?"

"Never mind."

"Damn your father, anyway! I know he had something to do with this!"

"He's dead, Mother. Neither one of us can blame him for our troubles—not now."

"Oh, you're impossible!" And Eileen did something she'd never once entertained doing in all her well-bred life. She hung up the phone.

After dinner, Dakota drove out to the track to check on Shameless, unable to keep away. She felt oddly triumphant, bearding her mother in her lion's den. Driving through the gate, she met Clay coming out. He waved. She hadn't seen him since Friday night, except at the track in the morning, when they were both too busy to talk. That was the way she wanted it. The man might be kind to animals, but he was hell on women. She had to remember that.

Shameless looked pleased with herself. No doubt her ears were still ringing from Lori's praise.

As Dakota cruised back down the highway toward Black Oak, her headlights picked up a truck parked on the verge. She realized it was Jerry Tanner's turquoise nightmare. Beside it, Lucy Tanner waved her arms. Dakota pulled up, hoping Jerry wasn't around.

"Thanks for stopping," Lucy said, her breath coming in

gasps. Dakota sensed she was frustrated to the point of anger, but hid it well. "The truck stalled and we couldn't get it going again."

"Do you want me to call a tow truck?"

"No. All we need's a push."

Dakota glanced at her Forerunner. It wasn't anywhere near as heavy as the truck, and she knew from experience (two fender benders in L.A.) how easy it was to crumple Japanese sheet metal.

Lucy seemed to read her mind. "I wouldn't ask you to use your truck." She looked wistful. "It sure is beautiful. I always wanted a truck like that."

"It has its limitations," Dakota replied.

"All I need's for you to drop me and my dad back home. We can get the truck started in the morning."

"You want to *leave* it here?"

The girl shrugged. "Look at it."

Lucy had a point. Dakota couldn't imagine anyone wanting to steal it. "Hop in."

An expression of extreme embarrassment crossed Lucy's features. "I need some . . . do you think you could help me with my dad?"

Dakota glanced at the truck and saw Tanner leaning against the passenger door, head in his hands.

"He's real tired."

Or real drunk. Anger streaked through Dakota, followed by pity so strong that it bordered on grief.

Lucy Tanner's expression was vaguely defiant. Dakota didn't blame her. It must be difficult to defend her father, to spend her childhood making excuses for him.

Dakota helped Tanner into her Forerunner, trying not to show her distaste. He reeked of tequila. She asked Lucy how he'd managed to drive this far.

"He wasn't driving. I was. I'll be sixteen in June and I've got my learner's permit," she added. "I've been driving for years."

Dakota wasn't surprised. It wasn't unusual for ranch kids

to start driving early. She herself had been driving her dad's truck since she was twelve.

The girl looked straight ahead. "I'm a good driver. You add it all up, I've driven thousands of miles, mostly on the freeway. Mountains don't even bother me—I'm better at them than my dad. You turn around and go back up this road." She motioned to the dirt road where Tanner's truck had died. "It's not far."

They drove in silence. The girl hugged herself against the cold, leaning against the passenger door. At last she said, "You can pull over there."

They had gone about a half mile up the dirt road. A corrugated shed attached to corrals loomed up on the right, and beyond it, an old silver trailer gleamed like a beetle carapace in the sweep of Dakota's headlights. The corrals were made of railroad ties strung with wire, here and there reinforced with warped tin. Dakota saw several dark equine shapes, one to each corral. Jerry Tanner's racing string?

Poor souls.

Dakota pulled into the yard, which was populated by undistinguishable hunks of machinery reduced by darkness to tortured shapes. An ancient Ford pickup with a 4-sale sign in the window brooded near a nest of rolled chicken wire, a stack of old tires, bales of hay, and an arthritic-looking hot walker. The water trough in the corral closest was a clawfoot tub whose innards were scabbed with black rust.

This was pretty much what she'd expected Jerry Tanner's place would look like.

Lucy clambered down. "Thanks a lot."

"You want me to help you—"

"No, he's wakin' up."

Dakota didn't relish talking to the man; she'd preferred his drunken stupor. She needn't have worried. He lurched against the door, climbed out, and staggered across the littered yard to the trailer, mumbling something she couldn't understand. Maybe it was "thank you," but she doubted that if he knew who she was he'd have anything to thank her for.

Lucy hung on the passenger door. "Can I ask you a favor?"

The girl looked like a plump pixie in that ridiculous hair-cut. Dakota's heart went out to her. "Sure."

"You need any help around your barn?"

"Well, I—"

She turned away dejectedly. "I didn't think so. Just thought I'd ask."

Dakota remembered that Judy, her father's groom, had just taken a waitressing job at the Steak Out. Black Oak, after all, was a dead end now.

"You have a groom's license?"

"Yup. But I'm really a trainer."

Dakota thought of the parallel, which seemed both incongruous and sad. Her father had been a racehorse trainer, and she had been his assistant. There the resemblance ended. Coke might have been stubborn and opinionated, but Dakota had always known, deep down, she could count on him.

There were no such reassurances for Lucy Tanner.

"I'm a groom, too. I'd do a real good job, honest."

Something inside Dakota made her quail at the thought of getting involved. She didn't want to be associated with Jerry Tanner in any way, even through his daughter. Perhaps that was selfish, but she couldn't help it.

Inside the trailer, a clatter and a yell; Tanner banging around.

Lucy darted a glance over her shoulder. "He wants his dinner. I'd better go." She looked down, dug her booted toe into the dirt. "I understand if you don't want to hire me, what with the way Dad is and all. You don't have to say anything."

Dakota was assailed by guilt. How could she be so damn petty? "Come by next Monday and we'll see how it goes."

Lucy Tanner smiled, and her face was transformed. Despite her weight problem, she could be a pretty girl.

As Dakota drove out of the cluttered yard, her thoughts remained with Lucy. It was a crime that someone could be born into such a horrible life, while she'd had all the advantages.

Life was patently unfair. But maybe she could even the odds a little.

Twelve

Derek Blue hopped down from the Santa Cruz County Sheriff's Department Bronco and motioned Dakota to follow him.

The oak tree stooped over the road, its dark tangled leaves reflecting the late afternoon sun like bits of twisted metal.

Dakota closed her eyes and thought briefly of the impact, and asked herself for the hundredth time what must have been going through Coke's mind as he hurtled to his death. "Thanks for taking the time to show me what you saw," she said.

"Hey, I don't mind." The deputy wore his hair short and sported a mustache that would have done Wyatt Earp proud. His hair and mustache were the same brown as his uniform, which was the color of an old manure pile in the sun. He was tall and lanky; Dakota wondered if he ever played basketball, but didn't ask. Probably everybody else had. "There are a few things about this case that don't add up."

Dakota perked up. "Like what?"

Derek Blue hitched his loaded belt up onto his hips, withdrew his big black flashlight, and slapped it against his open palm. "For one thing, there were skid marks."

"On a dirt road?" Dakota looked doubtfully at the hard caliche of Washboard Road.

"Think about it. You're going fifty miles an hour in a one-ton pickup, you're tryin' to stop—you just better believe you're gonna leave skid marks, even on a road as hard as this. He didn't hit the tree straight, either. People who are gonna kill themselves hit an object dead center."

Was he saying it wasn't suicide?

"Of course, he could've decided at the last minute that he didn't want to die after all, but it was too late. That's what the insurance investigator thinks."

"What do *you* think happened?"

He kept slapping the flashlight against his palm, like a pitcher slapping the ball into his glove before the windup. "We're going on the assumption that he'd had too much to drink, got going too fast, and wiped out. I can tell you right now that Coke wasn't a speed demon. He drove real careful, the whole time I knew him. Especially on Saturday night, after a couple of drinks."

He shifted flashlight hands. Smack, smack. "And there were all the retread fragments at the scene."

Dakota remembered the few black threads of rubber she'd seen earlier.

"It looked like somebody blew a tire, but Coke's tires were intact. Had about six months of wear on them, and they weren't retreads." He started down the road, which was blemished at intervals with spray paint.

"The paint marks places where I found pieces of retread. I didn't know if they were important or not, but I had to preserve the chain of evidence." He spoke the last words with obvious reverence. Whatever the chain of evidence was, it meant a lot to Derek Blue.

He must have noticed her puzzled expression. "Anything found at a crime scene—or accident—that wouldn't normally be there," he explained, "is picked up and bagged, and then the place is marked."

"And you think the retread has something to do with the accident?"

"I don't know. Probably not. There are a lot of people who use this road; ranchers, off-roaders, kids looking for a place to neck. The retread could've been blown anytime, but I thought I should pick it up. I had to preserve the scene, even if no one else thought the scraps were important."

Dakota couldn't help smiling. Obviously, "no one else" had to be the sheriff, Jimmie G. Arnette, who had been sheriff since she was a child.

"Now the thing of it is, the weird thing, is that I found scraps of retread all up this road for miles. A tire blows all at once," he told her. "The retread might be scattered over a few hundred feet, but that's it. And this retread looked like it had been sliced by something sharp."

"What does this all mean?"

For the first time, the eager-beaver look on Derek Blue's face diminished a little. "I don't know. But it's just weird. That's what I told the investigator the insurance company sent out. Most people, they want to kill themselves, they find a foolproof way. Like sticking a gun barrel in their mouth."

Dakota choked back her revulsion. She'd warned herself ahead of time to face the possibility that Coke might have committed suicide, but Blue's grisly word picture brought it home again that this was her father they were talking about. Her flesh-and-blood father.

Abruptly, she pictured him patiently fashioning a salmon egg around her fishhook. *This time try to keep it on awhile, okay, hon?*

Deputy Blue broke into her thoughts. "He wore a seat belt. Of course that could have been just habit."

Dakota drew on her memories of all the television cop shows she'd seen. "Did you have the retread scraps analyzed?"

"They're marked and stored in the evidence locker, so if anything comes up we can ship 'em off to the lab in Tucson. For now, we're calling it accidental death, but the investigation can be reopened at any time."

"What about the insurance company? If you're calling it an accident, won't they have to abide by the official ruling?"

"You'd probably have to sue them, and they can drag their feet for years."

Dakota thought of Black Oak, slowly sinking into a morass of unpaid bills. Her father's legacy to her. If she were ever to restore the ranch to its former glory—hell, even to keep it going—she'd need a lot of money. Already she was scrambling to meet the bills.

But you're not keeping Black Oak, a stern inner voice said.

No, she wouldn't keep Black Oak. But even so, the thought of people talking about Coke's suicide was unbearable. "Where does that leave me? If I wanted to pursue it?"

"Well, if we find out anything new, I'll surely tell you. Looks like I missed a piece," he added, nodding to a scrap of retread under a bush. He picked it up and studied it. "That's it, all right. Some kind of cut, real jagged."

A thought occurred to her. "Could someone have run him off the road?"

"Could have happened that way. But again, why take a chance running someone off the road when you could just shoot him? It's not a sure method."

Dakota persisted. "But if you thought it was murder, what would you do?"

The deputy handed her the retread. "I'd start by looking for the rest of this tire."

By the time Derek Blue dropped Dakota at her Forerunner, parked in front of the closed sheriff's office, sunset stained the sky red. She waved absently as the deputy drove off, her mind still on the retread and what it meant.

She unlocked the driver's side door and tossed the black scrap of tire onto the seat. That was when she noticed the sheet of paper on the windshield. Probably an ad. She slipped it out from under the windshield wipers.

Abruptly, a chill wind sprang up, flattening the piece of paper against her hands. The sky darkened. Dust shuttled across the dirt lot; debris pelted her legs. She started to ball the piece of paper up, then decided she might as well see what they were selling.

In the last red light of day, the letters might have been etched in blood.

Capital letters.

Short and to the point.

ACCIDENTS HAPPEN. ASK YOUR FATHER.

Dakota had to read them twice before her mind was able to grasp the meaning. Dread mounted in the pit of her stomach, and she was suddenly aware of how cold it was.

The words themselves were harmless, but the message was clear. In her politically correct world, Dakota had never encountered such an overt act of hostility. Even in Hollywood, cruelty and rejection had always been softened by a thin veneer of politeness.

Dakota prided herself on living life on an even keel. She'd always avoided confrontation. No one had ever hated her this much.

The idea that someone had slipped this note under her windshield right in front of the sheriff's office scared her even more. It was as if he were telling her that the sheriff couldn't protect her.

But that wasn't the worst of it. The worst was the grainy photocopy that accompanied the words. A picture of a wrecked truck, mangled beyond recognition.

Thirteen

"Looks like this photocopy came from a newspaper," Clay said.

Dakota had driven straight out to the Bar 66 Ranch, knowing she had to see Clay. It was pure instinct. "Was it . . ." Dakota couldn't finish the sentence.

"No. Your dad's truck was a Ford. This is a GMC."

Dakota sighed with relief. To see her father's truck, a jumble of twisted metal . . . the idea of it was unbearable.

"Let me get this week's papers." When Clay left the room, Dakota huddled deeper in the big leather recliner, still feeling cold. She clasped the hot mug of tea in both hands, her eyes fixed on the Anne Coe print on the burnt adobe brick wall opposite her. It mirrored her own roiling emotions; a disturbing vision of sly people and animals savagely cavorting and drinking outside a roadside tavern. Painted in dark, stormy colors, the print was entitled "Lust."

A nightmare vision of debauchery, drunkeness and death.

She thought of Coke, driving home from the Steak Out, a couple of drinks under his belt, maybe thinking about what he would do tomorrow. She thought of his fate swiftly encroaching like a pack of dark, slavering wolves at the edge of his vision, loping alongside his truck, waiting for the right moment to move in for the kill—

It would make a good T-shirt slogan: I PICKED UP DEATH AT A ROADSIDE TAVERN.

She looked up just then and got the shock of her life.

As if it had materialized from her imagination, a wolf stood on the Navajo carpet, not ten feet away. It was enormous—the size of a small Shetland pony. In the light from the fire, its eyes glowed like polished Mexican onyx.

Oddly, Dakota wasn't scared. Awestruck, yes. But not scared. She could sense that the animal wished her no harm. He wore dignity like a mantle, like the glorious bluish-gray pelage that furred his back.

Dakota felt suddenly guilty. She'd been thinking about wolves—the dark creatures of Anne Coe's fantasy—and had attributed terrible things to them. And now the real thing stood before her, as majestic as the desert, as remote as the moon.

"Imagine that," Clay said as he entered the room. "Azul doesn't usually let himself be seen by strangers."

"He's a wolf," Dakota replied, still numbed by the lack of reality in the situation.

"Mostly. About eighty-percent Alaskan gray wolf is my guess, and the rest is probably Husky. I only know of three people who've ever gotten this close to him, and one of them's you."

"Who else?"

"Coke."

Coke, gruff, opinionated, a rancher to the core.

"Azul must know you're related. That's the only thing I can think of. Better not," Clay warned, as Dakota involuntarily put out a hand toward the wild animal.

Azul padded over to Dakota and allowed her to sink her hands into his creamy thick fur.

"Damn, that's unusual."

"Where'd you find him?"

"Mexico. He was still a pup but twice the size of a regular dog. Someone had the mistaken notion he'd clean up at the dogfights. I happened to come across him left for dead in an alley after a dogfight. Took him to the local vet down there, he patched him up, and damned if the vet brought this guy out of the woodwork, said he owned the wolf and I'd stolen it. Didn't mind selling the pup to me, though."

"I've never seen anything like him in my life."

"Knowing him, that's what made me take those wolves. Can you imagine a world where these creatures didn't exist?"

"No." She shivered again, thinking how gratuitously violent mankind was. How much of its energy was spent on destruction.

"You okay?" Clay stood beside her, reassuringly solid. One thing she'd always known: You could count on Clay in a pinch. He might dump you as a wife, but he'd never desert you as a friend.

Swell.

She combed her fingers through the soft fur, the sheer tactile pleasure of touching the wolf blocking out her uncharitable feelings toward Clay. She had a feeling she could hug Azul and he would let her, but that she would never be able to truly know him.

"Sometimes when I touch him I feel like he takes me away from here," Clay said softly.

She understood what he meant, having just discovered that embracing a wolf was to touch the heart of wildness. The trick, she supposed, was to leave the heart still beating. What restraint it must take to play host to the Mexican wolves, yet never see them.

He handed her a stack of newspapers. "I throw 'em out once a week. You look through those, and I'll take these."

As if on cue, Azul walked over to the fireplace and lay down, resting his head on his paws.

Dakota and Clay leafed through the stack of *Arizona Daily Star* papers, paying particular attention to the front page and the section called "Metro."

She found the photo on page one, from three days ago. A man had lost control of his vehicle north of Tucson and it had flipped over three times.

"Three days," Clay said. "Whoever it was had to take the trouble to clip it out, photocopy it, and find your car."

"Someone really hates me."

"Either that, or you're some kind of threat."

"Why would I be a threat?"

"Did anyone see Derek Blue pick you up?"

"I don't remember."

"Maybe someone did have something to do with Coke's death, and they don't want you poking your nose in. You never did tell me what Blue said."

Dakota told him.

"So he thinks it might be more than an accident."

"To be honest, I think he doesn't know what to make of it."

Clay tapped his fingers against the chair arm. "You think you should tell him about this?"

"I don't know." She tossed the remaining newspapers on the floor. "When you look at it objectively, it seems kind of childish. Just someone playing a prank."

"A mean-spirited prank."

"Yes, a mean-spirited prank."

"Do you think it's a threat?"

Dakota shivered. "It feels real to me."

"Then tomorrow we'll see if this thing was photocopied here in Sonoita. Maybe we'll get lucky and get a description."

Cold seeped into her bones, despite the crackling fire. "I hope so," she said fervently. "I guess I'd better get back."

"You could stay here."

For an instant, Dakota pictured his arm encircling her, protective and strong, as they sat before the fire. She saw them as if they were actors in a play, talking through the night, unraveling the past. As in a play, their problems would be solved in a couple of hours, and then they would joyously resume their relationship and the curtain would come down. But that wasn't reality. "I couldn't do that," she said.

Clay stood up, retrieved his jacket from the coat peg. "Then I'll follow you home."

"There's no need for that."

"I want you safe."

He did follow her home, and looked through the whole house, checking the locks. Logically, Dakota thought he was going to ridiculous lengths, but in her heart, she was relieved. And grateful.

The following morning, as Dakota prepared Shameless for her gallop, Clay came by. "I should be done around one o'clock," he said. "We could get a bite somewhere, then see if we can find out who's got photocopy machines around here. If you still want to."

"Sounds good to me," Dakota replied as she rolled up bandages, which she would unroll again in a minute when she wrapped the filly's forelegs. She was glad he'd kept his word. It felt natural to be with him, as if they had been together all their lives.

"She's looking good," Clay said.

"I decided to aim her for the Santa Cruz Futurity."

He didn't say anything, but she could tell he was pleased she'd taken his advice.

"I thought that those races—the trial and then the Futurity—could be a dress rehearsal. Get her used to the crowds. Like a fast work, but in a race. I don't expect her to win, but it would be nice if we got through the trial and made it to the Futurity. Then she'd have two races under her belt before going to Ruidoso."

"Sounds like you've got it all thought out."

"She won't be ready for the Ruidoso. Even though it's run later, it would be her first race, and I don't know if she could run in company like that. Not with that layoff after Dad died."

"How's the trainer search?"

She knelt and started wrapping the near foreleg. "Not good. With everything that's been going on, I haven't had time to look." She didn't tell him that she'd gotten another list of possible trainers from a friend of her father's, or that she'd left it in Coke's desk, untouched, for several days.

All Shameless needed was to be galloped every day for a month or so. She was on automatic pilot. Dakota monitored her soundness, made sure she was feeling good. Who needed a trainer? Dakota told herself that she might save the ranch some money by supervising the gallops herself for a month, and then hiring a trainer when the filly started to run in earnest.

But if she left it too late, she might not find one.

She'd cross that bridge when she came to it.

"See you around one."

"Sure thing, Pearce." She said it automatically, her mind already returning to the one and only racehorse in the Black Oak stable.

Over Mexican food at El Vaquero, Dakota and Clay talked about old times.

"You remember that time we thought the pool was too tame?" he asked. "And we rode over to the stock tank?"

She shuddered. "It sure was slimy."

"That's not what I remember."

The fact that they'd been skinny-dipping—that's what he'd remember. It had been Dakota's first summer back on the ranch since she'd moved to California, and it was also the first time she'd seen Clay naked. He was sixteen; she fourteen. Immature, slim and tanned, Clay had unself-consciously revealed the mystery of manhood that had intrigued Dakota and her girlfriends for years. When they'd kissed, she had noticed that the little dogie he'd jumped in with had turned into a full-fledged steer—although she had tried not to look.

Now, skating along the surface of these memories, Dakota felt uncomfortable. The Clay across from her was not a boy of sixteen, or even the twenty-two-year-old she'd married. He was a man in every sense now, tempered and shaped by experience. Clay Pearce was at the peak of his manhood, and she couldn't help the ripple of pleasure in her stomach at the thought of what his body would be like now.

"You okay?" His dark eyes glinted with humor.

"I'm fine. This salsa is hot."

"Have some more water. That'll put out the fire."

She didn't say that the water would do more good elsewhere. "Remember how we'd try to get someone to buy us beer at the minimart?"

He shook his head. "Not real bright in a small town."

"Never did get any beer, just a bunch of lectures."

"I remember how you used to strap that Walkman to your saddle horn and sing Top Forty all the way to town. How'd you ever get interested in opera?"

"David—my stepfather—loves listening to it. It grows on you."

"I'll always like country."

As they talked, Dakota felt as if they'd opened a time capsule. Morning in America. Greed was good. Her friends had all been attracted to power ties and Beamers. Clay had been a cowboy. A darn good-looking cowboy, but he didn't fit the fashion of the times. Why couldn't he wear normal clothes, just once? Sure, he was sexy, and he always looked good in his jeans, but it got so she was embarrassed to introduce him to her friends at the University of Arizona. "This is my husband. He's majoring in Racetrack Management and rides bulls on the weekend."

And then her stepfather had offered her the money to go to USC.

A whole different world. Showing off her bikini on the boardwalk. Doing extra work and bit parts on sets and on location, hobnobbing with actors who had made it. Getting her SAG card. Darkened theaters, intense sessions with angst-ridden actors who smoked too much and ate too little. Some of the wittiest people in the world were actors, but there was always a razor-sharpness to their wit. They lived on the edge, something she could never do, because if she got desperate enough, there was always her stepfather's money to fall back on. After graduation she'd gotten a job as a waitress, lived in the Los Angeles equivalent of a garret, refused to touch her trust fund. Felt vital, alive, important—part of things. She'd come back that first Christmas, and there was Clay. She'd left him, literally, in the dust. He still looked like a hick to her. Still rode bucking bulls. And there was something else, something he was hiding . . .

"Could you tell me something, Clay?" She had nothing to lose, not now. When he nodded, she asked, "Did you have a girlfriend? When we were still married?"

He leveled his gaze on her. "There was someone, yes."

"I knew it!"

He said nothing, but his mouth was grim.

"Do you know how I knew?" She paused for effect. "I've never known a man to step off a boat unless the dock's in sight!"

"You must have had a lot of experience with men to know that," he said.

"Enough." Dakota refused to take his remark as an insult. She was twenty-nine years old. Of course she'd known a few men in her time. "Women grieve. Someone breaks up with them, they don't feel like going out with anyone for a long time. They face their feelings, get it out of their system. But men . . ."

"Men just find another boat."

"You got it. Was it a girl at the U. of A.?"

"Yup."

"Did you sleep with her? While you were married to me?"

She knew her tone was still lighthearted, but she was disturbed by the knowledge that suddenly, she needed to know.

His eyes darkened, and Dakota knew she'd gone too far. "No," he said at last. "I waited until after we were separated."

"Was it worth breaking up our marriage for?" This was going all wrong. What did it matter anymore? And yet she couldn't help the bitterness in her tone.

"Our marriage was already over."

"So you took the cowardly way out and found yourself a little *boat,* or was it the dock?"

"I'm not married to her, am I?"

"So that was why it was so easy for you to ask for a divorce. There I was in L.A., waiting for Thanksgiving, for Christmas, for spring break, thinking you still loved me, and all this time you were in love with someone else!" What was she doing? She sounded like the Grand Inquisitor!

"You were unfaithful, too."

"I was not!"

"You might not have gone out with anyone, but it didn't take a genius to figure out you were ashamed of me. You never introduced me to your acting friends. And then you took off for California and said you'd be back for Christmas." He leaned forward. "I may have been just a cowboy, but I had enough sense to know that if you don't water something it won't grow."

"I had to think of my career. What did you want, a housewife?"

"I wanted a marriage. That meant you and me in the same state."

"My life is in L.A." She realized she was speaking in the present tense.

"My life is here. Guess we were right, getting divorced."

"I guess so."

They ate in silence. Clay got the check. Dakota thought about protesting, then decided not to. If he wanted to pay, let him.

She'd be needing all the money she could hold on to.

There weren't many copying machines in Sonoita, but after asking around at the businesses that had them, Dakota and Clay realized that it would be impossible to find out who had sent her the note. Anyone with a nickel could use a photocopy machine. *The Arizona Daily Star,* a Tucson paper, was sold outside several establishments.

The note had been typed on a regular typewriter or computer printer. The message appeared to have been pasted to the newspaper photo and photocopied along with it.

Dakota could think of a couple of people who might do something like this. Jerry Tanner, for one. Rita. The look on her face that night at Er Pastaro . . . for one moment Dakota had seen through the mask to the pure hatred underneath.

She had no idea if either one of them would carry it any further. Tanner seemed like a coward—a petty, whining tyrant who had been ineffectual all his life. But maybe she shouldn't underestimate him. Ineffectual whiners were forever shooting up post offices.

Coke had fired Tanner. Someone had sabotaged Black Oak, to the point of getting Coke into trouble with the stewards at Los Alamitos.

"I'll drop you at the track, if that's all right," Clay said, interrupting her thoughts.

She nodded, still thinking about Coke. They bumped over the dirt weal cut into the hillside, and Clay stopped before Shameless's stall.

Dakota reached for the door handle. "Thanks—"

She felt his hand on her arm, gentle but solid, pulling her around to face him.

His eyes looked like the midnight sky on a sweltering desert night. There was a challenge in them. He leaned forward, as if he wanted to say something important. Then, suddenly, his mouth came down on hers. The pressure of his lips was brief, tantalizing—completely unexpected—and she reacted instinctively. Her own mouth parted without asking her, and the kiss deepened.

They fit perfectly, as she knew they would.

Dakota was seized by an anguish so sweet she thought it would topple her from sanity. And her heart—

Her heart.

The ache wouldn't go away.

When they finally came up for breath, Dakota was seriously shaken.

Clay's hand caressed her cheek, caught a sheaf of her blond hair in his fingers. The sadness in his expression made her heart lurch. It told her what she didn't want to know, that the kiss was finishing old business, not starting new. She looked away.

"I had to do that," Clay said.

"Okay," she said, knowing that she sounded stupid, that her voice strained. He knew how much she cared, he must have always known. . . .

She opened the truck door, jumped out, and walked toward the barn as steadily as she could.

She heard him put the truck in gear and drive away.

Fourteen

Dakota decided to pretend that Clay had never kissed her. She was friendly when they met. Even though she was aware that his gaze lingered a little too long at times, Dakota gave him no encouragement.

She tried not to think about the note, although unconsciously, Dakota found herself waiting for something else to happen. She couldn't shake the feeling that someone was watching her. Sometimes, as she went through her daily business, the hairs on the back of her neck rose and she was certain someone was following her—but when she turned around, no one was there.

A couple of times at the farm, Dan sneaked up on her and spoke in her ear, making her jump. He'd always walked as quietly as an Apache, but Dakota wondered if he got some pleasure out of scaring her.

One day she came out of the El Prado mall and saw a flier on her windshield. Her heart sped up, and blood pounded in her ears. She walked slowly toward her truck, morbidly drawn by the fluttering piece of paper. Swallowing, Dakota pulled it out from under the wiper and closed her eyes. She should crumple it into a ball and throw it away. She shouldn't let this person, whoever he was, terrorize her.

But she couldn't stop herself. She had to know. Taking a deep breath, Dakota looked.

Relief bombarded her. She leaned against the truck, weak-kneed. The flier announced that a new real estate company had moved to Sonoita.

As the first week came to a close, the note seemed less disturbing, more of a joke. Sometimes she wondered if she'd imagined the whole thing. She had a lot of other things to think about, like Shameless's training.

The month flew by. Dakota watched as her dark filly galloped a mile, then moved up to a mile and a half, then two miles. Shameless was building lean muscle mass. She looked athletic, and brimmed with energy, jumping and kicking out for the pure joy of it. Even now, she could gallop a mile and a half without breathing hard. Shameless would soon be dead fit.

Dakota had given up the pretense of looking for a trainer. She'd condition the filly first, then find one in time for the Futurity trials.

She'd found a regular rider for Shameless. Dakota wanted one person to ride Shameless every time, so that he would become familiar with her and be able to sense if anything was wrong. She'd watched the exercise riders every morning, and decided that the best person for Shameless was the nephew of Raul Acevedo, a respected trainer in Sonoita. Ernesto Acevedo couldn't be more than eighteen, but he had worked with his uncle's racehorses all his life. He wanted to be a jockey. He had the hands, the ability to rate a horse, the courage, the reflexes, but he was just a little larger than most jockeys. She thought he'd make a good trainer. His instincts were so good. He was always there, like a shadow, doing things before she told him. Because he spoke little English and her Spanish left a lot to be desired, he would point at things and then hold up his hands as if in a question. She was getting adept at communicating with him.

She would take him to Ruidoso with her. Although he had grown up in one of those isolated pockets of Arizona where the Mexican population spoke their native tongue exclusively, Ernesto was a U.S. citizen, for which Dakota was grateful. At least she wouldn't have to contend with Immigration.

And then there was Lucy. Dakota didn't really need her—

not with Ernesto right there, willing to do any chore. Lucy cleaned Tyke's and Shameless's stalls. She also helped ready Shameless for her gallops, but Dakota found herself resenting the time that, up until now, she'd spent alone with the filly. Grooming Shameless, bandaging her legs, bathing her, walking her—these simple actions helped Dakota figure out how the animal was doing mentally and physically. But now here was Lucy, brushing the horse because she had to earn her paycheck.

What I need is a bigger racing stable. Just to accommodate the help. How did she get herself into this?

It was a relief to Dakota when other trainers began to ask Ernesto to ride for them. At least he wasn't always hovering around, trying to please. Shortly after that, one of Clay's grooms quit, and Dakota sent Lucy over to his stable to work on five of his horses. That helped, but the girl always managed to finish up Clay's horses in record time and be back at the Black Oak barn, hanging around.

If Dakota didn't know any better, she'd think that Lucy had a crush on her. Sometimes she'd look up from bandaging the filly's legs to see Lucy standing there, an odd look on her face, as if she wanted to talk to Dakota but couldn't screw up the courage. Maybe the girl was just lonely.

At the end of March, Dakota flew to L.A. for the soap opera audition. The producer seemed to like her, but you never knew about these things. The producer who had auditioned her for the Yuma shoot had seemed to like her, too, but she'd never gotten a callback. She left a picture and resume with the casting director and drove back to her little house in Burbank. Her neighbor had watered the plants and taken care of Refrigerator, her black tortoiseshell cat, who had been named after the all-time leading money winner of quarter horse racing. Although Refrigerator was a female, she was muscular and compact, and walked like John Wayne. She could have easily been named for the other Refrigerator, William Perry.

It suddenly occurred to Dakota that she'd named all three

of her pets after racehorses. If she loved acting so much, why hadn't she named them Olivier, De Niro, and Streep?

What was going on with her? She felt so damn *restless*. Her mind kept wandering back to Sonoita. The farrier was coming out to shoe the filly; Dakota wished she could be there. Ernesto was good with her, though. There was nothing to worry about.

By Sunday night, Dakota was beginning to feel like an outsider; as if she were just putting in time here, waiting to go back to Sonoita and continue her life. Her friends were furiously scrambling to keep up with the L.A. scene, going to parties and being seen, dwelling with desperate hope on the offhand remarks of the power people. All Dakota wanted to talk about was the filly. How Shameless was slowly building up to racing condition, how in the course of her gallop next week Ernesto would ask her to run a short distance—just a quick blowout. Pretty soon she'd have to be schooled in the gate, relearn all her baby lessons, break and work in company. But Dakota knew her friends wouldn't be interested.

Feeling homesick, she called Dan to ask about Shameless. She should have known better. He made no effort to cover his disappointment. "You're coming back, then?"

"Is that all right with you?"

"I just work here." She could almost see him shrug those huge, stooped shoulders. And the sullen look on his face.

Annoyed, Dakota said, "You gave me all the files except the ones on the mares we kept. I'd like to see them."

There was a pause on the line. "Okay."

"Thanks." She hung up before he could reply.

Why did he dislike her so much? Well, he was right about one thing. He did just work there. And she was going home, whether he liked it or not.

On Monday, she visited her mother and stepfather in Laguna Beach. Eileen hectored her to stay in L.A., but David thought the change would do her good. She gave her neighbor all her plants, called the post office to arrange for her mail to be forwarded to Black Oak, and flew back to Tucson, where she'd left her Forerunner in the long-term parking lot.

Refrigerator came with her, yowling all the way from Tucson to Sonoita in her cat carrier, drowning out Jessye Norman.

Hard to do, but Refrigerator was one part Siamese.

It was a beautiful drive. As they reached the pass, the sky blushed a pretty apricot color, gradating to turquoise and then to deep violet-blue. Stars appeared, welcoming her; tiny glittering pinpricks. In the dying rays of the sun, the grass had changed from flaxen, to fiery orange, to ash-gray. Bighipped junipers looked as if they were on the verge of waddling down the hills toward the road, eager to tell her their secrets.

Back at home, she closed off the den and let Refrigerator out of her carrier. As the cat patrolled the perimeter, sniffing suspiciously at every piece of furniture in the room, Dakota noticed the blinking light on her answering machine.

Briefly, her pulse sped up. Maybe it was Clay, welcoming her back.

She pressed the playback button.

The malevolent voice oozed out of the speaker, loud and muffled at the same time.

"Take a look at your broodmares."

A cold needle of fear thrust into her heart as she heard the click of the receiver, followed by a dial tone.

Fifteen

She ran to the first broodmare barn, dreading what she would find. The night was cold now, and the wind raked at her face, her clothing. Her feet felt numb. She ran flat out, holding her gun close to her side, her heart going like a freight train.

It can happen to anyone. Somebody had threatened her, and she hadn't taken it seriously. She'd written it off as some crank. And now, just like her father, the horses—the innocents—had paid for her folly.

As she ran, her tortured thoughts ran alongside her like Anne Coe's canine companions. She pictured in her mind's eye a mare, lying on her side in a stall, dead. Or maybe she was still alive, in agony, her leg broken.

How many? All of them?

Breathing hard, she reached the first barn. Her hand fumbled for the light switch. Goddamn it, where was it?

Light bathed the barn. Dakota ran to the first stall. Her breath caught in her throat, suspended.

The light from the aisle seeped into the gloom, but Dakota heard rather than saw the movement within. A velvety nose poked over the stall door. She exhaled in relief.

At least one of them was safe.

She ran to the next, and the next, her heart starting to hammer more rhythmically. All of them were all right.

All right.

But the other barn—

"What's going on?" Dan Bolin appeared at the doorway, looking as if she'd awakened him, even though it couldn't be later than eight o'clock.

"We've got to check the other broodmare barn!" she said, running past him.

The second broodmare barn was a more modern structure which housed the best of the outside mares. As Dakota ran, she prayed. Please, let them be like the others. Please, God, please don't let them be dead.

They were the good ones. The expensive ones. If someone wanted to hurt Black Oak, they would be the target. She tried to block out the vision of dead mares, their beauty and grace gone, but couldn't. Could only say over and over: please God.

Dan reached the barn before her, and once again the glare of the overhead light yellowed the night.

Her gaze swept the aisle.

Inquisitive heads poked over the stall doors, ears pricked forward. All but in three of the stalls. In those, the square above the door was empty, opening into darkness.

Relief vied with dread as Dakota approached one of those stalls. She prepared herself for the worst. If there was slaughter, it had not been wholesale. Only three of them, she told herself, only three, but she knew that the number meant nothing. The last stall on the left belonged to Bar Counsel, a bay mare with the sweetest face on earth. Big doe eyes, so trusting and gentle. It was her first year as a broodmare.

Dakota's head pounded. She reached the stall, gripped the steel guard wrapped over the top, prayed.

Bar Counsel stood in the corner, dozing.

Run Bambi Run. Stall eight. She, too, was fine.

One more. Is She Cereous. Dan called her the PMS Queen. This mare hated people, hated her stall, hated her food, hated her water bucket—

The sorrel mare lay on her side.

Dead?

Is She Cereous lifted her head, then grunted as she struggled to her feet. Her nostrils wrinkled as if she smelled something bad. Her ears flew back. Head snaking from side to side, she scrunched her lip into her trademark sour leer.

"Don't change a thing," Dakota babbled. "You're beautiful just the way you are."

"What's going on?" Dan yelled.

Feeling suddenly foolish, Dakota told him.

"Who would do that?" Dan's eyes were the color of Wedgwood blue in his long face. She'd never noticed before. He towered over her, ponderous in his big denim jacket and big denim jeans—the Marlboro Man.

"I don't know."

"Well, the mares are all right. I checked 'em myself two hours ago."

"Maybe it was just a crank call." Dakota sensed that Is She Cereous was about to take a piece out of her. She stepped back, out of reach, and said, "Oh, no you don't! I'm not on the menu."

Is She Cereous turned her back on them.

Horrified, Dakota uttered a half gasp, half shriek.

The mare's tail had been hacked off.

Sixteen

Dan came up beside Dakota. "Good God."

"Did you cut it for some reason?"

"Why would I do something like that? She's not my horse."

The mare swung her head around and aimed a nip at him. "No wonder she's spitting fire," he said. "Look at her mane."

Dakota stared at the ragged hatchet job the clippers had made of it. The mare had lost her mane and most of her tail.

"You didn't do this?"

"You think I'm crazy?" Dan shook his head. "The owner's gonna be pissed about this."

"Her tail isn't hurt, is it?"

He went into the stall and felt along the mare's tail. "It's cut just below the bone and muscle," he said, obviously relieved.

At least she wasn't hurt. Stunned, Dakota tried to remember the words on the answering machine. Couldn't. She looked in the neighboring stall, and saw with horror that this mare's mane had been roached, too. Her tail was hacked off just below the bone, identical to Cereous's.

Eight of the twenty mares had been butchered this way— the most valuable ones. Someone had come onto Black Oak and done this to the broodmares, and she hadn't even known. Her fingers curled tighter around the gun, and she hugged herself against the coldness that came from within. "You say you checked on them two hours ago?"

Dan emerged from the stall, dodging Cereous's teeth. "They were fine. I would have noticed, if they looked like this."

"You didn't hear anything?"

"I was taking a nap. One of our mares is really close to foaling, so I planned to stay up tonight."

"What about Marcie?"

"She had the night off."

"Why would anyone do a thing like this? What would it accomplish?"

Dan shrugged. "Maybe someone doesn't like you."

She shot a glance at him, but he just looked thoughtful.

"Can you imagine how mad the owners will be?" he asked. "It'll take months to grow those manes out. They'll be stickin' up like one of those punk rockers," the stud manager said morosely.

"You think anyone might withdraw his mare?"

Dan shrugged. "Could be. They couldn't think much of our security."

"Damn!" Dakota kicked the raked dirt.

Raked dirt . . .

There hadn't been any footprints. Whoever had done this had had the time and presence of mind to rake after himself. She glanced into the stall. Snarls of black hair matted the sawdust. He wasn't so neat with the horses. She sighed. "I guess we'd better clean out these stalls. You don't think any of these mares are hurt, do you?"

He grunted. "Just their feelings."

It was the first time Dakota had ever heard him joke.

"You know how horses hate the sound of electric clippers." He stepped back into Cereous's stall and peered at her legs. "If any of 'em got scraped up, it'd be her . . ." The mare lashed out, and he dodged her expertly. "She whacked herself on her hind fetlock, probably kicking out. I'll treat the cut, if the bitch'll let me."

As he started for the tack room, Dakota called to him. "What possible good could this do anyone?"

"Who knows, when you're dealin' with a psycho?"

* * *

A different sheriff's deputy came and took the report. He told them there was nothing he could do. "Probably a crank."

Dakota took a deep breath to stifle her anger. "Can't you put a trace on my phone?"

"If you want to, you could call the phone company. But I don't think it'll do any good. Looks like random vandalism to me. Or maybe you made somebody mad, like cutting them off in traffic or something."

"My father was harassed. And then he was killed."

"We're pretty sure that was an accident."

"What about this?" She showed him the note.

"Someone has a mean sense of humor."

"That's all you can say?"

"Look, I wish I could help you, but there's only three of us holding the fort down here, and there's no way to tell when or if this guy's going to strike again. If any of your stock had been killed, then we'd take it more seriously. It sounds like this guy didn't have the guts to do anything that mean. You should count yourself lucky."

After he'd gone, she debated calling Clay. She remembered the last time she had run to him. When he asked her to spend the night, she'd been tempted. What could he do that the sheriff couldn't, except seduce her?

Suddenly, she realized that the man on the phone could have gotten to Shameless, too. She drove out to the track, fear clawing at her insides. She glanced at the truck phone. She could still call Clay. Maybe he could meet her there—

No.

The filly was fine, but Dakota wasn't taking any chances. She'd brought a sleeping bag, water, and candy bars. And her gun. It was a Smith & Wesson nine millimeter; her father had given it to her for her twenty-seventh birthday, to protect herself in that "Sodom and Gomorrah" of a city she lived in. Dakota had grown up with guns of all kinds, but she liked this one best of all; it was light and the grip fit her palm well. Although she hoped never to use it, she'd been taught to shoot to kill.

The following morning, still sore, Dakota supervised the filly's gallop, then went home. She showered, changed, and was making herself a quick lunch when the phone rang.

Dakota reached for the phone, but didn't pick it up. She really didn't want to hear that ugly, muffled voice. Didn't want to think what he might do next.

The phone kept ringing. It could be anyone. Owners were always calling, checking on their mares. Wiping her hands on a dish towel, she picked up the receiver.

"If I can get close enough to cut their manes, I can cut their throats. I'm not going to tell you again. Go home before someone gets hurt."

Seventeen

"Three owners have pulled their mares," Dan told Dakota. "Word gets around fast."

Dakota, patting her dogs absently as she watched the broodmares, tried to stem the feeling of panic rising in her chest. It had been a rough couple of days. Every time the phone rang she thought it would be that obscene muffled voice, telling her he had cut the mares' throats. She was a package of raw nerves. Whenever Dan sought her out, she expected to hear bad news. Maybe it was a good thing for people to take their mares; at least then they'd be safe. But it would mean disaster for Black Oak.

The mares—thank God—looked healthy and well-cared for, their coats glistening in the sun, but even from here she could see one of them trying to switch her short tail at the flies.

Beside her, Dan shifted his weight from one foot to the other. "Are you really going to send out that letter?"

"What else can I do? Tell them that hacking off their manes and tails is part of the service?"

Dan shrugged, his face blank. His shrug seemed to say, it's your funeral.

Dakota paused, trying to think of something friendly to say. She wanted Dan on her side. "They look good, though."

One of the golden retrievers, who had been sitting patiently at her heels, suddenly darted into the field. "Alydar! Come back here!"

He loped up to one of the mares, his tail wagging furiously. To Dakota's surprise, the mare didn't spook, but pricked her ears and touched noses with him. Alydar licked at the mare's muzzle, and she blew through her nostrils at him. He ran around her in circles, and she followed ponderously, obviously fascinated by him. They had an instantaneous affinity for each other.

The sorrel mare, heavy with foal, had an almost perfect white heart on her forehead. "Look. They're practically waltzing. That's a Black Oak mare, isn't it?" Dakota asked.

"I think she'll drop her foal soon. I'm gonna look at her in a little while."

Dakota whistled, and the dog returned, looking guilty. She'd heard about horses and other animals getting along, to the point that the horses couldn't bear to be parted from their companions. "That's one of the Shawne Bug mares, isn't it? Her name's Shawnes something—Shawnes Secret? No, that's not it."

"I've got to unload the hay," he said, brushing past her. Dakota watched him go, thinking how angry he looked. She supposed he had every right to be, considering his personal problems. Marie Bolin was getting worse. Alice had told Dakota that before Marie could get on the list for a heart donor, Dan would have to come up with a lot of money. The kind of money most people didn't have and couldn't get.

As Dakota drove out, headed for the track, she saw Dan Bolin leaning on the fence, rubbing his eyes tiredly. He stared bleakly at the mares, his anguish plain on his face.

She stopped for gas in Sonoita. As she reached into the glove compartment for the tire gauge, her hands touched rubber—the tire scrap. She'd forgotten all about it.

She remembered what Derek Blue had told her, and her own hazy conclusions. If Coke had been murdered, the most likely explanation seemed to be that someone had run him off the road. The blown tire could have come from the other vehicle.

Dakota realized that she didn't have to look at every car or truck in the county to try and match the chunk of tire. The only person she suspected of being involved in Coke's death was Jerry Tanner. She understood why the sheriff couldn't just go over there and compare treads—it wouldn't be legal—but she could.

When Deputy Blue had given her the tire scrap, had it been with his tacit approval to snoop? She'd be happy to oblige.

Suddenly, she had to know. The need to take control, do *something,* was overwhelming. She had been helpless to prevent the mares from being mutilated. She'd been impotent to stop the phone calls with their insinuating, slimy tone. Here, in her hands, was her chance to fight back.

She took the tire slice over to Tanner's truck. The shed-rows pretty much concealed her from view of the track, but there were always people and vehicles in the rear portion of the track area. When no one seemed to be looking her way, she slipped around to the far end of the truck so that its bulk hid her from view, then knelt down beside the tire.

The truck's tire was almost bald. Ol' Jerry would be driving on his rims before long. But the faint tread did not match the blown retread. She was surprised at the deep disappointment she felt. She had been so *sure.*

Damn! She stood up, brushed her hair out of her eyes. No one paid any attention to her. Horses walked in circles. The mournful sound of a radio, tuned to a country music station, drifted on the air.

Suddenly, she realized that a man like Jerry Tanner, who was too lazy to buy a rebuilt starter for his truck, wasn't the type to replace all his tires at once. More likely, he'd buy new ones only as each tire wore out. No doubt he'd pick the cheapest brand at the time. All four tires could be different makes.

Dakota walked along the truck to the left front. She pretended she was looking at it with an eye to buy it, although the thought of a Beverly Hills Rich Bitch buying this heap wouldn't make much sense if anyone thought about it.

A guy was taking his horse off the hot walker nearby. He glanced at her as he led the horse to the barn. She waved, trying to look innocent. Her smiled felt pinned to her face.

She looked around. A thin wedge of racetrack peeked out between the two closest shedrows. Squinting, Dakota tried to pick out a white shape on the track. Lucky for her the white mule Jerry used to pony his horses was easy to spot. Time slowed to a crawl. At last she saw the mule go by, way out on the backstretch. Even if Tanner was coming back, it would take him a good long time to get to the gap.

She knelt quickly and compared the tire treads. No match.

She'd have to go to the other one. It was closest to the track, and if Jerry happened to look over . . .

Taking a deep breath, Dakota bent down. As she stared at the tire, the certainty that she would be caught crept into her mind. Logic told her Tanner was far away, but her gut feeling didn't agree. It felt as if someone had pulled a wire in her stomach, setting off a chain reaction of heart-fluttering fear. Adrenaline pumped through her veins, making every extremity tingle.

Concentrate, dummy! She grabbed at the farflung tatters of thought, jerking herself back into the present. Stared hard at the tire, trying to make sense of the pattern there.

She couldn't tell. The tire was in shadow, the tread so faint it was difficult to see. She stood up, looking over at the track. Jerry must be on the turn, out of view. Dakota knelt down again, more nervous by the moment. The sliced tire in her hand was slippery with sweat. The flies around her were driving her crazy. She held it against one part of the tire, and then another. So hard to—

"What are you doing?"

Her thoughts froze. She was still staring at the tire, unable to fathom the reality of Jerry Tanner's voice.

"I asked you a question."

Galvanized by the anger in his tone, Dakota straightened up, her heart pounding like a sledgehammer. She'd had the presence of mind to let go of the tire scrap as she stood up, letting it fall in the shade of the wheel well.

"What did you think I was doing? I was looking at your truck," she said, shielding her eyes against the bright sun. Offense was the best defense.

Tanner held the halter to a scrawny thoroughbred with bucked shins. It was still wet from a bath. Someone else—Lucy?—must have been riding his mule.

"Why?"

"Lucy told me the shocks were bad. We happen to have some—they were on my dad's old truck. Brand new. I thought she could use them, since it's dangerous to drive with bad shocks." Not a bad lie, except Coke's truck was in an impoundment lot in Tucson. No doubt Jerry knew that; he wasn't stupid.

"Now why would you wanna do that for me?"

"I wouldn't do a thing for you," she said, forcing her tone to be calm. "But I don't want to see Lucy get hurt."

His eyes narrowed. "We don't need your charity."

She felt like saying that they'd lived off her father's charity for years.

Jerry leaned toward her. Hamburger with mustard and onions. "Just because you hired my daughter doesn't mean you're off the hook. You got that?"

"What do you mean?"

"I saved your father's life, that's what I'm talking about. It's plain as day, ain't it? You owe me, lady!" He waved his arm. "Now you come along with your la-di-da ways and all your money and think you can make it all up by giving my daughter a shit job. She might fall for it, but I don't. She knows which side her bread's buttered on."

"I gave her the job because she needed it."

But Tanner was on a roll now. "I know what's really going on. You think I'm blind? Your kind only care about yourselves. First you McAllisters took my livelihood, and now you want my daughter."

"Your daughter? I don't want—"

"It's hard enough to make ends meet, without her gallivantin' all over the place with you."

"I offered her a job. That's all," she said as coolly as she could. "If you'd rather she didn't work for me, that can be arranged."

He backed down at that. He certainly wasn't going to turn

down the money Lucy was bringing in. He glared at her for a moment, then yanked the chestnut around savagely and walked away. "Stay away from my truck," he yelled back at her.

Dakota decided she'd better leave the piece of retread where it was and pick it up later, when Tanner was gone. Still shaken from the encounter, she walked back to her shedrow.

One thing was certain: Jerry Tanner had a whole lot of hate, and it was all directed at her. Could he have hated Coke that much? He felt Coke owed him. In his mind, Coke had thrown him out on the street. What would a man like Jerry Tanner do about it? Would he be mad enough to kill?

She was pretty sure the tire she'd checked last wasn't the same, which left one more to look at. As she'd suspected, all three of the tires had been different brands and had different degrees of wear. It was feasible that the fourth one could match.

But later that evening, when Dakota went back for the tire scrap, it was gone. She looked over the whole area, but there was no sign of it. Either the maintainance man had picked up the trash, or else Jerry had found the tire tread and removed it—which would mean that he knew what she'd been doing.

That thought gave her chills.

Eighteen

Clay hooked one knee over the pommel and absently slapped his pants leg with one of the saddle ties as he stared at the track. His palomino mare, Goldenrod, pricked her ears as the sound of hoofbeats came closer. To the west, the Patagonia Mountains gleamed silver-blue above the surf of grassland, peaceful and aloof.

"I thought I'd find you here."

Clay glanced behind him, where Rita stood at the rail. He nodded to her, then returned his gaze to the track.

"Did you see the last bulletin on the wolves?"

He shielded his eyes against the sun, trying to block out her voice as Straight Eight, another of his All American hopefuls, came around the turn. Just before reaching the stands the exercise rider asked him for more, and the colt stretched into a run.

"Are you listening, Clay?" Rita had been talking all this time, but he hadn't heard a word. "There's going to be a meeting in Phoenix—"

"Rita, I'm busy right now." He'd been able to tell how fast the horse was going in his head—that was, until Rita had distracted him.

"One of these days you'll want me to pay attention to *you,* and I'll be too busy." Rita turned and walked away, her page-boy lifting off her neck in the breeze.

Clay watched his horse slow to a walk on the backstretch, turn around and walk back up the track.

He'd have to talk to her.

Clay realized he'd been a fool to believe that no-strings-attached crap, although at the time her act had been convincing. When she arrived last year, Rita cruised through Sonoita like a shark, flaunting her sexual prowess with reckless abandon. Her surface sophistication had fooled him into thinking she was the kind of woman who could handle a casual sexual relationship, that they would both move on when the attraction waned. Those had been the ground rules—rules *she'd* insisted upon. Too late he realized that her wildness was skin deep. About a month ago he noticed that she started making demands on his time, encroaching more and more into his private life. It wasn't a lighthearted fling anymore, if it ever had been.

He'd underestimated her—and himself. The moment he saw Dakota again, Clay had lost his appetite for sex with Rita. It wasn't fair to her, but he couldn't help his feelings. It was as if a light switch had been turned off.

Clay berated himself for putting off the inevitable. He should tell her that their relationship could go no further—today. He owed it to her. But what was he going to say? The minute he saw his ex-wife, he knew that Rita didn't fit the bill? There was little hope of reconciliation with Dakota—in fact, he wasn't sure he wanted one. But seeing her again, the kind of person she was—it was enough to show him that he could never seriously consider a woman like Rita.

They were too different. Rita hated to be alone; she needed people around to entertain her. Clay liked his privacy. Rita had to possess *things,* as if owning something expensive filled the void inside. Clay would rather involve himself in doing something—like training his horses. Rita wanted to be the focus of attention; she was always wondering what people thought of her. Clay didn't care for the frenetic level of Rita's life. He liked small pleasures, as Dakota did. If he had any ambition, it lay in becoming a better racehorse trainer. He loved the challenge of figuring out what went on in each horse's mind, and how to get the best out of him. Finding the horse's level—the class of horses he should run with and the distance that made him happy enough to win. Keeping him sound, eager, and strong. That was something that could take a lifetime to perfect.

Rita had a lot of good qualities. She cared passionately about certain injustices. She could run a fund-raiser like nobody's business. And yet she was a frightened little girl at her core, terrified of being abandoned. She'd told him she'd been adopted as the last resort of a childless couple. Ironically, soon after the papers were signed, her adoptive parents had two children in quick succession. They always compared Rita unfavorably to their natural offspring.

Maybe that was why she needed people so much. Clay sighed. It wasn't his job to psychoanalyze Rita. He was only qualified to psychoanalyze racehorses.

But it couldn't wait any longer. He'd have to talk to her today.

Hoofbeats sounded behind him. Up on Shameless, Ernesto Acevedo stood in the stirrups, gathering reins. Dakota rode beside him on Tyke.

They turned left and walked up the track, stopped near the far turn, before Dakota unclipped the pony shank from the filly's bridle. She rode over to Clay.

"This is it," Clay greeted her.

"This is it," Dakota agreed, her voice strained.

He glanced at her. Her face looked drawn and faint shadows nested under her eyes. She did not look like a person who was eagerly anticipating watching her All American horse run for the first time. "You nervous?" he asked.

"A little, maybe."

They watched in silence as Ernesto eased the filly into a gallop. Shameless went around once, nice and easy. She looked good. The second time, as they reached the homestretch, Ernesto let the reins out a notch. Not really asking her, just letting her run if she felt like it.

She felt like it.

Shameless took hold of the bit and put on a blinding burst of speed, her legs working like pistons. Clods of dirt flew up as she ran by them, a dark blur.

"Too fast," Dakota muttered.

Already, Ernesto was standing in the sitrrups, pressing his knuckles down into the filly's withers, taking back. Shameless fought him, shaking her head and almost pulling him out of the irons. Finally, she yielded to the pressure on her mouth, dropping back into a gallop. They made another circuit at a slow, hobbyhorse lope.

Clay realized he'd been holding his breath the whole time the filly was running. He couldn't remember seeing a horse that fast.

Dakota's strained expression was gone. "Did you *see* her?" she demanded. Her eyes shone with happiness. "Dad was right. She's everything he said she was!"

"She sure is."

Ernesto walked the filly back.

"I've got to go," Dakota said, reining her horse around and riding over to Shameless.

Whatever had been bothering her had been blown away, like birds scattered by a gunshot.

Exhilarated, Dakota bathed the filly, then started on a walking circuit of the grounds. Shameless seemed fine, except that she was jumped up. As excited as Dakota herself was.

"You liked that, didn't you? You wish you could do it every day," Dakota said, patting her neck.

"Dakota?" Rita DeWeil fell into step with her, on the other side of the filly. "I think I've found a trainer for you."

"Trainer?"

"His name's Jack Dougherty. I knew you were looking for a trainer, and I think he'd be great for you."

Dakota paused. "I'll have to think about it."

"Well, I know how much you want to get out from under—so I just thought, since I was looking for someone myself, to ask him for you. He said he'd be happy to talk about it."

The filly arched her crest and pranced, her eye ringed with

white, like an eclipse. Her nostrils flared salmon-pink as she pulled in the air, and Dakota could trace the filigree of delicate veins under her sweat-dark mahogany neck. God, she was beautiful! Beautiful, but a handful. Dakota jerked hard on the lead shank. "Walk!"

"She won't hurt me, will she?"

"Not if you stay back."

"Here's his card. He'd heard about Shameless, and he's eager to work with her."

"Thanks." But she didn't feel thankful. As a matter of fact, the thought of handing Shameless over to anyone was a depressing one.

Rita shot her a superior smile, and suddenly Dakota realized what this was all about. If Shameless had a trainer, Dakota would have no reason to remain in Sonoita.

"I've got to go. Clay's invited me to lunch. Give Dougherty a call, I have a feeling he'll be just the thing for you." She walked away, stunning in immaculate white jeans and a quilted vest, which depicted scenes of rodeo events in appliqués of suede, lamé, bugle beads and conchos. Dakota glanced down at her own chambray shirt, much the worse for wear, shirttail half in and half out of her jeans. Her hair felt like a wet dishrag under her Dodgers cap. A racing bat was stuck in the back of her jeans. Her running shoes were caked with dirt and manure. Very attractive. No wonder Rita had been so friendly.

So Clay and Rita were having lunch. Well, more power to them.

She had the next All American winner in her stable.

She headed for home, hot, sweaty, and victorious. Her limbs still trembling from the adrenaline rush, she threw her racing bat on the side table in the kitchen and poured herself a jelly glass full of orange juice.

Damn, but Shameless could run! And she'd come back in beautiful shape. No heat in the ankle, no swelling. And she wasn't even breathing hard. She wanted to run. She was born for it.

The phone rang. Dakota's heart lurched in her chest at the loud jangling. Three rings, four.

Every time she picked up the phone, she was afraid who might be on the other end. Even though she'd hired security guards for each barn, there was no one to keep *her* from being threatened. But nothing could bring her down today. She snatched up the receiver, prepared to slam it down immediately if need be, and sighed with relief at the sound of her mother's voice.

"I just talked to your agent," Eileen Wood said briskly. "You'll probably get a call later on today." She paused for effect. "You got it!"

"It?"

"The soap opera! 'Catalina!' The one you just auditioned for? They want you to play Tiffany Groves—"

Dakota pressed her fingertips against her forehead. "Mother, I can't deal with this now."

"What do you mean, you can't deal with it? Don't you understand English? You'll be starting on the ground floor of a new soap opera. This isn't a walk-on. This is a regular character, part of the cast."

Suddenly it hit her. What her mother was talking about was what she'd been working for for years. As much security as you could get in Hollywood. "You mean it?"

"Would I lie? They start production next week . . ."

As her mother babbled on, Dakota listened in stunned silence. After all these years . . . she couldn't believe it. If she packed up the truck, she could leave tomorrow morning—

Except that tomorrow morning Shameless had to be checked over, then walked for a good hour. Dakota didn't trust anyone to do it but herself.

When at last she put the phone down, Dakota stared out the window, her mind in turmoil. She found Jack Dougherty's card in her pocket, started to punch in the number. Hung up the phone. What did she know about him? What kind of trainer would he be? Shameless was doing so well, she didn't want to set her back . . .

All the joy, the exhilaration, went out of her day. It was as if a cloud had covered the sun.

Her big break had finally come, and she didn't know what to do with it.

Nineteen

Dakota couldn't sleep that night. After brewing herself some decaffeinated tea, she watched an old Nick and Nora Charles movie on television. She hardly paid attention to the movie; her mind was on other things. Around and around she went. One minute she was leaving for California; the next, she was staying here with Shameless.

Around midnight, she decided this chance was too good to give up. She could be out of here in a day. There was nothing stopping her. She'd pack some of her father's things and send for them later. Finding some boxes, Dakota put them together and started grabbing stuff, energized by her decision. The photo albums, a few of the best photographs on the walls.

She'd take her father's plates and glasses, the ones from the gas stations. As she reached up into the kitchen cupboard to pull down one of the frosted glasses, her hand brushed something that wasn't contact paper. She withdrew a small notebook from behind the glasses.

It was Coke's journal.

Dakota sat down on the couch and started reading. When she looked up again it was two A.M. Her head ached. The sheer number of incidents Coke recorded was chilling:

"*Ruidoso, July 5:* Thrilled with Yawl came back from a work looking good. While I was bathing him he keeled over dead from a heart attack. I'm getting an autopsy. *July 8:* Colt loose in the shedrow again. This time it was Elvis. He got into the feed. Thank God he didn't founder! I have a combination lock for the feed shed door. Jerry never did give me back all my keys. How's that for proof? If the cops would just search his place, but of course they won't. *July 24:* Cyber Cat's leg caught in haynet, he's hurt bad. He'll be out of action for a long time. *August 1:* Catch on halter broke on Fuel while I was ponying him, he got loose, spooked, ran into the rail. Torn up bad. *August 15:* One of our babies got loose again last night again. Replace bolts, latches."

Just a run of bad luck? It was said that if a horse will find a way to kill himself, he'll do it.

"*Ruidoso, August 24:* Bay filly had colic, nearly didn't make it. *September 10:* Shipped to Los Alamitos. Tire blew about forty miles outside of Las Cruces. Trailer ended up on its side in a ditch, took two hours to get Tiny's Garland out. Touch and go for a while, but we think she'll come out of it all right. Those tires were brand new. *Turf Paradise, September 18:* Drug test came back positive on Glamorous. What the hell's going on? She was a cinch to win. Everyone should know I wouldn't take that risk. *September 23:* Found three-inch nail in Benny's foot. Won't be able to run for a month at least. Still suspended, so I guess it's a moot point anyway. Horse got out again last night. I know the latches are good. I'm gonna get combination locks for all of them. *September 24:* Seems the stewards call me in every day. What have I done this time?

"*Turf Paradise, October 11:* Loose horse, again! No damage. *Turf Paradise, October 23: Another* goddamn infraction! I'm paying so many fines I could build them a new clubhouse. *Turf Paradise, November 3:* Twister broke down in a work. Had to be destroyed."

* * *

Some of these incidents could have happened to anyone, but not all of them. When Coke was suspended for drugging a horse at Turf Paradise, his outrage was real. He had been set up. Everyone knew it. There was little doubt that Jerry Tanner was the culprit. He had been fired in early June, and the recorded incidents started on July 5.

Dakota read on.

"There are a couple of ways he could of done it. Lucy worked over in the next shedrow to mine at Ruidoso. Her old man couldn've put her up to it. The apple doesn't fall very far from the tree. But I think it's Dave, who worked as a groom for me most of the summer. I fired him for laying down on the job, and later found out he worked for Jerry before me, both here and at Ruidoso. The bastard said the weirdest thing to me when I gave him his week's pay. 'Bet you think Velvet Elvis's gonna win you a ton of money tomorrow. I wouldn't bet on it.' The colt was the odds-on favorite in that race! Came in dead last, like he was waterlogged. Must've poured a gallon of water down his throat! The next week, the son of a bitch is back working for Jerry. One thing's for damn sure, Jerry didn't do it himself. I'd run him off with a shotgun if he ever showed his face at my shedrow. I don't know how he's doing it, but I do know why. Sour grapes."

From what Dakota had seen of Tanner, he didn't have a lot of discretionary income, but maybe he'd been willing to pay for his vice. He struck her as the type to be fueled by revenge fantasies.

She thought of the broodmares, and shivered.

If the journal was a record of the accidents that had befallen the horses of Black Oak, it also painted a clear picture of Coke's daily work with Shameless. Dakota smiled as she saw the way he did things, and how similar her own program was. Shameless was a project that she and her father shared.

* * *

"I had a feeling that breeding Dash to Judgment to Wicked would be a good nick," he wrote. "And it was. This filly has it all. I know it's not a good idea to tempt fate, but if this isn't a Grade 1 stakes winner, I'll eat my hat. I'll never forget the day I bred that mare. There was a partial eclipse, like the gods were telling me something."

As she read, Dakota fell into the rhythm of Coke's everyday life. She lived with him the long, thankless hours of hard work. Coke thought of little else but his horses; they always came first. But there was one other thing he thought about, especially in the latter part of the journal.

He thought about her. *Can't keep any good help. I wish Dakota was here.*

Dakota had the makings of a fine trainer.

I keep remembering her when she was little, before her mother turned her against me. She was the cutest little thing, with those pigtails and that Annie Oakley jacket, and she could ride just about anything.

In one revealing segment he wrote that he wished he'd fought to keep Dakota with him after the divorce. At the time, he was afraid of how much a custody battle would affect her. He did extract a promise from Eileen that Dakota would spend some time with him on the ranch and at the racetrack in Ruidoso. *I told myself I wouldn't push her, but she's made for this way of life and I got impatient. I just wanted her to see how much she fit, and I guess I scared her off. I guess it's just a pipe dream, but I could see Dakota and Clay raising Black Oak horses and training winners together. I'd be the grand pooh-bah, telling my grandchildren about the good old days at Rillito.*

Given the chance, Coke had written about everything that mattered to him. It might have started out as a record of vandalism for his lawyer, but it ended up as a diary. Tears filled Dakota's eyes. She could see it all, the growing sense of menace, his worry that something would happen to Shameless, his regret at not being closer to his daughter. He had been alone, fighting a battle he could not win.

She discovered the real reason Jerry Tanner was fired. Last summer had been an especially busy time for Coke. He ran his top string in California, and Jerry Tanner had charge of the younger horses at Ruidoso. Apparently, when Coke wasn't around, Jerry was sloppy. He never bothered to clean up his shedrow, and his trash accumulated. One day a plastic bag blew off the pile and got under a colt's feet as it walked on the hot walker. The colt had been playing with his halter fastener when the bag spooked him and he had cut his mouth. It had been a simple enough cut, but it had become infected. A month later, despite all efforts to save him, his most promising two-year-old, the one he'd thought would win the Futurity last year, had died in Coke's arms. His heartbreak was clear in the words on the page, for he had loved that colt.

Dakota set the notebook down and straightened up, rubbing her back. Last year, Coke had been cheated out of a run for the All American by Jerry Tanner.

This year, he had been cheated by death.

She stared at the blank TV screen, remembering the videotape of her father showing off his filly.

Dakota had no doubt that Jack Dougherty was a good trainer. He'd probably do right by Shameless.

But that wasn't what Coke had wanted. And, she was beginning to realize, it wasn't what she wanted either.

Dakota suddenly understood what had been there, under the surface, for some time. In her heart of hearts, she wanted to win the All American for her father. And she wanted to win it by herself.

Twenty

When she reached the track at six that morning, Dakota could barely keep from blurting out her news to everyone she met. The tension that had been her constant companion the last couple of months had evaporated, replaced by an almost unbearable excitement. Dakota became aware that she was holding the secret close to her chest, waiting to tell Clay.

I've decided to stay and train Shameless for the All American. She could hear herself say the words, but her mind wouldn't go beyond that point. Of course he would be glad. Hadn't he been pestering her to stay?

Not that it was important what Clay thought. He was her ex, remember? But Dakota glanced over at his shedrow every few minutes, hoping he'd see her and come over.

Ernesto had cleaned out the water buckets and kept out the feed bucket for Dakota to look at. Shameless had eaten well; she always did. When Ernesto led the filly out of the stall, Dakota caught her breath. Shameless was a superb balance of clean lines and solidly defined muscle; she might have been carved out of marble. Her coat, dappled with the effects of good nutrition and conditioning, shimmered like polished mahogany in the sunlight. *"Muy bien,"* Dakota told Ernesto.

"Gracias, señora."

Lucy was mucking out Tyke's stall. "You still want to go to the seminar?" Dakota asked her.

"Yes, ma'am," Lucy replied. She sifted the soiled sawdust through the pitchfork with clockwork efficiency. Her ability for hard work impressed Dakota, especially considering the junky environment she came from. "Are we still going to the Mountain Oyster Club?"

"That's the plan."

"Ernesto got some more rides," Lucy said, her forehead knitted with worry. "I hope he gets done in time. We can still go, can't we? Even if he's busy?"

"We can wait for him."

"Good." Going to the Mountain Oyster Club obviously meant a lot to Lucy.

Dakota gave Ernesto a leg up onto Shameless and ponied the filly out to the track.

Clay, on his palomino, was watching his horse gallop. Dakota reined in beside him. It had become a ritual, sitting their horses in companionable silence, enjoying the cool breeze blowing off the mountains, the sun warm on their backs. Today, however, Dakota was impatient with desultory conversation. She was just about to tell him her news, when he stood in his stirrups, watching as his horse galloped by.

The moment passed. This wasn't the time. She wanted some fanfare, and his mind was on his work—as hers should be.

There was a lull in the action. As they waited, Clay told her about his new barn mascot: a potbellied pig.

"Alydar's got a love affair going with one of our mares." As Dakota told him about it, the mare's name suddenly popped into her head. "Shawnes Soliloquy. It's been on the tip of my tongue since yesterday morning, driving me crazy."

"She's that's sorrel with a heart on her forehead? Nice mare." He checked his watch. "You going to Tucson for the seminar?"

"Yup."

"You could come with us."

"Us?"

He shifted uncomfortably in his saddle. "Rita's going."

"Oh. No thanks." Rita, again. If there was something going on between them, why couldn't he be honest about it?

"I'd like your company."

"To be honest, Clay, I'm not too fond of Rita."

"I can't uninvite her."

"I know."

He leaned forward and parted Goldenrod's cream-colored mane to the left side of her neck. "I don't think you should drive all that way by yourself."

"What do you mean?"

"I noticed your security guard. Maybe the horse isn't the only thing that needs guarding."

In a few words he had maneuvered her out of her good mood—and made her think of something that scared her to the core. She'd be damned if she'd tell him her news now. "So you feel it's your duty to be my bodyguard. When did you decide to switch careers?"

He looked straight ahead. "I know what happened with the mares."

"What?"

"I talked to Dan Bolin the other day."

"He had no right—"

"It's getting serious."

"It's nothing."

"Look at me."

She gritted her teeth. "Shameless is coming." She tried to concentrate on the filly's stride as Shameless galloped past, but it was impossible. Inside, she was quaking.

"She's gone. Now look at me."

Reluctantly, she faced him. Worry lines creased his forehead, and his jaw was set like stone. "Did you call the sheriff?"

"Yes. He thought it was a prank."

"What are you going to do?"

"You've seen the security guard."

"Why didn't you tell me?" he asked softly.

"It had nothing to do with you."

"Oh?"

"It isn't your business," Dakota replied as coldly as she could, and wheeled her horse around.

"Why are you so mad at me? Because I kissed you?" he called out.

She stiffened, realized that her legs were shaking like saplings in a strong wind.

"Don't get so bent out of shape, McAllister. It was just a kiss."

She turned to face him. "It's over, Clay. It's been over for ten years."

He didn't deny it. She rode out to meet Shameless and led her back to the barn. The words she'd been longing to say all morning now tasted like ashes in her mouth.

Lucy loved the Mountain Oyster Club. If she were rich, she'd come here every day.

She bet the members of the Mountain Oyster Club never had to worry about someone shutting off their electricity, or getting caught by some cop for not having registration tags. She bet they didn't have any problems at all.

Lucy stared at the western paintings on the walls, the photographs of racehorses. The motto of the club was *"cervesa y huevos para todos:* beer and balls for everyone," and the red carpet in the front room was patterned with bull balls and beer bottles. So totally lewd. She guessed rich people could get away with stuff other people couldn't. Her dad would be so jealous. He'd never made it to the Mountain Oyster Club.

Dakota must know everyone here, all the wealthy and powerful racehorse owners, big-time lawyers and judges, the ranchers, the politicians, their wives. People were constantly touching Dakota's arm and telling her how sorry they were about Coke. Lucy wished she was that popular. She could make people like her if she tried, but it was always an effort because she had to pretend. Pretending was easy; it was keeping it up that was such a bitch.

Too bad they'd had to leave Sonoita so late because of Ernesto's last ride. He kept trying to get her attention, pointing out stuff that she'd already seen, but she ignored him, even when he tapped her arm.

Lucy watched Dakota talk animatedly to a guy at another table. God, she wished she were like her. Beautiful, poised, rich. Dakota owned a champion racehorse, even if it hadn't raced yet. Dad would never be able to touch a horse like that. And Dakota had a boyfriend who was the handsomest man in Sonoita. Not to mention that beautiful ranch. Dakota said that when it warmed up she and Ernesto could go swimming. And of course, this summer Dakota would take her to Ruidoso. This time she wouldn't have to stay in the trailer. She bet Dakota would let her stay with her at the cabin, like she and Dad had done that summer before Coke fired him.

And maybe she and Dakota could be friends, real friends. She'd never had a friend before—never even felt the need for one—but she could see that being friends with Dakota would be fun.

Ernesto, of course, would always be hanging around. That was the downside. Dakota liked to include him, and Lucy didn't want to be shut out of doing things, so she went along.

The waitress set down a basket of crisply baked garlic toast. Lucy closed her eyes and chewed some, even though she knew her dad wanted her to watch her weight. God, what heaven! She *loved* food. She had four more of them, taking the last two when no one was looking.

Suddenly, she noticed Dakota stiffen. Following her gaze, Lucy saw Clay and Rita DeWeil come in. They didn't notice Dakota, and sat in the same room. After they were seated, Clay saw them and waved.

Dakota looked like she'd been hit by a truck. Not long after that, she excused herself and went to the bathroom. Worried, Lucy followed her.

Dakota was sitting on one of the green-and-white dressing table chairs before the mirror. She shook out two aspirin from a tiny bottle and dry-swallowed them.

"Are you all right?" Lucy asked.

Dakota glanced up into the mirror and smiled. "I'm fine. Just a little headache."

"I could get you a cup of water."

"No, I already swallowed them. I'm okay." She grinned. "Funny room, isn't it?"

Lucy glanced around, but saw nothing funny about it. It was exactly the kind of bathroom she'd have if she were rich; a princess's room, with wire-backed dresser stools and draperies and lots of fresh white paint on the walls. "Why aren't we sitting with Clay?"

"He's entertaining someone else."

"She's not as pretty as you."

Dakota didn't reply.

"He's been looking at you ever since they came in. I think he'd rather be sitting with you than her."

"Your imagination's working overtime."

"I could talk to them. Maybe they'd come sit with us."

Dakota smiled. "Thank you, but I'd rather you didn't."

"I heard her order the mountain oysters." Lucy giggled. "She'll probably throw up when she finds out what they are."

"I could do without that picture."

"I'm sorry," Lucy said quickly. "It's just that I don't like her. I like you."

Dakota sighed. "I should be flattered, but you don't have to choose between us. You can like her, too."

But Lucy had a feeling Dakota was secretly pleased. People cared about stuff like that. "If you want me to like her, I will," she added helpfully.

"That's not the point. I can't tell you how to feel about someone."

"I don't mind. You've been so good to me, hiring me even though my dad hates you. I'd do anything for you, including be nice to *her.*" Dakota was about to argue, but Lucy kept going. "You're the nicest person I ever met. You're even nice to *her,* when she's trying to snag your boyfriend."

"He's not my boyfriend."

Lucy grinned. "You'd like him to be."

Dakota was staring at her with a puzzled, not-so-friendly look on her face.

She'd said the wrong thing again. Sometimes she'd be going along, really impressing someone, and then, boom! The wrong word would pop out of her mouth and she'd get that strange look from people, like she had horns or something. She rushed on. "I saw a movie about people who were married once and got divorced. Fifteen years later they met again and fell in love, got married, and lived happily ever after. I think that's what'll happen to you and Clay."

"Lucy, we are not getting back together. I don't want to talk about it anymore. I don't want you to talk about it to anyone, either."

"Yeah, okay." Lucy took the hint and changed the subject. "These cartoons are really funny." She nodded to the bulletin board.

Dakota laughed, her annoyance gone. "Yeah, they are. I like the one about the bull."

They left the bathroom, passing the table where Rita and Clay were sitting. Clay glanced up just as the waitress set down their plates. "Dakota! Lucy."

Rita looked green. "Clay," Lucy heard her say. "These aren't oysters."

"I told you you wouldn't like them."

"What are they, then?"

Lucy winked at Dakota, who was staring at Rita, too. "They're scrotums," Lucy said. "You know the railroad tracks down the street? Transients are always getting run over by trains. Their balls are a real delicacy."

"Lucy," Dakota warned.

Rita looked horrified. Was she dumb enough to believe that?

"She's just joking," Dakota said.

Clay took a swallow of his beer. "Well, she's half right."

Lucy could tell he was getting a kick out of it. "They're really horse nuts," she volunteered. "You see the racehorses on the walls? Their owners get so attached to 'em they want to stuff 'em, but it's too expensive, so they eat their—"

"Come on, Lucy, let's leave them to their lunch."

"Makes 'em virile," Lucy called back.

When they sat down again, they both laughed until their

sides split. Even Ernesto laughed, too, although he only half understood the joke.

"Lucy, how in the world do you come up with these things? I swear, you're the smoothest liar I ever saw."

"She deserved it," Lucy said.

Rita sent a few smoldering glances their way, but it didn't bother Lucy. She was exactly where she wanted to be.

The seminar was as dry as dust. The speaker droned on about the threat of Indian gaming to the racetrack industry, but Rita wasn't listening. She didn't understand what he was talking about anyway. Or care.

She glanced at Clay. She could feel his forearm against her own, solid through the crisp material of his shirt. Even through her veil of depression, Rita felt the shock of pleasure race up her arm, goose bumps springing up like mushrooms after a rain. How she longed for those tanned, sinewy arms to embrace her again! She knew so well the things he could do with those strong fingers. It couldn't be over. Being near him again made her more determined than ever to get him back.

Yesterday might not have happened at all. She tried to block it from her mind. Clay was with her now, wasn't he?

He crossed his arms. His body was tilted away from her, leaving the armrest empty. Was he here with her against his will, because last week he'd promised to take her to the seminar? Because she'd called and told her car was in the shop? Because she finally wore him down with her begging? The desperate fear flared up inside her like a hot wind, and she saw his face in her mind's eye.

Rita, we need to talk.

The way he'd taken her hands in his, the serious look in his eyes. Some sixth sense had told her what he was going to say even before he even spoke. *It's time we saw other people.*

What do you mean?

I think you know. We both knew this day would come.

Clay shifted in his seat, his face still turned away. The man at the podium talked about something called "handle." Rita bit her lip; her lipstick tasted like crayon.

Oh? Well, maybe you'd better spell it out for me.

It's time to move on. Not see each other so much.

You're a conceited son of a bitch, do you know that, Clay? What makes you think I even want you anymore? That had been bravado, pure and simple.

If I got things wrong, I apologize.

His voice had been so damn *calm.* There wasn't a shred of emotion in it. That was what made her lose control. She'd screamed, railed at him, pleaded, cried, made a fool of herself in front of everyone in the track parking lot. He stood like a stone, absorbing all of it. Nothing could move him.

She glared at Dakota, who sat two rows in front of them. It was obvious that Clay would rather be with her.

He had somehow deluded himself into thinking he could start over with his ex-wife. It would never work out. Dakota had made it clear she didn't love him anymore. Clay was infatuated, not really in love. Once Dakota was gone, he'd come back down to earth. And realize where his real affection lay.

She had already tried to get rid of Dakota, but so far, it hadn't worked. It seemed the woman was here to stay.

Unless . . . Rita's lips thinned with determination. She'd just have to think of something else.

By the time Dakota, Ernesto and Lucy reached the Tanners' trailer, it was dark. Jerry's truck was gone. Lucy said he'd be either at the Steak Out or the Cowpony Bar and Grill.

"How does he afford to go out every night?"

"Veteran's disability pension," Lucy replied with chilling matter-of-factness. "It buys a lot of booze."

No wonder she was so strange, having a father who deserted her every night to get drunk while their place fell down around their ears.

"You want to come in?" Lucy asked.

"I'd better get Ernesto home."

"I could fix us some grilled cheese sandwiches."

"I can't." There was no way Dakota wanted to spend any time in that trailer. It gave her the creeps.

"I guess I don't blame you," Lucy said, glancing meaningfully at the mess in the yard. Dakota followed her gaze. The junk was distributed differently, but it was still junk.

As Dakota drove away, she felt a pang of guilt. Jerry Tanner was a real bastard, but it shouldn't make a difference how she felt about his daughter. The girl probably detested living in such squalor. Would it have hurt to eat one grilled cheese sandwich in less-than-pristine surroundings?

But deep down, Dakota was reluctant to encourage Lucy's all-too-obvious adoration. Hadn't she already betrayed the girl's confidence by sneaking around Jerry's truck, looking for evidence that he'd killed Coke? It was possible that down the road, Tanner might be arrested for Coke's murder. How would Lucy feel about her then?

Dakota couldn't shake the feeling that it didn't pay to get too close to the Tanner Family. Coke had learned that the hard way.

Twenty-One

At three years old, Viento Prieto—Spanish for Dark Wind—was already a Grade 1 stakes winner. Yet as he and Shameless made their way to the track, the experienced black colt was the fractious one. He pranced and shied and generally made a fool of himself. Shameless walked beside him, not a hint of nervousness in her springy stride. She reminded Dakota of a beauty contestant parading before her audience, well aware of the weight of her crown and its sundry responsibilities. She might have been born an adult.

Maybe Shameless had a precocious nature, but physically she was still a baby. A baby with fragile legs and a desire to run full out.

As Dakota sat Tyke near the stands, she tried to stem the nervousness rising in her chest. She always prepared herself for the worst, every time Shameless worked. It was the way the filly ran that both scared and exhilarated her. Shameless had a peculiar straight-up-and-down gait that appeared inefficient but covered the ground in a phenomenally fast time. Dakota winced as she thought of her own fingers drumming as hard as they could against wood. Shameless ran like that.

The clocker, standing nearby, asked the names of the horses to be worked. "Viento Prieto and Shameless," Clay called out, urging his palomino closer to Tyke. "Scared?"

"I feel like a parent dropping off her kid for the first day at kindergarten."

"She'll do all right."

"You really think so? She runs so hard."

"She's matured faster than most two-year-olds. It's in her breeding."

It was odd how comforting Clay's voice could be. Dakota realized how much she was beginning to depend on him; his presence, his advice, his many offers of help. She knew that her increasing reliance on him was dangerous, given her feelings.

At least he didn't flirt with her anymore. She wondered if he was still seeing Rita. Rita hadn't come to the track in over a week, since the seminar. Dakota wanted to ask Clay about it, but that would be prying. And it really was none of her business.

But the fact was, she still wanted him. Even a kid like Lucy could see through her. No wonder Clay had thought she was easy pickings.

Clay glanced over. Dakota blushed. Concentrate on the filly, she told herself sternly.

This was Shameless's first of two works that must be done in the company of another horse. The racetrack required two "works in company" of every horse that had not previously started in a race. Clay was nice enough to run Viento Prieto with Shameless, although at the moment Dakota wished she'd waited for a day when he was working one of his two-year-olds.

The two horses started out at a slow gallop, just before the far turn. Dakota lifted her binoculars as they picked up speed. She didn't expect much from Shameless, not running against an experienced three-year-old who had already won a stakes race.

They came at a fast gallop around the turn and headed for home. Now was the time. Dakota saw Ernesto hunch over the filly's neck and let the reins out a notch, asking her. She jack-rabbited forward.

"Holy Jesus!" Dakota heard the clocker mutter.

One second Shameless had been running alongside Viento Prieto, picking up speed, matching him stride for stride. The next, she took off like a rocket.

"That filly just hit Mach 1!" the clocker said.

Dakota could only look on in a mixture of panic and awe. It was obvious that Ernesto had been taken by surprise. He sensed her killing speed almost immediately and tried to take back, jamming his feet forward for leverage. Standing in the stirrups, he wrestled to get the bit back from the headstrong filly. Shameless would have none of it. She churned up the track with her explosive, punishing stride, one length ahead of Viento Prieto and widening as they headed into the first turn again.

Viento Prieto was running full out, his ears pinned back as he tried to catch the filly. The pounding of his hooves only spurred her on.

"He's got to stop her!" Dakota cried. But she knew there was nothing she could do. She was too far away to help.

Viento Prieto was pulling up, his breath coming in loud snorts. With relief, Dakota saw Ernesto slow the filly down, her neck bowed almost to her chest.

"He can't rate her," she said. "He's not strong enough."

"I think she's rating herself," Clay said. "She ran exactly one hundred yards."

That was the distance she was supposed to work. Dakota stared at the filly in awe. Shameless galloped along at an even pace. From here she didn't even look tired. How could any horse withstand that punishing pace, let alone a two-year-old?

The clocker pushed his cap back on his head and nodded to Clay. "That colt of yours is a three-year-old, am I right?"

"He won the Sun Country Futurity last year."

The clocker whistled. "And that filly made mincemeat of him. Me, I had a horse like that, I'd be sacred to death."

Shameless was quickly reaching peak running condition— faster than Dakota thought possible. Trainers who hadn't given Dakota the time of day were now stopping to talk to her, their eyes blatantly covetous as they looked the filly over. "How's she doin' today?" "You gonna be working her any time soon? Let me know." "What do you feed her, jet fuel?" There was no way Dakota could have kept her filly's exceptional talent a secret.

Having a great filly may have improved her relations with the other trainers, but it did not make her one of them. They were all polite to her face, but she knew that secretly many of them believed a novice shouldn't have a horse like that. She'd been around racetracks long enough to know how people talked. They'd admit she was lucky, but it didn't make her a racehorse trainer. Dakota was inclined to agree with them. It would take a lifetime for her to become as good a trainer as her father, if she had the talent and worked hard.

Training Shameless was a humbling experience. When you had a filly that did everything you asked, you just thanked God and tried not to get in her way. Outsiders might confuse a talented horse with a talented trainer, but Dakota knew better. One of Coke's favorite expressions was, "Any trainer can win with a great horse—for a while." Keeping the horse sound, *that* was the challenge.

Still, all the attention was exhilarating. Dakota couldn't help feeling the thrill of pride as she led the filly to and from her gallops.

For the second work in company, Dakota sent Shameless out with Dangerously in mid-April. Shameless ran away from the colt. After that, Dakota kept the filly to long gallops and a few brisk blowouts, just to keep the edge. She wouldn't let Ernesto ask the filly to really run again until the Santa Cruz County Futurity Trials in two weeks' time.

Then, she'd be running for money.

Meanwhile, Dakota hauled Shameless to another town to have her "gate okayed." Only when a horse showed he could act well in the gate, was he eligible to race. Until the Santa Cruz County Fair meet officially started at the end of April, all Sonoita had was a dinky little four-horse gate for trainers to school their horses. The actual racing gate, as well as the tote board, made the rounds from one county fair meet to another, towed by a semi.

Unable to continue paying the security guards and still

keep to her budget, Dakota set up Coke's old trailer near the filly's stall. Ernesto was only too happy to move in.

At the eye of the storm, Shameless was remarkably calm, although it was clear she felt good. Dakota sensed that Shameless knew what she'd been made for. She saved her energy for running. She broke well from the gate. She never acted up on the way to the track. She always accepted the saddling and bridling, bathing and bandages, medication and shoeing with stoic equanimity. She was perfect.

Except of course for the killing way she ran. This fear nagged at Dakota constantly, and many times she wished she could just retire Shameless before the filly had a chance to race. But more and more, she could see it wouldn't be fair to Shameless. The horse wanted to run; it was her destiny. Coke had been right, this time. Dakota only hoped her courage matched her filly's.

A week before the futurity trials, Rita DeWeil invited Dakota to lunch. Curious, she accepted.

Rita's stucco palace sat on a hill in a newly subdivided section of Sonoita; a ratio of one house to every six or seven acres. Like a tall wedge of white cake topped by an orange frosting of Spanish tile, the house towered above a grassy plot dotted by junipers and oak. Typical of the new houses going up in Arizona that owed their architectural style to Taco Bell. A new dark green Range Rover stood in the circular drive, a temporary license sticker in the rear window.

Rita answered the door herself. She wore a shocking pink exercise bra, matching headband, and a flippy skirt over tights. Dakota wondered if the effect was calculated.

Rita smudged at her face with a fluffy Southwest design towel. "I just finished my workout. Why don't you sit down while I freshen up. Would you like something to drink?" she asked as Dakota followed her across the off-white Berber carpet into a sunken living room. The air-conditioning blasted air cold enough to freeze the blood.

"No, thanks." Dakota sat on a Roche Bobois leather couch.

She glanced around the spacious, many-windowed house; white-on-white decor, Indian pots, serapes, hanging chilies, and a neckerchiefed coyote fashioned of paper-thin green copper. It looked as if Rita had bought out a Santa Fe boutique. Dakota would be willing to bet the kitchen was floored with saltillo tile.

When Rita returned, wearing a midriff blouse and Guess? jeans, she was accompanied by an enormous Arnold Schwarzenegger type whose massive jaw was framed by long blond hair. "I hope you don't mind, but I promised Mario I'd pay him." She went to a tall standing cabinet whose doors were striped with saguaro ribs, opening one side and extracting a checkbook. Dakota smelled the fresh, sweet scent of untreated wood.

Mario had come around the couch and was trying to make small talk with Dakota, his ocean-blue eyes full of meaningful looks. Dakota found herself looking lower, fascinated by the ridged muscles of his stomach, as well defined as the jointed torso of a scorpion.

Rita handed him his check and sat down, licking salt off a margarita glass that had materialized in her hand somewhere along the line. "Mario's my personal trainer. He's wonderful."

Dakota wondered if she had accidentally stumbled into a "Dynasty" rerun. At least she was no longer in the dark about what Rita wanted. Rita had decided to parade her gorgeous personal trainer before her like a prize bull at a stock show and see if she'd bid.

She leaned back on the leather couch and listened to Rita sing Mario's praises.

The onslaught continued at lunch in the "morning room" over pasta salad and white wine. Mario came in to make himself a blender drink. A towel hung around his neck and spandex shorts bisected his mountainous thighs.

Rita caught Dakota looking at him and permitted herself a satisfied smile. "What do you think of my Range Rover?"

"Very nice. But what are those bars for?"

"Bars?" For a moment, Rita looked puzzled. Then she

smiled. "Oh, on the front. The dealer told me they're used in Africa to deflect rhinoceros charges."

Dakota wondered how may rhinos Rita encountered on a milk run to the Circle K. "You must feel remarkably safe."

Dakota's sarcasm was lost on Rita. "It's the best," she said simply. "Mario, would you bring the rolls, please?"

Mario hopped to. He set the basket down near Dakota, brushing her shoulder with his arm. She could smell his clean sweat, and realized that she wasn't quite unmoved by the sinewy play of his muscles.

As he retracted his hand he managed (quite naturally, she thought) to knock over her water glass. "Imasosory," he said. He took a linen napkin and started blotting the shoulder of her blouse, headed for her breasts. She took the towel from him and smiled a thank you. He kept saying over and over how "sory" he was, and called her bella donna, which Dakota had always thought was a poisonous plant.

She glanced at Rita, sending her a clear message. Rita snapped, "That's all, Mario. Would you please take the Rover and fill it up, check the tires? I've got to go to Tucson tomorrow."

He bowed out, obviously disappointed.

"He likes you," Rita said.

"I'm not interested."

"Oh, all right, then." She shrugged, taking her glass of wine into the living room and sitting down. "That's not what I asked you over here to talk about anyway."

A Himalayan cat tippy-toed into the room and hoisted herself onto Rita's lap. Rita scratched the cat under the chin, making baby sounds. When she came up for air, she said, "I'd like to buy Shameless."

Dakota could only stare at her in amazement.

"Well?"

"She's not for sale."

"Have you ever seriously considered selling her? It would . . . get you out from under. I know how much you want to get back to L.A."

Rita would never make a poker player.

"I'm prepared to offer you a great deal of money for her. More than she's worth at the moment."

"I'm not interested."

"Look." Rita leaned forward. "What did you pay for her? Twenty-five thousand? I'm prepared to offer ten times that."

A quarter of a million dollars? Momentarily, Dakota's breath caught in her throat.

"Think about it."

Dakota did some quick mental arithmetic. If Shameless won the Santa Cruz County Futurity, she'd earn less than twenty thousand dollars. The Rainbow was far more lucrative. The winner's purse was over two hundred thousand. The big one—the All American—was one million dollars to the winner, but the odds against winning it were astronomical.

A quarter of a million dollars. What kind of idiot would turn down money like that?

Was Shameless worth that much? A cynical part of her said *no, but Clay is.* She had no doubt that leaving Sonoita was an unspoken part of the deal.

Dakota thought of what it would mean. The work she'd put in, the hours of preparing the filly: everything would be for nothing. She'd never get to walk on the backside again. Never get to stand at the rail, watching her filly run. Never get a chance to see if Shameless could win a big race. "I can't," she said simply, and realized it was the truth. Shameless was a Black Oak horse, and she would carry Coke's colors to the All American.

"Forgive me, Dakota, if I don't understand how you could be so cavalier about an offer like that. I understand your father's estate is in arrears. Shameless has never even run in a race. That's a lot of money to turn down for an untried filly."

Rita was right. It was getting harder and harder to meet all the bills. Black Oak needed a great infusion of cash if it were to survive. But Dakota had made a commitment to train one horse. After Shameless ran in the All American, Dakota might sell Black Oak anyway. "She's entered in the All American. If she wins, she'll make over four times that."

"Do you know what the chances are of getting a horse

even into one of those races, let alone winning?" Rita leaned
back, crossed one knee over the other, and bounced her leg.
Her Abrazo sandal slipped down to nudge her painted toe-
nails. "One million, then. That's what you'd win if she took
the All American."

"Are you nuts?" The words burst out of Dakota's mouth
before she could call them back.

"It's a legitimate offer."

They were in the stratosphere now. Dakota tried to picture
a million dollars, and what it could do for her, but couldn't.
The offer wasn't at all real to her. They might as well be
playing Monopoly.

Rita sipped some more chardonnay, her expression smug.
She acted as if it were a foregone conclusion that Dakota
would sell. "You could have the money in ten business days."

Dakota's head throbbed. This was too much. She thought
of Samuel Riddle, the man who owned Man-o'-War. He, too,
had been offered a million dollars for his horse, back in the
1920s, when it was worth one hell of a lot more. His answer
had been that there were plenty of millionaires in the world,
but there was only one man who owned Man-o'-War.

But Shameless was no Man-o'-War. She was just a very
fast filly. She could be injured tomorrow and never run a
race.

Rita seemed to read her thoughts. "Every time you run that
horse, it's a gamble. You know how easy it is to injure them,
especially at this age. I'm offering you the money, one million dollars, and chances are, she'll never make a fraction of
that."

"Why?"

"I have the money and I happen to like that filly. I want
her for my own. And I'd like a shot at the All American," she
added, almost as an afterthought.

"Would you be so anxious to pay a million dollars for an
untried horse if I weren't Clay's ex-wife?"

"That has nothing to do with it. You're old business."

Dakota set her glass down on the coffee table. "I think I'd
better go."

Suddenly, Rita's face twisted into a mask of hatred. "He doesn't want you."

"At least I'm not trying to buy him."

"I don't have to buy him. I'm just giving you a way to save face."

"Save face?"

"He's toying with you."

Dakota laughed. "Clay's not like that."

"Oh, isn't he?" Rita took another sip of wine. "What else would you call it, flirting with you while he's sleeping with me?"

Her breath went out of her, as if her lungs were a vacuum-packed can suddenly exposed to the air.

Rita's eyes glittered with triumph. "Why don't you take the money? You don't belong here. Clay will only hurt you if you stay."

"I don't believe you." The words tasted mealy in her mouth.

"Ask him."

Dakota knew then that Rita was telling her the truth. Betrayal crashed into her. Why hadn't he told her he had a relationship with Rita? Logically, she knew Clay didn't owe her a thing. He was her *ex*-husband, she admonished herself. But Dakota couldn't help the way she felt. The thought of seeing him every day at the track, spending time in his company—made her ill. God knew, he was probably laughing at her gullibility right now.

"Ten business days," Rita said.

It was tempting. Take the money. Get on a plane and head for home. Forget the filly, forget the ranch—there was no future here. She'd been fooling herself, thinking she could fit in again. And always lurking at the back of her mind, the ridiculous idea that she and Clay might . . .

Dakota closed her eyes to blot out the thought.

"It's dangerous here, anyway," Rita said. "There's talk that Coke's death wasn't an accident."

"What? Where'd you hear that?"

"Around. Somebody has it in for you. If you were wise,

you'd hightail it back to L.A. as fast as you can. With a million dollars you could go in style. You know what they say. Accidents happen."

Shock bolted through her. Those were the exact words on the photocopy.

An unfortunate choice of words, that's all, she told herself. A coincidence. Shaken, she headed for the door.

"Think about my offer."

"Go to hell," Dakota said. But outside, she didn't see the rolling grassland of Sonoita. She saw Rita writhing in Clay's naked embrace, her red lips stretched in a vulpine grimace of desire.

Twenty-Two

The official county fair meet opened a week before the futurity trials, and Dakota was no longer welcome on the backside until she was licensed as a trainer.

She had to take a trainer test administered by the chief steward. Since the test was scheduled for eight o'clock on a Thursday morning, three days after the meet opened, Dakota was not allowed on the track unless she came as someone's guest. Early Monday morning Clay came over to the gate to escort her onto the backside.

"Is this charade really necessary?" she snapped as they walked to her barn. "I'm sure you have something better to do with your time." *Like boff Rita.*

"You're not even supposed to be handling that horse. For all the state knows, you could be some bimbo who'd dash out onto the track right into the path of a runner. I've taken on a lot of responsibility."

"Yeah, right." She decided to take her cue from him. If he didn't want to talk about his love life, that was fine with her. She'd told herself it didn't matter, that Clay was a big boy now, but the ache in her stomach that had started Saturday at Rita's wouldn't go away. Logically, she knew there had never been any hope for a reconciliation, but the sense of betrayal was hard to shake.

Why the hell did he have to kiss her?

Clay leaned on the barn door as Dakota cross-tied Shameless for her grooming. "I forgot to ask. How was your lunch with Rita?"

She busied herself with the dandybrush, careful not to look at him. "The entree was a bit thick through the middle," she said, referring to Mario's impressive stomach.

"She served steak?"

"Italian beef, but I didn't have any."

"Are we talking about the same thing here?"

"She's got a man Friday named Mario. She kind of thought he and I would make an item."

"I thought Rita didn't like you. Why would she play matchmaker?"

A leading question if she ever heard one. She suspected he knew exactly how she felt about him, and was enjoying the thought of two grown women wrangling over him. Well, she'd be damned if she would confirm his suspicions.

Clay took the haynet down and started filling it with flakes of hay. "I'm not seeing Rita anymore."

"What's it to me?"

"I thought you'd like to know."

Dakota got the mane comb from the tack box. "So I know."

"You can't pull it off."

"What?"

"The tough act. It doesn't work."

She attacked the filly's short mane with a vengeance. "You've got it all figured out, haven't you? Every woman within fifty miles wants you. How can you stand it? You must feel like a wishbone!"

"What's with you, McAllister?"

"You annoy the hell out of me, that's what."

"Because it didn't work out between us ten years ago? We were kids! Different people. At least I know I am." He gripped her wrist.

She glared at him. "Let go of me."

His fingers tightened, causing white streaks on her flesh, before he abruptly dropped her arm. She could tell he was seething underneath. He passed a hand across his forehead.

"I'm sorry." He stared into the middle distance, his eyes dark and brooding.

Suddenly, the impulse to reach out and touch him was overwhelming. She wanted so badly to feel the warmth of his flesh against her fingers, the comfort it would give her.

While he's flirting with you, he's sleeping with me. The pain hit her in the solar plexus. How in the world had she ever gotten herself into this mess?

His eyes were dark with disappointment. "Blame me, then, if it makes you feel better." He walked away, leaving her feeling vaguely guilty and completely unhappy.

Dakota passed the trainer's test and was duly licensed as a horse trainer by the state of Arizona. The steward took her mug shot and fingerprinted her. All she needed now was an orange jumpsuit, and she'd be all set. Horse racing had to be the only job on earth where they treated you like a criminal.

As she emerged from the trailer where the test had been given, she saw Clay just outside the door, ostensibly talking to an official. When their eyes met, electricity quivered through her. Had he been waiting to see how she did? He stepped forward, a grin on his face. She walked right past him, trying not to notice how his smile turned into a grim line.

She "celebrated" by having an ice cream cone at El Prado. Alone. And found herself wishing that she hadn't snubbed Clay like that.

She sat on the tailgate of Coke's truck, licking her ice cream and staring at the Sonoita crossing. Her head told her to steer clear, protect herself. But her heart told her that Clay had never lied to her. He might not have told her about his love life with Rita, but then, she'd never asked.

Was Clay right? Had she been so busy blaming him for their breakup that she had never taken any responsibility for her own actions? Maybe he really had cared about her, but couldn't face being married at such a young age. What was the crime in that? Would it have been better for them to have stuck it out, and really grown to hate each other? Blaming him had been a reflex, one she'd nursed for so long that she had never even thought about seeing the other side. As far as she was concerned, there hadn't been another side.

She watched bleakly as an RV crawled down Highway 82 at a snail's pace, followed by six cars.

The wronged woman. That was the role she'd been playing all these years. No wonder it had been so damn difficult to get on with her life. Dakota realized she'd spent so much time blaming this man for ruining her future, that she hadn't bothered to enjoy the present.

On the way back to Black Oak, she stopped and bought a greeting card, a painting of a wolf, blank inside. It was time she put an end to this grudge. Clay had done nothing but help her since she came back. What had she done in return? Treated him like a pariah, because she couldn't handle her own feelings.

But as she sat at her kitchen counter, staring at the card, the words wouldn't come. Writing "Dear Clay" had been pretty easy. But now what? She didn't want to give him the wrong idea. This was an apology, not a proposition. Stalling, she addressed and stamped the envelope, poured herself some iced tea, sat on the bar stool and bit the end of her pen. Finally she managed, "I'm sorry for the way I acted today." After that, she didn't know what to say.

She glanced outside and saw the pool, inviting in the sun. Maybe a swim would help her think.

When the phone rang, Jerry Tanner hoped it was Rudy Gallego, coming back with an offer to buy Hatchet Job. Jerry had run the gelding all winter, and the horse got worse with every out. It was only a matter of time before his legs gave out—he probably had bone chips in both of his knees right now. Unless Gallego bought him, Jerry would have to drop him down in class to the cheapest claiming races at the bush tracks.

He didn't have to worry. Mexicans couldn't get enough of

stakes winners from the U.S., and Hatchet Job had once been
a big name. The Mexicans paid damn good money, too.
Couldn't buy 'em fast enough to fill the demand for match
races.

He'd let it ring one more time. He didn't want to seem
overeager.

"Hello? You the guy selling a Ford F-250?"

Jerry stifled his disappointment. "Sold it already." He
jammed the receiver into its cradle and closed his eyes. He
was *sure* Gallego had told him he wanted the horse. He tried
to remember, but it just wouldn't come into focus.

You blacked out again.

He tried to picture Gallego talking to him last night at the
Cowpony, saying he'd call, but it might as well have been a
dream. Shit.

He stared out the louvered window of the trailer, but saw
an internal landscape instead of the stable yard. Scraps of
thought passed behind his eyeballs, like Halloween witches
flying through the night. They fluttered just out of reach,
shrieking across his aching brain. He strained to remember.

At last a series of disassociated images scrolled through his
mind. Gallego leaning forward, the birthmark around his eye
looking like an angry burn; the lighted Budweiser Clydesdale
display revolving slowly above the bar; he remembered staring stupidly at the wall above the urinal, the pain in his blad-
der enormous. That tight-assed vet, Jared Ames, talking to
Rudy and Dan Bolin in the parking lot—he thought maybe he
and Ames had argued about a vet bill, but he wasn't sure, except that right now he could feel himself getting mad all over
again. And a dim memory of running up onto the side of the
dirt road, having to back up, start again, Lucy saying you
shouldn't you shouldn't drive—

Lucy wasn't there, was she? She had homework.

He really ought to cut down on the booze.

His gaze wandered to the newspaper photo of Coke's
smashed truck, which he'd cut from the paper and had decou-
paged onto a sawed-off piece of tree trunk. It hung above the

door, in the place where a decade ago Myrna's needlepoint, GOD BLESS OUR HOME, had been. The place of honor.

He toasted the photo with his coffee cup. "I'm doing a hell of a lot better than you, you goddamn old fart," he said. "At least I'm still alive."

He wondered if his ol' buddy Coke had felt the engine block slam his belly into his spine, or if he'd died instantly.

Wondering what made him such a devil for punishment, Clay sat down on the chaise longue by the pool and watched Dakota swim. She cleaved the teal-blue water like a pair of scissors through exotic, sequined cloth. The late afternoon sun burnished her shoulders as each arm flashed up and then slipped smoothly into the water. At the deep end, she executed a racing turn, kicking off powerfully.

At last she stood up, flicking water from her eyes, smoothing her now caramel-colored hair back against her head. And saw him.

She crossed her arms instinctively, like a virgin in one of those 1950 romantic comedies. "Who let you in? How long have you been watching me?" she demanded.

"Alice." He checked his watch. "About forty minutes."

"What do you want?"

He held up the greeting card. "I thought this would be worth more if you signed it."

Vaulting out of the pool, she strode up to him and grabbed the card out of his hands. Water pooled at her feet. "You're still a snoop, I see," she said coldly.

"It was for me, wasn't it?"

She blushed.

"I appreciate it," he said. "Although it's kind of soggy."

She glowered at him, shivering. He found her towel on the other chaise and handed it to her. Her nipples showed through the tight material of her black one piece. Just as he remembered them, although her breasts were a little larger. Rounder, fuller, but still upright, flattened as they strained against the swimsuit. They'd gone from pert to magnificent. He imagined pulling her to him, feeling the cold wetness of the suit battling the warmth of her body and his, imagined those nipples pressed up against him. He knew exactly where they'd come to on him, and his chest ached with a feeling akin to a ghost pain. Why the hell was he here?

Dakota toweled her hair and mirrored his thoughts. "Are you going to tell me why you're here, Pearce?"

He set the champagne bottle on the poolside table. "I thought we should celebrate. You're back in the fold."

"I don't think so." She wrapped the towel around her waist, covering her long, shapely thighs. "After the All American, I'm going home."

He waited for her to elaborate.

"This"—she waved her arm—"is an illusion. Sure, there are mares in the pastures, but they'll be going back to their owners as soon as they're bred or they've had their foals. Shameless is the only thing keeping me here. I promised myself I'll try to win the All American, and then . . . I'm going back home. I'm only doing this for my father."

"I thought you were doing it for yourself."

She turned away. "Think what you want, Clay, but those are the facts."

He reached out and clamped a hand on her arm. Why did she always duck out on him, like a spooked horse? Was she so afraid to face him, so afraid to look in his eyes and tell him what she was thinking? Had he really done this to her? "Do you have to be so bitter?"

"If I'm bitter, it's because of you!"

"If you're not careful, you might have to send me another card."

She said nothing. He could feel the warmth of her skin, the beads of cool water dissipating under his fingers. She made no move to extract herself. He eased his grip. "You're hard to figure out, you know that, McAllister? You take potshots at me and then hide for cover. Why can't you talk to me like I'm a human being?"

She closed her eyes. He thought he saw a tear at the corner

of her eye. She took a deep breath. "There's no excuse for the way I've acted. I know that."

"I don't mean you any harm, Dakota," he said softly. "Do you believe that?"

She lifted her chin, looking him full in the face. Her eyes were troubled, almost anguished. "I don't know what to believe."

She was irresistible. He didn't even try to fight the feeling. He leaned toward her, brushed her lips with his own. Dakota returned his kiss, deepening it. Her arms came up tentatively, clasped around his neck, pulling him closer. His own arms slipped underneath, circling her, his hands skimming over her back. She pressed against him, the cool suit quickly becoming warmer, a warmth that seeped into his flesh and sent a slithering sensation of desire to the center of his body. He delved into her mouth with his tongue, sensed her compliance. They were made for each other, interlocking, incomplete without the other's touch.

He felt as if he had come home.

Dakota's fingers were tangled in his hair. She strained against him, as if she could actually merge with him, and he gently pressed his palm against the small of her back, bringing her closer. She moaned, a soft, dovelike sound, fragile in her throat. He could feel the tears running down her face, mingling with their kiss, salty on his tongue.

He wanted to say, "I love you," but sensed it was too soon. Wasn't even sure if he meant it. There was so much about her he didn't know. But he knew he wanted her. He throbbed with desire, overwhelmed by it. He pressed against her, letting her feel his full intent. She moaned again. An answering groan crept into his throat. "I want you," he whispered hoarsely into her ear.

Dakota's breath quickened. She closed her eyes, letting herself be whirled away on the current of their passion. She couldn't get enough of the touch, the feel of him. Their tongues meshed in a sweet, familiar dance of ecstasy. The memories came back all at once, the steamy moonlit nights of summer, the cool breath of dawn, the torrid passion near the flickering fire in winter. So many good times.

One of his large hands cupped her skull, his fingers twined in her hair. The other roamed her body, molded her to him, bringing alive sparks as his knowledgeable fingers slid over her skin. He knew every inch of her, knew it well.

He knew her as no one else had. And she wanted him as much as he wanted her.

More, maybe. She'd always felt he was her weakness, the one desire she could not control. She made one more stab at resisting. "What about Rita?"

"I told you, I'm not seeing her anymore. I made a clean break . . ."

His words slapped her, hard, like a dash of frigid water. She remembered another clean break. Clay, telling her he wanted a divorce. The cold finality of those words, the look on his face.

At first she'd thought it was a joke, and she'd laughed. But he didn't laugh. She remembered the sick feeling in her heart, her stomach, as her disbelief suddenly burst like a dam, her whole world cascading down on her. It had cost her dearly to maintain her dignity, to accept his words, when what she had really wanted to do was beg him to reconsider.

Now he'd done the same thing to Rita. Slept with her until he got tired of her, until he decided to try for his ex-wife again. She could never let him hurt her like that again. Ever. She jerked away from him, tears starting in her eyes.

"What's wrong?"

"I don't think this is a good idea, Clay." Her voice shook. Why, *why,* had she ever come back here?

His lips narrowed into a line. He drew away from her, his dark eyes troubled. "What do you want from me, McAllister?"

"I want." She swallowed. What did she want? For him to leave her alone? Already she was too involved with him—already it would hurt. "I don't know." She pushed a strand of hair behind her ear. "You're pushing me. I'd like us to be friends, that's all."

"I guess now I know how it is to be on the receiving end."

"No, you don't. Rita knows what it's like to be on the receiving end."

He scowled. "You think I should have led her on?"

"No, but you seem to be pretty darn good at telling women you don't want them anymore!"

"Now there's a nice sentiment. You should've put it on the card." The bitterness in his voice matched her own. He grabbed the card from the table, crumpled it into a ball, and threw it on the ground. He strode toward the house.

She couldn't let it go like that. "Clay!"

He didn't turn around.

"I don't want to fight with you. I appreciate everything you've done for me, I want you to know that. I just can't—I don't want to get involved with you. That way."

He paused on the steps.

"If you broke it off with Rita for my sake . . . well, you shouldn't have."

His grin was sardonic. "Don't be so sure of yourself. I didn't do it for you." He flung open the French doors and disappeared into the house. Hugging herself against the cold, Dakota sat down on the chaise and stared at the bottle of champagne, feeling like a fool.

Twenty-Three

The starting gate at Sonoita had room for only eight horses, unlike the standard ten post positions at larger tracks. Four races would determine the eight fastest qualifiers for the Santa Cruz Futurity.

Clay's horse, Straight Eight, would be running in the trial against Shameless. His other horse, Dangerously, won his trial, posting the fastest time for 350 yards so far. It didn't matter if a horse won the race, as long as he had one of the eight fastest times. But the young colt had been impressive, winning his race by a length.

Dakota noticed that Jerry Tanner had a horse running in the second trial. He'd pressed Lucy into service as pony girl. He almost ran over Dakota at the soft drink stand. When he realized who she was, he scowled, his eyes as shiny and cold as steel BB's. She supposed he blamed her for his horse's poor showing; his colt had run dead last.

Rita had a couple of horses in the trials, but to Dakota's relief, she wasn't here. Apparently, she had to go to some big award ceremony in Phoenix, where her late husband would be honored for bulldozing half of Maricopa County and investing his earnings in a failed savings and loan. Dan Bolin was here, however, deep in conversation with an Hispanic man in a white straw cowboy hat. Dakota had never seen Dan so animated. When she waved to him, he nodded, his good humor extending to her. The man he was with glanced over his shoulder at her. A port wine stain ringed his eye like a fiery sun.

Shameless's race was up next. Stifling her nervousness, Dakota led her down the hoof-pocked ribbon of dirt toward the saddling paddock. The infamous Sonoita wind picked up, flirting at the filly's hooves and blowing streamers of dust around them.

The saddling enclosure was faced on one side by an open ramada divided into eight stalls, and a chest-high chain-link fence on the others. Behind the fence were bleachers brimming with onlookers. Trainers led their horses around the postage-stamp of faded grass or kept them standing face-out in their assigned stalls.

Despite its county fair status, the Santa Cruz County Futurity was known throughout the quarter horse industry as a testing ground for future stars. Many winners of the Futurity went on to major stakes races. And, as Clay had pointed out, there was another reason Sonoita was so attractive to those planning to run their horses later in the summer at Ruidoso. Sonoita, at almost six thousand feet above sea level, would help horses adjust to Ruidoso's high altitude.

Clay was already in the paddock, leading Straight Eight in a circle. When he saw her, he nodded curtly and kept walking. She didn't blame him for holding a grudge, after the disaster at the pool. If she could only figure out her own feelings, maybe she wouldn't keep sending him mixed signals.

Dakota led Shameless to stall number four. Four was a good post position, better than she'd hoped. Ernesto was already there, the saddle girths looped over his arm. Dakota decided to walk the filly around a little, let her loosen up. Shameless seemed outwardly calm, striding like a top fashion model down a runway, in complete control of herself as always. But Dakota sensed the energy just beneath the surface, like the dangerous humming of power lines. Shameless knew something was up.

Dakota glanced surreptitiously at Clay. He did look damn good in his gold long-sleeved shirt and faded jeans, a leather belt decorated with silver conchos, and a black cowboy hat. The hatband was also studded with conchos.

She, too, had dressed for the occasion, in turquoise form-fitting jeans and a belt with a heart-shaped buckle that she knew flattered her slim waist. She wore a blouse and matching bolero jacket of turquoise, flamingo pink, purple and royal blue in an Aztec design. Had she unconsciously dressed to impress him? If so, it wasn't working. He didn't so much as spare her another glance.

As she saddled the filly, her heart beat like bird wings in the cage of her throat. She prayed Shameless wouldn't run too hard—just enough to win the race. She'd given the jockey instructions to try and hold her back if they got far enough ahead to avoid any threat. Dakota knew the stewards often fined riders for keeping a horse under wraps, but if she won the race, who could complain? The bettors would still get their money, and it would keep Shameless sound. She swallowed. The thought of Shameless breaking down was unbearable.

I'm not cut out for this game, she thought, not for the first time. I'm not tough enough.

The jockeys filed into the paddock, as colorful as jelly beans. Melissa, the jockey Dakota had hired to ride Shameless, swung aboard. They followed the number three horse up the dirt aisle to the track. Ahead, Clay handed Straight Eight to his pony rider and stood at the edge of the track. She wished the card idea hadn't backfired. He was still her biggest ally.

She couldn't let things stay the way they were. Slipping under the rail, she joined Clay to watch the post parade. "Your horse looks good," she said, for lack of anything else to say.

He leaned his elbows on the rail. The tension between them was as tangible as a bunting board. "Yours, too."

She swallowed. "I want to apologize for the other day."

"You seem to be doing a lot of that."

"Well, look at it this way. I'm getting a lot better at it."

He said nothing, but continued to stare at the infield, which also served as an arena and holding pens for rodeos.

"What do you want? I said I was sorry."

He swiveled his head, his gaze level with hers. "Sorry doesn't cut it."

"What can I do, then?" She floundered for words. "Your friendship means a lot to me."

"Friendship. Is that what you think we have?"

"For now, that's what it has to be." *For my own sanity.* "If we can just agree on that, and still be . . . friends. Please, let's don't fight, Clay. You just have to understand—"

"I understand. You've made it all too clear. I hurt you a long time ago, and apparently, you have a memory like an elephant."

A void opened up inside her. "All right," she said quietly. She turned and walked along the rail, putting some distance between them. If he didn't want their friendship, she had no choice but to accept it.

She had a lot more to worry about right now. Lifting her binoculars, she tried to concentrate on the filly. *Shut him out of your mind, McAllister.*

Shameless cantered calmly beside her pony rider on the backstretch. Dakota wondered what it was about the dark filly, even at this distance, that made her stand out from the others. Some of the colts were bigger, flashier, breedier. They moved just as nicely. And yet Shameless was special in Dakota's eyes. She supposed that owners everywhere felt that way about their horses.

The tote board, it seemed, agreed with her. Although Shameless had never run a race, she was the favorite.

Dakota suddenly felt claustrophobic. What did they say? The best ones ran their hearts out. They didn't stop, even when they were injured. Swallowing her fear, Dakota tried not to think about it, but couldn't block the picture of Blue Kite from her mind. Why not just breed her? Why had she let it get this far? She wanted to leap the rail and run out onto the track, catch up with the jockey and tell her to dismount, there had been a mistake, she was scratching the filly. But she stood rooted to the spot. She would never make a racehorse trainer if she pulled a stunt like that.

She didn't know when she became aware that Clay had walked up to stand beside her. She glanced at him out of the corner of her eye. He stared straight ahead at the citron-hued grass, the brown ribbon of track, the voluminous blue sky. At last he spoke. "Want to make a side bet?"

Relief drenched her. "What kind of bet?"

"How about the winner buys dinner at the Cowpony?"

"You're on."

"You want to see the break?"

She nodded. They jumped into the starter's truck with the other trainers and were driven to the gate.

It took an eternity for the horses to load. Dakota stood beside Clay, her mouth dry. His arm touched hers and she nearly jumped a mile. She imagined her skin was composed of the tiny dots on a snowy TV screen, sensitive to the touch. Her pulse pounded in her ears.

Just friends, huh?

Everyone was in line. The gates would crash open at any moment. In fewer than eighteen seconds, the answers to all her questions would be realized.

"No, no! Not now!" cried an assistant starter. The colt next to Shameless reared up, almost went over backward. The jockey stood up in the gate, like a monkey clinging to a cage. They managed to bring the colt down and straightened him out.

Shameless faced forward, all four feet planted on the ground, oblivious to the other horse's antics.

"Good luck," Clay whispered in her ear.

"You, too."

The gates banged open to the clamor of the bell, the shouts of the jockeys, the popping of the riding bats.

From where she stood, the start looked like a fast break of pool balls. The babies broke clumsily, bouncing into each other and running toward both rails. All except Shameless, who broke cleanly and was ahead by a jump. She was long gone by the time the five horse came over and sideswiped the three horse. She headed the field in two jumps, drawing away with that incredible, punishing stride of hers, bashing the ground repeatedly like some motorized miner's pick gone haywire. She crossed the finish line, ahead by two lengths, her head bowed to her chest. Her only competition had been the tight hold on her mouth.

Straight Eight came in a respectable third.

Dakota's mind went blank. When Clay hugged her, she hugged back, clasping her hands around his neck and returning his kiss. It was a fast kiss, an excited kiss—not sensual at all. He hugged her tightly, picked her up, whirled her around.

"She did it!" Dakota cried. "I can't believe it. She did it!"

He set her down. His mouth crooked into a grin, and his eyes darkened.

Suddenly, Dakota realized what she'd done. "Clay—"

"We'd better get you to the winner's circle."

That night, after checking on Shameless and making sure she came out of the race all right, Dakota went with Clay to the Cowpony Bar and Grill. She ordered a Cattleman's T-bone, medium rare, baked potato and sour cream, and a salad consisting of lettuce, cabbage, carrot shavings, but no tomato. Dakota remembered that Coke had always complained that steak houses never put tomatoes in their salads. Coke had trained a horse for the owner of the Cowpony, and that horse had been named No Tomato as a joke. No Tomato had won the Santa Cruz County Futurity that year.

Clay and Dakota ordered margaritas and toasted both Shameless and Dangerously.

They scrupulously avoided talking about what happened at the pool. Clay was friendly and casual, without any apparent trace of regret. She was beginning to wonder if it really mattered to him how close they'd come to making love again. Maybe it wasn't as important to him as she'd thought. Maybe he'd just given it a shot, on the off chance that she'd fall for it. . . .

He drove her home right after dinner. He didn't even try to kiss her. Again, Dakota felt disappointed. This was what she'd wanted, wasn't it? His friendship. A platonic companion without risk.

But maybe the risk had been there all along.

Twenty-Four

Dakota swam up out of a deep sleep to the shrilling of the phone. Trying to shake free of the clouds, she remembered with a thrill that the filly had won the futurity trials.

She answered on the fourth ring. The panic in Lucy's tone slammed her into consciousness. "It's Shameless."

A thunderclap of pure terror exploded behind her eyes. Her fingers tightened on the receiver and she closed her eyes, trying to hear over the sledgehammer of her heart, wanting more than anything in the world *not* to hear. Because she knew what Lucy would say next. The words materialized in the air around her like a swarm of angry bees. She's dead. She's dead she's dead she's—

"Someone's been poking around her stall!"

Dakota went weak. The phone slipped from her ear as she opened her eyes to pounding blackness. Safe. She's safe. Her voice found purchase. "Stay there. I'll be there in ten minutes." She thrust the bedclothes aside. Her relief was short-lived as she realized the crisis wasn't over. Cold, gelid fingers of dread clutched her insides. Dakota pulled her jeans on over the shirt she slept in and put on her running shoes. She grabbed her keys and ran for the door.

It was more like fifteen minutes by the time she reached the stable gate. She asked the guard who let her through if anyone had come out in a hurry. "No, ma'am. It's been quiet tonight."

She told him what had happened, and asked him to keep anyone at the gate until she found out what was going on.

Dakota drove up to the stall, her headlights sweeping the barn. Lucy was there, pacing back and forth and hugging herself, rubbing her arms to keep away the chill. Ernesto had put a halter on Shameless and was leading her around, letting her pick at the weeds lining the shedrow. When he saw Dakota, he ducked his head in shame.

"What happened?"

Lucy seemed close to hyperventilating. "Dad was at the Steak Out and I had to bring him a message, and on the way back I decided to look in on Shameless, and when I got here I saw this man leaning over her stall, and he saw me and took off. I knocked on the trailer but Ernesto wasn't there, and I didn't know what to do!"

"Calm down," Dakota said, although she herself was far from calm. "What did he look like?"

Lucy shook her head. "I didn't get a real good look, but he was big. Tall."

"What was he doing?"

"He was standing at her stall, and then he saw me and he walked away real fast. He was holding a coffee can, like we use for grain? He was carrying the can, and I thought that was weird so I yelled at him to stop but he just kept on going."

Dakota's heart lurched. Had someone tried to poison Shameless? She opened the stall door and shined her flashlight on the grain tub. It was clean, as usual—the filly always cleaned up her grain—except for a few crumpled-up green leaves stuck to the bottom.

They shouldn't be there.

Dakota lifted one of them out of the tub and looked at it in the security light fixed on the roof at the end of the shedrow. The jigsaw piece of leaf was smooth and dark green, its leathery, cushioned surface silvered by the light. She had little doubt it was oleander, which was toxic to horses.

She looked at Shameless, who was taking advantage of her

night out and grazing, pulling Ernesto along behind her as she sought out the best tufts of grass.

How long before the poison worked? Had the filly eaten any of it, or had Lucy caught her in time?

"Was the filly eating when you came up?" she demanded.

"No. I put a halter on her right away and led her out. I didn't know what he did, but I thought maybe—because of the coffee can and all—he put something in her tub. Then Ernesto showed up and I handed her to him, got to a pay phone and called you."

"Good." Relief vied with the adrenaline rushing through her system. She turned to Ernesto, and in her broken Spanish, asked where he'd been. He motioned toward the trailer.

One of them was mistaken. "Are you sure he wasn't in the trailer?" Dakota asked Lucy.

"He didn't answer my knock. You're not mad at him, are you? I'm sure he's usually there."

She sighed. "No, I'm not mad at him." Disappointed, yes. She'd thought he was so gung-ho about looking after Shameless, but he'd let her down when it counted. It was hard to believe she'd been wrong in her assessment of him.

Dakota crouched down beside the stall. Maybe some of the stray leaves had fallen on the ground, inside or out. Her light played over the dirt, which was liberally sprinkled with hay and sawdust. It would be impossible to find the stuff. The whole stall would have to be cleaned out down to the dirt, and the sawdust replaced. Suddenly, she was aware that all of them had trampled the entrance to the stall, obliterating any footprints that might have belonged to the intruder.

She stood up, strode to her truck and dialed the car phone. It was time to call the sheriff. As she waited, Dakota started to shake. She was still shaking when he arrived.

"He was tall?" asked Derek Blue.

"Real tall," Lucy said. "Maybe six foot three. And he had broad shoulders."

"You said he wore jeans. You notice anything else?"

"He was wearing boots."

"What kind of shirt? Can you remember the color?"

"I think it was blue. Light blue. It was a western shirt, you know, with snap buttons. But I couldn't swear to that. I *think* it was blue. Could have been the light, though." She nodded to the light at the end of the barn. "But I'm sure of the cowboy hat. It was black."

"Were the jeans new or old?"

"They looked new. Dark navy, not faded at all. And he had on a belt, with a big silver buckle. Oval. I remember that because it caught the light when he turned around."

"You have quite a memory."

Lucy smiled, looking proud of herself.

"Do you know of anyone around the track who looks like that?" Derek Blue asked Dakota.

"The clothes are pretty typical. I guess the only thing that stands out is the height, and I've seen a lot of tall men around here." Even Clay might fit the description, if you fudged the height a little. And Dan Bolin must be six-three at least. He was broad-shouldered. But she couldn't imagine why he'd want to hurt Shameless. He didn't even have a license to get on the backside.

"Anything else?" Blue asked Lucy.

She squinted, as if that would help her remember. "His hair could have been dark blond, or brown. I only saw him for a second, and the hat hid his face." She turned to Dakota. "You won't fire Ernesto, will you? I'm sure he had a good reason for not being here."

"No, I won't fire Ernesto."

"Good. He's really torn up about it."

"We all are," Dakota replied.

"I guess that's it." Derek Blue put a foot on the bumper of his Bronco and wrote something on his pad. "I called the gate man. No one of that description has tried to drive out. But anybody could get over the fence around here." He motioned to the barbed wire that loosely surrounded the racetrack grounds.

"Aren't you going to dust for fingerprints?" Dakota asked.

"I don't think it's necessary. Fingerprints only work when you have someone in custody."

"Everyone at the track is fingerprinted. Wouldn't it be worth a shot?"

"I suppose we could take some, but I don't know that the racing association would let us—"

"I don't think it'll work," Lucy said. "I just remembered. He was wearing gloves."

"Work gloves?"

"I think so."

Blue shrugged. "I guess that's that."

The filly was back in her clean stall by two-thirty in the morning, and Dakota drove out the security gate, feeling as limp as a wrung-out dishrag.

She reached for the car phone, retracted her hand. It was late, and there was really no reason to wake Clay. The crisis was over, and she didn't want him thinking she had to rely on him for comfort.

As she pulled into the yard at Black Oak, her mind kept returning to Lucy's description of the intruder. It could have been Dan Bolin, although that didn't make sense. He had enough worries without trying to sabotage a racehorse.

Suddenly, she remembered Rita's man Friday, Mario. Any woman who would offer a million dollars for an unraced horse might be unstable enough to do something like this, just to get rid of Dakota.

If Shameless died, Dakota would go back to L.A., leaving Rita a clear field.

The woman was obsessed with Clay.

As Dakota jumped down from the truck, she saw headlights bouncing down the dirt road from the direction of Dan's house. She decided to wait for him.

"What are you doing up at this hour?" he asked brusquely.

Dakota told him what happened, watching his face. He had about as much expression as a cigar store Indian. "Lucky your girl was there," was all he said. He headed for the broodmare barn.

"What's going on?"

"Mare's about to foal. I set my alarm for three."

She was too wound up to sleep. "May I watch?"

"Don't see why not."

The mare was already in labor when they reached the box stall. Dan liked to leave the mares alone if they were doing all right; the less interference, the better. But he was always there in case there was trouble.

Within half an hour, a nose and two tiny dark hoofs appeared, and Dan took the legs in his hands and tugged gently along with the mare's contractions. The neck and shoulders appeared. The mare heaved one more time and the foal spilled onto the straw.

He looked as if he had been shrink-wrapped. Although the milky, bluish membrane covered him from head to toe, Dakota could tell he was a dark bay. Dan wiped away the membrane and cleared the little tyke's nostrils, positioning him close to his mama's head. The mare swiped at the foal's wet coat with her tongue, making him look a little less like a clump of seaweed.

"He looks like his daddy," Dan said, "except for that star and strip down his nose." He cut the umbilical cord and hovered as the foal attempted to rise, only minutes after his birth. The stiltlike legs stretched out straight ahead, bending slightly as the little guy's soft hoofs gained purchase. He almost made it, his front legs quivering with effort, but slid back down to sit on his hindquarters. He looked around, big brown eyes a study in comic surprise. The look on his face said, "What do I do now?"

The mare, standing now, neighed encouragement and butted him in the back.

He rested a moment, got his second wind, and hoisted himself to his feet. He took one tottering step, then another, before falling back down in a bundle of knobby knees and ramshackle legs.

"Ought to name him South," Dakota said.

"Hmnn?"

"The South will rise again."

Dan was not amused. When the colt made it up this time,

he guided him with big gentle hands to his mother's teat. The baby caught on quickly, nuzzling and sucking noisily, his little tail flicking from side to side.

Dan looked for all the world like a proud papa. Her own spirits soaring, Dakota caught his eye and grinned.

His smile lost its warmth like fast food left too long under a lamp.

He wasn't going to let her forget his resentment of her for a minute. But nothing could spoil the fact that Dakota had witnessed this remarkable miracle, or that Dan's heartstrings could be plucked, too.

She went to bed with the image of the newborn foal still in her mind.

Twenty-Five

Dakota awoke at ten. Still groggy, she walked out to get the newspaper. She started back toward the house, sifting through it for the sports section. A separate sheet of paper floated down onto the grass. Typed across the top of it were the words: TRY AND TRY AGAIN. Startled, Dakota dropped the newspaper.

Beneath the TRY AND TRY AGAIN, was a typed list of five names. Tulie Queen. Thrilled with Yawl. Mr. Texas Twister. Blue Kite. Shameless.

Her heart took a misstep. With shaking fingers, she picked up the note and stared at it. Blue Kite, she knew. The photograph was still vivid in her memory; a wild-eyed colt running on three legs.

Heart pounding, she ran to the house. Her father kept a ledger that listed his racehorses in alphabetical order. She pulled it from the shelf and threw it on his desk, the force causing the front cover to smack the tabletop hard. Dry-mouthed, she found the name Mr. Texas Twister. Her worst fears were confirmed: he'd fractured a sesamoid bone at Turf Paradise during a work and had to be destroyed. It had happened last year, after the accidents started.

Panicked now, Dakota snapped the pages forward.

Thrilled with Yawl, Tulie Queen, Blue Kite, Mr. Texas Twister. All of them dead. Two from broken legs, one from a heart attack, and one from colic. Every one of them had died within the last year, except for Blue Kite.

TRY AND TRY AGAIN. There was no doubt what that meant. She stared at the last name on the list. Shameless. The print wavered before her eyes as she thought of the gallant filly running her race. The fire, the vitality, the pure joy—it could all be extinguished in a second.

Her heart took off like a runaway horse. This time she didn't hesitate. Her fingers stabbed out Clay's number. She couldn't fight this alone.

"Whoever it was, he was *here,* Clay. Early in the morning, early enough to slip that note into the newspaper. Right outside the house."

Clay watched Dakota pace back and forth before the picture window. She spun around, her eyes as fiery as gems. "What happened? With Dad's horses? How much was sabotage and how much was bad luck?"

"It could have all been bad luck. I always thought someone helped it along a little, when he could."

"And you think that someone was Jerry Tanner."

"Isn't that what you think?"

"I don't know! Lucy said the man was tall. Taller than Tanner, at any rate." Frustrated, she ran her fingers through her golden hair.

He didn't want to say it, but he had to. "Maybe Lucy lied."

"Why would she do that? She saved Shameless's life!"

"Maybe she saw her father, what he was going to do. She could have been protecting him."

"You mean she made up that story?"

"I don't know. But it's possible, isn't it? She could describe someone who didn't look anything like Tanner."

"I'm so scared, Clay."

He stood up, went to her. She didn't object when he folded her into his arms. "I know," he said softly. He wished he could hold her forever, keep her from harm.

"It had to be Tanner." Her voice was muffled against his chest. To think that anyone else hated her that much—

someone she didn't know about—was unbearable. "He hated Dad for firing him, and now he hates me."

"I always thought he turned Coke's horses loose, broke his equipment, things like that." It would have been easy enough to do. There are a lot of people who need money at a racetrack. He could have hired someone with access—a groom, an exercise rider. But I don't know if he'd go so far as to injure a horse."

"He's spiteful enough."

"It would be hard, Dakota. How would he do it? How would he weaken a horse's leg so that it would break on the racetrack? I don't think Tanner is smart enough."

She broke away from him and waved the note. "You think that was just bad luck? All four horses?"

"I think whoever is threatening you is taking some poetic license. He might be able to take credit for giving a horse colic, or even giving him something that might cause a heart attack. But the other two—I don't think so. Stupidity destroyed Blue Kite. That was Jerry's doing, but it couldn't have been on purpose. He still worked for Coke then."

"But the oleander was real. She could have died, Clay."

There was nothing to say to that.

"Ernesto can't even tell me where he was, or why he was gone. I thought he was trustworthy. If Lucy hadn't been there . . ."

"But she was."

Dakota started pacing again. "Maybe I should fire him."

"I don't think he'll make the same mistake again. Have you seen him? He's dragging around like he lost his whole family."

"I was going to take him with me to Ruidoso, make him my assistant trainer. Now, I'm not so sure. Maybe I should take Lucy instead."

"You were planning to leave her here?"

"The truth is, I don't need her. Ernesto's the more valuable of the two. He can ride Shameless in her workouts. And up until last night, I trusted him to stay with her. I can't afford to take them both!"

"I wouldn't want to be responsible for a sixteen-year-old girl," Clay said.

"No. It's impossible. I'll have to break it to her soon." Dakota paced back and forth. "Some reward, huh? She saves Shameless's life and Ernesto's the one who gets to go to Ruidoso. I still can't believe he left the filly alone, after everything I told him!"

"Do you want me to ask him what happened? My Spanish is pretty good."

"Will you, Clay?"

"You know me, McAllister. I aim to please."

The day of the Santa Cruz County Futurity dawned sunny and already warm. The futurity was late in the day, so Dakota went over to watch the earlier races with Clay. She nodded to Dan Bolin, who was having a beer with the Hispanic man she'd seen him with last week. The Mexican wore the same straw cowboy hat, a guayabera shirt, and brown polyester western-cut pants. He had an apple-shaped figure—a large stomach and small rear end.

"Who is that?" Dakota asked Clay.

"Rudy Gallego. Trainer from Hermosillo. Ernesto's been picking up rides with his stable all week."

"Does he have good horses?"

"One of them's in the futurity. Gallego's got the money to buy the best." Clay frowned. "I thought he'd be at the dispersal sale. He likes Black Oak horses. With Coke gone . . ."

"Gone?"

"Coke wouldn't sell to him. Gallego makes a lot of his money match racing horses in Mexico."

Dakota shivered. She'd grown up with the sad fact that match racing existed on both sides of the border, although it was much more prevalent in Mexico. Match racing wasn't regulated; you could drug a horse up to its eyeballs. Consequently, a lot of horses ran without pain on unsound limbs, and broke down because of it. Horses were literally run into the ground, but a voracious appetite and unlimited money made sure that there was always a fresh supply of unfortunates for the meat grinder.

She changed the subject. "Did you talk to Ernesto?"

"He says he was asleep in his trailer. Lucy woke him up."

"That's not what she says."

"One of them's lying."

"Both of them have reason to." Ernesto, to keep his job; Lucy to protect her father. She sighed. "I'll have to talk to her soon about Ruidoso."

"If it's any consolation, I don't think ol' Jer would go for it anyway."

"Whether he cares or not, there's no way I'm taking responsibility for a sixteen-year-old girl at a racetrack in another state. She'll be upset, though." Dakota hated herself for putting it off. Lucy was getting too attached to her, and she blamed herself in part for encouraging it. She'd had Lucy and Ernesto over to swim on really hot days after work.

Lucy's company wore thin after an hour or two. Perhaps it was because she tried too hard. Or maybe it was chemistry—some people just didn't click, which was hardly Lucy's fault. But fair or not, Dakota sure didn't want to have her underfoot in Ruidoso. Perhaps she was being uncharitable, but this particular good deed had just about run its course.

She felt like a coward. A mean-spirited, selfish coward.

"You look guilty as hell," Clay said.

"I feel guilty as hell."

"She'll be all right. That kid's a real survivor."

"She has to be. No one should live like she does."

His mouth straightened into a grim line. "You're right, they shouldn't." He was about to say something more, when Rita appeared at his shoulder. She wore a red blouse with the state of Texas sewn across one breast in cobalt-blue bugle beads. Cowgirl fringe spilled in a yellow suede waterfall down the side hems of her tight jeans and off the tops of her red boots.

It must be Primary Color Day.

Rita touched Clay's arm. "Who's a survivor?"

"We were talking about Lucy Tanner."

"Your groom?"

"Unfortunately, she won't be for long," Dakota said, kicking herself for her compulsion to overexplain.

"My trainer needs another groom. Maybe I should tell him about her." She squeezed Clay's arm. "I have the most wonderful news!"

He grinned. "Oh?"

"You won't believe it! I'm going to Ruidoso! Isn't that exciting?"

Dakota felt as if someone had kicked her in the stomach. But she kept smiling until her cheeks hurt.

"I just talked to Jack today. He thinks that one colt, Mr. Moon Rock? He thinks he'll do well up there, so I've supplemented him into the Rainbow Futurity."

"You did what?" Clay demanded. "You'll have to pay fifteen thousand dollars!"

"He did so well in the trials, so I told Jack, I said, why don't we give him his chance? If he does well there, I'll supplement him into the All American." She looked pointedly at Dakota.

Clay shook his head. "He's not in that class. You're throwing good money away. There are other races at Ruidoso—"

"He was the second-fastest qualifier."

"He's a nice horse," Clay replied, "but, Rita, he got lucky in the trials."

"Talk about sour grapes! His time was faster than any one of your horses."

Clay's face took on that shuttered look. Dakota knew he wanted to say that good horses might run a slower time in a given race, but they always rose to the occasion when challenged. A horse's time didn't mean that much. Class did.

"Suit yourself," Clay said. "As you're so fond of saying, it's your money."

"You're damn right it is!"

Dakota, feeling uncomfortable, withdrew. She looked back and saw them still near the rail, looking like a married couple in the middle of an argument. The analogy made her wince.

* * *

Shameless won the Santa Cruz County Futurity by a length and a half. It was too bad Clay wasn't around to celebrate with Dakota this time, but Rita clung to him like a red, blue and yellow leech. Dakota couldn't be bothered dealing with that. Simple congratulations were exchanged. Dangerously was second. Rita's horse came in last, but from where Dakota was standing, the woman didn't look all that broken up about it.

Unable to shake the feeling that this race was somehow anticlimatic, Dakota led her filly to the test barn, where the winner was always checked for drugs. Two hours later, after Shameless had been bathed and walked and seen to, Dakota drove home, zapped herself a frozen dinner, and settled in to watch *Casey's Shadow*, the classic film about two subjects close to her heart and mind: a little-known trainer's bid to win the All American Futurity, and a father's love.

As she punched the video into the VCR, she wondered what Clay was doing, and if Rita was doing it with him.

Part Two

The Rainbow
Futurity

Twenty-Six

May

On the Friday morning following the Santa Cruz County Futurity, Dakota hitched the Black Oak trailer to her father's truck, loaded up Shameless and Tyke, and followed her ex-husband up the winding Sonoita road to Interstate 10.

When Clay offered to convoy with Dakota "for security reasons," Dakota was secretly relieved. Always at the back of her mind was the knowledge that someone had come close to killing Shameless.

If Lucy hadn't been there that night, the filly might have eaten the oleander and suffered an agonizing death.

At least she wouldn't have to worry about Tanner. Despite what he'd told her, he wouldn't be going to Ruidoso this summer. He'd be following the Arizona county fair circuit instead, where he'd have a better chance at winning races and making money.

Tanner might hate Dakota with a passion, but she counted on the fact that he was too poor and too cheap to drive all the way to eastern New Mexico just for revenge, when he could be winning purses at Prescott Downs.

And so it was with a light heart Dakota started out on the journey east to New Mexico. She'd always loved road trips. The drive from Sonoita to Ruidoso was a familiar one, although she hadn't driven this route in a decade. The last time had been with Clay, as his blushing bride. It was not something she cared to dwell on.

Ernesto would be riding with Clay's groom, they would be pulling one of three six-horse trailers for the Bar 66, so Dakota drove alone, which was the way she wanted it. She had Affirmed, Alydar, and Refrigerator for company. Refrigerator crouched in her cat carrier, glaring balefully at the dogs. The retrievers, naturally effusive, occasionally remembered Refrigerator's plight and curled up on the seat, looking guilty. Codependent dogs. How California.

Dakota punched in *Rigoletto,* turned it up to rock and roll levels, and settled in for the seven-hour drive. The morning sun glinted off the top of the horse trailer ahead. Tawny grassland and smoky-green mesquite shimmered in the golden morning light, enormous white wildflowers dotted the median. Cadmium-yellow billboards advertised everything from motel chains to "freeze-dried rattlesnakes" and "real Indian headdresses."

A combination roadside diner and filling station offered the weary traveler this dubious enticement: BURGER—FRIES—GAS!

And once in a while there appeared a reminder Dakota could have done without. Little white crosses, sometimes combined with heart-shaped wreaths of paper flowers, marked the places where traffic fatalities had occurred.

The caravan stopped to eat in Deming, New Mexico. They took up a block on a little-used side street, lining up along the curb. A few people came out of their houses and watched unabashedly as if the circus had come to town. Clay and Dakota watered the horses and left one of the grooms with them, promising to bring him back a hamburger and fries. They walked to the Sonic Drive-In on the main drag.

Menus complete with washed-out photographs of fried food were suspended in glass pods beside each parking space; a relic of *American Graffiti* days. "We ate here ten years ago," Clay said. "Remember?"

"It's not a real standout," she lied.

The humor in his eyes showed he didn't believe her. "I wonder if the cabin's the same."

That summer, she and Clay had honeymooned in her dad's cabin. Neither one of them had been to it since then. She wasn't too thrilled about facing all those memories again. They'd had a lot of fun that summer.

A lot of fun.

With every mile they seemed to drive deeper into the past. New Mexico's glory years had been the nuclear fifties and the space-age sixties, and the older motels and restaurants reflected that boon to their economy. The words satellite and rocket figured into more than a few of the old neon signs. Atomic symbols and phallic missiles dominated the scenery. Past Las Cruces, the barren pockmarked land did look like a moonscape. Ahead, leaden-blue thunderclouds boiled above the desert town of Alamogordo. Dakota glanced to her left, where bare, volcanic ramparts dropped away from the road. Clay had told her that the San Andres Mountains would be the most likely place for the release of the Mexican wolves. Later in the summer there would be a wolf rally at the White Sands National Monument nearby. Rita was one of the chief organizers.

They passed the White Sands, which washed up to the road like chalky surf, dotted with dune grasses and dusty-looking shrubs. Dakota shivered. She'd heard that farther into the park, it was a sea of white sand. It would be easy to get lost in there. Ahead, the storm clouds glowered in the hazy New Mexico heat. Alamogordo stretched out at the foot of the Sacramento Mountains, which, in this aqueous prestorm light, made Dakota think of the continental shelf dropping abruptly off to the ocean floor.

At a stoplight in Alamogordo she saw a young woman trudging along the side of the road, looking tired and defeated. She reminded Dakota of Lucy; baggy T-shirt, jeans, backpack, short pixie hair.

Dakota winced as she remembered the scene with Lucy earlier this week. The teenager had tried everything to convince Dakota to take her along. When it got through to her that there was no chance that she'd be going to Ruidoso, Lucy had hurled a dandybrush at Shameless and stalked off.

The brush had glanced harmlessly off the filly's hip, but it made Dakota mad as hell.

She tried to get the troubled girl out of her mind, but it was hard to do.

Dakota wondered if Lucy *had* lied to protect her father. Jerry Tanner struck her as the type of man who would use his own daughter without a qualm. If Lucy had seen her father trying to poison the filly, she'd probably do anything to cover it up. Dakota had read enough pop psychology books and seen enough talk shows to know that abused children did some pretty strange things to protect their abusers, and there was little doubt Tanner abused Lucy. Just living in that pigsty qualified as abuse in her book.

But what if Lucy was telling the truth? The only big, tall men she knew personally were Dan Bolin and Mario, Rita's Man Friday.

Accidents happen.

Could Rita hate her so much that she would try to kill Shameless? Dakota tried to shake that disturbing notion, but it clung to her like a noxious mist.

The rain caught them just as the sign for Tularosa flashed by. Dakota stared at the horse trailer in front of her through the brimming glass, past the squeak-snap of the windshield wipers. Almost there.

As she slowed for the turnoff onto New Mexico 70, she surrendered to the thrill that churned in her stomach like a caldron of witch's brew. The old excitement was back. Even the twin evils of Rita DeWeil and Jerry Tanner paled in comparison to the anticipation that increased with every mile. Rain pounded the roof of the pickup, but she saw holes in the clouds up ahead. She let out a whoop when she saw the first pine tree.

Dan Bolin drove home for lunch, feeling better than he had in weeks. Dakota McAllister was gone, and with her, half his worries. She wouldn't be underfoot anymore.

He stopped by to see his two-year-olds. The barn and

house looked a lot like the stables where he'd spent his youth back east. White colonial brick, gray slate roof, even spires—à la Churchill Downs—on either end. The barn had been built two years ago, before money got tight. Before Maria got sick from that goddamned virus that ruined her heart.

There were six two-year-olds in all. All had been broken to saddle, although they'd never seen a racetrack. He patted one here, checked the legs on another, putting off the moment when he would have to go home. He hated to see Marie so sick, just wasting away. It was as if part of him were dying slowly. Helpless, impotent, he could only watch her fade away.

As he reached the house, Marie's nurse bolted out the door and ran toward him. "Mr. Bolin! Hurry!"

Her face was flushed and her eyes were bright. It was either something very good or very bad. In the roller coaster his life had become, things seldom remained steady. He broke into a run, heart pounding in his chest. He always expected the worst, prepared himself for the words that would rip his life apart. He licked his lips, tried to speak. *Is she gone?* Couldn't say it. Couldn't put such a terrible thought into words.

"The hospital called a few minutes ago," the nurse gasped, her expression triumphant.

He couldn't believe it. Joy exploded in his heart, warmth spreading well-being to his limbs. It felt as if he'd just knocked back a shot of tequila.

He ran to the wall phone, fumbled with the receiver, punched the number he knew by heart. His knees were wobbly as a newborn colt's. The impersonal voice of University Medical Center asked where they could direct his call. "Dr. Clawson. Cardiology," he rapped out, feeling too important for this kind of byplay. Didn't they understand that time was of the essence?

An interminable wait as the line rang.

A receptionist answered. "Dr. Clawson," he said quickly. He identified himself, saying the doctor had called just a few minutes ago. Pacing, he was aware of the phone cord unraveling behind him. His heart surged like a locomotive in his chest.

Hurry, goddammit! Where the hell was he? He'd only called a few minutes ago. What'd he do, step out for a few holes of golf?

"Mr. Bolin?" The doctor's voice boomed on the line. "Good news. We've found a donor. Can you get your wife here within the next hour or two?"

He swallowed, closed his eyes. Thanked God. "We're on our way."

Twenty-Seven

Ruidoso Downs had been renovated since Dakota had seen it last. Painted a glistening tan color, the trilevel grandstand rose against a dark green backdrop of pines. The road leading to it curved gracefully in a long-limbed arc, echoing the natural bowl of land in which the racetrack oval lay.

The rain had stopped as quickly as it started, and the sun came out, edging the puddles with silver and steaming off the pavement. Dakota drove through the Horseman's Gate and down the hill, scanning the maze of long barns for Barn 31. She found it at the end of a winding dirt road, nestled into the mountainside beneath Highway 70.

Her two stalls were right on the end. She and Ernesto set up camp, putting down a fresh bedding of sawdust for Tyke and Shameless, filling water buckets, and hauling tack, medicinal supplies and feed into the tack room. While Ernesto measured out the grain and vitamins and filled the haynet, Dakota removed the filly's traveling boots and walked her around, letting her graze on the luscious weeds bordering the dirt yard, as the sound of cars whizzed by on the embankment above. Shameless had traveled well. She took in the sights, scents and sounds of her new environment with eagerness.

After registering at the race office, Dakota drove back up 70 and turned onto Sudderth, greeting the little town nestled in the mountains as an old friend. She loved the bright green poplars, which shimmied against the darker backdrop of pines, and the roadside flowers.

No matter what state they hailed from, when quarter horse people said they were "going to the mountains," they were talking about Ruidoso.

The town was strung along Sudderth Drive like a gaudy charm bracelet. Some of the charms were the real thing, and others were paste. Some, like Bubba's Bar BQ and Catfish—coffee, five cents—didn't pretend to be anything but what they were. An amusement park stood at the "Y," the junction of Sudderth and 70, setting the tone. Ruidoso was an adult amusement park, the capital of quarter horse racing in the summer, a ski resort in winter. The town catered to all kinds of tastes, from the wealthy horse owner whose wife shopped the trendy boutiques for denim, diamonds and lace, to the guy with a one-horse stable who dug a dollar out of his jeans for a breakfast of doughnuts. Ruidoso had several restaurants offering continental cuisine, and places like Olé Taco, a pink taco stand with a window full of baseball trophies and the sign: JESUS IS MY FRIEND. The Inn of the Mountain Gods offered fishing, sailing, golfing, casino gambling and fine dining; the Tepee Motel offered Cable TV and clean rooms. Motor court cabins built in the twenties gave the town a rustic feel.

Everywhere, the horse was king. The Winner's Circle Dance Club, Win Place and Show Liquors, The Paddock, the Finish Line—all paid homage to the town's mainstay. One fast-food place offered "Pete's Picks" along with the burgers.

Dakota drove down Sudderth in bumper-to-bumper traffic; Cadillacs and one-ton diesel trucks with dual wheels, headache racks and Texas Truck license plates. Bumper stickers declared that "Seven Days Without Meat Makes 1 Weak" and that the American quarter horse was "The World's Fastest Athlete." Roadside stands sold chili from Hatch, The Chili Capital of the World, and roasted corn, caramel apples, watermelons. One enterprising soul advertised FIREWOOD—DOG GROOMING—WE SELL HERMIT CRABS.

Some of the buildings were new, and the names had

changed, but it was still the same town. A little bigger, clogged with a lot more traffic, but essentially Ruidoso held within its boundaries the same spirit: that fairy tales did indeed come true. Anyone who had a good horse could go to Ruidoso and have a chance to win the All American. Now, *she* was taking a horse to the All American. When she reached Ruidoso Downs, all her worries dropped away, leaving only a deep, fulfilling joy.

Dakota followed Sudderth past the boutiques and stores, then past resorts and private cabins, until she reached Upper Canyon Road, where her father's cabin had stood since 1952.

It was just as she remembered it. Situated on two acres of ponderosa pine forest, it rose up out of tall meadow grass and wildflowers, still sweet-smelling from the thundershower. Harmless white clouds blew across the sky like freshly laundered sheets. Pine shadows flickered on the honey-yellow of the pine logs. At the foot of the drive, a dark green wrought-iron street lamp with a cluster of five globes was surrounded by a bed of petunias and geraniums. Inside, the Americana theme continued, lots of antiques from the thirties and forties, old signs, Coca-Cola memorabilia. Sunlight gleamed on varnished pine cabinets and fifties-era white appliances: a small gas stove and a round-shouldered refrigerator. Red-and-white gingham curtains in the windows, and cheap Early American maple furniture—cabin stuff. Rag rugs on the wood floor. A smoke-blackened fieldstone fireplace. Photos of horses, of course. Everywhere. The place smelled musty from having been closed up.

The toilet in the tiny paneled bathroom was new. Dakota remembered what Clay had told her this afternoon. Jerry Tanner hadn't taken his firing philosophically. Before he'd left, he trashed the place, and one of the things he'd done was take a cinderblock and drop it on the toilet tank. It had cost Coke a fortune to fix the cabin up, but unless her memory was faulty, it looked just as she remembered it.

She wasn't prepared for the pain that assailed her as she reached the doorway to the bedroom. The white chenille spread looked the same. Now, in late afternoon, the sun slanted across it, snowing dust motes. She closed her eyes, trying to shut out the memory, but saw it anyway, as if she were an outside observer. The two of them, embracing, kissing, their tanned bodies moving on that bed, young and healthy and gloriously happy.

I was never so happy in my life as I was that summer. She realized it was the truth. There was a lot of talk about growing up, moving on. Ostensibly, your life was supposed to improve as you became more mature. The infatuation of first love was supposed to fade as more practical things took over. But looking back on it, she felt the same deep longing that had hit her when she'd first seen Clay again. The void lodged just below her breastbone, spreading outward.

Nothing had changed. Certainly not for the better.

Tears pricked her eyelids. The memories rushed in like water over a dam: cooking together in the little kitchen, fishing in the river below, catching each other in the hallway and making love in a tangle of clothing without getting near the bed, talking until dawn. It had seemed then as if nothing could ever come between them. She remembered the time he'd made love to her on the couch. If she hadn't been nineteen, she would have had a stiff neck. She could see him looking down at her, tenderly touching her face. Telling her he loved her.

Suddenly, she had to get out of this cabin. She couldn't face all this now.

Picking up her purse, Dakota forged through the screen door, and almost ran smack into the object of her pain.

"Hey! Where's the fire?"

Dakota stepped back, letting the door slap to. "Clay. What're you doing here?"

"I'm in the mood for spaghetti, and I thought you might be, too."

She saw the grocery bag under his arm.

"Ragu with meat sauce."

Dakota started to say she was tired, that he should go away. But then she thought of the ghosts in the bedroom, and wished fervently that for just one night, she could pretend nothing had changed. The screen door opened with a squeak and Dakota stood aside. "Hope you brought some wine," she said.

They made dinner, slipping unconsciously back into the easy give and take of people who knew each other well and naturally divided up the chores, their motions as smooth and efficient as a choreographed dance. Not that the meal was anything special: just Ragu over pasta, the way they used to have it every other night so long ago. While Clay stirred the pot and measured out the spaghetti, Dakota chopped up stuff for the salad, her hands automatically going to the right cupboards for the collander, the knife. As one glass of burgundy became two, Dakota began to let go and have fun. Why *not* try to recapture the past? Clay was here, and so was she. Her longing for him was a physical pain. Bittersweet tension lay between them like a stifling blanket. He was so close to her, she could touch his hip, reach up and guide his mouth to hers, let him take her back to the bedroom with the ghosts, and maybe they could merge and time could stand still and they would be married again . . .

"You want to wash or rinse?" he asked her.

What a joy it was to do these simple tasks together. He was to her right, his arm occasionally sweeping against hers and igniting little brush fires.

After dinner they sat on the porch in the pine shadows and finished the wine, talking about old times. She realized she was flirting with him. Well, what was wrong with that? He'd been pressuring her all spring for precisely this kind of behavior. He kissed her, but the kiss didn't deepen. He seemed to be keeping his distance, and this confused her. Was he trying to hurt her again? Well, she knew she was beautiful. Hadn't he told her often enough? She threw caution to the winds and her arms around his neck. She asked him to hold her. Hold her tight. He did so, stroking her back, saying gentle, sweet things. The things he said made her want to cry, and pretty soon she buried her head in his chest and felt her hot tears course down his shirtfront, and his fingers pro-scribed firm, calm circles on her shuddering back, and then she was kissing him again, and tonight *she* was the aggressor, darting her tongue in his mouth with reckless abandon, rub-bing against him, exhilarated by his response.

He wanted her. Men couldn't hide a thing like that. They could go back to the bedroom and scare the ghosts away. Time seemed to whirl now, faster and faster like a carousel, all moonlight and the shadows of the pine needles against the log cabin, the warmth of his body, his kiss, and then in one dizzying moment he swept her up into his arms and was carrying her through the hallway, and it felt like a carnival ride in her stomach, so much better than emptiness, and then she was on the bed and she felt the mattress list as he lay be-side her, still clothed, and he was cupping her jaw in his hands, saying something, something she couldn't quite under-stand, and she reached for his belt, fumbled with the buckle, kissing him and crying at the same time.

She was awakened by chill air blowing through an open window. At first she didn't know where she was, and then it came back to her. She was in Coke's cabin in Ruidoso.

The smell of bacon wafted in from the kitchen. She heard the rattle of pans at the exact instant she remembered last night. Or most of it.

Clay was still here. He'd been here all night.

She sat up, rubbing her forehead, which ached mildly. How much wine had she had last night? Throwing back the covers, Dakota realized with horror that all she had on were her pan-ties.

That much wine. "Damn!" she muttered as she sprinted for her suitcase. She grabbed whatever was on top, which hap-pened to be a citron-colored tank dress. She tugged it over her head, trying to blot out the creeping dread that filled her. Had she gone to bed with her ex-husband?

Wearing his jeans and shirt from yesterday, Clay appeared

in the doorway and stared in the general vicinity of her chest. "You're up, I see."

Dakota didn't have to look down to know her nipples stood out in bas relief. The ribbed cotton shift barely covered her upper body. She wished she could run and hide. Instead, she stood her ground and raised her chin. "Who told you you could spend the night?" she demanded.

"You did."

"I did not." But she wasn't so sure.

His mouth quirked into a grin. "You insisted." He tucked his shirttail into his jeans. "I left you some bacon, eggs and coffee. I've got to get to the track. See you there."

"Wait—"

But he was already out the door.

She sat down, trying to ignore the throbbing ache in her head. Had she?

She remembered tugging at his belt. Remembered throwing herself at him, acting like she'd always imagined Rita would do. Obviously, she'd had too much to drink. She even remembered crying—a lot.

A crying jag. Jesus! She hadn't acted like that since college. Clay must have had a good laugh!

The question was, had he taken advantage of her inebriated state?

Feeling shaky, she walked into the kitchen. The bacon and eggs didn't appeal to her at all. But she should have some coffee. Glancing at the clock, she saw it was seven-thirty already. Great. Her first day on the backside at Ruidoso Downs, and she was late.

She'd slept with her ex-husband, made a complete fool of herself, and now she had gotten off on the wrong foot at Ruidoso. Not that anyone would notice, except of course, Clay.

Pouring coffee seemed like too great a task for the moment. Sitting down at the table, she pressed her fingers into her forehead and stared down at the Formica, hardly seeing it. Gradually, she realized there was a Post-it stuck to the table surface, just at the edge of her vision.

The handwriting was Clay's.

The note said, "In case you're wondering, we didn't."

The first thing Dakota did when she returned from the track that morning was to go to Wal-Mart and buy a new bedspread. As she replaced the white chenille with the Country French, Dakota hoped she'd taken a step toward obliterating those painful—and embarrassing—memories.

Fortunately, she hadn't seen Clay today. His stable was on the far side of the complex.

Wincing, Dakota remembered pulling at his belt and crying. What an attractive picture she must have made! Maybe he thought she drank like that all the time, and the reason she'd turned into a lush was because he'd dumped her all those years ago.

The thought of talking to him again was mortifying.

Dakota folded up the chenille spread and put it in the linen closet. Interacting with Clay couldn't be avoided, so she had to be prepared. Last night had been a momentary slip, that was all, brought on by exhaustion and too much to drink. The best thing to do was to pick up the pieces and move on, and try to regain what dignity she could.

But she couldn't get it out of her mind that he'd turned her down. She didn't know whether to be grateful, or insulted.

One minute, Trish O'Neill was having a great time, skating in the parking lot of the Stockman's Bank with her friends, and the next, she saw *it*.

The truck pulled up across the street, in front of the Sonoita general store.

Panic bolted through her system. Her mouth was suddenly dry. Her heart pounded.

"What's the matter, Trish?" Megan asked. Trish didn't—couldn't—answer.

There were two men in the cab, and two sitting in the bed

of the truck. She'd never seen them before. They were pulling a boat, probably headed for Parker Canyon Lake.

The men in the back of the truck stayed where they were. One of them glanced in her direction, but she was all the way across the highway, standing in the shade of the post office, so she doubted he would recognize her. He opened a cooler and took out a beer, popped the tab and drank.

"Trish?"

Trish was shaking. She tried to avert her eyes, pretend to be a teenage girl skating on the sidewalk. Tried to be as inconspicuous as possible, but it was impossible not to look at the truck.

It had to be the one. She'd forgotten until now what it looked like. If anyone had asked her to describe it before, she wouldn't have been able to. But when she saw it pull in, suddenly, she was back there at Dead Man's Curve, watching the killer drive up to see if Coke McAllister was dead.

It was the shape. Although she couldn't tell what color the killer's truck was, she'd had the impression it was dark. This truck was dark green. It was old and scraped up, with lights on the cab roof.

The two other men came out of the store, carrying a twelve-pack of Coors. Their backs were to her as they loaded the beer into the truck bed. One of them wore a Harley T-shirt and cammie pants. He had tattoos on each arm and his elbows bowed away from his sides. He was short and stocky.

It could have been the guy she saw.

She couldn't remember if the guy had been stocky, or if he'd just been dressed for cold weather. She hadn't been able to tell how tall he was, either. The only thing she remembered about him was that he'd stood there for a long time, his arms folded low across his chest. He'd rubbed his arms to keep away the chill. She'd realized that she'd been rubbing hers the same way, and that had spooked her.

She couldn't even remember if his hair was long under his cap. This guy's was.

No, it was impossible to tell. But the truck . . .

She saw them pull out, following 82 south toward the lake.

A sheriff's vehicle was coming this way. Trish raised her arm halfheartedly to wave him down, then stopped.

It probably wasn't the same truck, at all. And if it was, the guys in it would know who finked on them. They'd come after her.

The sheriff's deputy glanced her way, his face puzzled. She smiled and waved and let him go by.

Twenty-Eight

Dakota soon became caught up in the routine: mornings on the backside with Shameless, breaking for lunch, and a few stolen moments of reading or hiking along the Rio Ruidoso below the house, going back to the track for afternoon feeding, then spending a quiet evening at home. She didn't join the trainers who sat their horses near the clocker's stand and passed the time of day trading stories while keeping an eagle eye on their runners. She didn't know any of them, for one thing, and if Clay had a horse on the track, that was where he'd be. She'd nod to him as she led Shameless onto the track, then ride Tyke up the backstretch and wait for the filly there. It made her appear standoffish but also serious, and that was fine with her.

She was painfully aware of the looks she got from jockeys and exercise boys, and even a few of the trainers. A lot of the attention was sexual in nature, which she deflected by appearing naively oblivious. Dakota tried to do her job without letting it get to her, but it was hard. She might as well have a spotlight aimed at her. There were other female trainers—and plenty of female jockeys and exercise riders—but she was a novelty. First, she was new, and therefore vulnerable until she showed her mettle. But worse, she'd come here with a dynamite horse. That, alone, generated a great deal of resentment.

Although she ran Shameless as little as possible, Dakota had to work her to keep her sharp, and there was no hiding the filly's speed.

She worried every time Ernesto asked Shameless for more than just a gallop. The filly's legs seemed fine, and she came back feeling good, but Dakota was always on edge, waiting for something to happen. Shameless ran so hard, and Dakota worried that something was going on under the surface she couldn't see, and so she spent more money she didn't have on ultrasound tests. Even though the filly's legs appeared normal, she couldn't relax. There might be stress fractures too tiny to detect, but potentially crippling. There was no way to be absolutely sure.

The Rainbow Futurity Trials would be run in late June. Dakota concentrated on keeping her fit. Shameless was happy and eager to run. Her attitude was the best indication of soundness.

Dakota was cleaning the filly's stall one morning when Clay came up and leaned on the open stall door. "When's Shameless due for her work?"

Dakota tried to ignore the pounding of her heart. She couldn't look at him, so she concentrated on her work. "Sunday morning."

"I have a colt who needs to work in company. Would you send her out with him?"

"You have a lot of horses. Why don't you use one of them?"

"He's got a lot of talent and I want to see what he does if he's really pushed."

"Clay, I—"

"I know what you're going to say. You'd rather not." He stepped into the stall and took the pitchfork from her hands. "Don't you think you're being too hard on yourself?"

He didn't appear to be laughing. Or gloating. But her face burned as she remembered what happened her first night in Ruidoso. The worst thing was that she couldn't remember everything she'd said . . . or done. "I don't know what you're talking about."

"Bullshit."

She reached for her pitchfork. "Couldn't you just leave me alone?"

"Not until you tell me what goes on in that crazy head of yours." His were dark, stormy, like the ocean at midnight. "Do you think you're the only person in the world who feels anything? You had too much to drink that night, you think you made a fool of yourself, so you punish me."

"Punish you? You're the one who—"

"Who what?"

She grabbed the pitchfork away from him and stabbed at the bedding angrily. "Never mind."

"Turned you down?" His voice was quiet, as quiet as the thread of tension between them.

She glared at him. "How do I know you turned me down? I only have your word for it. You could have taken advantage of me and be playing some little game, waiting to see if I'd crack!"

"You really think that?"

"You hurt me before."

"Here we go again. I destroyed our marriage, I left you heartbroken, I came back into your life and tried to pull the same thing again. When are you going to face your own part in it?"

A stray lock of hair fell into her eyes and she swiped it away, feeling grubby. "I know it wasn't all your fault."

"Do you think I really care that you drank too much wine one night and told me how you really felt?"

She couldn't face the humiliation. Couldn't face him. She pushed past him into the blinding sunlight.

Clay didn't follow her. "The truth is, I don't care. It doesn't matter to me at all."

Dakota pulled her gloves from her jeans and put them on, grabbed the handles on the wheelbarrow. She didn't dare speak.

"For Christ's sake. You're only human."

"Only human? For throwing myself at you? I guess I'm no exception," she said bitterly.

He ignored the barb. "I miss you, McAllister."

She couldn't move. Just stood there, her hands on the

wooden handles of the wheelbarrow, her heart pounding. His words echoed in her mind. *I miss you, McAllister.*

She realized then that this problem was not going to go away. There were too many unresolved feelings on both sides. She couldn't ignore it anymore. They had to work this out, or she would go crazy.

"If you want to see me, I'm at Barn Fifteen." He strode past her.

"I do," she said softly. Why pretend she didn't? She wasn't fooling anyone.

"You still like fly-fishing?"

She nodded.

"How about we go out for an hour or so after evening feeding?"

Dakota swallowed. "Okay."

That evening they went fly-fishing in Rio Ruidoso below Dakota's cabin. They didn't talk about what had happened, and after a short period of awkwardness, slipped back into that easy companionship Dakota was beginning to realize was a part of her life, whether she'd planned for it or not.

It was on that evening that Dakota faced what she'd known instinctively for months: Clay was a man she could trust. He wasn't the boy she'd once known.

Twenty-Nine

The night before the Rainbow Futurity Trials, Dakota was too wound up to sleep. She and Clay had gone to the Inn Credible for dinner and then to a movie. He'd left her at the door with a kiss that had set her blood humming. For a moment she had been tempted to ask him in, but her head won over her body. This time.

Now she wished she hadn't been so demure. The pleasant ache his kiss elicted had deepened to an almost unbearable intensity, keeping her awake.

It was one in the morning, and she was in heat.

She gave up any pretense of trying to sleep, got up and padded through the cabin in her bare feet. Refrigerator hopped down from the bed and followed her. She poured some milk out for the cat and heated the rest for herself. Turning on the light in the tiny living room, she picked up her father's journal and sat down on the couch. Refrigerator curled up in a neat ball on her lap, the thrumming of her motor reverberating against Dakota's thighs. Affirmed, lying near Alydar beside the fireplace, lifted his head sleepily and thumped his tail once against the floor. Alydar sighed in his sleep.

Dakota leafed through the entries, restless and aching with bittersweet desire. The words blurred before her eyes, not making much sense:

Tanner came by today. Told me I'd better stop talking about him, or he'd sue me for slander.

Refrigerator shifted on her lap and dug her claws in. Yelping, Dakota pulled her terry cloth robe back over her bare flesh so the cat would have a pincushion. She didn't want to think about Jerry Tanner, so she turned the pages until she came to an entry concerning Shameless.

I let the filly run today for the first time. Man, she's got it.

Dakota's mind kept wandering to Clay. Would it have been so wrong to ask him in? She turned the pages, skimmed the journal. *Dan's away . . .*

Dan's away for two weeks and everything falls apart. Like the last time, when Judgment was ready to be bred and I couldn't find a drop of Something Wicked's semen anywhere! I took matters into my own hands that time and look how it turned out. . . .

Her eyelids grew heavier.

Had to send that kid back twice to find him. Imagine that, not being able to find Black Oak's top stud!

Dakota caught herself dozing off. She was half horny and half sleepy. It was increasingly difficult to concentrate.

. . . There was a partial eclipse, like the gods were trying to tell me something.

She'd read this before. Setting the journal down, Dakota turned out the light, gently spilled the cat onto the couch and stood up. A cool breeze flirted with the curtains at the open window; she could hear it way up in the pine tops, a soft exhalation.

Like silk rasping against flesh. Dakota touched the lace edge of her pink teddy, envisioning Clay's hand on her thigh. She pictured him standing outside her window, serenading her with a guitar. She'd open the window and call to him, and he'd climb in just like Romeo . . . on an impulse, she pulled one of the curtains back and peered out.

A hooded figure stood in the clearing, looking right up at her.

Reflexively, her hand shot back, letting the curtain drop away. Shocked, violently awake now, she sat down on the couch, crushing Refrigerator's tail. The cat yowled, scaring her even more, and jumped to the floor.

Panic sailed through her, gaining height like a kite in a high wind, crashing into her throat. Someone was watching her! He'd looked up into her window, perhaps seeing her shape behind the thin cotton curtains.

Her heart scrambled in her chest. How naive to think she'd left it all behind—that a few hundred miles could make a difference to whomever had been terrorizing her!

She stood up again, hugging herself. It was suddenly freezing in here.

She tried to recapture the fleeting image in her mind's eye. Medium height? Weight? She thought so. His hands had been in his pockets, she thought. The hood could have been from a jacket.

He might still be there.

Dry-mouthed, Dakota crept back to the window. Slowly, she eased the right curtain away from its mate. She told herself that the watcher couldn't see her, since the light was out. There was just enough of a slit to see through.

The figure was gone. All that remained was the moonlit yard, the vertical black stripes of pine trunks and tall grass.

It was almost as if she'd imagined it.

She couldn't believe this was happening, on the night before the futurity trials. But it did make some kind of sense. Shameless had nearly been poisoned a few days before the Santa Cruz County Futurity.

The filly.

Blood pounding in her ears, she picked up the phone and called Ernesto.

Thirty

The day of the Rainbow Futurity trials dawned rainy and cold.

Shaken from her encounter at the cabin, Dakota had stayed up until three o'clock in the morning, when she could no longer keep her eyes open. She'd seen the cold front come in, heard the first spatters of rain on the window that would soon turn to a steady downpour.

When the alarm awoke her at five, she dragged herself out of sleep like a losing prize fighter standing up for the last round. Fueling up on coffee, she gazed in despair at the rain pouring off the rainspout outside in a waterfall. She tried to swallow down her anxiety along with the coffee, but it remained in her throat like a knot. Rain meant a muddy track, a dangerous track. She'd planned to put bandages on the filly's legs for today's race, but that was shot now. Mud could pull the bandages off and cause the filly to trip and fall.

Blotting out visions of tragedy, Dakota dressed hurriedly in jeans, shirt, and jacket. She'd come back and changed around noon, since the filly's race would be later in the day.

She couldn't stop thinking about the figure outside her window. Maybe she'd imagined it. It could have been the tree trunks, the way the moonlight hit them—

But she didn't really believe that.

She wouldn't tell Clay now, not before the races. He had enough to think about.

Clay's colt, Straight Eight, would be running in the first

trial for the Rainbow Futurity. As Dakota watched his deft preparations, she tried to stem her nervousness.

Who would want to watch her? Her mind whirled with questions as she drove to the grandstand to watch Straight Eight's race.

Over a hundred and fifty horses were set to run in the sixteen futurity trials. The horses with the ten fastest times would move on to the Rainbow.

The first race set the tone. As the horses passed the finish line, one of them faltered, his leg snapping right in front of the grandstand.

It wasn't Straight Eight, thank God. But someone owned him, someone loved him. Dakota stood up, made her way through the crush to the restroom, and vomited. On the way back, she seriously thought of running over to the racing office and trying to scratch Shameless.

She couldn't do it. She remembered how the filly looked this morning. Shameless had known something was up, and there had been a quality to her that Dakota had never before seen in any of her dad's racehorses. It was electric—that keen, edgy quality only barely contained, that said: I can do this. Dakota could swear to that. Like a soldier who hears the trumpet call, Shameless had already girded her loins for battle.

It was that knowledge that set Shameless apart from other horses. Horses sensed when they were going to race, they got excited. But with Shameless, it was more than that. After only two races, this filly knew what her job was and approached it as a professional. Dakota sensed that keeping the filly from doing her job might destroy her, as surely as a broken leg would do.

She might be fooling herself, but that was the way she felt. "I'm not made for this," she muttered, sitting down at her table in the Turf Club. Her stomach tightened as she watched each race, expecting the worst. Clay joined her, his own expression guardedly optimistic. "His time was slow," he said, in answer to her questioning gaze. "At least he came back all right. That's the main thing."

"Why do people do this to themselves?" Dakota demanded. "There's so much damn risk, and so little reward. Most of those stables out there won't break even, and they're just setting themselves up for heartache. We're running for the big money, but think about all those people who run their horses in claiming races, that never have a good horse. They can lose their animal anytime. Or come back with an empty halter. And for what? A couple of thousand dollars that wouldn't pay for feed and vet bills? It's like the jockeys. Thirty-five bucks a ride to risk your life, maybe end up paralyzed for the rest of—"

"They can't help it. It's in the blood."

"Like my father," Dakota said bitterly.

"Like your father." Clay caught her gaze, his own eyes knowing. "Don't be too hard on him. That's the siren call of the racehorse business. It's older than God. My horse can beat your horse. The need to prove it is irresistible."

"It's nerve-wracking, is what it is."

He grinned. "You've been bitten by the bug."

"I guess so," she said gloomily. "I guess that's why I feel like I've got malaria."

Clay smoothed out the race program. "You ready to see Runaway Train in action?"

"Shameless can beat him," Dakota said automatically, then heard what she'd said and laughed.

"He's undefeated."

"So is Shameless." But she knew that the gray colt was trained by one of the top trainers in the business, and he had been running against the finest quarter horses in the nation. Shameless was still untested. Runaway Train had won the Ruidoso Futurity, the first leg of the triple crown—the race she's passed up for the less intimidating Santa Cruz County Futurity. Not for the first time did she wonder if she'd gotten in over her head. How would Shameless have fared against Runaway Train in the Ruidoso? She'd never know.

"That's the horse that'll win the Rainbow," the man at the next table said to his wife.

Clay handed her the binoculars. "Look at him. He ought to be in a painting."

Dakota had to agree. Runaway Train was slate gray, with a tail that started out almost black and ended up purest white. He was well muscled and mature for his age, with a springy step and a mind set on business.

He won his race easily, in the fastest time so far, despite the greasy, muddy track conditions and the blurring rain. Dakota stared gloomily at the track, trying to smother the dread that crept up like a rising water level in her chest. "I'd better go home and get ready."

"I guess that's it." She checked the girth one last time. The rain hadn't let up all morning. They stood under the overhang in the saddling paddock, waiting for the harrow to finish going over the track. The post parade had been scrapped because of the rain; they would go directly to the gate. There would be no time to warm up, which added to Dakota's nervousness. The wait was interminable, although Shameless stood as still as a statue. Only Dakota could feel the restrained power underneath the gleaming coat.

The paddock at Ruidoso resembled a circular courtyard. The saddling enclosure, divided into ten open-ended stalls facing the stands, made up half the circle. One or two horses trampled the radius in the rain, already too hyped up to stand quietly. The rain fell on the round terrace of flowers and brick in the center, where proud owners usually gathered to see their horses saddled. No one was there today.

The paddock identifier raised his hand. The first horse lunged out of his stall as the jockey swung aboard, followed by the two horse. Dakota had drawn the number eight post position—closest to the yelling crowds, which might serve as a distraction. But she was glad they hadn't drawn the inside rail, which looked like soup. She handed Shameless to Ernesto and walked to the end of the shed to get Tyke.

As Dakota led the filly down the track, she tried to calm herself. It would all be over in the space of a few seconds.

Four hundred yards, that was all. She prayed like crazy, from the foxhole of her own making. Please, please, please, God, let her get through this all right. I don't care if she wins, I don't care if she comes in last, but please let her come out of it all right.

Tyke lost his footing and nearly went down, sending Dakota's heart into her mouth. The filly had mud caulks on her shoes, but it wasn't slipping that Dakota was worried about. Shameless's punishing stride dug deep into a track, and moving all that extra real estate would add to the stress on those fragile legs.

Dakota saw Clay ahead, ponying his colt, Dangerously. She wished she could talk to him. He would know just what to say.

They reached the gate, walking in a circle as they waited to load. Right before she handed the filly to the gate man, Dakota whispered in the dark ear, "Go with God."

Then she rode her horse over to Clay to watch the break.

The gates clattered open and Shameless took off like a rocket. For a moment Dakota couldn't see any leader in the surging tide of horseflesh, especially from where she sat Tyke, behind the gate. She could barely hear the loudspeaker, but thought she could hear the word "Shameless."

The horse to beat (although technically, the only thing they really needed to beat was the time) was a filly named Rockette Fuel. Dakota knew she was running from the fifth post position, a flashy chestnut with a blond tail.

All thought of breakdowns was forgotten as Dakota watched Shameless run. The filly's hindquarters bunched, propelling her like a jackrabbit down her lane.

"Come on, girl, come on girl come on come on—"

The caller's voice broke through her mantra. "Africanized Bee at the extreme outside, Dangerously and Rockette Fuel, Shameless coming on strong now, pulling away, Dangerously and Rockette Fuel battling for second, Shameless a length in front—

"It's Shameless with an easy win over Rockette Fuel and Dangerously is third."

Dakota was strong and healthy, but for a moment she felt light-headed enough to faint dead away, if Clay hadn't already clasped her up in his arms.

His kiss was sweet on her tongue, like victory.

"For all I know, it was a neighbor just walking through my yard and looking at the stars," Dakota said.

Clay drummed his fingers on the table. They'd gone to the Cattle Baron's to celebrate, but suddenly he wasn't hungry. "Or it could have been the same person who cut the mares' tails."

"Jerry—"

"He's in Prescott. I talked to a friend of mine last week who's running his horses there."

Her lips parted in surprise. It made him want to kiss her again.

"You shouldn't be alone. Maybe I should move in with you."

Her eyes widened. He could tell that frightened her more than the intruder. "I don't think that's a good idea. The person didn't *do* anything, just stood outside my window for a minute. It might have been my imagination."

"You're hallucinating now? Do you really believe that?"

"I don't know!" She rubbed the bridge of her nose, reminding him briefly of Coke. Only she was far more beautiful than Coke.

He wished she wasn't so skittish, but he guessed she had a right. Divorce had scarred them both. "Describe him."

"I didn't really get a good look. It was just a dark shape, with a hood." She spread her hands. "I thought he might try to sabotage the filly today, but he didn't. Can't we get off this merry-go-round?" She lifted her glass of cabernet. "To Dangerously and Shameless." When he didn't follow suit, she said, "They're in the *Rainbow,* Clay. That's a big thing."

"To Dangerously and Shameless," he repeated, clinking glasses and making a mental note to drive by her house every night between now and the Rainbow. He'd also send a groom over to stay with Ernesto in the trailer.

It was the gloomiest celebration dinner he could remember.

Thirty-One

The weather for the Rainbow Futurity could not be more different from the time trials. The sun was a broiler today, roasting the pine needles on the forest floor to a crisp, filling the air with a smoky tang. Purple thistles crowded the roadsides along with weeds and meadow grass, ripened to green summer fullness. There was one white puffy cloud hanging above the town, as still as a blimp in the neon-blue sky.

Old Glory flew on every street corner and from most of the boutiques, and dresses of red, white and blue—the colors of the All American—shimmered in the windows, encrusted with an embarrassment of riches; rhinestones, sequins and bugle beads. Belgian horses pulled carriages full of tourists, blocking traffic and making Dakota curse.

After bathing the filly earlier in the day, she had treated herself by going into one of those fancy boutiques and mortgaging Black Oak for a new outfit—très Santa Fe, as Rita would say. Buying it had taken longer than she had expected, and now she was running late. Dakota wanted to be at Shameless's stall a full hour and a half before the race. Tapping her fingers nervously to "Amarillo by Morning" on the radio, she fought her way through town in bumper-to-bumper traffic, stopping at McDonald's to scarf down a Big Mac and some Diet Coke. She was so excited that she chewed without tasting, and wouldn't have known the Big Mac from its cardboard wrapper. Her nerves were like tinder, waiting for a spark. Whenever she closed her eyes she saw handprints of red, blinking on and off like a DON'T WALK sign. She hoped it wasn't a warning.

At the barn, Ernesto already had Tyke out and saddled. Earlier, Dakota had braided silver and turquoise pom-poms into his mane and tail.

When she led Shameless out into the sun, the filly's coat gleamed a rich, dark brown. Dakota groomed her some more and sprayed WD-40 on her hoofs to make them shine. As she wrapped Shameless's front legs with racing bandages, she had one ear tuned to the loudspeaker, the other to the barn radio, which gave the race results. "This is Bronko McGugan from the tall pines in Ruidoso Downs . . ."

At last it was time to go. Dakota walked the filly through the maze of dirt roads and hoof-pocked lanes toward the track, so jittery she couldn't concentrate. Someone yelled "hello" to her, and she looked up to see Lucy Tanner leading one of Jack Dougherty's horses back to the barn from the previous race.

A crushing fear blotted out all other thought. Was Tanner here?

Maybe Lucy had come to Ruidoso by herself. With relief, Dakota remembered Rita saying something about Jack looking for a new groom. It was possible—probable, in fact—that Tanner had remained in Arizona.

She wouldn't think about it. There was too much going on, and Shameless had a race to run.

Somehow she made it under the tunnel and into the infield, following the path to the saddling paddock, nodding automatically to the other trainers. She spoke to some of them, but didn't remember what she said. Everything was a jumble of simple actions that had become second nature but were now loaded with importance. Her stomach was a ganglia of tiny wires, each one connected to an emotion: joy, pride, fear, exhilaration. An electric fuzziness gloved her arms. Later, she would remember little about the day except a few snippets. Smoothing the special Rainbow Futurity saddle cloth across the filly's back, admiring Shameless's name and the rainbow emblazoned on it. Walking the filly in the post parade and then watching the jockey warm her up in a canter. The beautiful gray colt, Runaway Train, prancing like a carousel horse . . . She would never remember those agonizing few minutes as she waited at the gate.

A dozen images roiled in her mind—the way Shameless had dominated her Rainbow trial, the mud, the rain, and the image of the dark figure outside her window, the mares' tails—

The gates kicked open in slow motion. She expected the filly to break on top, as she always did. But this time, the four horse, Supercharger, came over and crashed into her, shoving her off course.

Shameless didn't stumble, she didn't fall. But she did lose her rhythm. She floundered, trying to take hold of the track. The other horses were two jumps ahead—an almost impossible distance to make up in a quarter horse race.

Dakota's heart sank. Shameless would not win the Rainbow.

It had all been for nothing.

Coke would have been so disappointed.

The loudspeaker sounded as if from a great distance: "Cash Your Chips goes to the front with A Bully Dash, Death Sun Bimbo on the inside, Runaway Train gaining ground."

The filly finally got going, but Dakota could only watch dully, sure that losing was a foregone conclusion.

And then Shameless put on the afterburners. Impressive, Dakota thought listlessly, but she'd never make up all that ground now. Dakota stared at the retreating horses, unable to dredge up any emotion at all as Shameless gained on the ragged row of stragglers spread across the track.

The filly passed them and homed in on the leaders.

Dakota began to think there might be a chance. But the finish line was too close. She'd run out of ground before she caught them.

Shameless, charging up the ribbon of dirt like the cavalry.

"Runaway Train moving now, it's Cash Your Chips and Runaway Train on the far outside, but here comes Shameless with a late kick, it's Cash Your Chips and Runaway Train, but here's Shameless coming down the middle of the track"

running, running, running for Coke, running

"Cash Your Chips and Runaway Train, Dashforatouchdown coming on, Cash Your Chips holding on gamely, but Runaway Train and Shameless are pulling away"

go baby

"Runaway Train and Shameless"

please

"Runaway Train and Shameless, neck and neck, Runaway Train and Shameless aaaand SHAMELESS! wins the Rainbow Futurity in a photo finish over Runaway Train in an incredible upset, Cash Your Chips holds off Dashforatouchdown for third.

"Hold all tickets."

Next, there was the interminable wait for the stewards to review the race and look at the photo finish. Despite what the announcer said, Dakota was sure that Runaway Train had won. That was what it looked like from her vantage point.

She rode out to meet Shameless, staring at the tote board and willing the flashing numbers to change. She was aware of the noise in the grandstand, a breeze on her hot face.

The numbers stopped blinking. The number on top was five. Shameless had won the Rainbow Futurity!

In a blur, Dakota met the filly and handed her horse to Ernesto.

Clay, meeting his own horse, gave her the thumbs-up sign.

"Can you find someone to take the horses?" Dakota called. "I want you and Ernesto in the winner's circle."

"We'll work it out."

Dazed, she led the filly with her jockey still up through the gap in the fence and onto the rubber bricks of the winner's circle. She stared out at the stands, and suddenly realized how tiny she must look out here, all alone with her winner. Usually, there were whole families standing in the winner's circle, but Dakota had no family, at least not here. She wished that Clay and Ernesto would hurry up.

And then Clay was there, hugging her, and she hugged him

fiercely back. Ernesto held the filly while she was presented with the Rainbow Futurity horse blanket and trophy.

She smiled for the cameras, unable to believe that this had actually happened. After the presentation, Tom Dawson from ESPN touched her arm. She stood beside him as he spoke into the microphone.

"The Rainbow Futurity was won today by a woman trainer with a one-horse stable. But the name McAllister is no stranger to quarter horse racing. Ms. McAllister, did this filly come from Black Oak?"

"My father bred her."

"I take it we'll see more Black Oak horses in the years to come?"

"I . . . don't know." She didn't want to spoil the moment by telling him the Black Oak horses had been dispersed.

"I understand Shameless is nominated for the All American. Are you still planning to run her?"

"I don't see why not." Something about the way he asked bothered her. She followed his gaze, as Ernesto led the filly from the winner's circle. What she saw drenched her in a freezing wave of terror.

Shameless stood with her right foreleg raised above the ground, obviously in pain.

Thirty-Two

Jerry Tanner was the first person Dakota thought of when she saw Shameless's injury. He had somehow found a way to sabotage the filly.

Clay reached for her as she ran past him. "Ernesto says she shin-bucked," he said. "She'll be all right. You've got to get her to the test barn."

Clay was right. She was seeing Jerry Tanners under every bed. It was an accident, pure and simple.

And so Dakota walked Shameless around the test barn, offering her water occasionally. Although she was worried, she couldn't help noticing that Shameless appeared to monitor her own heart rate like a human athlete, and kept moving of her own volition. The filly seemed to know when to drink and when to walk, pulling Dakota along as she limped purposefully around the enclosure. All business.

Considering how hard Shameless ran, she was damn lucky the foot hadn't been planted in the ground when Supercharger came over on her, or he would have twisted the leg as he knocked it, and possibly fractured her cannon bone. But she *had* shin-bucked, and it could mean the end of her All American hopes.

Dakota had the vet meet her at the barn, where he injected the site of the swelling with an enzyme that helped neutralize its effect. Shin-bucks happened often in young horses, and they were very painful.

"She's running in the All American," Dakota told the vet. "Do you think—"

"It's cutting it close."

Even though the All American was almost two months away, the challenge would be in keeping Shameless in racing condition. The filly could recover from the shin-buck in a week, or it could take much longer. Too long a lay off and she'd have to start all over again. Too short, and she could reinjure herself. It would all depend on how good a trainer Dakota was—and luck.

Part Three

The All American Futurity

Thirty-Three

July

The vet told Dakota to confine the filly to her stall for a few days. Dakota kept her in her stall for a week. He told her to walk her for a week and a half. She walked her for three. She knew Shameless would lose condition, but the painful blister on the filly's shinbone remained, and Dakota didn't dare stress the leg for fear that the trauma might cause the bone cover to separate from the bone. She didn't allow herself to think about the All American; if Shameless healed, they would see. But she would not run a sore horse.

Every day she took her to the creek which ran through the heart of Ruidoso Downs, and stood her in ice-cold water. They became a familiar sight; the young female trainer leading the horse who had come out of nowhere to win the Rainbow Futurity. Dakota and Shameless followed the maze of dirt lanes on the backside, occasionally straying onto the forest trails. Sometimes Clay could shake free and join them. Life followed a slow, easy pace. Dakota found herself cherishing the lull. No one stood outside her window—to her knowledge—and no more threats materialized. On the nights she didn't spend in Clay's company, she knew he cruised by her house.

If Clay wanted to move to the next step, he didn't show his impatience. But always there was that attraction between them, never alluded to. An undercurrent of passion, infusing the slightest word or touch with greater meaning.

She told herself they had to go slow, to learn each other again. Last time their passion had been so hot it had consumed them in its own fire. This time—if there *was* a this time—it would be different. This relationship was nothing like the last, and although she occasionally remembered their past with a melancholy yearning, she liked the Clay she knew now much better. It seemed to Dakota that the two people they'd been existed only in a long-forgotten dream. It was increasingly difficult to deny that inevitably, they would be lovers again.

The summer days ticked on, as inexorable as a clock. Roadside thistles gave way to bright masses of yellow New Mexico groundsel, tangles of broad-leaved buffalo gourd vines, and sunflowers. Crows called from the poplars and walnut trees, their harsh voices heralding fall. Dakota began swimming Shameless, to keep her in condition without putting a strain on tendons and bone.

Horsemen generally didn't have much extra time, but they managed to cadge a few hours here and there, abandoning themselves to play. They compiled good times, like photos in an album. The whiz and shimmer of their fishing lines as they fly-fished Rio Ruidoso. The warm smell of wildflowers and pine needles, dust and sweating horses as they explored forest paths. They played pool at the Hollywood Bar, line-danced at the Winner's Circle Dance Club. They tied flies and cleaned tack, studied the Racing Form and condition book, cooked steaks and corn on the cob on Coke's old Weber grill.

And no matter how many times he crunched up her drive, his dark hair unruly and his eyes glinting with humor, she always felt a flutter deep down inside.

She didn't know what would tilt the scale, and move them from friends to lovers.

Dakota usually ate her breakfast in the horsemen's cafeteria. Since she didn't have much to do except walk and swim Shameless, she had a chance to study the other trainers. She learned a lot from observing the successful ones, and she learned even more from the bad ones—they demonstrated clearly how easy it was to ruin a horse's prospects.

A couple of times she noticed Lucy sitting with Rita in the cafeteria. According to Clay, Rita had bought herself a groom's license so she could spend time on the backside. There was no sign of Jerry Tanner. Dakota had asked around. His string was not stabled at Ruidoso. Clay's friend in Prescott said he was still running his horses there, although conceivably he could have driven out here, stood outside her window, then driven back. But that didn't make much sense.

It was easy to forget that anything bad had ever happened. Maybe she really had left the evil behind her. The figure at her window had to have been a neighbor, enjoying the night air. She clung to that belief ferociously, and didn't permit any ugly thoughts to spoil this beautiful, miraculous summer.

Dakota had never felt so at home as she did here. When a representative from the Lone Star Stallion Station called, saying he'd like to meet her at Black Oak and look at Something Wicked, she wished she could say no.

"You have to go?" Clay turned the steaks, took a bottle of Classic Coke from the antique chest and leaned on the railing.

She sighed. "I'm the owner. I can't leave this to Dan."

"As I understand it, this is just a formality. They want to make sure Something Wicked is in good health. If they're paying that kind of money for a stud, I can see why they'd want to take a look at the merchandise. But Dan knows him better than you do."

Dakota slid down the bench out of the encroaching shadow and into the apple cider light of the late afternoon sun. "It'll only be a couple of days, tops. I'm not doing anything here. Shameless isn't due for her first gallop until the end of next week." Despite the warmth of the sun on her back, she felt oddly cold inside. "They'll be taking the last of our mares, too."

He held her in his steady gaze, as if he were trying to read her. "You should be relieved."

"I'm beginning to have second thoughts. I suppose I could stop it . . . no actual money's changed hands yet."

Clay brushed past her as he went to check the steaks, eliciting a fan of goose bumps up her arm. "You'll have a lot to think about on the drive over."

The way things were going, she would probably be thinking about him.

"Why don't you make Ernesto your assistant trainer? That way, if you get hung up, he can work the filly for you."

"I said I will, and I will."

His mouth crooked in a grin. "You're one hell of a procrastinator."

"I'll do it tomorrow, before I go. But I'll only be gone for a few days."

"You never know."

She didn't expect his words to be prophetic.

Thirty-Four

Dakota reached the turnoff to Black Oak in the afternoon. Before she left, she'd made Ernesto her assistant trainer, which gave him official authority to work the filly during her absence. She hated to leave Shameless, even for the weekend, but this trip couldn't be avoided.

If Lone Star had called just one week later, all the demons from hell couldn't have dragged her away. But the only thing Ernesto had to do was pony the filly at a walk and trot around the track. Ernesto had great instincts, and Dakota knew he would handle her filly like a Fabergé egg. She told herself to stop worrying.

As it turned out, there was enough worry to go around—in Sonoita.

When Dakota pulled up, she saw the vet's van parked outside the barns, along with a small knot of people. A backhoe stood off to the side, its very presence ominous.

Her sense of uneasiness turned to dread as Dan came toward her. His face had blanched so that even his freckles were invisible. Bad news. The broodmares?

She heard the oily voice on the answering machine again: I can cut their throats.

"What happened? Is it the mares?"

"It's Something Wicked."

She watched his lips move, unable to take in his words. Numbing fear filled her throat. "Is he hurt? What happened?"

Dan removed his hat. "He's dead."

Dead? Stunned, Dakota walked a few paces toward the stallion barn.

"He's not there. We just buried him."

"You buried him?" Dakota repeated. But the words didn't really register.

"Up on the hill with the others. Coke would've wanted that."

"What happened?"

"We think he hit his head. Hit it just right and it killed him. Found him this morning when I went in to feed."

The mists were clearing. "Hit his head? On what?"

"The roof of the stall, I guess. Something must have spooked him, he must've reared up, and bang, hit one of the struts."

Something about what he said didn't make sense. The ceilings were high, to prevent just such a thing from happening. Still in the throes of denial, Dakota walked over to his stall. It was empty.

There was no blood, but there didn't have to be. If a horse hit his head just right, the blow didn't have to be a bad one. A good hard tap on the poll would mean instant death. But he would have had to jump to get that high, and there was very little room for a horse to gather himself to jump like that. Horses kicked at their stalls, and sometimes reared, but they didn't jump.

Not usually. But freak accidents happened all the time with horses. She should know that by now. She started to shake from the adrenaline rush.

Dan came up beside her. "What rotten luck!" he said with feeling. Dakota studied him. He had the look of a shell-shocked soldier. He swiped at the sweat from the indentation above his upper lip and his hand shook. "We almost had him sold. Just one more day. I can't believe it."

"These things happen," she said, automatically trying to comfort him.

"I know, but this is too much. Goddamn it," he muttered. "I hate to see that kind of waste."

Dakota understood only too well. She felt ill. Her heart lit-

erally ached. Too many horrible things had happened at B___ ___
Oak. . . .

Too many. "Do you think someone might have done this?"

"What? Hit him on the head? Why would someone want to
do that?" He stared at her, his eyes turning bright as the realization hit. "You mean the threats? But they were against
the broodmares."

"No," Dakota said heavily. "They were against me. Maybe
this was the one way they could get at me."

"The sheriff said it was just a prank."

"This isn't a prank."

He shook his head slowly. "I don't know . . ."

"What did the vet say?"

"The same thing we thought."

"But he didn't do an autopsy."

"What was the point? The horse hit his head. It happens.
I thought I should bury him—"

Dakota brushed past him and walked over to Ames. "May
I see the report?" she asked.

He handed it to her. "I'm sorry, Miz McAllister. It's a terrible thing."

She looked at the paper in her hand, which was signed by
Dr. Jared Ames, DVM.

"You need to sign it," he said. The paper certified that one
nine-year-old bay stallion named Something Wicked had died
due to a trauma to the head. A string of long medical words
described the exact area of the injury.

"Just a minute. Shouldn't you have autopsied him?"

"The diagnosis was obvious."

"But you know someone has been threatening my horses!"

Jared Ames's mouth set in a stubborn line. "Don't tell me
my business, young lady."

She closed her eyes, remembering the day she saw Something Wicked breed the dummy mare. The thought of that
beautiful stallion lying in a grave, his nostrils and eyes
clogged with dirt, his coat dull and stiff—

Did she dare impose another indignity on him? He was
gone. Why not let him lie? Then she thought of Shameless's

close call. Someone had already made an attempt on her life. What if Something Wicked's death was planned, too? There might be some proof that someone had killed the stallion. She could not let it go. "You'll have to dig him up."

"Dig him up? Are you crazy?" the vet demanded.

"I shouldn't have to tell you your job," she replied stiffly. "When a horse dies of unnatural causes, it should be autopsied. Especially a valuable stallion like Something Wicked."

"What in the hell do you know about it? I've been taking care of Coke's horses for seventeen years, and I haven't had any complaints!"

"I want an autopsy done on this horse. If you won't do it, I'll get another vet, and if I do, he'll be taking care of these horses from now on."

He glared at her for a full minute. She matched him stare for stare. At last he yelled, "Fred!"

Fred Garvey, a local builder who owned the backhoe, detached himself from the crowd.

"Miz McAllister wants us to go back up there and dig him out!"

"You'd better use shovels," Dakota said.

He shot her a look of such enmity that she stepped back involuntarily. To hell with that. "I'll watch, if you don't mind."

"You're the boss."

They trudged up the hill. Dakota choked back tears as she saw the once-magnificent animal hoisted out of his grave. He'd been wrapped in a tarp, secured by straps. His legs stood straight out, reminding her of the plastic toy horses she'd had as a child.

Bolin removed the tarp and Ames stepped forward. He lifted the lip and called out the tattoo number. Dakota looked down at the tattoo to see for herself, then down at the clipboard through tear-blurred eyes. She might at least *look* like she knew what she was doing.

"I'll have to move him to the clinic," Ames said. "The way

his legs are sticking out, we'll need a cargo truck. It's going to cost you."

She swallowed her bile. "Then it'll have to cost me."

Later that afternoon, when Something Wicked had been hauled away, the full impact of his death hit Dakota.

Someone had killed him. She was sure of it. The same someone who had sent her the notes, the same someone who cut the mares' manes and tails. The same person who had put oleander in Shameless's feed.

They had struck her at her heart. The only thing that could hurt her worse was for them to have succeeded in killing Shameless.

Dakota dove into the pool and swam laps for over an hour. She swam like an automaton, back and forth, her mind clicking over like a stopwatch. She swam and she mourned, letting her grief propel her from one end to the other, her arms scything the water and legs kicking out behind her. Visions filled her inner eye, of the beautiful stallion that had been the heart's blood of Black Oak, galloping in the pasture, nodding his head over the stall door as the groom approached with his grain. His coat the color of polished mahogany, his black tail streaming out behind him as he ran, the play of sunlight on his rippling muscles. His inquisitive, liquid brown eyes. And then she saw him lying flat on the earth, lifeless, all the grace and beauty gone out of him.

Her tears mingled with the pool water. She felt cold at her very core. Violated, raped. Her heart was a tangle of twisted wires, burning with anger, with pain, with grief. That someone could do such a horrible thing . . . to destroy an innocent animal. Whoever it was, he had earned her hatred for all time.

When she emerged from the pool, her resolve had hardened. If the autopsy showed the horse had been killed, she would *make* the sheriff listen. If the sheriff's office could do nothing, she would.

But first, she had a phone call to make. It wouldn't be

pleasant. To everyone in the quarter horse racing industry, Something Wicked's untimely death would be just another black mark against Black Oak. To her, it was devastation.

Drying off and wrapping a towel around her waist, she went in to place a call to the Lone Star Stallion Station.

The autopsy showed that Something Wicked had hit his head against something solid and flat, about four inches across. It could have been a strut, but more likely it had been the top of the stall doorway.

For Something Wicked to hit his head at that angle, he would have to have been partway out the door. The most likely scenario, the vet told her, was that he was being led out of the stall, had reared up, and hit his head.

Someone had been in the process of leading Something Wicked out of his stall when he died between ten P.M. and midnight, the night before Dakota arrived.

Who would take a stallion out late at night, except someone bent on hurting it? The mark on the horse's head could have been made by a two-by-four, for all she knew, although from the angle, the person wielding it would have had to hit the horse from above.

Dakota remembered the note, TRY AND TRY AGAIN. She expected to hear from whoever was doing this, by phone or by note. Obviously, he was the kind of person who liked to gloat. But no note materialized, and the answering machine recorded only business calls and hang ups. Dakota hated waiting for the other shoe to drop. Monday morning she had breakfast at the Cactus Flower Cafe, trying to return her life to some semblance of normalcy. That was where she heard that Jerry Tanner had been barred from Prescott Downs. Wherever he was, he wasn't in Prescott.

Frightened and restless, Dakota wandered aimlessly around the barns. She found herself at Something Wicked's stall. Ruben, the stallion's new groom, was in the process of cleaning his stall out. The day before yesterday, a horse had lived here. Now the bedding was gone, the halter with his name on it put away, his water and feed buckets stored in the tack room.

As she watched Ruben rake the aisle, she wondered if he might be obliterating evidence.

"Ruben, when you started raking, were there any footprints outside the stall?"

"All over. Looked like Grand Central Station, you know?"

Dakota reached up to touch the stall door frame, and was rewarded for her efforts by picking up a sliver. She sucked her finger, tried to pick it out, then looked up again.

Was that blood? Or just a flaw in the wood? It was hard to tell. "Ruben, get me a footstool, would you?"

Footstool in place, Dakota ran her hand over the door frame. One patch was rougher, and she narrowly avoided getting jabbed by another splinter.

Something Wicked had hit his head on this door frame. It would be almost impossible to get a horse to rear up and hit his head in the exact spot that would kill him. Could it have been an accident, after all?

She went to look in on the other two stallions. Darkscope, Dan's horse, paid no attention to her. He paced around and around the stall, disappearing into the darkness every few moments to kick viciously at the back wall. His coat was dark with sweat and lather foamed the underside of his wringing tail like shaving cream. The stallion must have sensed Something Wicked's death, although he had been kept out of sight and scent of him. As she watched, he pawed the bedding of his stall, wheeled in rage, and let go a deafening whinny. He started pacing his stall again.

"He's been like that ever since Thursday morning." Marcie, one of the broodmare grooms, was lounging against the doorway. "Fighting mad. I don't think he likes his new groom."

"I thought Something Wicked had the new groom."

Marcie shrugged. "There's a whole lot of turnover around

here. What with most of the staff getting laid off after the dispersal."

Something else to feel guilty about. Sell off the stock and you ended up cutting jobs drastically. "How long have you been here?" she asked Marcie.

"Three years. Isn't he gorgeous?"

"He's a good-looking horse." A good-looking horse, but a dud. Dakota knew it was unfair to rail against fate, to wonder why Something Wicked had died, and this horse had been spared. She stifled the uncharitable thought.

"I like to come and look at the stallions, whenever I get a chance. They're so much more fun than the mares. It's like, you never know where you stand with a stud. They're unpredictable. But you take the time, you get to know 'em. This guy likes licorice. Gobbles it up. I'm not supposed to feed him, but I can't see it hurts anything." She walked up, pulled a package of black licorice out of her pocket. "Might calm him down," she added, holding the black candy out flat on her hand.

The horse came forward, sniffed the candy, then turned his back.

"That's funny," Marcie said. "He must be really ticked."

"It's been a bad week for everybody."

Marcie shrugged. "I guess so."

Dakota followed Marcie out, on her way to see Canelo Red, who had been her father's best stud for eighteen years. He looked so frail. She stroked his nose, telling him that she wouldn't let anything happen to him. It seemed a safe promise, since no one would have anything to gain by destroying an old pensioner on his last legs. But unreasoning fear for the horse swept through Dakota, and she clung to his neck, crying into his dark red coat. He stood patiently, and let her cry herself out.

Later that afternoon, when the phone finally rang, Dakota let the answering machine pick it up. It wasn't Something Wicked's killer. It was Clay.

"Why didn't you tell me?" he demanded.

"I don't know," she replied dully. "I guess I don't want to talk about it. I only called Ernesto to make sure Shameless was all right."

"She'll be doubly fine tonight. I'm bunking in with Ernesto."

"You don't have to do that."

"Someone just killed your top stallion. I wouldn't turn down any help, if I were you."

Weary, she didn't argue. "Thanks. I appreciate it."

"We'll sleep in shifts. You can call us anytime. What did the autopsy say?"

Dakota told him.

"It's not definitive, then."

"No."

"It could have been an accident."

"Maybe."

"Did you ask Dan if he had someone move the horse?"

"Why would he do that in the middle of the night?"

"Maybe Something Wicked had colic. Maybe he was nervous, and the groom felt he should move him for his own safety. There are a dozen possibilities."

"Wouldn't his groom say something?"

"Not if he was negligent. Handling a stallion is a tricky business at the best of times."

It occurred to Dakota that Ruben must have been assigned to Something Wicked since she left for Ruidoso. She was surprised, since Jimmy, the stallion's regular groom since March, had been working out well, according to Dan.

Could Ruben have underestimated Something Wicked, and let the high-strung horse get out of control?

"When are you coming back?"

"As soon as possible."

"I miss you."

She paused, then said with feeling, "I miss you too."

And later, as she lay in bed, she felt the familiar ache that was one part desire and one part loneliness. She wished he were here now, lying beside her, like two spoons in a drawer.

Longed for the strong circle of his arms, for the gentle rasp of his chin against her shoulder.

What purpose did their enforced celibacy serve? What had it accomplished, other than frustration?

Thirty-Five

Trish saw the guy again at El Prado Mall, where she and Billy had gone to get an ice cream cone.

He was standing in line behind her at the ice cream counter, so that when she turned around to say something to Billy, he caught her eye. As their eyes met, all the fear, the sheer panic, came back to her like a bad dream. She turned away hurriedly and bumped Billy, and the dollar bills he was using to pay for the ice cream fell out of his hand. "Hey, look out!"

Trish's legs shook. She could feel the guy staring at her back, imagined his gaze as death rays aimed at her shoulder blades. He was probably wondering where he'd seen her before. Any minute he'd make the connection. He *had* seen her that night when she and Billy had tried to hide among the oaks on the hill. She knew it.

Lynette, behind the counter, handed her the cone. Trish's mouth went dry, and the thought of eating anything made her distinctly queasy. But she took the cone anyway, feeling the sticky substance drip onto her fingers.

"You gonna eat that, or just look at it?" Lynette asked.

Trish felt as if she'd been submerged in water. She could barely hear Lynette, just see her lips move.

"You're dripping."

Trish looked blankly at the cone and her fingers. "Oh."

She heard the squeak of a sneaker on linoleum behind her and heard a long, drawn-out masculine sigh.

"Come on, Trish. The man wants to order."

The man. Feeling like a prisoner on death row, Trish allowed Billy to lead her away.

Once outside, adrenaline hit her. Galvanized by fear, she started around the side of the building in a run-walk. Billy caught up with her. "What the hell's wrong with you?"

"That was him."

"Who?"

"The *guy*. The guy who ran Mr. McAllister off the road."

Billy shook his head. "I don't think so."

"I know it's him!"

"Neither one of us got a good look at him. It could be anybody."

"I saw his truck a couple of weeks ago."

"What kind was it?"

"I don't know."

"Then how do you know it was the right one?"

"The shape."

He snorted. "The *shape?*"

"Yes! The shape. What's so funny about that? If you know so much, why don't you tell *me* what kind of truck it was?"

"It was a Ford. One of those older ones, late sixties, early seventies. With a tire strapped on the front."

The realization hit Trish hard. "You said you didn't know. You said there wasn't any point going to the sheriff because we didn't have any information. But you knew all along, didn't you? Just what kind of truck it was."

He waved his arm wildly. "Take a look around! They're all over the place. Hundreds of 'em. It was so dark I couldn't even tell the color."

"How many trucks like that have a tire in front?" She started toward the front of the mall again, her anger with Billy pushing panic aside. "I'll bet it's out in the parking lot right now."

"Jeez, Trish, you're full of shit."

"You scared to look?" she challenged him.

"No way."

"Well?" She stood there, her arms crossed. "Go ahead."

"I will." He marched around the side of the building.

Trish followed, her heart beating like a jungle drum. She paused at the corner and peered into the lot. She almost jumped out of her skin.

The truck stood all by itself, close to the road.

From here, she could feel its malevolence, as if it had a soul of its own. It radiated out toward her, unspeakably evil in the flat, ovenlike heat.

Sunlight glinted off the chrome strip above the windshield and gleamed opaquely on the metallic cucumber-green finish, which had been scoured dull by the elements in places and oxidized in others.

Billy skirted it gingerly, trying to look casual, then came back. He looked scared.

"I told you."

"Then where's the tire?"

"Maybe he took it off," she said.

"Maybe it was never there to begin with. It's just an old truck." But she could tell from his expression that he was nervous, too.

Trish felt suddenly cold, although it had to be ninety degrees. "He could come out any minute."

"So? We're not doing anything."

"He'll recognize—"

"Trish, he didn't see us!" Billy stepped out into the parking lot again.

"What are you doing?"

"If it had a tire on it, there might be something to show for it, like bolts or something."

"Be careful."

Hands in his jean pockets, Billy strolled over to the truck, glanced down. He looked around, then hunkered down near the front grill. He stood up again, his gaze darting right and left, then trotted back to Trish. "There was something on the front. Holes, kind of. Could have been made for bolts."

"It's the one," Trish said.

"Hey, not so fast—"

"I'm going to the sheriff."

"You can't! If our parents find out, we're up shit creek."

She started walking. The sheriff's department was just around the corner, and this time she wasn't about to chicken out. She couldn't live like this anymore, always worried that the guy would recognize her and kill her, too. At last Billy caught up with her, kicking at rocks and cursing a blue streak. But at least he came along.

Dakota was packing when Alice entered her room. "Dan wants to see you. He says it's urgent."

Dan stood in the foyer. His face was pinched and there were dark shadows under his eyes. "I have to go," he said. "Marie's taken a turn for the worse. They think she's rejecting the heart."

"Can I help in any way?"

He nodded. "Three owners are coming for their mares today, could you make sure they get them okay?"

"No problem."

"Two of the grooms are new this week, so they won't have a clue."

"I'll see to them. You'd better go. Don't worry about a thing."

He looked relieved. He opened the door, lost control of it so that it nearly slammed back into his face, and was gone.

Dakota's heart went out to him. What hell it must be to live from moment to moment like that. He had an hour's drive to Tucson, and at the end of it, who knew what he would find?

She sent up a fervent prayer for Marie Bolin.

"You sure that's the truck you saw?" Derek Blue asked, driving past the dark green Ford.

"It was dark, and there was a board across it . . ."

"It's got holes where someone bolted it to the front," interrupted Billy.

Derek noticed a sticker in the rear window—a temporary license. He wrote down the number and radioed it in.

"What about the man? You sure he was the driver?"

Trish looked doubtful. "I couldn't tell."

"He wears the same kind of cap," Billy said.

"What kind is that?"

"You know. A gimme cap."

That described half the men—and some of the women—in the county. As a matter of fact, there were probably a thousand trucks like this one in Santa Cruz County alone. The Ford F-100 through F-350 was a popular truck. They lasted forever and were great for farm work. He could name three racehorse trainers who had trucks just like it. His own brother-in-law had one, as a matter of fact. It looked like hell, but it could run on fumes. Better than that fancy new vet's van Jared held such great store by, which had been in the shop three times since he bought it new last year. They didn't make things like they used to, that was for sure. "What makes you think this is the one?"

"It's just a feeling," Trish said.

"Why don't you two come back and give me a statement."

Billy slumped in the seat of the Bronco. "Shit," he muttered under his breath.

After the kids had gone, he had Communications run the license number through Motor Vehicles.

The truck belonged to Blane Andrew Griffith, but the title had been transferred within the last month.

The previous owner was Jerry Tanner.

It was no secret that Jerry Tanner hated Coke McAllister.

Derek tapped his teeth with his pencil eraser. He'd had a feeling about Coke's death from the beginning. There was a certain vindication in all this, he thought, as he walked to the evidence locker.

He took the evidence envelope of tire scraps down from the cupboard. If what Billy and Trish said was true—and he had no reason to doubt them—then the tire scraps finally

made sense. They hadn't come off a tire on the ground;
they'd come off the tire in the front.

Derek knew a lot of people who put tires on their trucks to
protect the grill when they had to push things around. Judging from the pile of junk in Jerry's stable yard, he had a lot
of call for a rig like that.

He laughed, remembering Jerry's other truck, the one with
the faulty starter. Why go to a junkyard and pay money for
a rebuilt starter when you can just push it to get it going?
Tanner had always been a lazy son of a bitch, but that took
the cake.

The board and the tire were probably long gone. If Jerry
had shredded the tire in the course of running Coke off the
road, he wouldn't keep it around to incriminate him. He'd
sold his truck pretty damn quick.

Derek sat in his swivel chair, too excited to think about
anything else. At last he picked up the phone and dialed the
number for the impound lot in Tucson. The Pima County
Sheriff's department had a contract with Santa Cruz County
to store their vehicles there.

Coke's truck had been gone over by investigators when it
was first brought in, but the results were inconclusive. Now,
Derek knew what to look for.

Although the pickup was pretty beat up, most of the surface scrapes had happened before the accident. Even so, he
found new dents and one broken taillight.

The tailgate, which had been thrown into the truck bed,
had buckled in. The metal was flattened over a wide area, as
if it had been pressed, not rammed. There were also a few
isolated dents on each end, which Derek thought might be
glancing blows, but he had little doubt most of the contact
had been made dead center.

Coke must have wired the tailgate shut at one time. The
end of the wire was sharp enough to cut a tire, because bits
of black rubber still clung to it.

* * *

Dakota made sure the mares went off with their respective owners. Two of the owners had paid her on the spot, which was great news for Black Oak. That, plus the money from the Rainbow Futurity, would make life one heck of a lot easier.

She walked toward the house, detouring by Dan's office at the sound of the phone. It was a Mr. R. J. Price from New Mexico, who had bought one of the mares at the dispersal sale. Apparently, Dan had neglected to send him the medical records.

"Mr. Bolin's been called out of town on an emergency," Dakota told him. "I have no idea where to put my hands on them."

The owner said he could wait for the records, but he wanted to know if the mare had always had difficulty foaling.

Dakota realized that Dan had all the files up at his house, and was about to say she couldn't be of help. Abruptly, she remembered the ledgers in the bookcase, labeled by year. She'd looked through them before. The ledgers were really for financial record-keeping, but Dan used them to keep track of each mare; a day-to-day record of their progress. If Mr. Price's new mare had had problems foaling before, there was a good chance that Dan had written it down in the ledger. "Let me check and I'll call you back," she said.

She looked through the current year, but the mare was still in foal at the time of the dispersal sale. Dakota pulled down the ledger from last year. Last March, the mare had bled internally, but both she and the foal had survived under Dr. Ames's care. Dakota called the owner back and gave him the information, her gaze wandering down the page as she did so.

The owner thanked her. As her gaze trailed down the page, she told him that Dan would send him the medical records as soon as he got back.

Her gaze lingered on a familiar name. Shawnes Soliloquy, Alydar's love interest. Dakota smiled as she remembered the way the dog had cavorted around the patient, sweet-faced mare.

She was about to close the ledger when the words jumped out at her. "Shawnes Soliloquy did not take."

Did not take. That meant that last year, Shawnes Soliloquy did not conceive.

Dakota stared at the entry, her mind going ninety miles a minute. Shawnes Soliloquy *had* conceived. She'd foaled not long after Alydar had played with her in the pasture.

It had to be a typo. Intrigued by the mystery, Dakota jotted down the tattoo number and walked out to the pasture. Shawnes Soliloquy's tattoo matched the one in the book.

That was funny. Dan would have to look at the tattoo before writing it in his book. He'd have to know he had the wrong horse. Of course, he'd been distracted lately.

Dakota knew Dan didn't like her. He didn't want her here. But she'd always thought it was because he liked doing things his own way. Could he have made other errors besides this one? Perhaps that was why he didn't want her to see the broodmare files; to cover up his mistakes. Maybe there was more behind his dislike for her than she'd thought. Maybe he was afraid that if he couldn't handle things anymore she would fire him. He couldn't let that happen, not in his situation where every penny counted.

Alice called to her that she'd made some lunch. Dakota walked back to the house, wondering if her broodmare handler was falling apart, and what she could do about it if he had a nervous breakdown.

Thirty-Six

"Where the hell is he?" Derek Blue couldn't stifle his frustration. Jerry Tanner's trailer was gone and the corrals were empty.

"He's not in Prescott," Ray Garcia, Derek's partner, said. "I checked with them this morning. He left there two weeks ago, after he was suspended."

"Shit!" Derek kicked at a dirt-crusted can of baked beans. "Are there any other race meets going on right now?"

Ray shook his head. "Flagstaff was the only other one, and it lasted just a few days over July Fourth."

"So where is he?"

"New Mexico would be my guess."

"Might as well look around. Don't want to put the search warrant to waste."

Ten minutes later Ray called out, "I found something."

Derek walked over. Ray stood over a two-by-four lying in a ditch. One quarter of the way up was a dark substance, gluing red-brown hairs to the wood.

"Blood," Derek said.

"That looks like animal hair."

"Looks like old Jerry's still up to his old tricks."

"You think he killed that horse at Black Oak?"

Derek nodded. "Stands to reason. He hated the father and he hates the daughter. If we could just find that son of a bitching tire . . ."

"What kind of truck does he drive?"

"Old Chevy. Why?"

"Is that him?" Ray motioned to the dirt road, where an aqua-colored truck pulling a dilapidated horse trailer slowed to turn into the yard.

"Right this way, sir," the hostess said, leading Clay, Rita and Lucy to a table near the window at the Inn at the Mountain Gods resort. As they threaded between tables, Rita clung to him, the outline of her breast rubbing seductively against his arm under the light summer suit she wore. Her perfume was overwhelming.

To the people in the restaurant they must look like a family—an idea that made him uncomfortable.

Rita had chosen to ignore the embarrassing scene in Sonoita, when she had yelled at him for leading her on. Since Dakota left, she called him constantly, trying to get him to do things with her. Today she'd used good old-fashioned guilt.

"It's Lucy's birthday, and she doesn't have a soul here to celebrate with. Her father hasn't called her in a month. She had to hear from a stranger that he was warned off at Prescott."

So here they were. Clay felt like a boy dressed up to go at a function that bored him. He resolved to get through it the best he could and, after Lucy was gone, tell Rita again that there was no future to their relationship. At this rate, he'd have to tell her over and over again. Until she got it.

Being here didn't help his case. He stared dismally out the window at the lake sparkling in the sunshine, and thought how good it would be if it was Dakota across from him instead of Rita.

It didn't help that Rita was a beautiful, alluring woman. It didn't help that he felt a sexual stirring as he watched her remove her jacket. What did he expect? He wasn't a eunuch.

When Lucy excused herself to look around, Rita leaned forward, her lips glossy and her voice low. "You'd think her dad would call her on her birthday. I know he's got his troubles, but he *is* her father."

Clay leaned back to keep Rita's perfume at bay. "Do you know if he left Prescott?"

"I have no idea." Rita shook out her linen napkin and placed it on her knee. Every movement was calculated to entice. "Thank God Jack had an opening at his stable. I shudder to think of her living in that squalid little trailer, not to mention the humiliation! I hope this lunch cheers her up. She's been let down so many times, it's important for her to know we're not going to dump her."

Her message was clear. Dakota had dropped Lucy like a hot potato, consigning her to a horrific existence with a man like Jerry Tanner. In comparison, Rita looked unselfish and loving. It was a pity, he thought, that her seductive clothing precluded her from also appearing maternal.

"I bought her a little something—a necklace from The Ghost Shaman. A running horse—all gold."

"She should like that." The Ghost Shaman was one of the most expensive boutiques in Ruidoso.

"The poor kid. She just needs a little guidance, and she could become anything she wanted. I think coming to Ruidoso has made all the difference in the world to her."

He had to admit that Lucy looked happier than he had ever seen her. There did seem to be real affection between the beautiful, wealthy widow and the lonely child. They'd come a long way from their shaky start at the Mountain Oyster Club.

But Rita had to get it through her head that he was not the third component in this happy little family. Throughout lunch, he maintained his distance, physically and emotionally. Lucy opened her present and read her card aloud, then the three of them explored the resort and walked along the lakeshore after lunch, and all the time he wished he were somewhere else. At least he had the excuse of evening feeding.

He dropped Lucy off at the apartment she shared with two other grooms, and then drove Rita to the Champions Run condominiums.

"Would you like to come in? I've got some new coffee that is out of this world."

He wanted to refuse, but realized that this was his opportunity to end this charade. He followed her in.

"Just let me check my messages," Rita said, brushing past him. She moved like a panther, svelte in her tailored suit, which was more about sex than business. The skirt fell about midthigh and molded to her hips like a second skin. She walked to the answering machine and bent forward at the waist, exaggerating the long, fluid line of her body and displaying an enticing rear view. Her skirt rode up, revealing a smooth expanse of thigh and the creamy lace of her half slip. "This'll only take a sec—"

The answering machine beeped. "It's Jack. I'm trying to get a hold of Lucy." Dougherty cleared his throat. "Her father's been arrested in Arizona."

Clay stared at Rita's stricken face, but his mind was elsewhere. If they'd arrested Tanner, had it been for Coke's murder?

"Oh, God," Rita said. She tottered on her stiletto heels, reaching out for him. If he didn't catch her, she would have fallen. She steadied herself against him and tucked her head against his chest. "She's going to need us more than ever now," she said.

Thirty-Seven

Dakota couldn't believe it. After all this time, they'd caught her father's killer.

"We're holding him for questioning," Derek Blue told her. "The kids saw your dad run off the road, and they ID'd the truck. We're trying to match the tire up now."

Dakota closed her eyes, sighed with relief.

"We also found a two-by-four we believe he used to bludgeon your horse. He says he beat a dog to death with it, but he can't remember where he buried it. Said he got mad at the dog when he was drunk. Pretty convenient, huh?"

Dakota couldn't speak.

"Just thought you should know, so you won't worry."

"Thank you." She set the receiver down, feeling suddenly weak. It had been Jerry. She'd been right all along. He had killed her father out of spite, just as he had killed poor, harmless Something Wicked. Just as he had tried to kill Shameless.

Relief drenched her like a bucket of cold water. Jerry was in jail. She hoped to hell he rotted there.

Dan returned to the ranch later that day. The crisis was temporarily over, although the doctors thought there might be something wrong with the new heart. They were looking for a replacement, but it didn't look good.

"I can stay here a little longer," Dakota said. "If you'd rather be in Tucson with your wife—"

"No! No, it's all right. She's stable for now. I can't be any help there. I just don't know what to do . . ." He turned away from her in anguish, hands in his rear pockets, a big man laid low by circumstances. "It's going to cost so much, but I can't think about that. If we can't find another donor, there's not much they can do."

"Maybe I could help," Dakota said. "I have some money—"

"We're talking hundreds of thousands of dollars! You have that kind of money? Anything else is just a drop in the bucket. Oh, Jesus!" He covered his face with his hands. "I can't believe this, it looked so good, why the hell did it have to happen now?"

There was nothing Dakota could say. He was distracted by his grief, and the only thing she could do was let him work it out. "The offer's there," she said quietly, and withdrew.

Later, Dan came to apologize.

"No apologies are necessary. I don't know how you've borne up under it this long."

He cleared his throat. "I just need to get back to work, get my mind off it."

"Then you want me to go?"

He looked at her gratefully. "There's no need for you to stay around here. You have to get that filly ready for the All American, and there's nothing you can do here. Really."

"I'll go back tomorrow, then."

His relief was palpable.

Later that evening, Marcie caught Dakota as she walked toward the house. "Can I talk to you a minute?"

"Come on in." Dakota opened the door to the office and led Marcie to the study. Marcie sat down, looking at the Route 66 sign on the wall. "Your dad had such great stuff!"

"What did you want to talk to me about?"

Marcie smiled triumphantly, as if she were about to deliver

a bombshell. "The horse in Darkscope's stall isn't Darkscope."

Dakota was at a loss for words. At last she managed to say, "How do you know?" It came out in a croak.

"Well, see, it was simple once it occurred to me. I was real puzzled that Scope didn't like the licorice, you know? I mean he really scarfs that stuff. So I tried him again today, after he'd calmed down a little. No deal. Wouldn't touch it."

"But that doesn't—"

"He wasn't acting like Darkscope, either. Nothing I could put my finger on, but when you're around a horse, you just know. If I wasn't at the wrong stall, I'd swear it was Wicked. So I looked at his night eyes."

"His night eyes."

"You know what they are, don't you?"

"Yes, I know." Night eyes was another name for horse chestnuts, the putty-colored pads on the inside of a horse's legs that had been second and third toes eons ago, when the horse had been a tiny animal called eohippus. "Darkscope has a real unusual one. Looks just like an hourglass."

"How'd you know that?"

"So let me guess. You didn't find an hourglass. Couldn't you have been mistaken?"

"Nope." Marcie stood up. "I'm positive the horse in that stall is Something Wicked."

For a long time afterward, Dakota sat in her chair, stunned. The implications were incredible. If what Marcie said was true, then Something Wicked didn't die. Darkscope had died in his place. How could that have happened?

Hope struggled to the surface, like a spring shoot poking up through the earth after a long winter. If Something Wicked was still alive—

No. Impossible. She'd seen the horse buried. Checked the tattoo herself.

There was an easy way to find out. She had the original AQHA birth certificate for Something Wicked. She also had a copy of the bill of sale to Dan for Darkscope, showing the horse's tattoo number, which matched his tattoo number in the catalog.

She went down to check the horse in Darkscope's stall.

Marcie was wrong. The tattoo didn't match Something Wicked. It matched Darkscope.

Stifling her disappointment, Dakota tried to reconcile what the girl had told her. She'd been here three years; she knew the horses well. Probably as well as a mother would know her identical twins. On the face of it, it didn't make sense that she'd be wrong about something like this.

Still, it didn't alter the facts. Tattoos didn't lie; that was why the American Quarter Horse Association used them. It was impossible to change a tattoo; cutting that part of the lip could cause a horse to bleed to death. The horse in that stall was Darkscope. The horse at Dr. Ames's clinic had to be Something Wicked.

Dakota didn't know what to do. The facts were irrefutable, but her gut told her that Marcie was right.

There was one other way of telling for sure. She could have Something Wicked blood-typed. Blood-typing didn't lie, either.

Jared Ames still had Something Wicked's corpse. She could ask him to do the blood-typing, then send it to AQHA and see if it matched their records.

Dakota remembered the stubborn set of Jared Ames's jaw when she'd told him to autopsy Something Wicked. No doubt he'd give her a fight over this request, as well.

Dakota decided to stay for another couple of days. She needed to find another vet, and wanted to supervise Something Wicked's blood-typing before he was buried again. Her change of plans didn't make Dan happy, but he could hardly argue when she suggested he could go to Tucson and be with his wife. She kept her own counsel regarding Jared Ames. She knew Dan and Ames were good friends.

Gearing up for unpleasantness, Dakota called Dr. Ames to tell him that he would no longer be working for her.

"That's fine by me," he replied curtly. "By fall, you won't have a farm anyway."

"Then you shouldn't mind so much." When she hung up, her stomach ached. She called Clay, got his answering machine. No doubt he was at the track.

Damn, but she missed him! It would have been nice to talk to Clay about what was going on at Black Oak. He'd lived here all these years, so he'd have a better feeling for what was going on.

Dakota remembered that Clay's vet was Beverly Johnson. She called the vet and asked if she would go out to Ames's clinic and do the bloody-typing.

"That could be awkward," Dr. Johnson told her. "Perhaps you'd better have the horse sent to my clinic."

Dakota tried not think about the gruesome aspect of all this. The poor horse was being moved around like an MX missile. She called Dr. Ames back and told him that Something Wicked would be going to Dr. Johnson's clinic. He told her to arrange it herself and hung up.

She ought to write a book on how to make enemies.

Restless, she called Clay again that evening, got the machine again. He called her back late.

"Where were you?" Dakota asked, annoyed.

"Would you believe go-carting?"

"What?"

"I got dragged into going with Rita and Lucy."

The feeling of jealousy that wormed into her heart was unworthy of her. She ignored it, telling Clay about Marcie's revelation, and her decision to fire Doc Ames.

"You've got guts, I'll give you that. Ames worked for your dad for—"

"Seventeen years. So he's told me on numerous occasions. But what else could I do?"

"You really think there's something in what Marcie says?"

"I don't know! It's pretty far-fetched, don't you think?"

Clay was silent for a moment, then said quietly, "That kind of thing's happened before."

"You think Dan and Ames switched the stallions?"

"It wouldn't be the first time. Say you've got five mares ready to be artificially inseminated by Something Wicked, but you only have enough semen for three of them. And there, in the refrigerator, is some of Darkscope's semen. You're under the gun, these mares have to be bred today or it'll be too late. Who's going to know? Especially when those studs look so much alike. Their colts won't be all that different. And you're making out like a bandit, getting paid a Something Wicked stud fee for a Darkscope service. That's two thousand dollars profit on each mare."

"If Coke had done it, it would make sense—not that he would. It was his stallion, and the money was paid to him. But how would it benefit Dan?"

"I don't know. Unless he's got a percentage of Something Wicked."

"I don't think so." But Dan was secretive. If he and Coke had some kind of handshake agreement, she would never know. "Why would they bother to switch the horses at all? If you're artificially inseminating the mares, why not just switch vials?"

"You're right. It doesn't make sense. Something Wicked's a proven producer. They'd only need Darkscope if they ran out of Something Wicked."

"If they did switch horses, wouldn't someone notice the tattoo on his lip?" Dakota asked. "A groom or someone?"

"What's Shameless's tattoo number?"

"I don't know."

"Could you pick Shameless out in a herd of horses that looked just like her?"

"Of course I could."

"Because you know her." He cleared his throat. "Think about it. A groom starts working for Dan. Dan points out the horse he'll be working with. That's Something Wicked, he says. Is the groom going to think any different?"

"No. He's going to accept at face value that Something Wicked is who Dan says he is," Dakota finished for him.

"To that groom, the horse *is* Something Wicked."

"Right."

"But I checked the tattoo on Something Wicked. It's the same as the number on his papers."

"Then I guess we just indulged in a flight of fancy. It's getting tougher to do that kind of thing anyway, with the blood-typing of stallions, and now they're doing it with the foals. With DNA testing up the road, soon it will be impossible to cheat." Clay changed the subject. "When you coming back?"

"I could leave day after tomorrow. I want to make sure Something Wicked gets over to Dr. Johnson's clinic, and it looks like I'm going to have to find someone to take over for Dan while he's in Tucson."

"He's not going to like that."

"I'm thinking that Marcie could do it. He needs an assistant. Someone who knows what's going on here, so that when he has to go to Tucson, everything around here doesn't fall apart. It's only temporary. We won't have any mares left in another month," she added glumly. "So we won't be needing a stud farm manager much longer. He could keep up the grounds, see to old Canelo Red and Cochita, but I don't think he'll like that. Lone Star's taking those last seven mares sight unseen."

"I wish you hadn't agreed to that."

Dakota said nothing, although she regretted it, too. With Something Wicked dead, and the outside mares going home, Black Oak was slowly winding down. Soon it would be empty.

Clay must have sensed her desolation. "The wolf rally's on Friday evening. If you're coming through about that time, why don't you meet me there?"

"All right."

He told her where in the White Sands National Monument the rally would be, and Dakota wrote it down. She wanted to get out of here, before the last of the mares left. Wanted to be with Clay, in Ruidoso, working with her filly, preparing her for the All American. She wished the summer would never end. Because she knew after Shameless's campaign was over, there would be no Black Oak to come home to.

Thirty-Eight

On her way out of town, Dakota stopped by Dan's place to catch him up on what had gone on at Black Oak during his absence. His truck wasn't there, even though he'd called her early this morning to say he would be back for morning feeding.

Dakota was surprised by the uneasiness she felt as she stepped out into the quiet of the morning.

The Bolin house had an empty, shuttered look, as if its occupants had left for good, even though there were several improvements obvious to even the casual eye: a newly blacktopped driveway, a front walk, half completed, the remaining bricks stacked to the side. Even the satellite dish looked new. Coke hadn't paid for his employees' insurance, but had tried to make it up to Dan by giving him a high salary. Still, Dan's private insurance must be enormous, in light of Marie's illness. And yet he was adding improvements to the house.

Dakota wondered if Marie Bolin would ever see these improvements.

A breeze sprang up, making her shiver. She couldn't shake the feeling that she was an intruder here. It was almost as if the house were watching her, a colonial brick extension of a grim, secretive Dan Bolin. Silly, she thought. It's just a house. And a nice one at that. What was scary about privet hedges, carriage lamps, white shutters? Or the covered speedboat in the shiny new driveway?

She was here; she might as well try the barn. It, too, was colonial brick with a gray slate roof. Such a neat stable. Compulsively so.

"Dan?" she called, stifling the urge to whisper. At any moment she expected him to come around the corner, and—

And what? Chase her with a pitchfork? Her imagination was working overtime. She raised her voice. "Dan? Anybody here?"

The barn was as empty as the morning. Dakota walked down the center aisle, surprised to see he had so many young horses. She noticed that all of them were blanketed and wore traveling boots, which was strange—

An engine droned. Dakota shielded her eyes and saw a puff of dust in the distance, coming this way. Her heart went from a trot to a gallop in the space of a second. Her first instinct was to hide. Dan sure as hell wouldn't want her snooping around his barn.

Stupid, the truck's out there in plain sight. All you have to say is you came looking for him before you left for Ruidoso. Which is God's honest truth.

Dakota strode to her truck, started the engine and drove onto the dirt road leading back to the main house.

An unfamiliar pickup pulling a six-horse trailer met her on the brow of the hill. As they drew abreast, Dakota recognized the driver as Rudy Gallego, the horse dealer from Hermosillo. Jared Ames sat on the passenger side. She waved cheerily, hoping she didn't look guilty as hell. The vet's double take was almost comic.

The trailer's brake lights flared and the rig slowed to a halt. Dakota's pulse quickened.

Jared Ames got out of the truck and walked over. "You looking for Dan?"

"I was. I'm headed out for Ruidoso now."

"He's been delayed. Can I give him a message?"

"What? No. No message. I just came to say goodbye." Dakota knew she sounded lame. She had a tendency to babble when she was nervous. "I was just looking at Dan's colts. They sure look good, you can tell they're in perfect health.

You taking them somewhere?" she asked, remembering the traveling boots.

Ames tapped his fingers on the roof of her cab. "Nope. We're just picking up Dan's roping horse. I'm borrowing him for the rodeo in Douglas today. I'll tell Dan you came by."

"Okay." She didn't know what else to say, and he was already walking back to the truck. In another minute the rig started forward again. The horse trailer swayed as it rattled over a cattle guard before disappearing over the hill.

On the drive back to Ruidoso, Dakota's mind lingered on her conversation with Jared Ames. She could have sworn they had come for the colts, since the colts all had traveling boots on, and Gallego was pulling a six-horse trailer. She knew it wasn't any of her business, but it made her uneasy. *Dan Bolin* made her uneasy.

Dakota wondered if there was any link between Dan's colts and Marcie's belief that the horse in Darkscope's stall wasn't Darkscope. She couldn't think of one. Besides, tattoos didn't lie, did they? That was the bottom line.

Just beyond Las Cruces, a black GMC truck with dark windows hurtled past her at eighty miles an hour, making her own vehicle sway in its wake. It looked a lot like Dan's truck.

She had Dan Bolin on the brain.

She reached the gates to the White Sands National Monument around six-thirty in the evening. The rally had kicked off at five o'clock; obviously a plan to beat the heat.

The park ranger had circled the site of the rally on the White Sands map. It was far into the park, she'd told Dakota. After ten minutes of driving, the dusty tangles of saltbush and sage petered out, until there was nothing but huge alabaster swells of gypsum. The road was packed hard and rutted by thousands of tires, looking like a rock-salted patch of slushy highway in the dead of winter. Turnarounds were shallow depressions in the featureless immensity of the dunes.

She passed one of the picnic areas. The ramadas could be

a modern artist's impression of covered wagons. Behind them, the dunes undulated to a backdrop of the Sacramento Mountains to the east, the last rays of sun glittering off the sugary crystals of gypsum. To the west, what little sky was left under the swollen storm clouds made her think of the gradated stain of a toilet bowl after someone has tossed a cigarette in it: grainy, muddy.

Dakota must have traveled miles before she found the wolf rally. A banner stretched across the entrance to the picnic area, declaring it MEXICAN WOLF DAY. One side of the banner depicted a blue and green earth, the other, the sad-eyed face of a wolf.

She'd missed the speeches; they were setting up for the picnic now. Dakota looked around for Clay's truck, but the only vehicle she recognized was Rita's Range Rover.

Cramped from her drive, Dakota slid down from the truck. She was surprised at the stillness of the air, as invasive to her skin as a warm bath. The light was fading, the dull black clouds closing the gap in the sky. As she watched, the sun, a fierce yellow disk, dropped below the San Andres Mountains. The day turned dark. The dunes were a solid gray now, almost blending with the horizon.

There was a stillness about the air, a heaviness, as if the gods were holding their breath.

Dakota tried to pick Clay out at one of the ramadas. Booths had been set up in two rows like a western movie town, and there were knots of people around each one. He must be here somewhere. Her heart beat faster with anticipation as she headed for the booths, barely noticing the neat ranks of colorful environmental T-shirts and outdoor equipment on the tables. Until she came to the WAG booth, which displayed heart-wrenchingly vivid blowups of wolves in traps and hunters standing beside pelts. Her heart flip-flopped and she felt ill to think what had been done to the beautiful, wild predator. She paused before the table bearing petitions, bumper stickers, and fliers.

"Are you a registered voter in Otero County?" asked the fortyish man behind the booth. There were enough ponytails (male and female), beards and baggy pants to fill a Grateful Dead concert, and he was typical.

Dakota shook her head, but put some money in the jar. Now she was flat broke. Smoke drifted across her path, the enticing aroma of barbecued chicken filling her nostrils. She suddenly realized she was starving.

Rita broke from a group of people at the farthest ramada. "Dakota!"

"Hello, Rita."

Rita's lean, tanned body was sheathed in a crisp FREE THEM NOW T-shirt, khaki walking shorts, and new hiking boots. A white plastic visor crowned her hair, which had been frosted blond and was pulled back into a ponytail. A new look. "I have a message for you from Clay," Rita said.

Dakota tensed. She could imagine the spin Rita would put on any message Clay had to give her.

"He has a horse down with colic, so he can't make it. He asked me to go by later," she added. "For support."

Dakota had no answer to that. She might as well leave. It was only another hour to Ruidoso, at the most, and she suddenly longed to see Shameless.

"Dakota! Is that you? Dakota McAllister?" A slender redhead carrying a baby in a denim knapsack on her chest strode toward her.

"Jennie?"

"It's got to be seventeen, eighteen years!"

"What are you doing here?" Dakota couldn't believe her eyes.

"The same thing you are!" Jennie hugged her so hard that Dakota was afraid they would crush the baby, who seemed oblivious to it all.

"Who's the little one?"

"Danny T. Melrose the third. Isn't he gorgeous?" Jennie's grin was infectious. They had been best friends until the seventh grade, when Jennie's family had moved away from Sonoita. "You've got to meet Danny the second." She grabbed Dakota's hand and led her to the green ramada.

"I can't stay long," Dakota said, but Jennie ran over her

like a steamroller. Before long, the two of them were talking old times over sweet, spicy chicken and potato salad. Dakota had forgotten how fun, how full of life, Jennie was. And Dan T. Melrose the second was a perfect mate for Jennie; Dakota felt as if she'd known him all her life.

Dakota hardly noticed that people were gathering up their picnic things and driving away one by one. The wind had sprung up, whistling through the eaves of the ramada, sending streamers of dust down from the dunes.

"Sorry to break this up," Dan said, "but we've got to get this guy to bed."

"I can't believe you live in Las Cruces now." When Jennie had left for North Carolina, Dakota had been positive she'd never see her best friend again.

"Now that you know we're so close, don't be a stranger."

"I live in L.A.," Dakota said. "Or at least I did."

"Take my advice, kiddo. Clay was the best guy—other than Dan—I ever knew. I knew it in the fourth grade and I doubt he's changed. Don't let him get away again."

Dakota walked them to the car and saw them off. She'd loved Jennie like a sister. No, better than a sister. Imagine such a twist of fate getting them back together after all these years!

As she headed for the truck, she noticed Rita and Lucy breaking down the booths. Lucy rolled up the banner and piled it onto a flatbed trailer hitched to a truck that looked a lot like Clay's. Although Lucy also wore khaki hiking shorts, her figure bore a closer resemblance to Magnum P.I.'s Jonathan Higgins than to Rita.

Dakota grinned. Lucy had certainly changed her mind about Rita. She had to give the girl credit, though. Lucy wanted to go to Ruidoso, and here she was. If the teenager was ever to shake Jerry Tanner's influence, that kind of single-mindedness would stand her in good stead.

The wind was strong now, blowing more and more sand up from the dunes, almost obscuring the newly risen moon. Dakota checked her watch. Eight o'clock!

As she walked to the truck, sand blasted her legs and the

wind whipped her hair. The dunes shivered in the pale moonlight, the wind stripping away veil after veil of sand, like Salome's dance before John the Baptist.

That opera had always given Dakota the creeps.

She started the truck and put it in gear—and realized almost immediately that the left front tire was flat.

"Damn!" Getting out of the truck, she surveyed the damage. Completely flat. The tire was much bigger than her Forerunner tires. It would be a real bitch to change.

She located the tire under the truck bed and pulled it out.

"You need some help?" A man in a Cubs cap she recognized from one of the booths stood beside her.

"Please. I can do it," she added hastily. "But I can't do it fast."

The man removed his cap and rubbed his balding head, studied the sky. "Looks like we're in for a storm. Gonna be dark soon. Why don't you sit down and make yourself comfortable, and I'll fix this tire."

"I could help."

"Don't need it." He hunkered down near the tire, dismissing her.

Well, she wasn't about to turn down his aid. There were only a few cars left, and most of them were leaving. The wind howled now, like an angry cat, and the sand whirled around her. Headlights stabbed through the white scrim of sand as cars continued to file out of the picnic area. It was unsettling to be out here so late, but it would be worse if she were all alone. She was glad the man had stopped to help.

Rita drove by, honking her horn. She didn't bother to offer any help. Dakota could swear she was smiling. Lucy followed, towing the trailer stacked with wood and tables. In another fifteen minutes, the place would be deserted.

She sat on the picnic table under the ramada, head bowed and eyes shut against the stinging wind. It would be a nightmare just driving out in this, but she sure as hell wouldn't stay here. She'd ask the good Samaritan if she could follow him out.

"All done," a male voice said right at her elbow.

"I don't know how to thank you."

"It's nothing. Wouldn't want to be stuck out here much longer," he said. "I live in Las Cruces, and I know what these sandstorms can do. You take care, now."

The wind rose to a scream as if to punctuate his advice.

"Can I follow you out?"

"No problem. I'll pull out first and wait for you."

Exceedingly grateful, Dakota hopped into the truck. She turned the ignition, relieved to hear the strong hum of the big engine. The lights didn't cut through much—she figured visibility to be about five feet ahead. Her truck had yellow fog lights low on the bumper, but even these did little but reflect yellowly off the road. The moonlight made things worse, catching the tiny particles of gypsum and spinning them crazily, like a snowy TV screen.

She felt all alone, wrapped in a cocoon of strange bluish-white light.

Putting the truck into gear, she drove forward until she saw two pinpricks of red: the taillights of her good Samaritan.

Visibility got worse. She had to creep up to within three feet of the car in front of her, squinting against the incredibly luminescent whiteness. The wind screamed at the edges of the windows, clawed at her nerves.

The drive was taking forever. Dakota's eyes strained as she tried to pick out the two red lights, her only frame of reference in a white world. The whistling wind tore her nerves into rags, and her neck ached from stretching it out as she peered through the windshield. They were crawling, which was just fine with her.

The heater wasn't working. Damn. She looked down, saw the problem, and moved the knob. Warm air flooded onto her knees. Her glance darted forward again, automatically seeking out the taillights of her good Samaritan, which had been her umbilical cord to the outside world.

They were gone.

Just like that.

She'd only looked down for a second. How could they have disappeared so quickly?

Panicked, she hit the brake. The truck died. She turned the key and the starter growled a bit, then caught. Dakota put it in gear, and the damn thing stalled again. She waited for a few moments, wondering if she'd flooded the engine.

A loud thump! sounded simultaneously with a jolt that banged her chest against the dash, and the Ford rocked on its wheels.

Someone must have been following her, and ran into her when she stopped. Great. Now she'd caused an accident! She peered into the rearview mirror, saw nothing but iridescent whiteness. Well, she knew someone was behind her, which was a comfort. The thought of being alone out here was unbearable.

She doubted there was much damage to the truck's bumper; it was built like a locomotive, but who could tell what she'd done to the other vehicle? Whoever had run into her would probably be waiting for her to go back and exchange insurance information. Unless he was already coming to meet her. Expecting a knock on her side window at any moment, Dakota turned on the interior light. She grabbed her purse from under the seat and rummaged through it for her wallet, withdrew her license from its plastic holder.

No one came. That was a pretty hard bump. Maybe the driver was hurt. She pushed the door open against the tangible crush of wind, reluctant to get out into the dust storm.

The wind almost knocked her over. She could barely make out the outline of her hand a foot from her face. The sandstorm was more like a snowstorm, blinding white, and so gritty she had to peek through her lashes.

"Hello!" she called. Her voice sounded strange and high in the wind.

There was no answer. Panic gripped her. Was the driver all right? She placed her hands on the truck body and felt her way back toward the rear. Standing near the back bumper, she squinted into the whirling sand, expecting to see the shadowy shape of a car behind brilliant white disks of light.

There were no headlights.

The air was uniformly white, except for the spinning particles of gypsum that caught the moonlight. She wouldn't have known a vehicle was there at all, except for the rumble of an idling engine and the eerie warmth it gave off.

"Are you okay?" she shouted. "Stay there. I'm coming back."

For answer, she heard a grind of gears, and the higher whining sound of a truck backing up.

Panic slammed into her. Why was he backing up? To drive away? "Stop! Wait!" Couldn't he hear her? She waved her arms, although she was positive she couldn't be seen.

The vehicle stopped abruptly.

That was a close call. She couldn't stand the thought of being alone out here.

Headlights switched on, as bright as spotlights, pinning her to the rear bumper of her truck. Her arm flew to her eyes.

She heard the truck door open.

Relief drenched her. He wasn't leaving her here alone. "Hello?"

No answer but the crunch of feet on the gritty road. Then silence, except for the howling wind.

The headlights were blinding. She felt exposed, naked, terribly alone. Something wasn't right. Fear trickled like ice under her armpits. "Hello?"

A rolling noise, like a foot on gravel. Another sound she did not recognize immediately, a stealthy but mechanical *snick,* like a bolt sliding home. A familiar sound, a sound she associated with something deadly.

But she couldn't remember what it was.

The vehicle was idling, she imagined she could feel the heat of its engine blasting her knees. She smelled oil. Alarm bells rang in her head, along with a voice from nowhere, a singsong melody in her ears saying it's deadly, deadly, get out—

get out of the light

She pitched to the side as glass shattered behind her. A

crack like a backfire sounded dimly in her ears, rocketing through her soul as she fell in slow motion. She was aware of raw pain as her palms slammed against the road. Disbelief and terror warred in her as she realized that the sound she'd heard was the cab's rear window exploding.

Someone had shot at her!

That realization seared through the shock, exploded through her limbs. She rose to her knees, fear thudding in her heart. She had to get away from here.

The truck? Could she get in and start it up and drive away?

A bee stung her. Then she realized it wasn't a bee but a bullet, whizzing past, kicking up shrapnel off the hard road. The report came a split second on the heels of the bullet, so close it deafened her.

She flattened against the ground and scrambled as fast as she could alongside the truck. If she could reach the driver's side door, she might be able to get away, or at the very least find cover and defend herself. Her gun was under the seat.

Every moment she expected to feel the bullet that would end her life.

She heard the front tire explode near her head. Another bullet banged off metal, ricocheting with a whine. She reached up for the door handle, felt along the cold smooth metal door—

Another bullet ripped the air in half, right next to her cheek. Like a fly in a web, she was caught in the headlights. She had to get away from the truck.

Dakota got to her feet and ran.

She ran away from her only means of transportation. She ran away from her gun.

Her heart thumped in her chest, her head, her throat. She couldn't catch her breath. Her terror was so great she wished she could curl into a ball and let the danger pass, but knew that soon her stalker would stop firing and look for her. She poured every ounce of will into running, trying to ignore the firing squad sounds directly behind her.

And ran smack into a dune. Grabbing handfuls of powdery sand, she shoved her feet in to her knees before gaining purchase on a rind of crusted sand. She scuttled up the dune on all fours, her breath coming in ragged gasps. Get to the top of the dune, she told herself, he'll never find you up here.

He'd stopped firing, which was worse. It meant he was choosing his shots. Could he see her? Was she an easy target?

She had to believe that he could see just as well as she could—which was nothing. Completely blind, she scrambled up the dune. Some places were hard-packed ripples and she could move much faster, but there were a few pockets of deep, powdery sand, and her feet would sink to her socks. When she reached the top, winded, she sat down, breathing hard.

Silence.

He must be on foot, looking for her.

It'll be like finding a needle in a haystack, she told herself. But she stood up anyway, holding her breath. She had to keep moving, as quietly as possible. He could stumble on her by accident.

She crept along the top of the dune, trying to stay on the hard-packed area. Once, her foot plunged through the crust, a loud crumbly sound.

Her heart lurched. She froze, listening for footfalls.

Couldn't hear anything in this screaming wind. Maybe he hadn't heard her, either.

Dakota didn't know how long she sat there, waiting. It seemed like an hour, but she guessed it was only ten minutes in real time.

In the distance, she heard a door slam. The engine gunned. She sat down on the dune and stared in the direction of the sound, trying to pick out a shape. A weak beam of light glimmered, only slightly yellower than the whirling whiteness. The shape behind it displaced white air like a shadow.

He was leaving!

She kept her eyes fastened on the spot. That was the road. If she had any chance at all of getting out of here, she had to get back to the road.

Either that, or stay here and wait for morning.

The sound of the engine receded. Dakota kept staring at the same spot, willing herself to concentrate. When the sound disappeared entirely, she started down the dune.

And stopped. What if it was a trick? There could be two people in the vehicle; the shooter and the driver. Or he could be parked just around the corner, waiting to hear her walk down the road. Waiting to spring his trap. . . .

She sank back down, uncertain what to do. Finally, she decided to wait.

Dakota covered her head with her arms, closed her eyes against the grit, and waited. The howling wind was the loneliest sound she'd ever heard. She tried to stem the panic in her heart, counting the moments until she could go down to her truck and get the hell out of here. A glance at her watch told her fifteen minutes had passed. Surely, the killer was gone by now.

Uncertain, she decided to wait another fifteen minutes, just to make sure.

At first she thought the droning was part of the wind. Then the ghostly lights appeared on the road below her, insubstantial in the sifting sand. The vehicle stopped, cut the engine, its lights picking out a glint of metal, a blocky shape. Her truck.

A truck door opened. He must be searching the truck for her. After a while, she heard the clank of the door again. Maybe he'd give up now, go away.

The engine didn't start. Instead, the headlights suddenly blinked out.

He was going to wait for her.

Her gun was there. Her truck. She would have taken a chance and driven on the rims, just to get out of here.

That was what the killer was counting on, and why she must turn her back on the only haven she knew.

Shivering from the adrenaline rush, Dakota put two dunes between herself and the road—at least she thought she did. In this storm, it was hard to tell.

Too exhausted to move or think, she finally sat down in the

lee of a dune, and tried to make herself as small as possible. She'd wait the storm out, then walk for it.

She would not go back to the truck.

Thirty-Nine

Clay was tired. It was a good kind of tired, because he'd managed to save the colt's life.

He reached his cabin around midnight, poured himself a well-earned drink, and sat on the couch. The wind rushed around outside, making him restless. Dakota should have been here by now. He called her cabin and got the answering machine.

He hoped Rita had given her the message. You never could tell what Rita would do. He called her, but there was no answer there, either.

Pinching the bridge of his nose, he closed his eyes. In another minute, he was asleep.

Dakota dozed, drifted, awaking to calm. The sandstorm had abated, and she could get her bearings.

Where she was, was the middle of nowhere. She felt like a castaway set adrift in the ocean, each swell larger than the last. Huddled against the desert cold, she felt lost and alone.

The moon grinned above her, its clotted-cream smile malevolent with false promises. The sand shivered off the dunes, but she could see now. Dawn was the faintest blush above the Sacramento Mountains.

At least she'd survived the night.

Damn, it was cold. She thought of the truck heater. It wouldn't hurt just to sneak up the last dune and look over . . .

Except that that was what the killer wanted her to do.

Dakota trudged onward, her mind lingering on the heater. Up one dune and down the other, hoping to connect with the road at some other point. She planned to watch the road from the top of a dune and wait for the first tourist to come by.

She paused to get her bearings, staring back at the growing rust-red stain above the Sacramento Mountains.

That was when she spotted the rectangular speck. It was too perfect to be other than man-made. Reversing direction, she trotted toward it. Soon, the speck turned into a metal roof, surrounded by a tall chain-link fence topped by concertina wire. As she approached, the top third came into view.

She jogged faster, her legs pumping as the heavy sand sucked at them.

When she reached the top of the next dune, she could see the whole thing.

The shed wasn't much bigger than an outhouse, built of gray cinderblock. A sign on the gate read: US ARMY— UNAUTHORIZED PERSONNEL KEEP OUT.

Beside the gate, two soldiers in army camouflage sat in an olive-green truck.

When the phone rang, Clay hurtled out of sleep, his heart pounding. He glanced at the clock. Eight-thirty! He should have been at the track three hours ago.

He must have been so tired last night, he'd forgotten to set the alarm.

Cursing, he grabbed the phone.

"I didn't see you at the track," Rita said. "What's going on?"

"I slept in. Have you seen Dakota?"

"No."

"You gave her my message? To come by here?"

"Of course I did! Maybe it was late when she got back and went home instead. She had a flat tire at the wolf rally."

"You didn't help her?"

"What do I know about flat tires?" Rita's voice took on a sulky tone. "There was someone there already."

"Did you know him?"

"No. So?"

Clay kept a rein on his temper. He didn't want to say what he thought of her.

"I'm sure she'll turn up." Rita dismissed Dakota's plight with an audible yawn. "Did Lucy return the truck?"

"I don't know." He glanced out the window. "Yes."

"Do you know she's been hanging around with Eddie Dejarlais? He must be twenty-one at least, and I hear he's—"

A knock shook the screen door. Dakota raised her hand to knock again, looking as if she'd been sleeping in a cactus. "She's here now," he spoke quickly into the phone. "I'll talk to you later."

"Clay! This is impor—"

He hung up and unlatched the door. "What happened?"

Dakota's face was an odd color of gray. "Someone tried to kill me," she said.

The phone rang immediately. He tried to ignore it, but the shrill bleating cut through his brain like a buzz saw. He picked up the receiver, staring at Dakota, still trying to digest what he'd just heard.

Rita's voice. "Clay, I—"

He slammed the phone down, jerked the cord out of the wall.

Dakota stared at him in shock.

"I'm sorry," he said, wanting to fold her in his arms and comfort her. But the way she stood, her arms folded over her chest, shaking, made him stay where he was. She looked as fragile as crystal. Illogically, he feared that one touch might shatter her into fragments. "Sit down," he said, standing back for her to enter. "Let me get you some coffee."

She made it to the couch on legs that looked as if they'd give out any minute. Shivering like a china cup in a saucer.

Hurriedly, he put on the coffee and grabbed a blanket from the bed, draped her with it. He didn't know what to do after that, so he sat down opposite her, reached for her hands. They were cold. "What happened?"

Dakota swallowed. "There was a sandstorm at the Monument. I was driving back after . . . I had a flat tire . . ."

He silently damned Rita DeWeil to hell.

"A man helped me change the tire—"

"What man?" he demanded, wincing inwardly at his overreaction.

She shook her head. "It wasn't him. He helped me. I was following him out and we got separated . . . the truck stalled and someone ran into me. I thought I caused the accident, I didn't know if the driver was hurt, I couldn't very well just leave them there . . ." She trailed off helplessly.

"Don't blame yourself."

She continued on as if she didn't hear him. She told him how she'd gotten out, called to the vehicle behind her, the eerie sound of the engine idling . . . "Something just told me to get out of the way. If I hadn't . . ." She shuddered. "I could have been shot."

The image of her lying in her own blood almost drove him out of his mind. Despair, fear, a blinding, righteous anger bolted up through him, flapped and clawed into his throat like a vengeful bird of prey. "Jesus," he muttered. In that instant he crossed the space between them without conscious knowledge, and she was in his arms, the blanket accordioned between them, and she pressed her face into his shoulder and he held her as close as he dared, as if she were a bird whose life lay in his hand, a fragile, beating heart.

He was surprised when she shifted against his chest and her arms came up around his neck. She pulled him down to meet her lips.

Dakota didn't think. It was pure instinct, this need to assimilate him into herself, to mold him to her body, to hold on for dear life to his strength. She kissed him savagely, with a bruising intensity that came from some feral place deep within. In an instant, like a brushfire consuming a single stalk of dry grass, he caught her fury. His response was swift and violent. He crushed her to him, his mouth drinking her in, his hands sliding along her body as he sought handholds. His restless, strong, plundering hands. One palm cupped her spine and she arched her back up to meet him, her breasts brushing the hardness of his chest, and she felt a carnival thrill as his hand slid down further, over her jean-clad hip, up and over the long hill of her thigh, delving gently inward. His tongue was forceful, demanding, and she forgot her terror in a frenzy of desire. Her fingers twined in his hair, sifted through the dark feathers—she'd dreamed of doing it for so long—and then she felt him rise above her, caging her between one arm and the couch back, the palm of his other hand finding her center, describing deliciously sinful, lazy circles through the soft fabric of her old jeans. She closed her eyes, letting the ecstasy pool and ripple from his touch, an aching want so deep she thought she'd pass out. She writhed underneath him as the waves of pleasure mounted, and his breath was ragged, short, as their lips fastened and came apart, and all the while he was punishing her with his tongue his palm clamped down with warm pressure on her sex, his fingers coaxing her open like a flower to the sun. She wished the barrier of clothing between them would magically disappear.

"Oh God," he muttered against her hair, "I can't believe . . ."

She shushed him with a kiss, reaching up to undo his belt.

The buckle wouldn't give. "Let me," he said. His strong fingers expertly tugged the belt over the prong.

While he was busy with his belt, his hand had left her aching, and she couldn't stand the lack of contact. She raised her hips and her body slid along his length, hitching lightly on the jutting heat of him, and she heard him groan, felt the quiver that ran through his body. She heard the snap of his jeans, felt the wellspring of his passion meet the palm of her hand. Above, he shifted slightly, poised with arms on either side of her head, and rocked against her, eliciting a frisson of desire. "You like that?" he asked, his eyes gleaming like the devil.

"I love that," she moaned.

For answer he lowered his head and kissed her softly, tousling her lips lazily before sitting back on his haunches. She couldn't keep her eyes off him.

"Let's get these things off you," he muttered, pulling off first her shoes, then her socks, and then reaching for the zipper to her jeans. She moaned as he gently pulled the tab and the material parted, revealing the silk and lace. "Clay . . ."

"What?" He looked so innocent, but she recognized the teasing depths in his midnight eyes.

"Hurry . . ."

"You got it, sweetheart." He leaned down and kissed the silky smoothness of her belly above the panties, then hooked his fingers over the waistband of her jeans. He pulled gently and they glided down her legs. He discarded them on the floor. The panties followed. She held her arms over her head as he pulled her shirt up and off, and unsnapped her bra. He kissed one breast and then the other, nuzzling her gently, drawing out the anticipation until she thought she would go mad, and just then he pushed up on his palms, his strong, muscular arms like pillars on either side of her shoulders. He poised above her, gently lowering himself so that his chest brushed against hers. Tantalizingly, inch by inch, careful to keep from crushing her. Once more he rocked forward and back, first merely grazing her, then nudging, finally cradling himself between her hipbones, until she couldn't stand his teasing anymore. "Please!"

"McAllister, your problem is, you never can wait."

"I've waited ten years for this."

"Me," he gasped ". . . too."

He groaned as he took her, and she held him tightly, amazed at the way he filled her, every nook and cranny, their bodies like silk and iron. They melded together, each giving the best to the other, until the lazy rhythm gave way to frenzy, and the building passion, the pounding fury of it, threatened to maroon her on an island where there was no time, no mind, only pleasure.

He gripped her shoulders, driving into her with his tongue and with his sex, hard and deep and totally encompassing, and when his spasm came it shook them both, setting off a chain reaction that took her far and away above the world, and her love for him sang in her ears, filled her with light, brought tears to her eyes.

He lay against her, his breath slowing. Still careful to keep his weight on his arms. "McAllister?" he muttered.

"Yeah, Pearce?"

"Damn but if I don't want to marry you all over again."

The second time they made love, it was gentle, like the light rain that tapped on the roof. This time they explored each other, remembered old haunts, sampled the sweetness of a leisurely stroll down memory lane. The horses were forgotten. Their responsibilities were forgotten. And most of all, for the first time in a long while, Dakota felt absolutely secure.

Later, still lingering in the warm glow of their lovemaking, Dakota and Clay drove to the Otero County Sheriff's Office in Alamogordo. Dakota's truck had been towed in. The back window was gone, a tire shot through, and four bullet holes peppered the tailgate. Dakota couldn't believe she'd survived. If she hadn't jumped when she did . . .

Sitting in Detective Pete Molino's office, she had to pluck her thoughts back from that precipice and pay attention to his questions.

"You believe the person who made an attempt on your life also killed your father?"

She glanced at Clay, who squeezed her hand. "I think so. It doesn't make much sense, otherwise."

"Why do you think someone would want to shoot you?"

"I don't know."

"Someone just killed a valuable stallion of hers," Clay said.

Molino's salt-and-pepper eyebrows knitted together in a V. "What has that got to do with it?"

"I've been getting threats for months." Dakota told him

about the photograph of the mangled truck, the broodmares' manes and tails. The attempt on Shameless's life.

"But you think the person responsible for this has been arrested."

Dakota nodded, feeling a headache coming on. She didn't know what to think anymore.

Molino picked up the phone, leaned back in his swivel chair, and placed his feet on the desk. "Is this the Santa Cruz County Sheriff's Office?" He identified himself. "I understand you have a man in custody named Jerry Tanner? He was charged with the murder of—What?" His coffee-brown eyes sought Dakota's, but she could tell he wasn't really seeing her. "When was this? No, that's all right." He set the phone down.

Dakota's heart lurched. "What is it?"

"Tanner was released last week."

Clay stood up. "What?"

"The County Attorney felt there was insufficient evidence to convict."

Little more than a shadow in the gathering dusk, the intruder walked up the steps to the cabin and peered through the darkened window.

Empty. The cabin was empty. It was hard to see the inside, but some objects materialized in the gloom: the stove, the maple rocker, the fireplace.

A car drove by. For a moment, it looked like it would turn in here.

The vintage Coca-Cola chest hummed by the back door. The figure followed the deck around to the back, boots clumping on floorboards that rang hollow above the rushing night.

Open the lid, plunge a hand into the chill water and pull out a bottle with the lumps of ice still clinging to it. Drink the sweetness, let the bubbles congregate on the tongue, silvery needles of delight. Drowning in the sensation, the animal pleasure, the figure walked back and forth along the deck.

The Rio Ruidoso trickled over rocks down below, familiar-sounding, comforting. Cold damp air rose from the river. Somewhere there was a rustling sound. Had to be a bird. Birds were the only animal that didn't bother to hide their noise.

Inside, the phone rang. It rang a long time before the answering machine picked up.

She'd come home and gone out again. If things had worked out, she might never have come home at all.

Luck had been with her. This time.

Somewhere, a siren pierced the stillness. An ambulance?

If she was scared enough, if she gave up and went back to L.A. now, everything would be fine. But that didn't look like it was going to happen.

Not after this morning.

The Coke had lost its edge, started to cloy. The familiar void returned, along with the bone-deep knowledge that something was wrong. The something wrong remained out of reach, just at the edge of conscious thought, like a huge, spreading ink blot. It was never gone for long.

Fuck it. Pitching the half-full bottle over the railing, the dark figure walked back to the front of the cabin.

The bedspring croak of a cricket shivered in the air. It was cold after the rain. Rubbing arms against an inner chill, the intruder walked back down the steps and melted into the darkness.

Forty

Dakota had to get away by herself and think about what had happened. The following morning, after supervising Shameless's gallop, she slipped away to ride Tyke on one of the forest trails. The feel of a responsive horse under her and the flickering pine shadows soothed her frayed nerves. On a sunny day like this, it was hard to believe that someone had just tried to kill her.

But someone had. What was she going to do about it? Wait for him—or her—to try again? But there weren't any options, when it came right down to it. The only thing she could do was watch her back. Literally.

Suddenly uneasy, Dakota glanced over her shoulder and touched her gun, which rested in a zippered carrying case slung over the pommel. She didn't like carrying it—didn't like the idea that she needed a gun to survive—but she wasn't about to be caught flat-footed again. *I'm the NRA,* she thought bitterly. *I'm Charlton Heston in a bra.*

A rustle in the tall grass.

Dakota froze. She strained her eyes, peering into the barred shadows of the pines. *I'm scaring myself silly. Maybe I shouldn't have come out here.* Clay wouldn't want her riding out here alone. You could bet the farm on that. She *was* vulnerable, riding a splashy paint horse that made an easy target.

But she needed to think, and she did her best thinking on horseback. Dakota nudged Tyke's sides and he moved forward again.

She was fairly certain that the same person who had tried to kill her had murdered Coke. It was doubtful there were two killers running around Sonoita. Tanner had always seemed the best bet—although she didn't know enough about her father's past to know if he had any other enemies.

She checked Tyke as they reached a road. A car flashed by. They crossed the blacktop and followed one of two dirt roads through the forest. It was the wrong choice, because it dead-ended at a house and they had to double back.

As they headed back, she tried to put the harassment in some kind of order. First came the photocopy of Coke's truck. Then, the mares' manes and tails had been mutilated, followed by the warning on the answering machine. After that, someone had tried to poison Shameless. The next morning Dakota had gotten the note with the list of deceased horses. TRY AND TRY AGAIN.

Then Something Wicked was killed.

And Friday night, the whole thing had escalated again, when whoever had been harassing her decide to play for keeps.

Something about the pattern bothered her. The attacks seemed inconsistent, almost random. One minute, he tried to kill Shameless, the next, she was the target. He threatened the broodmares, but never carried through. Yet he had killed Something Wicked without compunction. What did he want? Dakota was so busy trying to work it out, she almost missed the trailer backed into a clearing in the pines.

Tyke didn't, though. He spooked, his hooves clattering on the hard dirt road.

Dakota's heart seized. She was immediately transported to the night she drove Lucy home.

It looked like Jerry Tanner's trailer: the dull silver patchwork of rivets, like an airplane fuselage; the strange skirt at the back that flared outward. The trailer looked somehow malevolent in the pine shadows, the sun gleaming off the front window, which was so dirty she couldn't see in.

Dread crawled over and through her. He was here. Maybe

he'd followed her to White Sands. Or he could have known she would be there. All he'd had to do was talk to Lucy.

She stepped down from Tyke and led him over to the trailer, wondering if Jerry was watching her. At any moment she expected him to catch her.

The trailer sat in the sun, insulated from her curiosity by blank windows and dull aluminum. Dakota thought of a frog, waiting patiently for an unsuspecting fly to buzz by and them—snap! No more fly.

She cupped her hands and peered into the side window. Although the window was nearly opaque with dirt, she could see the stuff piled up against it; a racing bat, a cooler, several cardboard boxes crammed with stuff. Dakota thought she saw white piping and two buckles sewn to canvas—a horse blanket?—in the jumble.

She touched the door handle, looked around. Tugged on it. Locked.

Relief made her legs weak. She really didn't want to break and enter. She stepped back, almost tripping over a large boulder opposite the door. An iron skillet sat on the smoke-blackened rock, silted with grease. He must have cooked his breakfast outside.

He could come back any minute.

She got the hell out of there.

A few days later, Dakota saw Jerry Tanner lounging by the rail when she led Shameless onto the track for her gallop.

He stood next to the poplars right near the Gap, his eyes seething with hatred. She'd never believed in the evil eye before, but now she wasn't so sure. Jerry Tanner was here, and he hated her more than ever.

Dakota met Clay at the Rio Ruidoso, where he was standing one of his horses in the ice-cold water. "Did you see Tanner?" she asked him.

His eyes darkened. "He's here?"

Dakota folded her arms over her chest, trying to hug away

the chill. "Damn straight he's here. I saw him at the Gap. He's following me, Clay."

"Damn!" Clay kicked at the tall grass, startling his horse.

"I don't know what to do." Her gaze rested on a man ponying a thoroughbred along the white-railed lane above them. It seemed so peaceful here. Armfuls of bright yellow sunflowers and groundsel nodded in the breeze, stippling the banks of the creek like a Monet painting. She should enjoy it here, but all she could feel was the suffocating fear that had taken hold of her heart.

"He could be here to see Lucy," Clay said.

"You didn't see the way he looked at me today. He must blame me because he was arrested. He can't get a license here, can he? After what happened at Prescott Downs?"

"I don't think so. He must have some kind of guest pass or something to get on the backside. Maybe Lucy got it for him. Obviously, he gets a charge out of scaring you."

"Well, it's working." She shuddered as she remembered the odd light in his eyes. He enjoyed the hell out of hating her.

Clay pulled her to him, held her close. He stroked her hair, his mouth drawn in a grim line.

He caught up with Tanner at the Hollywood Bar. Jerry's rattletrap Chevy was easy to find.

Tanner sat hunched over the bar, already drunk.

Clay bought a drink and sat on the stool next to him. "What are you doing in Ruidoso, Jerry? I thought you were in Prescott."

"It's none of your business."

"You got runners here?"

"Fuck off, Pearce."

Clay picked up Tanner's beer and poured it in the bar well. "You don't want to talk, that's fine," he said quietly. "But you can listen. I don't want you bothering Miz McAllister."

"It's a free country."

"Do the stewards know you're hanging around the Downs?"

"I got a license. I can go anywhere I like. If I want to say hello to an ol' friend of mine, I got that right." He motioned for another beer. "What you gonna do, get a restraining order? They're not worth the paper they're written on."

Clay leaned close. "I don't need a restraining order. If I catch you bothering Dakota, the police won't even know about it."

"Are you threatening me?"

"Threats," Clay said, sliding off the stool, "are about as hard to prove as ignoring a restraining order." He shoved Tanner's hat down over his face.

But as he walked out into the gathering dusk, Clay knew Jerry was right. There was no way he could legally stop him from harassing Dakota.

The next day, soiled and tired from her work at the track, Dakota sorted through the mail as she walked back to the cabin. Among the bills and circulars was a letter from the AQHA—the results of the blood test on Something Wicked. Mounting the steps, she tore open the envelope.

The blood types matched. The dead horse was indeed Something Wicked. Although it saddened her to know for certain that her top stallion was dead, she breathed a sigh of relief. It was one less worry to take up her time.

The phone rang. Dakota raced into the house, hoping it was Clay. She'd tried to reach him last night, but got no answer. An uncharitable voice inside her head told her he was out go-carting with Rita and Lucy.

The voice on the phone didn't belong to Clay. It was Derek Blue, returning her call regarding Tanner's release. "There was nothing we could do," he told her. "We had insufficient cause. The judge dismissed without prejudice."

"Without prejudice?"

"It means he can always be charged again, if we find more evidence."

"But what about the witnesses?"

"It wasn't enough. The tire's long gone by now, and there's

no damage to the front of his truck. Those kids could have been mistaken. It was dark, and they couldn't identify him in a lineup."

Dakota felt the tears gather at the edges of her eyes. She would not cry. She would not give in to that kind of weakness. But she thought of him standing at the rail, as if he belonged there. Watching her. Telling her with his eyes: "I got away with it. And now I'm going to get you."

"There's something else," Derek Blue said. "He has an alibi."

"But he was there at the bar that night. That's common knowledge."

"That's right, he was. But he was so drunk there was no way he could get his truck out of the parking lot, let alone run someone down. Whoever ran your father off the road must've been a good driver. Otherwise, he'd've wiped out, too."

"But I don't understand—"

"His daughter drove him home that night. That's what clinched it for the County Attorney."

"His daughter." A lump formed just below her solar plexis.

It wasn't Jerry Tanner. At least, it wasn't Jerry Tanner who murdered Coke.

Which meant it was someone else. And that same someone had now tried—and almost succeeded—in killing her.

"I'm sorry," Derek Blue said. "You want my opinion, he's guilty as sin—of killing your horse, at least—but I can't prove it."

Dakota hardly heard him. She set the phone down, dread spreading through her. Jerry Tanner, at least, had been the devil she knew. She'd never realized before that her conviction that he was the enemy had taken the edge off her fear and allowed her to get on with training Shameless, despite her worry for her horses. But if what Derek Blue said was true, Jerry couldn't have killed Coke.

Whoever wanted her dead was still out there, and there was no way of knowing how to stop him.

Forty-One

Although Shameless had come out of her injury sound, Dakota sensed the filly was not quite there yet. She needed conditioning. Long gallops built stamina, but stamina alone didn't make a racehorse.

Dakota had blown out the filly a few times and worked her seriously once. She didn't dare do more. Shameless's punishing stride might undo all the good. If there was even a tiny weakness in that hind leg, Shameless's jackhammer style of running might stress it too much—and she could break down.

Although she was sound, Shameless wasn't the same horse who ran in the Rainbow Futurity. And in this kind of company, a horse had to be at his best—and then have the luck of the devil

If Dakota didn't have enough troubles, Jerry Tanner continued to come to the Gap and watch her horse gallop. She knew he was waiting for her, and she had to prepare herself for the sight of him. He stood in the same place each time, looking toward the stables until she arrived, turning his head slowly as his eyes followed her. She knew he enjoyed the effect he was having on her.

It was a subtle kind of harassment that went unnoticed in a venue where double entendres and meaningful (and sometimes downright lascivious) glances ruled the day. She wished she could complain to the racetrack officials, but knew that would only brand her as a troublemaker. She'd thought he wouldn't be able to stick around the backside very long without a license, but he was there every day.

One morning he stood at the Gap and waved something at her as she rode by. His grin was friendly.

It took her a moment to realize what it was: a branch of oleander.

Goddamn him to hell! She had had enough of this harassment.

When she'd finished with Shameless, she marched over to Jack Dougherty's stable. "Is Lucy around?" she asked Eddie Dejarlais, one of Jack's bug boys.

Eddie jumped down from the horse he'd been exercising, the strap on his crash helmet swinging. He sighted down his racing bat as if it were a paper airplane and tossed it onto one of the tack room chairs. "Not today. She's moving."

"Moving?"

"Yeah." She felt his lascivious gaze travel down to her chest, then back to her face. "She's going to live with one of the owners." As she walked away, he called after her, "Hey! You doin' anything later?"

Dakota caught up with Lucy unloading boxes in the parking lot of Rita's place, the Champions Run Condominiums.

"Hi, Dakota, what's up?"

"Lucy, I want you to give your father a message."

The girl set down the box she'd been carrying. "Sure."

"If he comes near me again, I'm going to slap him with a restraining order, and if he comes near me after that, I'll see he never races *any* horse at *any* track in the country. I'll make it my *career* to see he can't even run 'em in the bushes!"

Lucy stared at her, mouth open. "Okay. Sure."

Dakota left her standing there, squelching the urge to tell her to shut her mouth before a bug flew in.

Ernesto moved into Dakota's cabin, and she moved out, into the trailer next to Shameless's stall. More often than not,

Clay spent the night with her. Two people in such a small space might get on each other's nerves, but the close quarters merely gave them an excuse to brush enticingly against each other in the tiny hallway, or fall into a rapturous tangle on the dinette cushions. They were on an extended camping trip. Everything would be wonderful if it weren't for Jerry Tanner.

Dakota hadn't slept very well since Tanner waved the oleander branch at her. Often, she would awaken from vague, frightening dreams to Clay's concerned scowl and strong arms.

But her resolve didn't crumble. If Tanner tried anything with her filly, she would be ready.

She knew her show of temper with Lucy wouldn't have much impact. What could she really threaten him with? As Clay pointed out, a restraining order was a joke. The idea of Jerry Tanner flaunting his power enraged her. If he touched a hair on Shameless . . . the visceral part of her wanted to shoot him. For the first time in her life, she understood how people killed one another without compunction. Someone cut you off in traffic? Riddle their car with bullets. Some son of a bitch threaten to kill your horse? Blow his head off.

It was not like her.

It scared her.

On the morning of the All American Futurity Trials, Clay cooked a breakfast of eggs Benedict on the trailer's Magic Chef stove. He served it to Dakota on a silver tray (she'd won the tray in a horse show) along with a bud vase bearing a single red rose. When Clay was done with his horses, he helped bathe Shameless. With a soft cloth, Dakota polished the filly like a fine antique. She sprayed Shameless's hooves to a shine, rubbed the inside of her nostrils with Mentholatum, bandaged her front legs carefully, pulled her forelock under the bridle headband and smoothed it neatly down the center of her forehead. She stood back and surveyed her work, thinking that Shameless was the most beautiful filly in the world.

But looks wouldn't win her the race.

* * *

As Dakota led Shameless around the saddling paddock before the race, her eyes unconsciously scanned the crowd for an Arizona Feeds cap, which Jerry Tanner always wore. She didn't see Tanner, but thought she recognized Jared Ames. He liked to bet on the ponies, and Dakota guessed that Ruidoso was the logical place for a horse vet to take a busman's holiday.

"Jockeys up," the paddock judge called.

"See you in the winner's circle," Clay said, bussing her on the cheek. Ernesto gave her the thumbs-up sign.

Dakota ponied the filly, letting her stretch into an easy lope up the backside. She prayed that Shameless's lack of conditioning wouldn't cause her to reinjure the leg.

They loaded the horses into the gate. The colt next to Shameless acted up. He reared and almost flipped over, but Shameless stood calm and focused, all four feet planted firmly on the ground.

Dakota held her breath.

The bell clanged and the doors sprung open.

Shameless shot out like a cannon.

Dakota closed her eyes and prayed harder.

The horses fanned out over the track in a ragged line of browns, blacks, golden-reds. Shameless took the lead, stretched it to a length.

Hoofs drummed against the biscuit-colored earth. Jockeys hunched over whipping manes, hides glistened and stretched like Mylar over bunching muscles and straining tendons.

The sun was warm on Dakota's back. It smelled like summer.

Shameless was going to do it again.

And then, halfway up the track, the filly lost ground. Her stride shortened. Her head bobbed with effort. The length of her seemed to telescope; her trademark up-and-down style added to the impression that she was running in place. The jock scrubbed at her with his whip.

A fifteen-to-one longshot named Dreamcatcher caught her

at the wire, winning by a nose. Although it was her first defeat, Shameless's time was still fast. But would it be fast enough?

Dakota went out to meet her, feeling like a wrung-out dishrag. Shameless looked as tired as she felt. The filly's sides quaked and her nostrils flared as she tried to get breath, and sweat poured down her dark coat.

Shameless was the eighth-fastest qualifier—so far. Throughout the day Dakota and Clay listened to the results. A horse in the tenth race came in at a faster time than Shameless. That knocked her down to the ninth fastest qualifier. If two more horses beat her time, she'd be out.

But at the end of the day, Shameless's time stood. She would be running in the All American Futurity.

By the skin of her teeth.

The Ruidoso News ran the results of the trials, and called Shameless, who had been "decisive" in the Rainbow, a "disappointment." One swallow, they said, did not make a spring.

Forty-Two

Jerry Tanner popped the tab on another Pabst Blue Ribbon. Christ, he felt good. Everything had gone as planned. The only fly in the ointment was the fact that the McAllister bitch had a horse in the All American.

He should have trained Shameless. He'd been looking for a horse like that all his life, and just when he found it, they'd cheated him out of the big one. The All American would have made him as a trainer.

Too bad Lucy didn't poison the filly when she'd had the chance. Not that it mattered now. He had bigger fish to fry.

Still, he'd had his fun. The oleander branch was a stroke of genius, if he did say so himself.

He wiped his lips and stared at the photograph of Lucy he'd put up on the cupboard above the sink. It burned him that she'd defied him. A kid should obey her father. He didn't believe the garbage she fed him about being caught, either. He knew the real reason Lucy didn't poison Shameless. She just didn't want to do it.

"But I like Dakota," he mimicked in a high voice.

You had to give the kid points for originality. He didn't know if he would have been that quick on his feet. The big man. It sounded like the one-armed man on "The Fugitive." No wonder nobody on that show ever believed Richard Kimball, with a screwball story like that.

He lit a Lucky, then realized one was already burning in

the ashtray. The ceramic ashtray was shaped like a cowboy boot; Lucy had made it in school when she was younger.

She'd been a good kid then. Looked up to him. Now she didn't listen to him at all. Moving in with that DeWeil bitch, living high off the hog while he sat here in this dump. But he'd shown her that he was still the brains of this outfit. She'd dance to *his* tune, all right, and next time he asked her to do a little job like putting oleander in a horse's feed, it would get done.

His empty joined a row of them on the windowsill.

Well, there were big changes in the air. Lucy would learn to mind him soon enough. He was finally going to come into some money, much more money than Coke ever had.

Ka-chunk. The muffled thump seemed to come from just outside the door. The trailer swayed gently on its springs. He stood up and looked out the window. It was a dark night, but he thought he saw the pine branches move in the wind.

His thoughts turned back to Coke McAllister. It sure was ironic that Coke's death might just provide his old friend Jerry with money to live comfortably for the rest of his life. That was the ultimate irony.

He lay back against the dinette seat, feeling warm and cozy. It was cold tonight, but the space heater he'd saved from the dump sure did the trick. As he dozed, his last conscious thought was: just how much money would a person pay to keep the status quo?

Dakota accompanied Clay to the clubhouse for dinner at the Turf Club. A bash was thrown for the owners, trainers, and jockeys of the horses running in the All American Derby and the All American Gold Cup. For Dakota, the evening was a dress rehearsal for Sunday night, when they would return for the All American Futurity Pre-race dinner.

Dakota rolled down the truck window and put her hand out to catch the cool breath of evening. The sky above the mountain was apricot, with a few flamingo-pink clouds that were quickly turning plum red as twilight fell. They followed the graceful arc of road around the racetrack, watching the fading light glimmering in the infield lake. Dakota couldn't help feeling thrilled. *I'm here, Dad,* she thought. *Just like you wanted me to be.*

She'd never in a million years really expected this to happen. It had been her goal, but now it seemed more like a fairy tale come true.

Situated on the top level of the grandstand, the Turf Club was open to the air. A light breeze swirled through the breezeway, lightly caressing Dakota's bare back.

Svelte women in evening gowns, cocktail dresses, and cowgirl dresses milled around, sipping chardonnay and tasting the shrimp and brie at the center table. Men wore everything from Brush Popper shirts and western-cut suits to Saville Row. Seven X Stetsons and hand-tooled boots dominated. Dakota wore the new outfit she'd bought, the rich autumn colors setting off her glowing skin. After standing in line at the buffet, she and Clay searched for their table, which was decked in white linen emblazoned with the name VIENTO PRIETO on twin strips of red and blue satin.

Next time, the letters would spell out SHAMELESS.

She sensed her father's ghost in the room, beaming with pride. "I hope you're paying attention, Dad," she muttered, spearing a shrimp. "Not very many people get here."

"You talking to yourself?" Clay asked, sitting down beside her.

She let him think she was.

They topped a perfect evening with a long session of lazy lovemaking at Dakota's trailer. As she drifted in Clay's arms, Dakota thought how happy she was. This was her life. Clay, the horses, racing.

She knew then that she wouldn't go back to L.A. when the All American was over.

Clay stirred, pulled her closer to him. Dakota reveled in his touch, holding the good secret safe in her heart, and fell asleep smiling.

* * *

A knock on the door tore her out of sleep.

Dakota shot up in bed, gripped with fear. Clay sat up and pulled on his jeans. "I'll get it."

Stark naked, the sheet up to her chin, she didn't argue. When Clay answered the door, she strained to hear. The muffled voice belonged to a woman. "Is it Shameless?" she asked when Clay padded back to the bunk.

"No. But I've got to go."

"What do you mean, you've got to go? It's almost one in the morning!"

He pulled on his boots. "Rita's here. Lucy's been picked up by the sheriff. She was with some guy at a bar, he got drunk and caused a scene when the bartender cut him off. The sheriff took both of them in."

A lot of things ran through Dakota's mind, but the words that came out of her mouth must have made her look mean-spirited. "Why do *you* have to go?"

"Rita needs my help." He stuffed an unbuttoned shirt into his jeans.

"I still don't understand. Where's her father? What's this got to do with you?" She regretted the words even as she said them. She should be worried about Lucy, not bean-counting to see how many hours Clay spent with Rita as opposed to her. But she couldn't help it. Another ugly thought popped into her head. "How often have you been playing surrogate dad?"

"What are you talking about?"

"The three of you seem awfully cozy." Damn! What had gotten into her?

He stared at her, his eyes like midnight. Unreadable. "I can't believe we're having this conversation," he said at last. He strode to the door, and in another moment Dakota heard a car pull out of the stable yard.

She sat on the bed, shivering and miserable. How in God's name did Rita know Clay was here?

Rita must have heard them arguing. Dakota knew she'd sounded like a harpy—a jealous, insecure harpy. Just a while ago, she'd planned to spend the rest of her life in Sonoita, presumably with Clay. How could she act that way?

Her gaze fell on the Black Oak Dispersal Sale catalog. She picked it up and leafed through it. Anything to keep her mind off the fool she'd made of herself. It didn't take long for her to realize she'd chosen the wrong medicine. Looking at the catalog depressed her.

All gone, she thought. All the mares, all the foals. The yearlings, the two-year-olds. Something Wicked. She realized how foolish she'd been. Why hadn't she listened to Norm and waited awhile before selling? She wanted to go back to Black Oak, but what was left? She'd sold off the ranch's life's blood. Wicked Witch. Palomita. Go Mango.

Go Mango had been her father's joke. The mare was a daughter of the great running sire, Go Man Go. Dakota forced herself to read the dry statistics on the page. It might put her to sleep, and she wanted to sleep. She didn't want to sit up all night waiting for the sound of Rita's Range Rover. She didn't want to appear dependent, or codependent, or whatever they called it these days. When he came back, she wanted to be dead to the world, with a peaceful smile on her face.

Go Mango had produced some fine stakes winners, but her produce record had slipped recently. Well, she was an old mare. In the last five years, only one of her foals had lived to see a racetrack.

Dakota glanced at the clock. Clay had been gone for an hour, and she was wide awake. She turned the page, surprised at how familiar she was with each mare's history. As she read, her mind kept returning to Go Mango. What was it that bothered her about the mare? Whatever it was, it eluded her now.

Three broodmares later, Dakota understood.

She knew what Dan Bolin had been doing.

She wondered if Coke had found out. And if he had, what Dan would have done to protect his secret.

Suddenly, she was very, very scared.

Forty-Three

Jerry Tanner dreamed he was burning a mattress behind the house. As he swam up to consciousness, the boiling smoke of the dream followed him. His eyes opened to dense, ominous blackness. He could smell something burning, and his open mouth sucked at air as thick as cotton candy.

It took a moment for his beer-addled brain to make the connection. Smoke. Burning. The trailer was on fire!

He staggered to his feet, breathing in fumes and coughing them right back out. It was okay. The dinette was at the front of the trailer—the door was only a couple of yards away. He couldn't see a thing, but he knew where it was.

He stumbled over some junk, went sprawling. Found a pocket of oxygen. Don't panic. When people panicked, that was when they died. The door was right here. He could reach out and touch it.

His hand fumbled for the handle. He screamed, jumped back and shook his hand, amazed at how quickly he'd been burned. He'd need ice for that.

Right now he needed something to open the door with, an oven mitt, a blanket—anything.

The horse blanket was right by his knees. Closing his eyes against the stinging heat—he couldn't see anyway—Jerry grabbed a handful of horse blanket and clamped it on the door handle. This should do her. He wrenched it to the left.

It didn't budge.

Calm down! Try again.

The handle was frozen in place.

What was going on? One good pull and the locking mechanism should come free and the door should open and he should be out in the fresh air, saying what a close goddamn call, I almost bought it this time, and tomorrow he'd find a cheap motel and stay in it until he could work out a deal, and then he'd stay at the Inn of the Mountain Gods if he wanted to if only this goddamn door handle would get with the program and turn—

But it didn't. He tried pulling to the right. Nothing. Kicked it. The door rattled in the frame. "Open, you goddamn-piece-of-shit-door!" he yelled. He shoved his full weight at it. The door wouldn't budge.

Disbelief clawed at his insides. He was locked in here! He couldn't get out. *He couldn't get out!*

He started pounding, shrieking for help. The screaming was only in his mind because by now he couldn't get enough breath to make a sound. His brain was sluggish and he could almost feel all the little cogs and pistons and belts in his body freeze, refuse to obey him. He'd pass out any minute and then he'd be done for.

Then he heard a rumbling. He turned to face what was coming.

In the split second before it hit him, he knew it was over.

The gust of superheated flame barreled down the hallway and slammed into him, lighting him like a straw effigy, and his last thought before he exploded in a ball of fire was: he'd known it was too good to be true.

It promised to be a busy All American weekend for the Lincoln County Sheriff's Office. Only Thursday night, and already there was one drunk-driving accident and three bar fights. At ten thirty, they answered a call at a trailer fire near the racetrack.

By the time the Ruidoso Downs Volunteer Fire Department and the sheriff arrived, the trailer was engulfed in flames. The black skeleton caved in under a whoosh of bright sparks.

Undersheriff Robert Millar watched as the sheriff's department arson investigator pulled up near the old turquoise truck.

Bonnie Jardin emerged. "Any word yet who owns the trailer?" she asked as she approached.

Robert scratched his neck. "The truck belongs to a racehorse trainer named Jerry Tanner."

"You know him?"

"I've scraped him off a bar stool or two in my time," he said.

Dakota awoke to the crowing of a rooster. Automatically, she reached for Clay. His side of the bed was empty.

She remembered last night, their argument. Was he still at the sheriff's office? Dakota rose to one elbow, her hand crushing the catalog. Something bothered her, something frightening—

Dan.

A spear of reflected sunlight flashed on the cupboard above the sink, and she heard car tires outside. Startled, Dakota jumped up and rapped her head on the overhanging bunk.

She saw Clay close the door to Rita's Range Rover and walk toward the trailer.

She met him at the door.

"Sorry I didn't call, but I didn't want to wake you."

Unreasoning anger shot through her. Even so, she tried to keep her voice calm. "Where were you?"

"I promised Rita and Lucy I'd take them home."

"Well, that's—"

"Dakota, Lucy's father died last night."

His words hit her like a punch in the stomach. "What?"

"They're pretty sure he was in the trailer," Clay amended. "They'll go through the rubble later today. We just got Lucy to bed. She was . . . upset."

"A trailer fire," Dakota repeated.

"She was at the station when it came over the dispatch."

"Oh God. Poor thing." Dakota closed her eyes, but couldn't obliterate the grisly vision just behind her eyeballs: the silver skin of Jerry's trailer engulfed in flames, turning charred and black. She dared not think of the man inside.

That morning, the medical examiner, the fire marshal, all thirteen members of the sheriff's department and their arson investigator, the state police and *their* arson investigator, and the Ruidoso Downs Volunteer Fire Department converged on the scene, giving Jerry Tanner considerably more than his allotted fifteen minutes of fame.

They found the body just inside the door. Foreshortened tendons had caused the arms to curl up to the chin like a praying manits. Although a positive ID would take time, the sheriff's department had run the truck's registration and learned from the daughter that the trailer belonged to Jerry Tanner.

An empty gas can, wiped of prints, had been thrown into the grass near the trailer.

The sheriff, Davis McGrath, hunkered down near the doorway, which had been reduced to something resembling a messy floorplan. "You thinking what I'm thinking?" he asked Bonnie.

Her gaze followed his to the charred two-by-four, lying beside the boulder opposite the trailer door. "It could have been wedged against the boulder and propped under the door handle."

McGrath stood up. "The first murder in Lincoln County in three years."

Forty-Four

"Marcie, I want you to do me a favor," Dakota said into the phone. She paced by the picture window of her father's cabin, watching a Steller jay peck at the bird feeder. With Tanner dead, Dakota thought no one else would try to hurt the filly, so she'd moved back into the cabin this morning.

"Sure."

"There are some broodmare files on my father's desk in the study. I'd like you to find the files for Shawnes Soliloquy, Go Mango, Narcolepsy, Globe Mallow and Jimsonweed, and call me back. Okay?"

Mystified, the groom replied that she would, and Dakota hung up.

Clay looked up from his seat on the couch, where he was rolling clean bandages. "You think the files will be different from what's in the catalog?"

"I have no idea." She'd already told him her theory, which seemed far-fetched in the light of day.

"Those two-year-olds," Clay said. "The ones you saw at Dan's place. You think they're from Black Oak mares?"

Dakota sighed. "I don't know. They could be his. He could have bred his mares to Something Wicked at the regular fee. Or Coke could have even let him breed his mares for free—as a perk. It could all be perfectly legitimate. Except I know Rudy Gallego and Ames were shipping them somewhere. I think Ames was lying when he told me he'd come for Dan's roping horse. Where do you think they are?"

"Mexico."

The heaviness in her heart told her he was right. "Do you think we could get them back?"

Clay passed a hand over the back of his neck. "It would be hard."

The phone rang—Marcie calling back. Dakota asked her to read the produce records of each mare. She wrote everything down to make sure she wasn't hearing things.

Clay looked over her shoulder. "Holy cow."

Two of the five mares were listed as not conceiving the previous summer, and yet those same mares had foals at their side in the dispersal catalog this spring. Another mare's foal died after only two days. Like Lazarus, he'd returned from the dead to appear at the dispersal. And Shawnes Soliloquy, Alydar's friend, had dropped her foal while Dakota was there.

Clay cradled her in his arms and grazed his lips over her hair. "What are you going to do?"

"I don't know. Marcie said that Dan's wife is dying. He's been with her night and day for a week. I can't confront him now."

"I don't think you should, either. You've got to concentrate on the futurity."

"And the derby," she said, thinking of Clay's horse Viento Prieto.

"And the derby."

But all that weekend, Dakota felt an encroaching sense of doom. Which was ridiculous. Dan was in Tucson. She was safe, at least for now.

Still, the questions ran through her mind. Was Dan a good man desperate for money to save his wife? Or was he a killer?

She thought of the satellite dish, the boat. How many years had he been siphoning off colts from Black Oak? Coke had never paid much attention to the breeding program, delegating all the responsibility to Dan. Her father was a racetracker at heart, and spent all his time at Los Alamitos, or Ruidoso, or Turf Paradise.

But what if he'd found out? What if Dan had killed him to keep the whole thing from blowing up in his face? What if he wanted her dead, too, to cover up what he'd done?

Should she feel sorry for him, or should she fear him?

Forty-Five

As it turned out, Dakota didn't have to call Dan Bolin. He called her. "I have to see you." It was very early Sunday morning, the day before the All American Futurity. Dakota had come back for breakfast after walking Shameless.

Dakota could tell he'd been crying. Alarmed, she asked him how Marie was.

There was a pause. "She didn't make it." When he continued talking, his voice was dull and faraway. "Did I tell you they had a heart for her? It was being flown in from California. I asked her to hold on, but she couldn't hear me. I don't think she ever knew. It was some young guy, twenty-two years old, a motorcycle crash, he had a good strong heart. I really think if she'd held on . . . but I guess it wasn't to be." He sounded as if he were discussing the weather. Obviously, it hadn't hit home yet. "She died this morning, around six. They were just about to prep her, and now, now I don't know what to do."

Dakota swallowed. She couldn't bring up the mares now. "Don't worry about a thing. Do whatever you have to do. Marcie can take care of things at Black Oak. If there's anything . . ."

"No. Nothing. I don't need money. Not now."

Not now, the niggling little voice said again. *But he did need the money. And by the way, who killed Coke?*

They talked for a while longer before Dan hung up. Dakota sat down, her heart heavy. There was too much sadness in this world. Jerry, burning to death, leaving a sixteen-year-old daughter behind. Dan, losing the wife he adored. Coke. Oh, God, Coke. She felt the tears come.

The phone shrilled. It was Dan again. "Look, I have to get out of here. I was thinking maybe I could drive out to Ruidoso, talk to you. There's something you should know, I've got to tell you in person."

"But what about the arrangements? This is hardly the time to—"

"Screw the arrangements! I'm leaving now. I should be in Ruidoso by three."

"Are you sure this is wise?"

"We can meet at that coffee shop on Mecham. The one across from the shopping center. Four o'clock."

"I have to be at the pre-race dinner—"

"I have to get this off my chest. I'll see you then." And he hung up.

Dakota stared at the phone, wondering if the man she'd just talked to was a distraught husband, or a killer.

Dakota parked outside the coffee shop, twenty minutes late because she'd just watched Clay's horse run in the All American Derby. Although she would have liked to have Clay with her, he'd had to go to the test barn when Viento Prieto came in second. Things were so hectic, she'd told him she would be back at the cabin in time to change for dinner.

She wondered if she was making a mistake in meeting Dan. A coffee shop was safe enough, as long as they stayed there. She would not leave with him, no matter what reason he gave.

The man just lost his wife.

But he still had a lot to lose. Her heart thumping wildly in her chest, she crossed the parking lot and opened the glass door, wondering if she was about to face Coke's killer.

I wish Clay were here.

Dan Bolin sat on the vinyl seat that ran around the front of the coffee shop, head in his hands, apart from the rest of the people waiting for tables. Dakota almost didn't recognize him. Once a big man, he seemed lost in his clothes. His freckles stood out in stark relief against his white face, and puffy half circles couched dazed eyes.

She couldn't see him running Coke off the road, or shooting at her.

He stood up, looking uncomfortable. Dakota took his hand. "I'm so sorry."

"It's all right." He might as well have said "it's nothing." He probably didn't even understand her words; he must be in shock.

The hostess led them to a booth and they ordered coffee. "You didn't have to come all this way," Dakota said.

He looked down at his big hands. "Driving was kind of therapeutic."

"I can find you a place—"

"No, no. I'm okay. I got a room at the Apache Motel. I'm really okay, you know?"

The coffee came, and he spent a long time tearing the lids off the little plastic creamers, pouring and stirring, shaking in Equal and stirring again. At last he couldn't do any more to the coffee unless he added the Tabasco that had been set next to the salt and pepper, so he stared with fierce concentration into the cup, as if it were a TelePrompTer. He sighed heavily. "You might as well know. I've been cheating you."

"I know."

The first sense of real awareness stirred in his eyes. "You know?"

"You've been listing some mares as unable to conceive, and then selling off their foals."

He rubbed his eyes. "How'd you find out?"

She told him. About Shawnes Soliloquy, and Go Mango. "Shawnes Soliloquy might have been a mistake, but *three* mares listed as barren in one place and in foal in the other?"

She didn't add that the best-bred mares were the most unlucky when it came to producing dead foals. The best mares of Black Oak. Dan Bolin was taking Something Wicked's most promising progeny and pocketing the money. "That's why you didn't want me poking around."

"I didn't think you'd notice, but I wasn't taking any chances."

"So you tried to keep me from seeing those files. Why didn't you just change them?"

"I thought you'd go back to L.A. right after the dispersal. It was too much work, and I wasn't thinking too well at the time." He toyed with his wedding ring as he spoke.

"Let me get this straight," she said, trying not to look at his wedding ring. He had cheated her, and she had to remember that, despite the pain he was going through now. "The dispersal sale threw a spanner in the works. You couldn't very well separate a nursing foal from its mother or hide a pregnancy, so you wrote the mares' true conditions in the catalog and took a loss on the foals."

"I didn't think you'd notice."

No doubt. Running Black Oak as his own private fiefdom, he hadn't bothered to alter the files. When Dakota had asked to see them, he must have banked on the fact that she wouldn't know what to look for. He was almost right. It took Alydar's attraction to a broodmare named Shawnes Soliloquy to make her look closer. How could she feel sorry for him? He'd cheated her father!

"I planned on doing it only once, when Marie first got sick and we needed a heart transplant. The insurance company flat refused to pay for it. I needed hundreds of thousands of dollars, and there was Rudy Gallego telling me about his rich owner who wanted Something Wicked's get. I sold him five yearlings, averaging twenty thousand dollars. Can you imagine that? He bought them without papers for twenty thousand dollars. We'd be lucky to get half that here. Forget NAFTA. In this business, the Mexicans have the money. So I did it. I bought her time. We waited three years for that heart, and then it was no good." He sighed. "What are you going to do?"

"I don't know," she said in all honesty.

"I don't care if you go to the police. My life is over now."

He said it simply, and Dakota believed him. He honestly didn't care.

"Did Jared Ames help you?"

"It was his idea. He was the one who wanted to switch the stallions."

Stunned, Dakota stared at him. It *was* true.

"You didn't know about that, did you?" There was a rueful smile in his eyes. "Jared thought you'd guessed."

"I had Something Wicked blood-typed. It had to be him."

"It was him. The horse we buried was Something Wicked."

"Then I don't understand . . ."

His big hands started fiddling with the coffee mug. "It's a long story but I'm not going anywhere." He took a deep breath and launched into it.

Something Wicked's first two seasons at stud were a disappointment, he told her. The stallion didn't seem to pass on his blinding speed to his colts, and the percentage of foals indicated his sperm count was low. Despite that, Dan didn't discourage owners from sending their mares.

Then disaster struck. Something Wicked came down with a virus that laid him low for several weeks.

Mares were ready to be bred. One owner in particular, an influential force in the quarter horse industry, was threatening to withdraw his mare, a World Champion. When Dan palpated her ovaries and realized she had to be bred that day or not at all, he panicked. The owner—a bellicose know-it-all—had shown up to watch the procedure, and if he knew about Something Wicked's virus, he would make waves throughout the industry.

That was when Dan, walking past the stallion paddock, noticed Darkscope. He'd often joked about the two studs, how they were practically identical, except that one stallion had been a barn burner on the track, and the other had been a dud. Coke was hoping the younger stallion would at least pass on the bloodlines he shared with Something Wicked.

The owner was shouting at Dan. He had a meeting in Phoenix, and he didn't want to waste any more time. Dan was sick to death of the pushy bastard, so he went to the refrigerator where the semen was stored and picked out the vial labeled "Darkscope." He changed the labels and inseminated the mare under the owner's watchful eyes.

It served the son of a bitch right. And the deception went off without a hitch. It went so smoothly that he decided to try it again with the other mares to be bred. He began to store Darkscope's semen, marking it as Something Wicked's. It was easy.

Then Jared Ames, who had just returned from a three-week fishing trip to Alaska, noticed the semen containers marked "Something Wicked" in the refrigerator. He knew that the horse was still suffering from the virus. At first he accused Dan of breeding a sick horse, which could endanger the mares and any potential offspring.

Dan's face reddened. "I wouldn't do that."

"You sly dog. What're you doing? Breeding Darkscope as Something Wicked and pocketing the difference?"

That was how Dan got a partner. After Something Wicked recovered, Darkscope wasn't used as often, but Dan and Jared managed to make some money off the discrepancy in the stud fees.

And then a remarkable thing happened. Darkscope's colts started winning at the track, while Something Wicked's progeny lagged far behind. And so they switched the horses permanently. Dan fired the stallion grooms and put Darkscope in Something Wicked's more spacious stall. He even put the halter, the one with the brass plate emblazoned with "Something Wicked," on the pretender to the throne.

Everyone benefited. The "Something Wicked" colts were doing well for their owners, so Coke should be happy (if he'd known). Dan had saved his job, and began to siphon off a little money on the side—just a little, here and there. After all, hadn't he saved Black Oak from disaster? Something Wicked wasn't half the stallion Darkscope was.

Jared Ames made out like a bandit. So far, they'd been lucky; there was no reason for the people at the AQHA to compare records, so the discrepancies in blood-typing hadn't been noticed as yet. Dan knew he was playing a dangerous game, that one of these days he would be caught, but by that time his wife was sick and he needed all the money he could get. He continued to play Russian Roulette with every spin of the centrifuge.

Everything was going along smoothly until Coke died, and the dispersal sale was scheduled. That was the beginning of the end. By then, Marie was very ill, and Dan was buried under hospital bills. He'd already sold two crops of colts. Dakota had called him from Ruidoso, telling him that the representative from Lone Star was on his way.

"So Marcie always thought that Something Wicked was Darkscope and vice versa," Dakota said.

Dan nodded.

"When they were switched, she thought that the horse in Darkscope's stall was Something Wicked, even though he really was Darkscope. She just didn't *know* he was Darkscope." It was all so confusing. She was missing something in all this. Something important. It sat right at the edge of her mind, like the tip of an iceberg almost covered by murky waters. She shook her head. It eluded her.

Dan was playing with his wedding ring again. He was quiet now, after talking so long and freely about his deception. He wouldn't look at her.

Then it hit her. Something Wicked was dead. She'd always thought Jerry Tanner had killed him, but now . . . "You didn't have to kill him!" she said. "Why couldn't you just switch him back? Why did you have to kill him?"

"I didn't kill him on purpose," he said in an anguished voice. "I tried to switch them back. He was always hard to handle, being a stud. I was kind of in a hurry, it was dark, and he didn't like the smell of that stall. He knew another stud had been in there, and he got agitated." Dan tore more lids off more coffee creamers, splashed them into his coffee, but didn't drink. His hands started tearing up the little foil lids, his big, clublike fingers surprisingly gentle. "We had a tug-o-war—I was trying to get him into the stall, and he reared up and hit his head on the beam. Just right." He shook his head.

"It was an accident?"

Dan nodded.

"So Jerry Tanner didn't kill Something Wicked."

"There's something else I have to tell you. I was so scared, when you wouldn't leave. I wanted you to go. So I sent you those notes."

Dakota's blood ran cold. "The picture of the wrecked truck?"

"I had to, don't you see?"

"But I know Jerry tried to kill Shameless. He practically admitted it," she said, remembering the way he'd stood at the rail, waving the oleander branch.

"I didn't know who tried to kill Shameless. I just took advantage of it."

Dakota remembered picking up the morning paper the next day, throwing it down in fear. TRY AND TRY AGAIN. "How could you?"

"I had to do something. You were around too much, I had to scare you off."

"I can't believe it," she breathed. She felt betrayed. "That was cruel . . . What about the broodmares? Did you do that, too?"

"I had to. You wouldn't leave—"

"Would you have hurt them, like you threatened?"

"No," he whispered. "I could never do that. That's why I only cut their manes and tails."

"And yet you sold young horses down into Mexico, knowing that within the year they'd be running in match races!"

"I had to," he repeated, his mouth drawn into a stubborn line.

Dakota had a headache. She'd been prepared for the broodmares, but the stallions? That meant that all the horses they'd sold in the past several years were fakes. Black Oak had defrauded the public by passing off Darkscope colts as Something Wicked's. The enormity of it was impossible for her to grasp.

That something at the edge of her consciousness crowded

in again. Something she instinctively shied away from, something she didn't want to know.

"I don't know how to make it up to you."

"You can't," she said brusquely.

The torment in his eyes made her feel small.

"I guess we'll muddle through all this somehow." She couldn't think about this now. The All American was tomorrow. She'd have to sort this out later, if it could be sorted out. But even now, she had the terrible feeling that there would be no easy answer.

They had defrauded the public.

All of Something Wicked's foals were actually Darkscope's . . .

It was so hard to believe.

Something, something really bad, just at the edge . . .

And then it hit her, with the sound of the world caving in around her.

Shameless was Darkscope's foal, too.

Forty-Six

As Dakota hurried home to change for the pre-race dinner, she tried to deny the obvious. There had to be some kind of mistake, something she was missing.

Well, she'd be damned if she wasn't going to the dinner. This was the biggest night of her life, and she would not be cheated from it. *Coke* wouldn't be cheated from it. Every time her subconscious tried to bring it up, she shied away. Slam the door, bolt it shut. It wasn't true, it *couldn't* be true.

Think about the dinner. Coke would be so proud.

"Where've you been?" Clay asked when she walked through the door. He buttoned a crisp white shirt and tucked the tail into pleated pants.

Dakota didn't know what to say. If she told him now, her decision was made. Denying Shameless her chance to win the futurity would haunt her for the rest of her life. She needed time, serious thinking time to ponder all the ramifications, before committing herself. "I had errands," she lied.

Dakota saw the disappointment in his eyes, and knew he was wondering why she hadn't stuck around with him to celebrate Viento Prieto's good showing. What kind of errand was more important than that? "I'm sorry, Clay. They were things I had to do, or you know I would have stayed," she added lamely.

"Sure," he said.

This time, the drive to the clubhouse was a tense one. Dakota knew that Clay didn't buy her explanation, but he didn't say anything. And all the time the little voice in her head chanted like a mantra: impostor, imposter, imposter, imposter, until she thought she'd go mad.

This time the sunset looked like a gaudily painted backdrop, the shrimp was tasteless, the band dissonant. She took no pleasure in her surroundings, or the glorious man at her side. There was her table, just as she'd pictured it, with the name SHAMELESS running down the center in satin. It mocked her now. The night had an unreal feeling to it, as if she were swimming in an aquarium, and everyone could see in.

After they ate, the racing secretary spoke about the many changes for the good that would be coming to Ruidoso, then told the story about how the All American started. Dakota had heard the story many times before, but concentrated on the racing secretary's words, hoping they'd drown out her own inner voice.

In 1953, he told them, some of the West's top horsemen were swapping stories in the Hilton bar in Albuquerque, and boasted about their fine racing mares. These mares read like the *Who's Who* of quarter horse racing; Stella Moore, Shue Fly, Miss Princess, and High Deal. As horsemen had done for centuries, they argued about which was the best, finally agreeing on a race that would decide it once and for all. The following morning, in a more sober frame of mind, they realized their mistake. All the mares were in foal. And so they decided instead to race the foals that were *in utero* in two years' time. That was how the All American Futurity was born.

"Now, let's take a look at our ten qualifiers. As you know, Runaway Train, owned by Sid Lasco and trained by Dwayne Carouthers, was the fastest qualifier, followed by . . ." The secretary read the names in order of their times: First Down Dallas, Chamiso Te, Can't Touch This, Money Bunny, Yawl Yeller, Rampaging Ronda, Dreamcatcher, Shameless, and Dashforatouchdown.

Dakota stared up at the monitors until her neck hurt,

watching the qualifiers run their races. Runaway Train was the most impressive, winning his trial by one length at a blistering speed, just an eighth of a second off the track record for a two-year-old. In Shameless's trial, the filly seemed to strain to catch Dreamcatcher. But the extra week and the tough race had made a difference, and Dakota believed the filly was back to her old self. Shameless was ready to run.

If she were allowed to run.

They drove back to the cabin in silence. When Clay started to undress, Dakota stopped him. "I'm sorry, Clay, but I'm really tired. I'd like to be alone."

His forehead knitted into a scowl. "Dakota, are you all right?"

"I'm fine. I just need to be alone."

"What's going on?"

Don't tell him. "I just want to get a good night's sleep, and you know if you stay . . . I need the rest. Honestly." She smiled wanly. "Big day tomorrow."

He left, but she could tell he didn't believe her.

When he was gone, she stared at the wall, where a photograph of Coke in the winner's circle at Los Alamitos hung in all its glory. Tears blurred her eyes. "I'm sorry, Daddy," she muttered. "I don't know what to do."

It was good she hadn't involved Clay. This was her decision to make; she couldn't burden him with it. Besides, if she decided not to tell the stewards—and there was that possibility, she had to think of every possibility to be fair—she couldn't bring Clay into the deception.

But of course she would scratch the filly. She had to.

Dakota shivered. All that work, all that risk, down the drain. . . . It wasn't as if she were drugging the horse, or pulling in a ringer. The filly was the real thing. So she wasn't sired by Something Wicked. But she won the Rainbow on her own, didn't she? She got into the All American fair and square. It wasn't *cheating,* exactly. . . .

And Dakota was as much a victim in this as everybody else. She hadn't planned to defraud anyone. This was not her doing. She was innocent—

Until now. Now she knew.

Again, the enormity of what Dan Bolin had done hit her. How could she ever untangle this mess? There were hundreds of horses out there with fake pedigrees. The lawsuits would bankrupt her. This was the legacy of Black Oak, she thought bitterly. This was how it would end for one of the finest old quarter horse ranches in America. The reek of corruption would follow her father's name down the years.

Her father hadn't bothered with his breeding operation, and this was the result.

"Why the hell didn't you pay attention?" she cried, kicking his favorite chair. "It serves you right, you old bastard!"

Coke's apathy—that was the cause of all this. He loved racing, so that meant he had to belittle the breeding part of Black Oak. Leave it in someone else's hands, treat it like an unwanted child. It was typical of the man she knew. Everything in his life had been set into an adversarial context. He'd played Dakota against her mother when she was younger, before they'd both escaped to California. He found it impossible to believe that Dakota could love them both, equally but differently. His intolerance had made her mother's life unbearable. And now his apathy toward the breeding operation had, to quote the Bible, reaped a whirlwind.

She found herself crying, sobbing, her shoulders shaking as the pain burst through her. She was crying not for a lost chance at the All American, but for the man who had hurt her and loved her at the same time. She cried out her betrayal, her rage, her loss. The tears had no beginning and no end; she felt as if she would drown in them.

Grief was its own sedative. Mercifully, she fell asleep, her tears still wetting her pillow.

She awoke to the sun slanting in through the windows. It was All American Day. On the heels of that thought came the ugly reality. There would be no All American for her.

She picked up the phone, punched out the first three digits of Clay's number, then set the phone back down. The thought of reciting the story again, the tangled skein of lies and deceit, was too much to bear. She'd tell him after she talked to the stewards.

And, the niggling little voice at the back of her mind insisted, *if I don't tell the stewards, he won't be a party to it.*

She went around and around the issue like a mouse on a treadmill. One minute, she decided to go to the stewards. The next, she was equally determined to run the filly no matter what. Give her her chance. As the Nike ad said, Just Do It.

But in the end, she knew she could not. The taint would follow her for the rest of her life, even if no one else knew. And Clay . . . She couldn't start her new life with Clay like this. There would be other races. Probably not the All American, but they would have to be enough. Her decision was made.

Dakota ran cold water, dabbed puffy eyelids with a washcloth. Her eyes felt like grapes that had been dipped in sand. She turned on the "Today Show." There was no point in going on the backside this morning. Shameless was through as a racehorse. She would go later, scratch the filly, and then head for home. The next several days would be ugly, but she had to face them. She'd have to call every one of the owners who had bought horses at the dispersal sale. And what about the mares that had been bred to Something Wicked over the last few years?

She supposed she should try to buy back as many of them as she could. It wouldn't take long to run out of money, but she had to do something. No doubt she could get a good price for Shameless after her win in the Rainbow, no matter what her breeding was. Too bad she wasn't a colt. The money from a promising stallion prospect just might have been enough to pay back all the people Black Oak had cheated . . .

Swallowing back her panic, Dakota took her suitcases down from the closet and began to pack her things.

As Derek Blue pulled into the parking lot of the sheriff's office, he recognized Ken Daltry's truck. Ken stood beside it, one foot on the rear bumper.

"Hey, Ken! What can I do you for?"

Daltry, bartender at the Cowpony Bar and Grill, blinked against the early morning sun. He was pale as a cadaver. "I've been trying to figure out if it's important or not," he said, following Derek into the office. "It's probably just talk, knowing Jerry, but I thought I oughta pass it on."

Derek waited. Ken never got around to anything important right away. He was the second-guessingest man Derek had ever known.

"If you think about it, a bartender's kind of like a father confessor, you know? I probably shouldn't even be here."

Derek sat down and folded his hands over his lap.

Daltry scratched his neck. "I guess it won't hurt none, since a couple of other guys heard him. He was in my place not too long ago, drinking too much as usual."

"Go on."

"I wouldn't say this except it might have something to do with Coke's death. I heard about how you arrested him but had to let him go. He was going on and on about how he knew what happened to Coke and how the stupid cops wouldn't figure it out in a million years—sorry, Derek, but that's what he said—and when I asked him straight out he clammed up and said he'd already said too much and he was by God gonna keep his mouth shut."

"He had to keep his mouth shut about Coke's death?"

"That's what he said. He said a lot to things—boasted about coming into some money soon. Said how he deserved that money because he was, how did he put it? Family. That's what he said. He was family and she damn well wasn't going to shut him out."

"She? Did he say who 'she' was?"

"Nope. But he mentioned her a few times. I can't remember his exact words, just the general idea he had a real grudge going for this lady."

A terrible thought occurred to Derek, one that on the face of it seemed impossible. He leaned forward. "Could 'she' be Dakota McAllister?"

"I guess."

"What else did he say?"

"It was all kind of snarled up. He didn't make a lot of sense, on account of his drinking. Mostly, he talked about how he was going to be rich. How they'd have to pay him to keep him from telling everything he knew. Sounded like blackmail to me."

"Anything else?"

Daltry frowned. "Something about how it was all coming back. It was like a dream, but now he was remembering more and how he didn't think it was a dream anymore. Called it a fun ride—no, that wasn't it. A joy ride."

"Did you ask what he meant by that?"

"Yeah. He thought it was real funny I didn't know what he was talking about. All he'd say was he was taken for a real ride all right, but it wasn't going to end there."

"That's it?"

"All's I can remember. Does it make any sense to you?"

Derek shook his head. "Sounds like he knows who killed Coke, though, doesn't it?"

"That's why I came."

After Daltry had gone, Derek pondered what he'd been told. What was Dakota not going to get away with? Could she have killed her own father? Had Jerry witnessed it, maybe in a blackout state, and now remembered?

That didn't make any sense at all. Dakota had been in Los Angeles at the time of her father's death. And he'd had enough dealings with her to know that she didn't act like a murderer.

But there was that insurance policy. He supposed he ought to look into it.

Forty-Seven

Zipping up her suitcase, Dakota glanced at the clock. Eleven-thirty already. She couldn't put it off any longer. It was time to head for the track.

She was almost out the door when the phone rang.

"Dakota! I'm so glad I caught you!" Lucy Tanner sounded agitated.

"I'm just leaving—"

"Clay's had an accident!"

"What?" Shock slammed into her. "Is he hurt?"

"I don't know. I think so. Yes, he's got to be hurt because he can't get back up the mountain—"

"Mountain? Where are you? What happened?"

"I'm up on Sierra Blanca. Near that barbecue place . . ." She paused, as if getting her bearings. "I'm not sure where, it's on the main road. But he's not here. He's down below."

Dakota was confused. Confused and scared to death. She closed her eyes, trying to marshal her thoughts. "Lucy, calm down. You're not making any sense. What happened?"

Lucy took a deep breath. "You've got to come. He's asking for you."

"Is there anyone there? An ambulance? What's wrong with him?"

"I don't *know*," she wailed.

"Is the ambulance there?" Dakota repeated. "It might be faster if I met him at the hospital. For God's sake, Lucy, how bad is it?"

"Look, I've got to get back to him. I called the paramedics. They should be here by the time you get here."

"Where do I go?"

"You'll see Rita's Range Rover on the side of the road. There's an old mobile home in a field. Just past it, on the right. Hurry!" She hung up.

Five minutes later, Dakota turned onto Mecham and headed toward Sierra Blanca, her heart in her throat.

After Daltry left, Derek Blue checked his messages. One was a bombshell—a call from the Lincoln County Sheriff's Department. They wanted information on one Jerry Tanner, whom they believed had been killed in a trailer fire.

Derek whistled through his teeth. If Tanner had black-mailed someone, he hadn't been careful enough.

As Dakota turned off 48 onto Ski Run Road, she tried to think rationally. It was difficult, considering how scared she was. Her heart pounded so hard she could hear it in her ears. She had no patience for slower cars, passing them as soon as she was able, often on a double yellow line. She drove Coke's Ford as if it were a race car.

He has to be all right, her frenzied brain repeated over and over. *Has to be.* She couldn't lose him now. She loved him, God how she loved him! She wanted to spend the rest of her life with him. The gods couldn't be that cruel, to let her finally find love again only to take it away!

Think! she told herself sternly. She tried to sort out the jumble of Lucy's words. He was alive. Lucy had said that much. If she could just get there and see for herself.

She accelerated out of a turn, realized too late it was one of those hairpins that went on forever. The truck's tires screamed as she braked, hit the shoulder, spewing up dust.

She fought the wheel, accelerated, letting centrifugal force take her out of the turn. Slowed down just a hair, her mind going a thousand miles a minute as she scanned the road, looking for a mobile home in a field, and a dark green Range Rover parked on the verge.

He's alive. Hold on to that.

What had he been doing up here, anyway, on All American Day? He should be at the stable, not halfway up Sierra Blanca—

First she saw the barbecue place, and a little farther up, the mobile home. Stripped to the frame, rusting in the field. The Range Rover was up ahead on the right. Sunlight arrowed off the back window, almost blinding her. She pulled over, slamming the truck into park before it had stopped completely.

Lucy leaned against the Rover's driver's door, appearing oddly cozy in a saddle blanket jacket and jeans.

"Where's Clay? she demanded. "Is the ambulance here?"

"He's just up this road," Lucy said, pointing at the dirt road just beyond the Range Rover.

"Where's the ambulance?"

"They're already up there. I thought I'd wait for you. You can ride with me."

Just then the Range Rover's car phone shrilled.

Ignoring the phone, Lucy opened the door and got in. "It's unlocked," she said.

"Aren't you going to answer that? It could be more help."

"I told you, they're already there." Lucy backed the Range Rover up, spun the wheel expertly, and sped up the dirt road.

The phone kept ringing.

"I think you should answer it."

Lucy sighed. "All right."

Rita had a nail appointment at eleven. She didn't notice the Range Rover was missing until then. The first person she called was Clay. She paged him at Ruidoso Downs, but got no answer. Maybe he was out on the track.

Damn! She wanted to talk to him so badly. It couldn't wait until tomorrow, when he'd promised to meet her for lunch. She needed his opinion now. Things were getting out of hand—she'd really painted herself into a corner with this whole foster mother thing.

It suddenly occurred to her that she could reach the Range Rover by phone. If someone had stolen it, of course, he wouldn't answer, but it was worth a try.

The phone rang forever. She was about to hang up, feeling foolish that she'd tried to call a car thief, when someone picked up.

"Hello? Who is this?" she demanded.

"Uh ... who's this?"

Relief drenched her. Lucy had taken her truck without asking. *Stealing,* the small voice in her mind said. That was one of the signs. "What are you doing with my truck?"

"I had to see if Clay was all right."

"Clay? What happened?"

"There's been an accident."

Rita clutched the phone cord. "What? Is he all right?"

"I don't know." The disembodied voice sounded dull.

"What's going on?"

"I told you," Lucy said coldly. "Clay's been in a car wreck."

"Where are you? How bad is he? What's going on?" Rita could taste the fear in her mouth.

Faintly, she heard Dakota McAllister's voice. "Tell her we're on Ski Run Road."

"Ski Run Road? What's he doing up there? Lucy? Can you hear me?"

"Uh, I gotta go." And she hung up.

Rita looked out the window. What was going on? Why were Lucy and Dakota up on the mountain? What had happened to Clay? God, if anything had happened to him—

You can't believe a word she says.

But Dakota was there.

Rita sat down, her mind a whirlwind. Had Lucy heard her talking to the counselor? Did the girl know that she was having second thoughts about adopting her?

Lucy wouldn't hurt Clay, would she? The counselor she'd

talked to had said that she was probably harmless. *Probaby* harmless.

When Derek pressed line two, he heard Ken Daltry's apologetic voice on the other end of the line. "I asked Jolyn—she was working tables that night—if she knew who Tanner was talking about."

Derek pulled a legal pad toward him.

"The 'she' I told you about? According to Jolyn, it was his daughter. Lucy Tanner."

Forty-Eight

Although she'd tried to deny it, Rita had begun to dislike Lucy weeks ago. The little things got to her. The way the girl lied about anything and everything. Lucy was a chronic liar, and could do it without turning a hair.

She'd deluded herself into thinking that Clay would leave Dakota when he saw what a cold-hearted bitch she was, but that wasn't how it happened. It was a nice fantasy, Clay marrying her and the two of them taking in Lucy as a foster child, shutting Dakota McAllister out in the cold. But Rita was no fool. The more time she spent with Lucy, the more the girl bothered her.

Lucy was just plain unpleasant.

Rita had begun to feel trapped.

When Jerry died, Lucy naturally assumed that Rita would start adoption proceedings immediately. It would be the three of them, Lucy said. They would be a perfect family.

If Rita was honest with herself, she couldn't blame Lucy for talking that way. Hadn't she filled her head with that fantasy? Of course, that was before she got to know the girl better.

Rita had decided that if she was going to go through with this—and she wasn't at all sure that she would—she'd at least talk to a couple of Lucy's teachers and see if they could get to the bottom of this lying problem.

Rita did not know what she was in for.

Last week, a woman had called, identifying herself as a

school counselor at Patagonia High. "I understand you're interested in adopting Lucy Tanner," the woman said. "I could lose my job for this, but I thought I should warn you . . ."

What Margaret Whiting told her chilled her blood. There had been problems at school with Lucy's lying, and that wasn't all. Hard to believe that a girl who looked like Lucy was promiscuous, but it was true. She'd slept with several boys at school, and told more than a few she was pregnant by them, causing all sorts of trouble with their families.

She hadn't been pregnant at all.

Lucy shoplifted from local stores, and manipulated other children into stealing, too. In fact, they were usually the ones to get in trouble.

Lucy had a crush on one of the boys at school, but he dated a pretty cheerleader named Ashley Snipes. Ashley Snipes swore that Lucy was following her around and giving her the "evil eye." She even claimed that Lucy had killed her puppy. At the time the accusation seemed fanciful, but something happened to make an A student like Ashley fail her courses and lose weight. Finally, her parents took her out of school. The following day, Lucy asked Ashley's boyfriend to take her to the prom. Ashley's parents complained that Lucy had been persecuting their daughter in order to go to the prom with her boyfriend, and since they had been on the school board, the counselor was called in to talk to Lucy.

"There was so much trouble that the school paid for a psychiatric evaluation—and I'm telling you, they don't put out money unless there's a reason."

Rita asked her what was in the evaluation.

"It was sealed. I wasn't allowed to see it, but I know my *DSM III.*"

"Excuse me?"

"That's *the* book on abnormal psychology. There's no doubt in my mind that Lucy suffers from Antisocial Personality Disorder. The layman's term for it is sociopath. She fits the profile like a glove."

Rita's blood froze. "Sociopath? Wasn't Ted Bundy a sociopath?"

"I've done a lot of reading up on the subject—I'm this close to getting into the doctorate program at the University of Arizona, so I know my stuff—not all sociopaths are killers. They're just . . . well, it's as if there's something missing. They feel no remorse for their actions. They don't have empathy for other people. Con men are almost always sociopaths. They're users."

Users. Well, Lucy had certainly used her!

"Manipulators. Lying is as natural as breathing to a sociopath. They don't care if they get caught in the lie a few minutes later, it doesn't mean anything to them. They can be charming, but sooner or later people begin to sense there's something not quite right about them. Sociopaths try to be like other people, emulate what they see, but it never quite works."

That was Lucy. Sometimes, when Rita talked to Lucy, she had the oddest impression she was looking into a distorted mirror.

Sociopaths, Margaret Whiting said, manifested their unusual behavior early on. Girls somewhat later than boys. Boys were more overtly dangerous. Fighting, abusing drugs, starting fires, maiming or killing animals, lying and stealing were all signs of a possible Antisocial Personality Disorder.

The counselor went on to tell her that Lucy hadn't shown any signs of being dangerous, but she thought that it would be an "unrewarding relationship" at best. "You can't change a sociopath. There really isn't any hope. She won't love you like a normal child would, and I'm afraid that taking on responsibility for someone like that would only frustrate you. I felt I ought to warn you, even though by doing so, I'm skating on ethical ice. Please don't tell anyone I told you. It could mean my job."

Rita had been stunned. But when she'd given it time to sink in, she realized that Margaret Whiting's assessment of Lucy Tanner was right on target.

And so last night, when Lucy had prattled on about how happy she'd be when Clay married Rita and the adoption went through, Rita had humored her.

"Now that Daddy's gone, you won't have any trouble adopting me, will you?" Lucy had asked her. "If you're married to Clay, it won't be hard at all."

No remorse. The girl acted as if she didn't give a damn that her father had burned to death.

Rita had answered her carefully. "I shouldn't imagine we'd have any trouble. Assuming Clay and I get married." That was her out. Let Lucy blame the whole thing on Clay; he was strong enough to handle it. She wanted out, but she had to be careful. Looking at her beautiful Himalayan cat, Rita thought of Ashley Snipe's puppy and shivered.

She needed time to figure out how to get out of this without angering Lucy. She needed to talk to Clay. He would know what to do.

Rita tried the racetrack again. Clay didn't answer his page. Maybe Lucy hadn't lied after all. Maybe Clay was up on the mountain. Why else would Dakota be there?

Rita decided she'd better go up to Sierra Blanca, just in case. She left a message on Clay's answering machine and headed for the door.

She was almost to the garage when she realized she'd have to rent a car.

Forty-Nine

"What happened?" Dakota asked Lucy as they jounced down the rutted dirt road.

"I told you. He fell."

"He was hiking? Today?" Clay wouldn't have gone hiking up on Sierra Blanca on All American Day. "I thought you told Rita he was in a car wreck."

"I said he was in a wreck. A rock fall. He fell a long way. Here we are." Lucy stopped the vehicle abruptly. She got out and followed a wide path leading into the forest.

"Where's the ambulance?"

"They're already down there. Come on."

Hugging herself against a chill that seemed to come from within, Dakota followed Lucy through the tall meadow grass. They followed the slope down between black trunks of ponderosa pine until they reached an outcropping of lichen-carpeted granite. Lucy clambered up one rock that rose up from the forest floor like a whale's back.

Dakota saw no car tracks. Heard nothing but the breeze soughing through the pines, high up. Her uneasiness increased. What game was Lucy playing? "Come on, Lucy," she said in as stern a voice as she could summon. "What's going on?"

Lucy stood on the rock, her breath coming in ragged gasps. "We've got to hurry."

"No."

Lucy stared at her, and then her eyes filled up with tears.

"Dakota, what's wrong with you? You've gotta come. He told me he had to see you. I promised him." She swiped at her nose. "Please?"

"Not until you tell me what's going on."

"There's another way down," Lucy said through strangling tears. "The ambulance followed the road—they're down there now. Come on, we gotta hurry, before they take him out. He might not make it. That's what I'm scared of. I promised him you'd come—please?"

He might not make it.

Lucy's tears had to be real. Dakota felt the void open up beneath her, the boundless fear. Lucy looked so forlorn, standing there. Forlorn and frightened and desperate. *He might not make it.*

Dakota climbed up the rock. It must be an overlook, because Lucy was staring down. Cautiously, Dakota walked to the edge.

Expecting to see ambulances and police cars like matchbox toys down in the canyon, her thoughts were wiped clean of her agony for Clay in an instant. There was nothing there. Nothing but forest. A steep dropoff studded with sharp boulders and choked by ferns and blackjack pine.

Relief drenched her, followed by a deeper, more visceral fear as all the pieces fell into place. Lucy had lured her here.

Her mind exploded with the image of the headlights at the White Sands, the rifle report—

The command from her brain took its time, wending its way in agonizingly slow motion through all the checkpoints, the misfiring synapses, past the drumroll of her heart, all the way to her legs but at last they tensed, the balls of her feet prepared to push away from the rock, to run—

Air displacement behind her. She spun around just as Lucy's hands shot out and shoved her, hard.

"He's down there," Lucy said, as her hands came into contact with Dakota's chest.

Fifty

The more Rita thought about it, the more certain she became that Lucy was indeed dangerous.

As she drove, she thought back to her confrontation with Eddie Dejarlais. He'd come by yesterday, swaggering up to her place as if he owned it. He had the nerve to try to see Lucy, even though he was the one who took her to a bar and got them both arrested. Rita told him Lucy wasn't around, and that even if she was, he couldn't see her anymore.

"It's a free country," he'd replied, narrowing his mean little eyes. "You ask her. She wants to see me. Can't get enough of me, as a matter of fact."

"Get off my property."

"You think she's such a good girl," he jeered. "The night her dad kicked off, she couldn't get enough."

"What do you mean?"

"It was her idea to go to the bar. She said she wanted to celebrate—"

"Celebrate?"

"Yeah. She woke me up, and boy, was she hot. A little wildcat in bed." He paused to let that one sink in. "Then she got me to take her to the bar. Ordered champagne."

"Champagne."

" 'Cause she was celebrating. She said all her problems were over, and we'd be hearing about it soon."

We'd be hearing about it soon.

The conversation hadn't meant much at the time, but now Rita saw it in a different light.

What was she celebrating? Jerry Tanner's death?

Steering with her left hand, she fumbled in her purse for her Mace.

Derek Blue looked at his notes from Ken Daltry's visit. If "she" was Lucy, why would Jerry Tanner talk about blackmailing his own daughter?

Derek doodled on the pad, drawing a caricature of Jerry in his beat-up truck, a fifth of Southern Comfort dangling from one arm as he held it out like a turn signal. Derek had gone to art school before he'd decided on becoming a law officer, but now he confined his art to doodling. He was quite pleased with his artistic rendition—the Southern Comfort in Jerry's outstretched hand looked real enough to drink.

Those kids had been so sure that the truck had been used in the McAllister homicide, but he'd dismissed it because Jerry had the perfect alibi. Tanner was too drunk to drive, and his daughter had driven him home that night. Derek had accepted Jerry's alibi at face value.

But what if he looked at it another way?

On an impulse, he erased Jerry Tanner, and drew in a plump teenager with pixie hair instead. He put Jerry in the passenger seat. Staring glassily ahead. The more he drew, the more it made sense.

Ken had told him that Jerry had been taken for a carnival ride—no, that wasn't it—a *joy* ride.

Kids took joy rides. They stole people's cars and they drove around for kicks.

"Good God," he breathed. She ran down Coke McAllister with her father passed out in the truck—or at least she thought he was passed out.

She was either very smart or very stupid.

He picked up the phone and called the Lincoln County Sheriff's Office.

* * *

Dakota lost her balance. She tried to throw herself sideways, but it was too late. Pitching over backward, she experienced in slow motion the sensation of flying, and before she reached the violent thump at the end there burst through her mind all the car crashes she'd ever seen in the movies, only her disbelieving brain told her this time it was her, she was the body hurtling through space like a missile and hitting the ground with bone-jamming force.

Dazed and bruised, her mind registered the hit, the rock ramming into her side, and then she bounced up again and flipped over, crashing shoulder first through the brush and ferns before coming to a sliding stop against the rough bark of a tree in the canyon.

Her side was bleeding, so were her hands, there was a throbbing in her shoulder and one foot, but essentially she was all right, unless something had happened inside.

"Dakota?" Lucy called from above.

Dakota tried to appear motionless. Maybe Lucy would go away.

No such luck. She heard the trickle and slide of rocks as Lucy started down the hill.

Clay walked back from Dakota's barn the third time that day, wondering what the hell was going on. Ernesto, in the process of scraping the excess water off Shameless after her bath, told Clay he hadn't seen her.

After lunch Clay had tried to reach her at home, but she wasn't there, either. It was going on two-thirty and the All American would be run around four. She should be at the stable.

She should be with him. This was the biggest day of her life, and he wanted to share it with her.

He had her paged, but there was no answer. Stifling his frustration and the first small beginnings of worry, he went back to his own barn.

* * *

Dakota felt Lucy's shadow on her back, but kept herself from flinching.

"I know you're alive," Lucy said in a conversational tone. "I can see you breathing."

Dakota heard Lucy's boots scuff the ground as the teenager shifted her stance. Turning her face to the side, Dakota saw Lucy standing above her, arms upraised, holding a rock the size of a watermelon. Poised to drop it on Dakota's skull.

Instinct made Dakota twist away, just as the rock crashed onto the stone where her head had been. She scrabbled through the choking ferns, trying to get enough purchase to rise to her feet.

Lucy reached her just as she stood up, just as she put her weight down on her right foot and felt the excruciating pain arrow up her ankle.

She couldn't run. Her ankle was broken. Lucy bulled into her, knocking her to the ground. Her head cracked against another rock, she felt the warm ooze of blood. Stunned, she watched as Lucy bent to pick up the rock again.

"Tell me why!" Dakota gasped. "At least tell me why!"

Lucy considered her, then let the rock drop. Brushed her hands on her jeans. "You promise you won't try to run?"

"I promise."

"You're not going anywhere. Your ankle's broken."

"You're right. I'm not going anywhere."

Lucy sat down on a boulder. "It's not like I *want* to kill you. I just have to."

The pain in her ankle was making her dizzy. She didn't know if she was hearing right. She was sweating from the pain. "Why . . ." she felt herself slipping out of consciousness, brought herself back with gritted teeth. "Why do you have to?"

"Rita says if Clay marries her she'll adopt me. You're in the way."

"That's crazy!"

Lucy stared at her a moment, as if gauging her true feelings. "All right. I want revenge."

"Revenge? For what?"

"Because you fired me." Her voice was flat. "You kept Ernesto, even though I took better care of Shameless, and you didn't let me stay in the cabin—that reminds me. Do you still have that lamp, the one with the stagecoach base?"

"Yes." This had to be a dream.

"It's so cool. Do you mind if I have it? You won't need it."

"I'll tell you what, you can have your old job back."

"Why would I want a piss-poor job like that? I've already got everything I want. But I'd kind of like the cabin. It was nice there, those summers Coke let us stay. You should have hired Dad. It's your fault, Dakota. I gave you plenty of chances."

Dakota tried to hold on to the thread of reason. "Did you kill Coke?"

"Daddy ran him down in the road like a dog. I was there, though."

"It *was* Jerry." She was really fading, now.

Lucy took a stick and drew on the ground. "Maybe Rita and Clay will buy the cabin when they adopt me. How much do you think it'll sell for?"

"Clay won't marry Rita."

"He will if you're dead."

"You really meant it, didn't you? You're going to kill me because Clay loves me?"

"Sure. Why not?" Suddenly Lucy looked worried. "Don't you think it will work?"

Dakota almost laughed aloud. What was Lucy doing, asking her advice regarding her own murder? "No. It won't work. Clay won't marry Rita, not even if you kill me. He doesn't love her."

Lucy looked angry. Her face wavered in and out. "You're just trying to trick me."

"It's true." Dakota drifted.

A while later, when the pain drew her back to consciousness, she was surprised to realize she was still alive. Lucy was flinging rocks at trees.

"Did you see that? Bull's-eye! I'm a good shot, too."

"What are you waiting for?" Dakota asked.

Lucy came over and hunkered down beside her. "I wanted to ask you something." She looked completely innocent, her eyes bright with hope. "Did you ever think of adopting me? I know you liked me, and you felt sorry because of my rotten childhood—I heard you talking to Clay about it. That's why I didn't kill Shameless when Dad asked me to, because I thought you and Clay would be my family."

"We talked about it," Dakota lied.

"If I'd met you earlier I wouldn't have had to kill Coke."

This was crazy. Was she still alive, or had she gone to some weird place suspended between heaven and earth, where the inmates were all insane? "I thought you said your father killed Coke."

"Nope," Lucy said proudly, sitting on a tall rock and swinging her legs. She looked like any teenager on a picnic. "I did. I ran him down in the truck. It took some good driving, let me tell you."

"I'll bet."

"I almost wiped out on that turn, though. It sure was a close call." She sighed, her face softly reminiscent.

"Why'd you kill him?"

"Because," Lucy said.

"Stop playing games!" The pain was getting to her.

"He was going to the sheriff. He had proof that Dad was hurting his horses. Dad said that if he was in jail, I'd get thrown out on the street, I'd have to live out of garbage cans. Of course, that was bullshit. It wouldn't have been that bad, but I'd have to get a job—a real one, not just taking care of horses. At McDonald's or something. Yuck!"

"So you killed my father because he *might* have gone to the sheriff, and they *might* have had enough evidence to put your dad in jail, and you *might* have to go to work? That's why you killed my father?"

"Isn't that a good reason?" Unsure of herself again. Dakota noticed that Lucy was watching her for cues.

"I guess, if you wanted to keep your father out of jail."

"You know, Dakota, you could have saved yourself all this if you'd just offered to take me off Dad's hands. He would have been glad to see me go—especially if you gave him the trainer's job at Black Oak. You and I and Clay could stay in the cabin, we could train racehorses and the three of us would've had a great time, doing all those great things, like that time we went to Nogales? That was so much fun!"

"We can still do that," Dakota said, trying to keep the hope out of her voice.

"Yeah, and pigs will fly. You shouldn't try to fool me like that, Dakota." She stood up. "I've gotta go." She picked up the rock.

"Wait a minute!" Dakota cried. "What about your dad? Did you kill him, too?"

Her eyes grew muddy again with cunning. "I told you I gotta go." But Dakota's question was enough for her to drop her guard. Dakota reached out and grabbed her foot, pulled up with all her might. Lucy toppled over backward.

Dakota thrust her hands into the dirt and shoved herself up onto all fours, pushing off with her good leg and dragging the other. It was impossible, Lucy would be on her in a minute, but anything was better than waiting to die.

A crack of a branch as a rock hurtled past her. Dakota tried to ignore it, her nerve endings screaming in agony as she pushed away with the bad leg. She had to run. Had to run on this broken leg or she was dead.

Lucy crashed through the brush behind her. With every ounce of courage she had, Dakota thrust off and up like a runner from the starting block. The pain screeched inside her, like guitar strings strung too tightly, deafened her with an agony so great she forgot everything else.

Lucy was gaining. She could hear her breath. Lucky she was chubby.

Up ahead she saw a patch of blue. Too blue to be a lake, or even the sky. It was a tent.

Dakota ran toward the tent, screaming as loud as she could. She screamed "fire"—something she'd heard was more effective than "help!" or "rape!", and couldn't believe her eyes when a man burst out of the tent and grabbed his camp shovel.

All this she saw like a kaleidoscope—the man, the shovel, the tent, while Lucy's fingers reached out and yanked some of her hair out like ripped stitches and clutched at her clothing.

And then all dissolved into blackness.

The All American was the next race on the card.

On the way to Dakota's barn Clay saw Fern Sawyer, the former all-around champion cowgirl and a fixture in the All American post parade for over thirty years, warming up in the infield. She wore red, white and blue; sequins and rhinestones shimmered in the mellow late summer sun. The grandstand was filled to capacity, and Clay could feel the buzzing excitement from here.

Dakota still wasn't at the barn.

He remembered how strange she'd acted last night. Withdrawn, prickly, distracted. At the time he had put it down to her being nervous about today. Now, he wondered if she'd been hiding something.

Where the hell was she? He knew her as well as he knew himself. Dakota would be here if it were humanly possible.

Something had happened.

He thought of the White Sands. Pulse pounding, he strode to his truck and placed a call to the sheriff's office. He told them he wanted to report a missing person. Predictably, the officer replied that a person who had been seen last night was not technically a missing person. He got the same results from the state police.

"But you don't understand," he said, biting back his anger. "She's running a horse in the All American. There's no way she wouldn't be here."

"You'd be surprised at what people do."

Clay hung up.

What could he do? Where could he look for her? Maybe her car had broken down, maybe she'd overslept, maybe the moon was made of green cheese.

Clay paced the barn area. If Shameless was going to run, they'd have to get her ready *now*.

The filly was cross-tied outside her stall. Ernesto wrapped her legs carefully, soothing her with gentle Spanish words.

"*La has visto?*" Clay asked him.

He shook his head.

"*¿Que vas a hacer?*"

Ernesto met Clay with defiant eyes and spoke in precise Spanish. "I will race the filly for her."

Rita thought she recognized Dakota's truck. The Range Rover was gone, but since the truck was parked right before the dirt road, she decided to try it. But first, she'd take a look at Dakota's truck.

It was unlocked. She found a Dunkin' Donuts cup on the dash, a lead rope that had seen better days, and a black zippered bag on the seat. She opened the bag and saw the gun.

Rita had never shot a gun. She was afraid of them, as a matter of fact. But the thought of Lucy on the same mountain gave her the creeps. She lifted it gingerly, tried to ascertain if it was loaded. Well, loaded or not, it would be a deterrent.

Carrying it away from her body, careful to point it far away from her own limbs, Rita walked to the car and drove up the logging road.

A mile and a half down the road, she found the Range Rover.

Gary Brandt had been spreading out his bedroll when he heard the woman screaming there was a fire. He crawled out of his tent and grabbed the camp shovel leaning against the tree at the edge of his campsite.

The woman pelting toward him was covered with blood.

He couldn't see her very well; she was running through sunlight and the deep dark shadows of the pines, and there was a lot of tall brush and scrubby trees that seemed to be tearing at her as she ran. "Where's the fire?" he called, running out to meet her.

She was still a long way from him when suddenly she fell to the ground, like a bird falling out of the sky.

He dropped his shovel and ran toward her.

She was unconscious, bleeding from a wound at the back of her head. He thought of the first-aid kit in his Blazer.

Best not to move her. But if he could clean her up a little and see what kind of wound it was ... Gary stood up uncertainly, then turned and walked for the truck.

The last thing he saw was the shovel swinging up into his line of sight. He was killed instantly.

Clay accompanied Ernesto and Shameless down the infield path toward the saddling paddock, still expecting Dakota to show up any minute.

There she'd be, wearing her All-American finery, walking up to him at the paddock, her golden hair bouncing on her shoulders. "I'm sorry I gave you such a scare," she'd say, and Ernesto would hand the reins over to her and the three of them would saddle the filly for her greatest triumph.

But there was no trim figure, no golden hair. Time ticked inexorably on. His eyes constantly scanned the paddock, the stands, the jockey room, but she wasn't coming. The paddock judge checked Shameless and nodded to Ernesto to saddle her. And still she didn't come. Clay walked the filly around, more nervous than any horse. The paddock judge called "jockeys up," and Shameless's rider swung aboard. And still she didn't come.

Fern Sawyer led the post parade on her prancing gray horse. Clay mounted Tyke and led Shameless to the post, swiveling in his saddle to scan the stands.

Something had happened to her. He knew it.

With a sick heart, he watched them load the gates for the All American.

He wanted to do something. Go somewhere. Look for her. But where would he start? Ernesto, in his colorful cowboy shirt and flowered gimme cap, stood by the rail in a small knot of anxious trainers, shoulder to shoulder with the likes of Jack Brooks and Sleepy Gilbreath. He, too, had a horse in the All American. That knowledge made him appear bigger, his shoulders broader, his posture straighter.

Clay swung down from Tyke, ducked under the rail, and handed the reins to Ernesto. He knew he wasn't needed. Ernesto, as assistant trainer, was the only person who could run the filly anyway.

As he sprinted to the parking lot, Clay wondered where the hell he should start looking for the woman he loved—and feared he had already lost.

Dakota remained unconscious only a few moments. She heard the man's voice telling her to lie still, it would be all right, and he would be right back.

Safe at last. But the pain was beginning to drive her crazy. The adrenaline that had helped her run on a broken ankle had disappeared with her relief, and she feared she had done herself a lot of damage.

Painfully, Dakota sat up. Convinced that the bone was sticking out, she suddenly had to see her foot.

That was when she heard the thump, like someone hitting a melon with a hoe, and looked up to see her rescuer fall backward into the ferns. Lucy stood over him, the camp shovel in her hands.

As Dakota watched, Lucy turned slowly and trudged toward her, the blood-spattered shovel riding on her shoulder.

Fear shoved up into Dakota's throat, blocking her scream. She knew the man was dead. And in moments, she would be, too. The expression on Lucy's face was enough to send her into madness. There was no psychotic glee capering behind her eyes; no pity, no excitement, no hatred. Just a work-manlike frown of concentration. One down and one to go.

Lucy's boots swished through the grass. The sun brought out the highlights in her hair, limned her soft baby-fat cheeks. She could have been any teenager doing a chore, carrying out the garbage or feeding the chickens. Her Pendleton jacket glowed in the flickering sun and shade, a saddle blanket of vibrant reds, yellows, greens, blues, deep pink. So pleasing to the eye. It was a beautiful day, Dakota thought with an odd, detached wistfulness. The way the ponderosa shimmered, their needles tipped with silver where the sun hit them, that deep, achingly blue sky. A squirrel chortled in a tree, so normal, and here was this sixteen-year-old kid, walking toward her, about to end her life.

Suddenly, Lucy stopped. She might have been a wild animal, frozen, listening.

Dakota heard it, too. The droning of a car engine. She looked up the incline, saw light glancing off metal. Someone was driving down the forest road, and it was obvious that the road came down here, because the dead man's Blazer was parked only fifty yards away.

Lucy stood there, blinking. Confused.

Dakota gauged the distance to the Blazer. She'd have to run to the right, to avoid Lucy. It seemed impossible, but it was better than waiting.

She thrust to her feet, staggered, almost fell. The adrenaline that had left her returned, surging through her like quicksilver.

Startled, Lucy's gaze swung back to her. Dakota didn't care. She darted to the right, sideswiped a tree trunk, half ran and half shambled for the Blazer.

Almost there . . .

She felt breath on her neck, thought she heard footsteps behind her . . .

Please let it be unlocked please please please.

Thirty feet. Twenty feet. Almost there. She swung her gaze backward, like Lot's wife, knowing it was a stupid thing to do, that it could slow her down, make the difference—

Nothing there.

Lucy wasn't behind her, breathing down her neck. The forest was empty.

Dakota didn't pause to contemplate this new wrinkle. She hurtled into the side of the Blazer, shoved her thumb into the door handle, yanked the door open and clambered in, pulling the door shut behind her and hitting the lock pin, hitting all the lock pins, and then, only then, did she look around.

Lucy was gone.

The car must have spooked her. She'd melted into the forest, must be hiding there somewhere. Waiting for the car to go on.

Dakota searched under the dead man's seat, hoping for a gun. Nothing. No CB, no car phone, either.

She leaned on the horn.

Rita heard the car horn. She braked, peering down into the forest in the direction of the sound. It came from the red Blazer in the clearing below. The horn didn't let up, so she assumed it had something to do with Clay, Dakota, or Lucy.

Could it be one of Lucy's tricks?

Cautiously, she followed the road, looking off to the left to see if there was any way down. She found a weedy track and took it, hoping the rental car wouldn't get stuck.

The car was coming down! Dakota kept her elbow on the horn, waving her other arm. She heard the pop of rocks under tires as the car inched along the road, so agonizingly slow—couldn't they drive faster?

At last the car pulled up beside her.

Rita DeWeil was the most beautiful thing Dakota had ever seen in her life.

Rita started to get out. Dakota motioned her to stay where she was. There was a remote possibility that Lucy was still here, could be lurking behind a tree or concealed by brush.

Rita rummaged on the seat for something and lifted up a

gun with the tips of her fingers, her red nails flashing in the
sunlight. Her questioning gaze sought Dakota's.

Dakota rolled down her window. The passenger's side of
the rental car was only a couple of feet away. "Unlock the
door!" she shouted.

Rita didn't seem to hear. She looked puzzled.

Dakota motioned to the lock. Rita unlocked the door.

Almost out of here. Dakota unlocked her own door, looked
around one more time. Pushed it open, stepped out onto the
cushion of pine needles. Her adrenaline was still a humming
power line throughout her limbs, urging her to throw herself
across the distance between the Blazer and Rita's car.

Silly. The danger was over. Lucy was probably over the
next hill by now.

She stepped forward, her leg in agony.

And landed flat on her face. Something held her foot in a
vise.

Her broken foot.

Dakota screamed.

She felt a hand clutch at the leg of her jeans, pulling her
backward through the dirt, under the car. Lucy scuttled out
from underneath the Blazer, dragging the shovel with her, and
Dakota glanced up to see the horror on Rita's face as Lucy
bulled to her feet, overbalanced and staggered backward, her
hip connecting with Rita's car. She planted her feet solidly,
her face a mask of determination, and swung the shovel back,
her colorful coat filling Dakota's whole vision, and Dakota
ducked her head, remembering the man who had almost
saved her, and the sickening wet smacking sound of his skull
caving in, and she squeezed her eyes shut, waiting for the
blow. She heard the whicker of steel, the loud ding! the
shrieking scrape of metal as the blade hit the Blazer, heard
Lucy grunt with effort and lift the shovel again, and she realized her eyes were no longer shut, her vision swimming
back into focus as some reflex, some form of self-
preservation made her reach for Lucy's foot, and the shovel
hit the top of its arc just as she saw the dull surprise on
Lucy's face. Dakota heard the gunshot, punching through the

Blazer door and fragmenting the air around her. The colorful saddle blanket coat bloomed dark red as Lucy toppled forward, falling like a tree. She crushed Dakota, slippery and warm and smelling of blood.

"Good shot," Dakota said, and fainted.

Fifty-One

Shameless exploded from the gate, her hind legs propelling her forward with incredible force. Her hide gleamed like dark mahogany, smooth as satin over the bunched muscles of hindquarters, chest, shoulder, forearms.

She jackhammered down the lane, the jockey hunched on her back, urging her on to glory. One jump out of the gate and she was a head in front. In one hundred yards she had increased her lead to a length. Her feet flirted with the dust, her tail flaunted her power, and the other horses fell back as if awestruck. The Black Oak filly tore a hole in the air as she powered down the track.

Aside from the hard running style that characterized her, Shameless ran easily. Her ears tipped forward and back, relaxed, her muscles bunched and unbunched, her belly stretched like a rubber band. She continued to draw away, like a hare before hounds, a shimmering ribbon of speed, connecting the line between the starting gate and the finish wire in one smooth motion. Four hundred and forty yards of continuous motion.

By the time she flashed under the wire, she was three lengths in front of her nearest competitor, Runaway Train.

The crowd went wild. A woman with a one-horse stable had won the All American. Not only that, but she had dominated it, humbling the best horses in the country.

Ernesto's family had come to see the horse run, and now they filled the winner circle—grandparents, uncles, aunts, father and mother, brothers and sisters, children. The filly was led onto the rubber bricks to great fanfare, so excited she almost took down the photographer. It was her one and only gaffe, and she was forgiven; she had a right to be effusive. She wore the All American winner's cooler, and it fluttered around her like a prize fighter's robe. Ernesto beamed for the camera as he held up his end of the giant check for one million dollars, as he accepted the blanket and the trophy, as he spoke through an interpreter to the reporter from ESPN. Chris Lincoln pondered aloud the mystery of the absent owner-trainer, Dakota McAllister, who just might be the real story behind this year's All American.

After the presentation, Ernesto was ushered up to the VIP room off the press box for champagne and congratulations. Although he didn't say much, he fit right in. Quarter horse trainers were renowned for the brevity of their speech. Many an All American winner had answered the inevitable question, "How does it feel to win the All American?" by looking into the camera and mumbling, "Good." Sometimes he elaborated: "He run good."

Clay heard that Shameless had won the All American on the loudspeaker as he exited the grounds. It only increased his urgency to find Dakota.

He took the steps to his cabin two at a time. The answering machine light blinked.

He cursed when he heard not Dakota's voice, but Rita's. "Clay? Clay? I couldn't raise you at the track, so I thought I'd call here." There was a pause. When Rita spoke again, she sounded worried. "If you get in, please call me. I heard you were in an accident on Sierra Blanca. I guess I'll go up . . . just call me if you're all right."

He had to listen to the message twice to understand her meaning. Sierra Blanca? How did she get a damn fool notion like that? Who would—

Dakota wouldn't miss the All American unless there was

an emergency, unless she thought something had happened to him. Like an accident.

He raced for the truck, rammed it into gear, and spun out of the drive in a rooster tail of gravel. Headed for Sierra Blanca.

He was almost to the turnoff for Ski Run Road when the news came on the radio. A teenager had killed a man and terrorized two women up on Sierra Blanca. The women, Rita Deweil and Dakota McAllister, had survived the ordeal, and one of them had killed the girl, Lucy Tanner, in self-defense. Dakota McAllister had a broken ankle, and had been taken to the hospital for observation.

With a screech of brakes, he spun the truck around and headed for the hospital.

He detoured to the hospital gift shop, bought some flowers, and jogged through a maze of corridors to Dakota's room.

She'd taken several stitches in her scalp, and her fractured ankle was reset, but other than those injuries, had survived the ordeal well. When she saw him, her face grew radiant as a sunrise. "Clay!"

He wanted to take her in his arms, but was afraid he might hurt her. And so he stood there like a fool, holding the flowers in front of him like an offering.

She reached up and tugged on his sleeve. "For Christ's sake, Pearce, I'm not made of china. Hold me."

He did as he was told. She clasped her arms around his neck and held on for dear life. They remained that way for a long time, just holding each other, shutting out the world. He couldn't believe the goodness of it, the joy that filled him, knowing he might never have had the chance to enjoy this simple pleasure again. Her cheek pressed against his chest, and he stroked the soft spill of honey-gold hair, marveling at its silky texture. Marveling at everything about her, the solid feel of their bodies pressed together, the beat of her heart against his.

Thank God.

He would never let her go again. "You scared me, McAllister."

"I know."

He kissed the top of her head. "I love you."

"I love you more."

"No you don't."

"Yes I do."

"You know, you could thank me," Rita said behind him. She walked into the room, carrying two cups of steaming coffee. For an instant, Clay saw a bone-deep sadness in her eyes. And then she smiled. "I missed my nail appointment because of her."

"I'll buy you your own salon. How's that?"

Rita gave Dakota her coffee and sat down on the chair by the window. She looked tired. Tired and resigned.

Clay clasped her hands in his. "I can't thank you enough. I heard on the radio—"

"Let's not get into that, shall we? It's making me think of one of those 1950's westerns, you know the kind? The whore with the heart of gold loves the hero but he loves the innocent blonde, and so the whore saves the hero at the end of the story by taking the bullet meant for him? I don't like playing that role, and I'm not into consolation prizes."

Dakota grinned under her pallor. "You saved my life."

"First time I shot a gun in my life," Rita said. "And I hope to God it's my last." She sipped the coffee and made a face. "Invite me to the wedding. I just might come." And with that, she walked out of the room.

"You know, she kind of grows on you," Dakota said.

"I think we should invite her."

"Oh? And when will this spectacular event take place?"

"As soon as you're off your crutches. If we're inviting half of Arizona, I want it to be esthetically pleasing."

"The first one was nice."

"Too bad it didn't work out." He pulled her to him. "It will, this time."

"There are no guarantees in this life, Pearce."

"I thought about that. You might wonder if I'm marrying you for your money."

"My money?"

"Didn't you hear? You just won the All American."

Epilogue

Dakota rose early, although the appointment with her lawyer was for ten o'clock. The cast wasn't due to come off for another two weeks, and she needed to schedule in maneuvering time.

Dakota had decided to stay on in Ruidoso for a while and rest up after her ordeal. She still didn't completely understand why Lucy had done what she had, although one of the detectives had explained it to her. Sociopaths, as a rule, were governed by one appetite, an overriding desire. Some—the serial killers—desired power over life and death, or to possess a person before they killed. Lucy's desire was to be supported all her life. She wanted security. Lucy had killed to protect her father, not because she loved him, but because he represented security. Apparently, the better the lifestyle, the more secure she would feel, because she transferred her allegiance first to Dakota, and when that didn't work out, moved on to Rita.

It was a naive way of thinking, but to Lucy it made perfect sense.

Lucy had killed Jerry because he tried to blackmail her. He thought that Rita would adopt his daughter, and as Lucy's family, he wanted some financial compensation. Lucy must have thought that Jerry's demands would cause Rita to have second thoughts, so she killed him.

It was still hard to believe that Lucy would have the audacity to run Coke down with her own father in the truck. Sociopaths acted on impulse, Detective Sykes had told her, they didn't think about the consequences of their actions. Lucy wanted Coke dead and saw an opportunity to kill him, and so she acted. As she had acted in the White Sands, puncturing Dakota's tire and waiting at another turnout for the yellow fog lights she knew set Coke's truck apart from the rest.

Well, Lucy was dead, and Dakota need never fear her again. Too bad her other problems wouldn't go away so easily.

Dan Bolin had turned himself in to the authorities, but for the moment he was out on bail and was helping her contact the owners. He had agreed to implicate Jared Ames, who had fled Arizona, and Dakota believed that Dan wouldn't serve much jail time, if any.

Dan Bolin didn't care, one way or the other. He was a shadow of himself now that his wife was gone. But he did try hard to untangle this mess, and had spent hours on the phone with Dakota, probing his memory and his records to sort out just which horse belonged to which sire.

Clay had managed to track down four of the colts Dakota had seen that day at Dan's. He had bought them back for her, and she was hopeful he'd find the rest. For her part, Dakota had contacted most of the new owners from the dispersal sale and offered restitution. Some were angry and threatened to sue, some sold their animals back at the same price plus the feed and board they'd paid out, and others, it seemed, thought their horses were good enough to keep, requesting only new papers with Darkscope's name as sire. Darkscope was a good stallion; as a rule, he'd produced better runners than Something Wicked. Dakota had decided to stand him at stud.

It might take years, but she would find a way to make restitution to everyone. And as things stood now, Dakota had the money from the All American and the Rainbow to offset the tremendous financial problems she faced.

Although she doubted she'd have that money for long.

Rumors were flying. If the other horses at Black Oak were fakes, didn't it stand to reason that Shameless was, too? Already, some of the owners whose horses ran in the All American were talking lawsuits. After that would come the lawsuits from the owners of the ten horses who ran in the All American First Consolation, because the fastest horse in that race had missed the tenth slot in the All American, and then there were the horses in the Second Consolation . . . any day now, Dakota expected the stewards to summon her for an explanation.

She checked her watch. She was meeting Clay and Norm at the office of Clay's lawyer in twenty minutes. Clay said there was some news that she really needed to hear.

She arrived at the office of James, Monroe, and Brady right at ten, knowing that she would have to end this charade once and for all. She wouldn't wait for the stewards to call her in. Today she would tell them the truth about Shameless.

She walked toward the office, glancing at the sign across the street, which read: DAYLIGHT DOUGHNUTS CHRISTIAN CHURCH. It was such a beautiful day—the pines, the sunflowers, the blue sky, but a feeling of dread spread outward from her heart. If only Dan hadn't told her the truth.

Clay met her at the door. "You look grim," he said.

"Bankruptcy isn't the best way to start a marriage."

"You can't have everything."

"I mean it, Clay. I'm going to the stewards today."

"Just wait and hear what Norm has to say."

They sat down in Jim Brady's office, who had obligingly let Norm have it for this meeting. "First of all, thanks for letting me look at your father's journal," Norm told her, after they exchanged amenities. "It bears directly on some legal issues that are extremely important to Black Oak."

Dakota was determined to be polite. Norm could be stuffy, but he was a good guy. "Look, I've got to get this off my ch—"

"Did you read the journal carefully?" Norm asked.

"I read it several times over." What did this have to do with the price of sweet feed?

"Then I guess you must have read the part about your father breeding Dash To Judgment to Something Wicked."

"Darkscope," Dakota corrected him.

Clay squeezed her hand. "Listen," he suggested.

"It says here that the groom, who was new, didn't know in which pasture the stallion was kept. He brought the wrong stud. Coke looked at the horse, checked his tattoo, and sent the groom back for the right horse. Something Wicked."

Dakota stared at him. Her heart kicked over, then began to soar. *Don't get your hopes up,* she told herself. *See for yourself.*

Norm Fredman obligingly pushed the journal across the desk. "That highlighted passage, there."

There was a partial eclipse, like the gods were trying to tell me something. I collected from the stud and inseminated Judgment right on the spot, the way they used to do it in the old days before they added all these newfangled antibiotics. Danny Boy would have a heart attack if he knew.

She read it, reread it. "It's not conclusive, though, is it? It's just some writing in a book. Legally, it wouldn't stand up in court." Why was she playing devils' advocate? She needed that money if Black Oak was to survive.

"But blood-typing will," Clay said. "I sent to the AQHA for the records on the blood types on Shameless, Something Wicked, and Darkscope. I got them back this morning. Shameless could only come from Something Wicked."

Dakota tried to digest this.

Shameless wasn't an impostor. Dan Bolin had almost single-handedly ruined Black Oak, and her father had single-handedly saved it. "You know what this means?" she asked Clay.

"We've got our first stakes winner—an All American winner—for the new Black Oak. And with the mares, foals and yearlings you'll be buying back, and my own horses—"

"But the lawsuits—"

"We'll make it," Clay said. "Together, we'll make it."

And as they walked out into the morning sunlight together, and Dakota drew in a breath of mountain air, she suddenly knew that they would.

YOU WON'T WANT TO READ
JUST ONE — KATHERINE STONE

ROOMMATES (3355-9, $4.95)
No one could have prepared Carrie for the monumental changes she would face when she met her new circle of friends at Stanford University. Once their lives intertwined and became woven into the tapestry of the times, they would never be the same.

TWINS (3492-X, $4.95)
Brook and Melanie Chandler were so different, it was hard to believe they were sisters. One was a dark, serious, ambitious New York attorney; the other, a golden, glamourous, sophisticated supermodel. But they were more than sisters—they were twins and more alike than even they knew . . .

THE CARLTON CLUB (3614-0, $4.95)
It was the place to see and be seen, the only place to be. And for those who frequented the playground of the very rich, it was a way of life. Mark, Kathleen, Leslie and Janet—they worked together, played together, and loved together, all behind exclusive gates of the *Carlton Club*.

Available wherever paperbacks are sold, or order direct from the Publisher. Send cover price plus 50¢ per copy for mailing and handling to Penguin USA, P.O. Box 999, c/o Dept. 17109, Bergenfield, NJ 07621. Residents of New York and Tennessee must include sales tax. DO NOT SEND CASH.